"Sunday is the only day I have free from lectures and tutorials. Is it a good day for you?"

Penny nodded. Even her ideas about the days of the week were going to be changed in London: Sundays had always been a day of church, family dinner, duty visits. Sunday looked now as if it were going to be the day in the week when she was happiest.

David said, "You'll keep them free? All of them?"

"Yes."

He kissed her.

"David!" she said instinctively. But her voice was happy, happy and relieved.

"Better get used to it, Penny," he said happily, and took her arm towards the door.

Fawcett Crest Books
by Helen MacInnes:

ABOVE SUSPICION
AGENT IN PLACE
ASSIGNMENT IN BRITTANY
CLOAK OF DARKNESS
DECISION AT DELPHI
THE DOUBLE IMAGE
FRIENDS AND LOVERS
THE HIDDEN TARGET
HORIZON
I AND MY TRUE LOVE
MESSAGE FROM MALAGA
NEITHER FIVE NOR THREE
NORTH FROM ROME
PRAY FOR A BRAVE HEART
PRELUDE TO TERROR
REST AND BE THANKFUL
RIDE A PALE HORSE
THE SALZBURG CONNECTION
THE SNARE OF THE HUNTER
THE VENETIAN AFFAIR
WHILE STILL WE LIVE

HELEN MacINNES

FRIENDS
AND
LOVERS

FAWCETT CREST • NEW YORK

To Gilbert

A Fawcett Crest Book

Published by Ballantine Books

Copyright © 1947 by Helen Highet. Copyright renewed 1974 by Helen MacInnes

ISBN 0-449-21072-3

This edition published by arrangement with Harcourt Brace Jovanovich, Inc.

The poem "The Second Coming" from *Collected Poems of W. B. Yeats* is reprinted by permission of The Macmillan Company. Copyright, 1924, by The Macmillan Company, copyright renewed 1952 by Bertha Georgie Yeats; and by permission of M. B. Yeats and The Macmillan Company of Canada.

Manufactured in the United States of America

First Fawcett Crest Edition: February 1967
First Ballantine Books Edition: November 1983
Second printing: August 1986

chapter i

THE MORNING mist had cleared. Now a fresh wind was blowing, curling the edges of the waves, touching them lightly with flecks of white. The sea had lost its cold gray look; the blue waters were a darker reflection of the smiling sky, intensifying its color and emotion by their great depths. The mainland, wide stretches of heather and bracken sloping down from barren hills, ended abruptly in red granite cliffs. On this part of the coast, there was no sea loch or ragged inlet to distract the swiftly moving tide in its course between the mainland and the scattered islands. There was no sign of house or croft. There was nothing but the uneven hills, silent, watchful, folding eastwards, one behind the other. To the west and north and south was the Atlantic with the lonely islands jutting out of its deep waters to break the force of its rolling waves and turn them into swirling currents.

The men in the boat—single-sailed and small, speeding swiftly with the wind and racing tide—had not spoken since they had left Loch Innish on the mainland. But then, David Bosworth thought, this was the kind of place where conversation was hardly necessary. He was content to watch the wide-winged gulls wheeling overhead.

George Fenton-Stevens, who was standing upright with an arm hooked around the mast, oblivious to wind or spray or gulls, suddenly looked down at David sitting securely in the well of the boat. "What do you think of all this, David?" There was a smile of enjoyment on his face, possessive pride in his voice.

David studied Fenton-Stevens for a moment before he replied. Perhaps if he waited long enough, no reply would be necessary. George's eyes and attention were once more fixed on the islands lying ahead of them. When in Rome, David was reflecting, old George could always be counted on doing more than the Romans did. In Oxford, for instance, George wore more twists of scarf around his neck, trousers both baggier and more stained, a gown torn into more tatters than the usual undergraduate adopted. In London, at Christmas, he had appeared more Foreign Office than Anthony Eden; never had there been so black a hat, so neat an umbrella, such impeccable shoes and gloves. And now, in the Western Highlands of Scotland, he was the Celtic sea-reiver standing proudly before the mast as his ship bore down on an unsuspecting island.

"What do you think of it?" George asked again.

David buried his chin in the upturned collar of his jacket as he tried to avoid a sudden shower of cold sea water. "Ninth century," he answered. "Definitely. Kishmul's galley and all. If I could see properly"—and he wiped the spray ostentatiously from his brows—"I could perhaps give you the decade as well."

George relaxed noticeably and his very Anglo-Saxon chin was less pointed towards the prow. "I hadn't thought of that," he said, "but it *is* ninth century. Nothing has changed. This sea, and these hills." His flight of fantasy failed, and he was left with embarrassment. He sat down beside David Bosworth.

"That's better," David said. "With you swaying up there above me, I couldn't concentrate on equilibrium."

George was watching him with amusement. And the red-bearded Highlander sitting at the stern gave almost a smile. In all the jokes against oneself, David thought, there was always a particle of truth. Ever since they had left the shelter of Loch Innish, his mind had been persuading his stomach that this was all perfectly normal and was even considered enjoyable by some. But it was difficult to forget the hideous groaning of the wooden planks, the labored creaking of the mast, or the pool of water washing about in the bottom of the boat. All quite normal, of course, if you were accustomed to this kind of thing.

"There's Inchnamurren," George said suddenly, and pointed to the larger of two islands lying close together. For company, David thought; they would need that in winter. George was explaining that the smaller island was uninhabited, and that Inchnamurren's houses couldn't be seen yet. They were hidden by the sharp hill, on the north end of the island, which fell steeply into the sea. "Devil's Elbow, they call it," George said. "Nasty piece of work, isn't it?"

"Sounds ominous," David agreed. He spoke lightly, but his

thoughts were serious enough as he looked at the crook of black rock thrusting itself so evilly out into the Sound. *Full fathom five . . .* The grim sea-raiders, the quiet fishermen who once sailed around these islands, and then sailed no more— *The sea-wrack their shroud . . . Back to back they lie, lifeless lie . . .* The lines from the sea dirges which George's mother kept prominently displayed on the piano at the Lodge were haunting him today.

David looked at the red-bearded owner of this boat, Captain MacLean, retired from the Seven Seas to spend his remaining years sailing around his own islands. David wondered what the Highlander thought of them, the intruders. His blue eyes, bright beneath the heavy brows, met David's gaze. He nodded slightly as if in greeting. He raised one hand slowly to his pipe, and removed it from his lips.

"Fine day," he said.

"Fine," David answered, conscious of the strange fact that he felt just like a schoolboy trying to win the friendship of an austere headmaster. Then the pipe was replaced, the blue eyes looked beyond David once more, and the conversation was over.

They passed the Devil's Elbow, and entered the island's sheltered bay. Here, in sunlit peace, colors sharpened. The water, shallow, flowing over white sand, became a broad band of jade edging the shore. At its edge was a row of whitewashed cottages. Farther back, there were other houses equally white and gleaming, scattered widely over the green fields and rugged ground. The heather was beginning to bloom; one rough hillside was already covered with reddish purple.

"Every time I see this island, I wonder why Mother didn't buy a house here rather than on the mainland," George said.

David didn't reply to that. There was only one obvious answer which George was too good-natured to see: there wasn't a house on the island big enough to suit Lady Fenton-Stevens. The Lodge at Loch Innish, on the other hand, had Scots baronial turrets which photographed well for the August and September issues of the fashionable magazines.

"You really ought to see it when all the heather is out," George was saying. "Look, David, why don't you stay for August? Mother and the girls will be here for the Twelfth."

"Can't be managed, George," David said firmly. Lady Fenton-Stevens had no doubt invited some really eligible bachelors to amuse her daughters.

"I hope it isn't because of Eleanor," George began, and then halted awkwardly. He frowned as he thought of his very pretty sister who had such an enchanting time, always—so it seemed—at the expense of his friends' emotions.

"Good Lord, no." David gave a short laugh which sounded almost genuine. Eleanor wasn't within his price range, even if he had still wanted her.

"I still think you ought to have a few weeks of proper holiday," George said stubbornly. "London in August is hideous. You'll never be able to work there."

I've got to, David was thinking: I've only myself to depend on. George would never know what grim urgency that small fact gave to life. But he smiled and said, "God, isn't it bright? I am seeing all colors in the spectrum now, black-dotted." He watched the boat as it was carefully eased along the jetty where two brown-legged, barefooted children halted in their game to see the foreigners arrive. A white-haired man was working on the seams of an upturned rowboat. Two women gathered seaweed on the shore. Three men leaned against the wall of a cottage.

"A hive of industry," David remarked. "George, are you sure there is a hotel?"

"Over there beside the church. They'll give us a decent enough lunch, and then we can call on this Dr. MacIntyre of yours."

"Not mine," David said hastily. "This is all Chaundler's idea."

Walter Chaundler was David's tutor at Oxford. When he had heard in June about his pupil's visit to this part of Scotland, he had been delighted. "You must go to see MacIntyre and take him messages from me," Chaundler had said. "I shall write to him at once and tell him that you are tutoring this summer at the Fenton-Stevens place on Loch Innish. That is almost next door to Inchnamurren, as far as I remember. I spent a summer on the island, three years ago in 1929, when MacIntyre and I were collaborating on that book on *Mysticism and Its Influence on History*. Quite a remarkable man, really. He was born on that island and went to school there. Then he went to Glasgow University, and after that came up to Oxford. He became a don here and, later, he was a professor in London. And then, quite suddenly, after his wife died, he went back to his island again. Quite remarkable." And when David had remained silent, wondering if retiring to an unknown island in a forgotten part of the world was the depressing proof of

8

failure after so much effort, Chaundler had sensed the young man's doubts. He had urged in his kindly, gentle way: "Do go. I am sure MacIntyre would be delighted." And that was how this visit had been decided.

David had not been altogether happy about it, though. He had postponed it until almost the last week of his stay at Loch Innish. And he would not write to Dr. MacIntyre, either. His excuse was that if Dr. MacIntyre lived on a small island he would always be easily found. Better keep the whole thing as informal as possible, he had thought: then it would seem less of an invasion.

As they began walking towards the village, David found that he was following George and MacLean with rather a slower stride. Either George was being too enthusiastic about this whole place, or he was taking charge of this visit too efficiently—anyway, it was all becoming a forced pilgrimage. It had never seemed to dawn on George that Dr. MacIntyre might find them rather a nuisance.

"George," David said very quietly—and, as Fenton-Stevens halted while MacLean went over to talk to the three men outside the general store, he went on: "Look, why don't we call the whole thing off?"

George stared at him. "Rather late to think of that. But just as you please." He gave a worried glance towards MacLean and his friends, now deep in conversation.

David touched George's arm. "All right," he said, "I agree we did arrive rather obviously. Let's see this medieval historian on his medieval island, and justify Chaundler's letter of introduction about us. Let's get that over and done with." He watched George's transparent relief at not being forced to do the wrong thing.

"Good!" George said. "Now we had better collect Captain MacLean. He has invited us to visit his sister, as we've arrived here earlier than we thought. I couldn't very well refuse." He looked anxiously at David, but David was smiling now quite openly. "Well, come on, then." George said with a touch of sharpness.

They walked over to the group of islanders, who stopped speaking Gaelic and watched the foreigners gravely as Captain MacLean introduced them with as much seriousness as a *grand seigneur* presenting two young protégés at court. There was a brief exchange of polite phrases, the Highlanders now speaking in English with their soft voices and careful pronunciation. It was very far removed from the coarse dialect of the stage Scotsman. David was noting, too,

9

that there was not one inch of tartan displayed—that was probably kept for dress occasions—and he was thankful that George had not worn his Clan Stevenson kilt today. That was best left for the Lodge, where the natives had become more inured to tourists.

MacLean measured the necessary length of the slow, simple conversation with considerable skill. As they were led away from the group, along the narrow earth road which ran in front of the row of cottages, David had the feeling that George and he had been weighed in the balance. And not found wanting, he hoped.

A white-aproned, square-set, apple-cheeked woman was waiting for them at a cottage door. "My sister, Mistress McDonald," MacLean explained.

"Will you not come in and have a cup of tea?" she asked. "The kettle's singing on the hob." She stood aside, waiting for them to enter, but with no trace of curtsy in her gesture. She had a gentle voice with music in it, and her eyes were as placid as her brother's.

George Fenton-Stevens looked anxiously at David. But, for once, David needed no urging. He was saying, with that rare smile of his which lighted up his serious, guarded face with sudden warmth, "Thank you, Mrs. McDonald, that's kind of you." He stepped over the carefully whitened step which led into the cottage, and Fenton-Stevens followed.

Inside the cottage was the smell of a peat fire and freshly baked scones. The kettle was hissing cheerily, a clock ticked loudly on the high crowded mantelpiece decorated with an edging of crochet. The table was covered, and waiting. Through the small open window, the cries of the cormorants and harsh-voiced sea gulls blurred into the background murmur of breaking waves. The blazing colors of heather and grass and sea were exchanged for a gentler light.

A girl rose as they entered, more startled by the unexpected guests than Mrs. McDonald had been.

"It is Mr. Fenton-Stevens from the Lodge at Loch Innish with his friend Mr. Bosworth, who have come to see Dr. MacIntyre himself," Mrs. McDonald was explaining. David found that he had held out his hand, and afterwards he remembered thinking how very odd it was that he had made that gesture so impulsively. But at the time, he was looking into a pair of very blue eyes in a very pretty face, and that was all he could seem to see. He did not break that look, as he should have, and besides he didn't want to. He did not even hear the girl's name, as Mrs. McDonald's soft precise voice made the introduction. Then he suddenly became conscious that George was saying something to him about one of the curios which littered the mantelpiece, and remembered to drop her hand. He glanced quickly at George, and he was relieved to see that he had noticed nothing. Neither had MacLean nor Mrs. McDonald. He relaxed, but he found he was watching the girl as she moved towards the door, and he felt a sudden stab of disappointment. The girl halted at the doorway. Perhaps she wasn't leaving after all, he thought hopefully. But she was saying that she was so sorry to leave, that she was so very late. Her voice was gentle and yet clear, gentle and low, an excellent thing in woman. Her dark hair had strong auburn lights, almost dark red and yet not quite. The sun was gleaming on it now as she stood at the threshold. There was a natural grace to her body as she looked back into the room over her shoulder. And then she was gone.

He saw her pass the small window, hurrying as if she were indeed late. But even now, that last glimpse of her through the window, that color of the sweater which she wore, reminded him again of her eyes. He looked sharply at George, but Fenton-Stevens was helping Mrs. McDonald to clear a chair of magazines, and Mrs. McDonald was saying that Miss Penny was always so thoughtful about bringing her something to read, which was a nice change from the knitting. It was clear from her matter-of-fact words, and George's equally sensible reply, and Captain MacLean's practical absorption in the excellent soda scones and fresh butter, that none of them realized they had just seen a miracle of a girl.

David concentrated on the difficult problem of eating a newly baked oatcake. He was thankful that George had noticed so little, or else there would have been much leg-pulling for days—perhaps even weeks—about his sudden aberration. He could hear George saying to a group of Oxford friends, when the subject of women came up, "Remember David and his neat speeches on women being a snare and delusion? If they are pretty, they have no heart, no brain. A pretty girl doesn't need them: she doesn't need anything except her face-value, which she has calculated to the last shilling. Well, don't listen to him .... You should have seen him, holding on to her hand, no doubt supporting himself, for he would have fallen flat on his back if he had let go." At least, David now reflected, he had been spared that.

11

"You are very quiet, David," George remarked, with a slight touch of prodding. Sometimes David was really too difficult socially. He had entered this cottage with good enough grace, but here he was in one of those preoccupied moods of his.

"I am wrestling with this," David said, and indicated the mess of golden crumbs which covered his plate. "It looks as if I needed a spoon, doesn't it?"

That amused his hostess; and her brother remarked, as he tactfully demonstrated how to spread butter on oatcake by placing the cake on the flat tablecloth rather than on the curved surface of the plate, that Mr. Bosworth was a great one for the joking. David saw a gleam in George's eye, and knew that if any reminiscences about this visit were to be created in Oxford—for George rather fancied himself as a storyteller—then MacLean's summing-up would be the chief reason for mirth. George would develop a masterly rendering of the Highlander's pronunciation of the initial consonant. "He's a crate one for the choking," George would say at the right moment after David had produced an attempt at wit. But that was the kind of leg-pulling that David could take.

So now David smiled around the table as he thanked MacLean for the excellent advice, and began to talk about the mantelpiece, crammed with some particularly hideous presents from Shanghai and Singapore which the late Captain McDonald had brought home from his voyages.

"It is rather pleasant, I must say," George began, and then thought better of saying it. They were walking up the winding road which would take them to Dr. MacIntyre's house.

"What is?"

"To see the island from the inside, as it were. I've visited this place each summer, but I've always left MacLean at the jetty and then strolled inland. But this is the first time I've got to know any of them. They are very polite, but very remote to strangers."

"Foreigners, you mean."

George looked as if he did not like to accept that idea. After all, he was English, and these islands were part of the British Isles. And he had been coming to this part of Scotland each summer for six years, now. "Well," he said, "they accepted us all right, today."

"Because we had the right password, I suppose."

"Dr. MacIntyre's name?"

"I'm afraid so. Quite a blow to admit it wasn't for our

12

sweet and charming smiles, isn't it? But cheer up, George: the right password is the key to any fortress. Here, it is quite simply a matter of friendship. It wouldn't have mattered to Mrs. McDonald who we were, or what we did or thought: we came as friends of Dr. MacIntyre's, and that was good enough for her."

"I must tell that to Mother," George said. "She is completely baffled by these Highlanders, you know. When we first came here, she tried visiting the cottages in the village at Loch Innish, taking the people some fruit from our garden and that sort of thing. But some weeks later, they returned the visit bringing homemade scones and heather honey. It set Mother back for weeks."

David let out a roar of laughter, and George joined in eventually. He had the uncomfortable feeling that David was laughing at quite a different side of the story.

"You do throw yourself into things, old boy, don't you?" George remarked when David had recovered. "No half measures for you in anything, it seems." Then, thinking of his mother, with a hint of guilt for having laughed too, he said, "Might be rather nice to bring Mother and Eleanor over here some day. It would be definitely a new experience for them."

David said quickly, "Good God, not that." And then more slowly, tactfully, "They will be much too busy, anyway."

"Yes. One always is busier than one imagines." George paused. With a sudden flash of sensitivity he said, "Women are such damned snobs, come to think of it. They just couldn't have tea in a kitchen without feeling all the time that it *was* the kitchen. Now men, for instance, enjoy a pleasant hour anywhere, and they don't care where it is as long as it is pleasant."

David nodded. He was thinking again of the girl he had met in Mrs. McDonald's kitchen. Her voice had no Highland intonation. Was she a summer visitor, and where was she staying anyway? He halted suddenly, and looked back at the village. What an idiotic way to behave, he told himself angrily, and turned quickly to walk on with George.

They said "Good day" to two children, an old man and a young boy. But of the girl with the blue eyes and the dark auburn hair there was no sign.

chapter ii

SILENCE fell on the pleasant room. Dr. MacIntyre, sitting in his favorite armchair by the side of the large brick fireplace, wondered just how long they had been talking. The conversation had been interesting enough: it was always a delight to hear the news from Oxford, or to catch an echo of his own experiences when he had been an undergraduate, or to watch a young man's ideas and enthusiasms suddenly reveal themselves in spite of pretended diffidence. For it was the fashion among young men, these days, to be diffident. But every now and again their natural exuberance would break down the pretense. And a damned good thing, too, Dr. MacIntyre reflected.

David suddenly thought of looking at his watch. He rose quickly to his feet. "I'm terribly sorry, sir," he said. "I've taken up far too much of your time. I had no idea..."

"Then we both enjoyed the afternoon," Dr. MacIntyre said tactfully. He rose, too, and knocked the ashes from his pipe into the fireplace. He was a tall man and he still carried himself erectly, but he had become thinner since he had ordered his tweed suit, for it hung loosely on him. His age, in spite of his white hair, was only noticeable in his deliberate movements. His blue eyes were unfaded, and there was youth in them: they were interested and amused. The flesh on his face was firm over the strong bones, and there was a fresh healthy color in his cheeks. He had surprised David when they had first met: he gave the impression of vigor and of enjoyment, as if his life had been completely successful and surprisingly entertaining.

David hesitated, looking around the room, knowing that he really must take his leave and yet regretting to go. It was a room to work and talk and think in, a large room that was friendly and comfortable. Bookcases, tightly filled with books—and not all scholarly books either. A piano and a heavily filled music rack. A wireless set beside the fireplace. A gramophone, and a good variety of records. At the west window, there was a large desk. At the east window, looking over the Sound towards the mainland, there was a low table with a game of chess in progress and two comfortable armchairs. David's eyes traveled back to the desk, with its busy disorder of work interrupted.

14

He said, "I'm afraid I have been rather a nuisance."

"Not a bit of it, not a bit of it," Dr. MacIntyre said. He was satisfied with his pipe tapping. He straightened his back, and then stood for a moment looking at a photograph on the mantelpiece. He seemed lost in thought, and David felt he was being politely dismissed. This was the way in which Chaundler, in Oxford, gave him warning. I've stayed too long, and I've talked too much—God, much too much— David thought miserably, and all the pleasure in the visit vanished as he realized how bored Dr. MacIntyre must have been.

But Dr. MacIntyre, taking a keen look at the embarrassment on the young man's face, said, "If you wait until I find my tobacco, I'll take a turn with you in the garden. I have some surprising hollyhocks." He noted the relief on David's face. Young men did not change very much, after all, in spite of fashions in behavior .... No doubt Bosworth had come here out of a sense of duty, not really expecting to enjoy himself. And now, because he has enjoyed the visit, he is having an attack of guilt in case he has bored me, Dr. MacIntyre thought. "I believe he likes me," Dr. MacIntyre said to himself, and then shook his head over his own vanity. "Now, where did I put that tobacco tin?" he asked.

David was looking at the three healthy children in the silver-framed photograph which, along with a faded picture of a very pretty woman in Edwardian dress, held the position of honor on the mantelpiece.

"That was my wife," Dr. MacIntyre remarked quietly. "And these are my grandchildren," he added, straightening the silver frame to let the three young faces smile directly into the room. "Charming," David said politely, but he was much more interested in the photograph of Mrs. MacIntyre. She reminded him strangely of someone.

"Brats," Dr. MacIntyre said, not without affection. "Thank heaven it was decent weather today, or we shouldn't have been given a moment's peace. Chopsticks on the piano, cuttings from magazines scattered all around, portraits of me being made ... I can't even fall asleep in my own armchair in case I am drawn with my mouth open. Ah! Here it is!" He retrieved the tobacco tin from the side of the chess table. He filled his pipe thoughtfully, looked down at the chessmen on the board. "I'll have to watch out, or I'll be running into difficulties. The schoolmaster plays a canny game. Of course, I can always blame my mistakes on the view." As he lit his pipe, he raised his eyes and looked out over the Sound and its shining waters.

David came over to join him. The two men stood in silence for a few moments.

"I envy you living here," David said suddenly, and was surprised to hear his own words.

"You are seeing it at its best today, I might warn you," Dr. MacIntyre said deprecatingly, but he was pleased all the same. And now, he thought, Bosworth will say it must be quite awesome in the winter months. His visitors always did. But David's next remark made him turn to look at the young man with surprise.

"Beautiful, but cruel," David was saying. "So much land, so few people, so little for even those people to live on. And why? Fenton-Stevens says it was always wild land, only good for grouse and deer. True, you can't do much with mountains except admire them or climb them. But where there are mountains, there must be valleys. And where there are valleys, there could be good roads and small towns and light industries. When we motored from Glasgow to Loch Innish, we passed enough torrents and waterfalls to give electric power to the whole of Scotland. Then why aren't there electric railways opening up the whole place? They'd bring more than they would take away: they don't have to make a place ugly. I'm thinking of Switzerland, you see." He stopped abruptly, aware that he was perhaps suggesting something that Dr. MacIntyre would deplore. Many people, even Scotsmen, would be annoyed by such an idea.

Dr. MacIntyre was watching him with interested eyes. He said nothing, as if he were waiting for David to go on. And David realized that Dr. MacIntyre's surprise was not caused by any new ideas that had been presented to him, but by the fact that David—an Englishman—had actually thought of them.

But David didn't speak. He was telling himself gloomily that whatever he could say about the Highlands—their neglect for almost two hundred years, the fact that as far as they were concerned the Industrial Revolution or the prosperity of the nineteenth century might never have existed in the British Isles, the lack of any large-scale plan with real determination behind it—well, Dr. MacIntyre had already thought of all these things. Anything David said might only look as if he were trying a little show for Dr. MacIntyre's benefit. Perhaps he *had* been enjoying that moment too much, when he felt he had captured Dr. MacIntyre's attention. Yet, it was more than that. He glanced sharply at Dr. MacIntyre to see if there was any trace of amusement in his eyes.

"Of course," David said, "I should admit that I never even thought about all this until I came to visit this part of the world."

Dr. MacIntyre looked at David thoughtfully. Visitors usually accepted what they saw, and asked no questions. Either they praised the scenery and the beauties of the simple life—and then after three or four weeks they went home to modern conveniences—or they remarked how isolated and desolate it all was, how very primitive, and never stopped to wonder why. I have a weakness, Dr. MacIntyre thought, for young people who ask an intelligent why.

He laid his hand on David's shoulder and said, "I have something here that might interest you." He led him to a bookcase, with more photographs and snapshots placed on its top. He chose one and handed it to David. It was a group of young men in the dress of forty years ago.

"Do you know anyone there?" he asked. "I'll give you a clue. It was taken in our last year at Balliol."

David recognized MacIntyre's direct eye, strong nose, and determined jaw line. But Walter Chaundler was not so easy to find. David's unsuccessful attempts amused Dr. MacIntyre.

"There he is!" He pointed to the most elegant young blade of them all. "Of course, the photograph hasn't aged very well." He examined its yellow, faded surface. "We all look as if we were giving imitations of William Tell's son mixed with Oscar Wilde."

"And a touch of George Washington after he cut down the cherry tree," David suggested.

"After he confessed," Dr. MacIntyre emended. They both looked at the photograph and laughed in agreement. "It is a nice old horror," MacIntyre said affectionately, as he replaced it carefully in its exact place on the bookcase. David was thinking of Walter Chaundler. He was remembering the quiet, thin face, imperceptible in a crowd, vague even to the pupils he tutored. David glanced towards the photograph again, and felt a sense of depression. On the surface, Chaundler's was the more successful life compared to that of the man who had suddenly retired to the simplicity of this island. On the surface . . . but the photograph pointed him out quite clearly as the less successful man. Perhaps not in his career; but somehow, some way, in himself.

David said slowly, "Strange how one changes."

17

MacIntyre seemed to read his thoughts. "If I were a young man again, there is one bit of advice I would like to get." He paused then, and smiled. "Now that's an old man talking, if ever I heard one."

"What would that be, sir?" David asked.

"Well," Dr. MacIntyre said, "a man's life is divided into two parts: there is his work and there is his own private life. Two small worlds which he has to make for himself. And it is only when he is old, and the time for decision is over, that he may realize he did not need to neglect one for the other. For if he concentrated too much on one of them, then he really confused their purpose. He had thought that either a successful career was life, or life itself was a career. He hadn't realized that his work and his own private life should be given the same amount of thought, that they should grow along with each other, each influencing the other, each developing the other. Without that balance, he will find himself an incomplete man. That's the tragic thing about age: to realize you have somehow never seen what *is* happiness until it was too late to start building it up. For it has to be built. Pleasure is a simple thing: you can choose it, buy it, even have it as a gift. It only depends on your taste. But happiness is much more complicated: you have got to build it yourself."

"But what about the uneven start in life?" David asked.

"Oh, I know that even those who get that head start have to work pretty hard if they want to achieve anything for themselves. But—"

He paused. That was cold consolation. You might have contempt for those who depended on their father's name or their grandfather's money—the "borrowers," you could call them—but they still had an easier time of it, even in the smallest things. They could go to a concert, buy a ticket for a theater or a copy of a book they wanted, without having to miss lunch for the next three days to pay for each of these pleasures. Yet, even the man who could make the choice of feeding his mind and starving his body was lucky in his way: he had his head start, too, over those who had to starve both mind and body. There were plenty of them. Too many ... David stared angrily out at the blue sea with its rim of clear bright green.

"But it is the small worries that all link up to form a chain round your ankles. It isn't easy to run, that way. And if a man manages it, in spite of all the handicaps, he gets more sneers than praise. We all make jokes about the self-made

18

man; you'd think in Britain that the wealthy families had never been *nouveaux riches* at one time, too. If snobbery is as important as we assume it is, then we should be quite thorough about it. If it is age and custom that counts, then the descendant of the Saxon manor house, who is called plain 'Mr.,' is certainly more noble than any of the family of a fifteenth-century earl. Our mental habits are ludicrous. And damned unfair. Sorry, sir. But that is how it looks to me."

Dr. MacIntyre said, "I used the same sentence, many a time." The past tense was definite. There was kindliness and understanding in his eyes. He seemed to be telling David to accept the unfairness and the inequalities, not as a proof that difficulties were too big ever to be overcome, but rather as a challenge which, if well met, promised its own private reward. It was the inner success—the sense of striving for completeness—and not the outward signs of success which really mattered.

In that moment, a lot about Dr. MacIntyre became clear to David.

And then the door opened. Mrs. Lorrimer, Dr. MacIntyre's daughter, came once more into the room. She had the same expression of worry on her face with which she had welcomed Fenton-Stevens and David this afternoon when they had first arrived.

"That boat is in sight, Father," she said warningly. She was middle-aged, tall, and thin, with her fading blond hair caught in a heavy knot at the back of her head. Her blue eyes had faded, too, and so had her skin. There was the same bleached vagueness about her whole appearance. She was dressed in brown. She always dressed in brown because she had been told at the age of twenty how well she looked in brown. David couldn't know that, of course. All he knew was that her dress was very correct, very safe, and dull enough to be very expensive. She looked old enough, he decided, to be the mother of the three young children on the mantelpiece.

"Is it, Mary?" Dr. MacIntyre said, refusing to be hurried. On a clear day like this, the little steamer which brought mail, merchandise, livestock and occasional passengers to the various islands could be seen miles away. There was no need to get worried about it. "Where's Fenton-Stevens?" he asked. "I thought he was with you in the garden."

"That was a long time ago." There was a note of remonstrance in the cool, precise voice. "Eventually," it went on,

"Mr. Fenton-Stevens went over to explore the west shore with the children. I've been reading upstairs." Somehow, there was a slightly complaining effect, just a touch of self-pity, in the way she phrased her words. But Dr. MacIntyre either ignored or preferred not to notice.

"How nice," he said. "The rest would do you good, Mary."

His daughter did not acknowledge that probability. Father, she decided, was having one of his annoying moods. "Have you that letter ready for the boat, or can it wait until next week?" she asked.

"The boat won't arrive for another hour, Mary. I have plenty of time."

"I told the children to be sure to return for the boat," Mrs. Lorrimer said. "They can take the letter down to the jetty, and perhaps Angus will slip it into the post-bag for you."

"He always does," her father said genially. "We've a damned good postman, here, Bosworth. He never breaks a rule because he has never made any." David saw Mrs. Lorrimer flinch slightly at her father's choice of adjectives. But its purpose was achieved: no further suggestions were made to plague Dr. MacIntyre. And having established his own unflustered world again, the old man turned towards his desk with a glint of humor in his eyes and picked up his pen. "I'll join you later," he said to David. "Have a look at the holly-hocks."

That sounded a very pleasant way of spending a half hour. But unfortunately Mrs. Lorrimer was a very polite hostess, and insisted on accompanying David towards the garden.

chapter iii

Dr. MACINTYRE's house had been originally a row of three small cottages. The thick walls had been kept, the unnecessary doors had been plastered over, the windows had been enlarged and given shutters for protection in the winter, and a deep-gabled slate roof had been substituted for thatch. It stood very white and brightly smiling in the sunshine. A gray stone wall had been built across a short field to join the southwest corner of the house at right angles, and within the sheltered crook of this arm a garden had come to life. Here, all the warmth in the air was trapped and held and the hollyhocks grew.

David looked out over the bleak hillsides and then back at this smiling corner. "How remarkable to see anything growing except heather," he said.

Mrs. Lorrimer seemed hardly to notice the pleasure of the soft green grass underfoot. She ignored the excellent crop of vegetables, and looked critically at a rosebush which showed symptoms of withering. "It is very limited gardening, of course," she said. "There are so many things that simply refuse to grow here." She sounded as if it were necessary to concentrate on what couldn't be grown in the garden, rather than on the things that could. David wondered if her garden at home could grow bananas or coconuts, and if it could not, did that prove it was not a very good garden?

"Fine crop of hollyhocks," he said tactfully.

Mrs. Lorrimer looked frowningly at their bright reds and pinks, glowing with all the warmth and life of a Renoir painting. "It is so very odd," she said almost apologetically, "that Father ever came back here."

"Perhaps he likes living here."

"But he is so out of touch with everything."

David thought of the room which they had just left.

Mrs. Lorrimer's exact voice continued, "We thought he should retire to some place near us in Edinburgh. My husband is a Writer to the Signet there, you see." There was a slight pause to allow that fact to sink in. "Edinburgh really would have been much more of a spiritual home to him. Or Oxford."

David had flinched at the phrase. He said quickly, "I've always thought that a—a spiritual home is just not a matter of geography." He cleared his throat nervously, and was thankful that none of his Oxford friends had heard him use the phrase.

"You mean, it does not matter *where* one lives?" Mrs. Lorrimer was shocked: she was probably thinking of Glasgow.

"Emotionally or physically, yes. We all feel happier or less happy in certain places. But if there is any spiritual home, surely it is what we have collected inside our own heads? After all, Descartes thought out half of his philosophy when he spent a day in a Bavarian stove. And he lived much of his life in foreign armies although he wasn't at all warlike.

21

I don't think he would call the stove or the barracks his spiritual home: they were just places that suited him for examining his own thoughts. He didn't have to talk to people there, I suppose." Now, he thought, let's drop all this stuff about spiritual homes and enjoy the garden instead.

"Really!" Mrs. Lorrimer murmured. Inside a stove—but how ridiculous. Was he being facetious? Surely he didn't mean that people who talked of spiritual homes had few resources inside their own minds? She stared at him blankly. He was looking now at the row of hollyhocks against the wall, his hands deep in the pockets of his gray flannel trousers. She admitted with a certain amount of effort that he was not disagreeable to look at. He was tall, and carried himself well. Even when he was standing negligently, as he was at this moment, he did not slouch. He wasn't handsome like George Fenton-Stevens, of course, just as he had not his charm of manner either. Gray eyes under strong eyebrows. Black hair, thick and rather too long, but then barbers were difficult to find in this part of the world. A mouth which was pleasant enough when it smiled, but it seemed to fall naturally into a firm line. Rather too strong a face, Mrs. Lorrimer's taste decided as she completed her inventory. Still, he was not unattractive. Mrs. Lorrimer determined to try again.

"Were you at school with George Fenton-Stevens?"

"No." David turned away from the hollyhocks.

"Where did you go to school?"

"In London." There was a fleeting smile. This insistence on schools always amused him: the safe conversational gambit, becoming suddenly less safe when London was given so broadly. That might, people always thought as they withdrew their cloaks just an inch, mean even a board-school. Mrs. Lorrimer obviously thought so.

"Oh!" She was vaguely distressed, as if she had been talking to a legless man and had asked him how he liked dancing. "But you are at Oxford?"

"Yes." This time he looked at her very directly. "On a scholarship," he said very clearly. Just as your father was, he thought. Just as more than half the men at Oxford are.

"How interesting," she was saying, but her voice was far from interested. "And what are you going to do after Oxford?"

"That isn't decided yet." It wouldn't be, until he had First Class Honors. If he didn't get that, then his choice of career would narrow down.

"Really?" Mrs. Lorrimer was amazed. "I thought young men always knew at this stage of their lives what they were aiming for."

They know, he thought. Most of them know, but only some of them can talk about it. There is nothing like a nice little private bank account to let one talk confidently about the future.

Mrs. Lorrimer was saying, "Mr. Fenton-Stevens is thinking of the Foreign Office, I hear. A diplomat's life must be so interesting, don't you think?"

David agreed politely, but there was a strained look about his mouth.

What an odd young man, Mrs. Lorrimer decided. He talked so little about the things that really mattered. This was not what George Fenton-Stevens had led her to expect from his friend. Brilliant talker, editor of this magazine, secretary of that Society, leading light in the Union. . . . Why, he had made David Bosworth sound really quite interesting. She picked one of the roses, and looked at its soft petals without seeing them. She liked young men handsome and well-mannered, with nice families and definite careers and high hopes. Who didn't, with three growing daughters to be launched into successful marriages?

She tried once more. "And how is Lady Fenton-Stevens?"

David turned to look at her with some surprise.

"Charming woman," Mrs. Lorrimer said, on the strength of one chance meeting some three years ago in Edinburgh. Not that Mrs. Lorrimer approved of all the publicity which Lady Fenton-Stevens managed to attract in the newspapers.

David only smiled, and Mrs. Lorrimer felt uneasy. If she had been a mind reader, she would have been horrified.

"You are a friend of the family's, aren't you?" she asked.

"Not exactly. I'm staying at Loch Innish as a tutor. George's young brother and his cousin need some grounding, and George and I are doing some reading together too when we get time for that." David made an effort to end this question-and-answer conversation. "The Lodge is an interesting old place. It must have seen a lot of fighting in the days when the McDonalds owned it. Their coat of arms is carved over the entrance, you know." And a Margaret McDonald is the housekeeper, and a Malcolm McDonald is the head ghillie—but let that pass, he thought tactfully.

"Oh, these McDonalds were very good sheep-stealers and pirates, themselves," Mrs. Lorrimer said lightly. "It isn't wise to investigate any of the past history around here. All these Highlanders were very wild."

"Fortunately for us!" David said with a laugh. "Or England might have found herself being attacked by Norsemen who had settled quite cosily in these mountains."

There was a tolerant silence. Oh God, David thought, isn't that letter finished yet? And then, as his eyes left the garden, searching for some possible piece of conversation which would not leave them feeling this hidden antagonism, he found his release. "Hello!" he said. "There is someone in rather a hurry." He pointed to a small thin figure scrambling over the hillside with more energy than grace.

"That's Betty," Mrs. Lorrimer said. "I wonder where the others can be?" There was a motherly note of anxiety in her voice which made her sound human for the first time.

"Oh, they'll be all right, Mrs. Lorrimer," David said. "George is really awfully good with children. He handles his small brother and shrimp of a cousin very well."

Mrs. Lorrimer looked strangely at the young man beside her. But she did not reply, for her attention was gathering on her daughter, now within polite calling distance.

"Don't jump like that, Betty. It's dangerous. You'll sprain your ankle."

The girl, one of those long-legged polelike creatures who haven't yet become conscious of their sex, waved cheerily back, but she stopped leaping from mound to mound obediently and settled into a jogging run.

"I wish I had had three boys," Mrs. Lorrimer said as if to herself. "It would not matter if they were to thicken their ankles, or break a nose, or have a scar on their cheek. Just look at you, Betty!"

Betty, red-cheeked and breathless, looked. She had sea-weed stains across the shoulders of her blouse, her skirt was wet at the hem as if she had waded in the sea and had misjudged the height of a wave, there was a long red sore on her leg still bleeding slightly, and her shoes were caked with the black earth of the peat bog.

"Doesn't hurt a bit," she assured her mother cheerfully, looking down at the cut on her leg. "We were exploring the rocks, trying to show George the seals, and I slipped into a pool. It's nothing." She surveyed David gravely, with frank curiosity. To her, a man meant someone who could run more quickly and climb more rocks than she could. He also meant someone who paid no attention to her, but just let her

24

come along with her sisters. But this man was smiling as he watched her. She felt he was sort of on her side.

Mother was asking questions again. Betty said wearily, conscious of her audience, "Oh, Moira and George have gone to the village to see the boat come in. I came to get Grandpa's old letter."

Just wait until I can talk to you alone, my girl, Mrs. Lorrimer thought. "*And* to wash and change." She looked angrily at the scarred leg. "Put some iodine on that. And wear your stockings. You are much too big a girl to go running about with bare legs."

Betty's red cheeks deepened in color as she was disciplined in public. She glanced nervously at the man standing so silently beside her mother.

"Yes, Mummy," she said dutifully.

Old letter, indeed, Mrs. Lorrimer thought. "And where's Penelope?"

"She stayed to see if the seals came. Don't worry, Mummy," she went on quickly seeing the frown on her mother's face. "She isn't climbing over the rocks. She's sitting on the shore. She can't fall off there." Betty, with her natural good humor once more regained, moved towards the house. She called over her shoulder to David, "Aren't you going down to see the boat come in? There are horses on board, today. Once, there was a storm and the waves were so big that when the horses were swimming ashore—"

"Betty! You are late," Mrs. Lorrimer interrupted.

"Yes, Mummy." Betty moved another three feet. "You couldn't see their heads," she finished for David's benefit, and then ran.

David felt himself abandoned once more to Mrs. Lorrimer's quiet disapproval. If only she would go away and do what she wanted to do. It would be pleasant to stretch out on the grass and wait here for George to return. Or it would be pleasant to explore the island. This was a perfect day for exploring.

He said suddenly, "I say, Mrs. Lorrimer, why don't you let me go over to the Atlantic shore and bring your daughter home? She may forget all about time, over there." David looked towards the western path across the island. "I suppose if I follow that, I can't go wrong?"

"There is a stretch of sand at the end of that road. She is probably there. I suppose she will be all right, really. But I never know what these children are up to, next. Cave-exploring, rock-climbing, diving through Atlantic breakers.

They think they are indestructible." Mrs. Lorrimer spoke with a certain relief. She really had wasted so much of this afternoon already.

"I'll find her, and bring her home to tea. Don't worry. No trouble at all. I should like a walk. Yes, really I should," David said quickly, and started towards the road. Just at that last moment, he had felt Mrs. Lorrimer was about to change her mind after all.

He was perfectly right about that. She remained standing there, hesitating. But she was too late now. She turned and went indoors.

He would have been amused if he had known that Mrs. Lorrimer had already started worrying about him, and worrying all the more because she couldn't imagine why she should be worrying. But all he was thinking about was the fact that he was free for the next hour, that he was actually going to be left alone. He never seemed to be able to be alone over at the Lodge, not until the others went to bed. They were gregarious animals and assumed that everyone wanted to be like them; an afternoon spent by themselves would seem to them intolerable. This, David decided as he looked with keen pleasure around him, is sheer luxury. The air tasted of heather and bracken and sea. There was silence, so much silence that it was almost a sound; for here, in the middle of the island, the murmur of the waves had faded in the sloping moorland, and the solitary falcon overhead made no cry.

He remembered his errand, and increased his pace slightly. If he must play nursemaid to get this hour, he was quite willing to do it: the walk across the island was well worth it. For somehow, from the photograph in MacIntyre's study, David had formed the idea that Betty was the oldest child— she was easily identified, freckles and all. So he must keep his eyes open for some pigtailed creature with a passion for seals. But perhaps, he thought hopefully, she had gone home already, taking a short cut, like Betty, across the hills. That would make things perfect.

On the west side of the island there were no houses whatever. The scattered trees had disappeared too—the last ones he had passed had only been man-height, with all their meager branches growing eastward. The sun's reflection dazzled his eyes for a moment; and then he saw, at either end of the stretch of shining sand, black rocks bared like giant teeth jutting boldly up against the enormous breakers. As he watched, a small fragment of the black rock moved and dived into a spent wave. Another piece of glistening rock raised itself and then lay down again. Good Lord, he thought, there *are* seals after all. He stood still; if he moved, they would take fright. He remembered, dutifully, to look for the Lorrimer child. She wasn't there.

Instead, he saw the girl with the auburn hair and the bright blue sweater. She was sitting on the sand, so motionless that the outcrop of black rock beside her had partly hidden her, and she was looking at the seals. She hadn't noticed him.

His first impulse was to leave. You don't have to see her again, he told himself. He waited, perhaps hoping that she might turn her head. You don't have to see her, he told himself again.

And then he began to walk slowly towards her.

chapter iv

As HE reached her, his heavy shoes sank into the harsh sand, and the sound made her turn her head.

"Hello," he said—hesitated, and then dropped casually down beside her on the sand. She smiled, but she did not speak. She lost the startled look which had greeted him.

David said, "Sorry, I'm afraid I've frightened off your friends." After his first quick glance at her face, he had looked away, and now all his interest seemed to be focused on the seals as they dived into the water and stayed there.

She was silent for some moments. And then, as if she had suddenly realized that it was her turn to say something, she spoke quickly, still clinging to the subject that he had given her. "They are easily frightened." She hesitated, but as he seemed to be perfectly happy just sitting there, waiting for her to speak, she gained confidence. Her voice became more natural. "They *are* funny, you know. They love showing off, and they will flap up on these rocks and pose for us because they simply can't help it. Then, if we move, they'll dive into the sea. But a little later, if we keep quite still once more, they'll come back on to the rocks. They'll look round, as if they were making quite sure we were still there, and they'll start posing again."

"Disappointing for them, when they find their audience has gone home to tea. What were you trying to do, sitting so still? Tame them?"

"I don't always sit quite so still." She looked at him with her blue eyes smiling. The nervous tightness in her throat had altogether disappeared now, and she no longer felt as if each word were being strangled. "You see," she admitted, "sometimes I get tired of them on the rock. They aren't so very pretty bouncing around on land, and their fur gets dried—all sort of brown and spotty. So I move, and they dive. They really are beautiful when they dive. And when they come back on to the rocks, they are black and glistening. Much more attractive."

He found he was laughing, partly because of the vivacity in her face, partly because she was laughing at herself. "One-woman society for the preservation of the beauty of the seal," he said. "And what else do you do over here? Fascinate the waves?"

"They do the fascinating," she admitted.

And then her conversation crumpled under her like a treacherous mountain path, and she was left stranded, afraid to go back, unable to go on. That was the kind of remark which her mother and Moira called silly. Her cheeks flushed. There was a pause. The more things she tried to think of, the less she found to say.

"What *do* you do?" he insisted gently. Did she just think about herself? Wasn't that what girls thought of, mostly? Even when they went out with a man they couldn't lose the habit: you'd see them looking at themselves in mirrored walls in a restaurant, comparing other women with themselves. In cinemas and theaters they still found another kind of mirror, measuring their own lives by what they saw. And even when they read, there was that conscious reflection: this heroine is like, this villainess unlike, me. But what did they think about when they could sit and watch this sea with so much real interest?

"Oh . . ." she said. "This and that." She pretended to be unaware that he was watching her, and she turned her face to look out to sea. But she knew that his eyes were still on her. She felt a strange mixture of excitement and tension and embarrassment, and it wasn't altogether unpleasant. She seemed to be mesmerized by it, for all she could do was to stare at the sea, and at this moment she could think of nothing at all.

Sugar and spice, David was thinking, was that all girls were made of? Born with good bones and healthy blood, three well-chosen meals a day, no worries. That produced prettiness, the kind of perfect hair and skin and coloring which Eleanor Fenton-Stevens had too. But this girl—she had turned her eyes away, and he could look at her now quite openly without being seen—this girl . . . This, he realized in amazement, this is what I think is beauty. He stared at her unbelievingly. If he were another man, he might never have even thought she was beautiful: ideas of beauty were as varied as the men who looked at it. What he felt, now, as he looked at this girl, depended on what he himself was. It was the proof of some strange link. This morning, he had thought he was irrational. Now he knew that he had only met a strange and new experience, as overwhelming as that of a man who has lived on the plains all his life and has been well content with them until, suddenly, he comes upon the high ranges of mountain peaks.

He became aware that she had been speaking. She must have asked a question, for she was now looking at him, waiting for his reply.

He said, "I'm sorry. I didn't quite . . ." He recovered his sadly misplaced wits. "I was thinking about the sea," he said. "You can hardly help thinking about it, can you?"

"No; it is sort of everywhere. At first, you notice its colors and sounds, and you feel its power. Then you think of the sky, too, and how the sea and sky reflect each other, each influencing the other. They are two separate things, and yet they aren't separate. I mean—" she looked at him quickly to see if he were amused at her, but he was listening politely and quite seriously. "I mean, a bright sky makes an angry sea less terrifying. Or a dark sky will make a calm, peaceful sea quite forbidding. So when you start thinking of all the variations they can produce on each other, then—well, that is what I really meant when I said that the sea did the fascinating."

He was still looking at her, but there was another kind of interest in his eyes. "Yes," he said, "fascinating. Just as its power is terrifying. Sailors love and hate it, you know."

"Yet they keep going back to it. Few leave it."

"I expect they find they start to worry too much when they live on land. The sea is so dominant that we can't help remembering how small all our problems and worries are.

The sea will still be there when they are all buried with us." He grinned and said, "Perhaps that is why some people, including me, never feel quite comfortable when we look at the sea. It takes away our sense of importance."

"Or perhaps they are poor sailors." It was as if she had said, "I don't believe *you* have a sense of importance," and he felt ridiculously pleased. Then, remembering worries and problems and people who did not like the sea, he thought of Mrs. Lorrimer, who would rather be spending a summer somewhere else.

"Good Lord!" he said, "I was sent over here to collect a child. I quite forgot." Damnation, he thought, and rose hastily to his feet. But there was no one else on the shore, not even behind the small isolated rocks cropping through the bed of powdered shells.

He looked down at the girl, realizing then who she was and saw by the look on her face that he had indeed blundered. There was amazement—well, he deserved that—and there was also a hint of disappointment. He could have understood annoyance. But why disappointment? He started making appropriate excuses: he hadn't caught her name this morning ... awfully bad at names: the photograph in the study; Betty's likeness to the oldest girl in it. ... But he ended them by feeling he had only made matters worse.

He rubbed the back of his head and looked at her ruefully. "Too many 'I thoughts' in all this, if you ask me," he said.

She was smiling now. But as she rose to her feet and then brushed the hard particles of shell down from her skirt, there was some change in her manner. The warmth and the ease had gone. She was merely polite and charming and very practical.

"If you were sent over here to fetch me, then we are both in disgrace," she said. "The boat must have arrived ages ago and tea is probably over."

"Shocking," he admitted. "But then I never did do the right thing. I'm especially glad I didn't, today."

She didn't seem to hear that last sentence, mumbled as it had been. He was relieved in a way, because he was embarrassed now that he had said it. It had just slipped out, somehow. All in all, he reflected moodily as they walked towards the road, he was in rather poor form today—at least, with this girl. That idea depressed him.

But Penelope Lorrimer had heard the sentence all right. And she was feeling happier once more, yet not so happy as she had been. Disappointment still was there in her heart, mocking her for her foolishness. That was what came of imagining things the way you wanted them to happen. For she had thought, when he had appeared on the shore so suddenly behind her, that he had walked across the island to meet her. She had imagined the scene when the others returned to the house—where's Penelope, oh still over on the shore, now you know I don't like her to be there alone, Penelope's my second daughter who is studying painting, I believe you met her for a moment this morning in the McDonald cottage... And it hadn't been at all like that. Instead, he had come to look for a stray child. He hadn't even known her name.

And she had stayed on the shore, thinking that perhaps he might come, thinking—as the others left her—that surely he and Grandfather had finished talking and there might be time for a walk over to the west shore, and perhaps, just perhaps, but what fun if he did, perhaps he would come over here. And he had, but not in the way she had wanted it. If I were a man, she thought, and if I, as a man, had felt anything the way I felt in the McDonald cottage this morning, then I would have walked across three islands to meet the girl again. But either what she had felt had not been felt by this man, or men just did not think this way. She wondered, still remembering the McDonald cottage, if he said how d'you do like that to every girl. Surely he couldn't, simply couldn't, go about staring at people when he first met them as if his whole life had stopped for a moment. And first, she had stared back at him, and then she had felt as helpless as if she had been drowning, and then she had panicked, and then she had rushed out of the cottage saying she would be late for something or other. Late, and an idiot, imagining—when the first wild surge of feeling had subsided—that he had known that strange emotion too. Surely anything so strong as that must have been shared. But it hadn't been. She felt a warm flush spread over her cheeks.

Her color deepened still more as she heard him laugh. He was saying that now they were even: *she* hadn't been listening, this time, and his question was left floating in the air.

"It wasn't worth answering, anyway," he said. "Questions and answers are a dull way of learning about people." Damn, he thought, I am always saying more than I should to her. That had been a particularly naïve approach. He racked his brains for a quotation or two—this scenery called for some, and he had been quite free with them as he had walked over here by himself. Usually, there was always some poetry lying around in his head to be picked up and presented. But today, or now at least, his memory was failing him. He searched for his pipe and tobacco.

But that failed, too. The matches flickered and died in the strong southwest breeze. He paused, turned his back to the wind, and then as the match was still blown out before the pipe was set going, she suddenly cupped her hands around the pipe to form a windbreak. He looked up from the flaring loose strands of tobacco in surprise. She had been completely natural in her action: she was watching the tobacco as critically as he himself might have done.

"That's it, I think," she said. "My grandfather is always having the same kind of trouble with damp matches." She looked up at him and smiled. She had dropped her hands as soon as the tobacco was lit, but her eyes were still held by his. It was the McDonald cottage all over again.

She turned away hurriedly, and said quickly, "We really ought to hurry. We are frightfully late."

"Yes," he said.

They started walking towards the village, but their pace was just as slow as it had been before. He began to talk. Gradually, she was made to talk too. A strange mixture of talk about people and food and pictures and plays and novels. Little things, trivial things perhaps, never definitely with an end or a beginning, always merging as their minds set out to entertain each other and were in themselves entertained. But they were all somehow vitally important to both of them, as they unconsciously strove to build up the shadowy outline of each other's life. It would have been simpler if they could have said directly, "Who are you? What are you?"

David, if he had found any time to rationalize—his favorite method of defense against women in these last months at Oxford—would have found himself in grave difficulties. He was talking, and listening in his turn, without any fashionable pretense or attitudes. His words came easily, as they did when he was alone. Now he could quote himself without fear of a misplaced interruption or of a dazed tolerant smile, or—worse still—of the supercilious smirk which warned you that everything you said was being taken down *and* would be used against you. And if he talked well, it was not for the old reason that he wanted to talk well, but also because he wanted to hear her replies.

As for Penny, even her most critical mother—if she could have listened—would have had to admit in spite of alarm that her daughter had never been more charming.

They came at last to the path that led to the house on the hill. It was only when they saw the group standing at the doorway that they realized how late they must be. For Captain MacLean was there. David remembered with sudden guilt that there were such things as tide and current to be considered. MacLean had warned them to be ready to sail at six o'clock.

Betty came running towards them. "You're late, awfully late. What went wrong? Penny, Mother's simply furious. You missed tea."

David noticed Penny's suddenly grave face. "I'm sorry about this," he said. "It's my fault."

"No, it wasn't. It was mine, too. The time seemed so short."

"Did it?" He was pleased.

"Yes," she said simply. They had forgotten about Betty. But she reminded them quickly enough.

"It was both their faults," she called to the waiting group as she ran back to them.

Penny said furiously, "That's torn it. I sometimes wonder if I was really so impossible at her age."

"We all were. Come on, cheer up." David still looked bewildered at the peculiar reactions to a harmless walk. God, he thought, does that old dragon think I was seducing her daughter? Then he saw that Penny was more embarrassed than he was. "Aren't you ever allowed out alone?" he asked half-jokingly.

"We have pretty strict rules," she said in a low voice. Now he would think that she was only a schoolgirl. That would be enough to damn her in the eyes of any University man. She wished the hillside would open and swallow her up.

As they reached the group at the door, she forced a disinterested air which deceived neither her mother nor Moira. Moira was looking very much elder-sister. By one year, Penny thought angrily. She ignored Moira, and said to her mother, "Sorry we were late."

"We had no idea of the time," David said cheerfully. "My watch stopped. I'm awfully sorry if we kept you waiting."

"Captain MacLean has been waiting," Mrs. Lorrimer said with marked dignity, "for almost fifteen minutes."

"We've time enough yet," MacLean said with his usual slow smile. "Time enough."

"My fault entirely," David said, conscious of Fenton-Stevens's amused eye. "I didn't believe that seals would appear. So we waited until they did."

33

"They actually did?" George was interested now.

"A regular squad, complete with sergeant major and waxed mustache."

Penny laughed, and the others smiled, all except Mrs. Lorrimer, who thought the remark quite meaningless.

"Well," Dr. MacIntyre said, "I'm glad you did have time to see the Atlantic coast. Good-by. And come again. Delighted to see you. We all might have a picnic together, some day." He waved a friendly hand to the two young men, and retired into the house with an abruptness which David thought admirable.

"That would be grand," George said to Mrs. Lorrimer. "We shall have another free day in a week's time."

"But we are leaving at the end of the month, and that's next week," Betty said. There was exaggerated disappointment in her voice. Mrs. Lorrimer made a mental note to speak to Betty really severely this evening: far too much play-acting in front of people, far too much consciousness of an audience.

"Well, perhaps we could arrange an earlier date than that," Fenton-Stevens said. "What day would suit you, Mrs. Lorrimer?"

David let George do all the arrangement. George liked that kind of thing, anyway. David stood silent, near Penny, not looking at her and yet conscious of her. He moved restlessly as George and Mrs. Lorrimer, then Betty and Moira and even MacLean, were all drawn into the whirlpool of discussion. First the day, then the time, then the place... what did it all matter? He and Penny would not be allowed one moment together. They would have to listen to others, talk to others, and hardly dare look at each other. Even now, the family's influence was trying to check the current of intimacy which had flowed so easily between them only half an hour ago.

It was with relief that he heard MacLean say that they must leave.

The good-by was as disappointing as he had feared. Their hands touched briefly. Her eyes wouldn't meet his. George, he noticed with some bitterness, was given a longer handshake and a generous smile.

David was sullen, and he knew it, which made him even more bad-tempered as he walked with Fenton-Stevens and MacLean to the jetty. He had begun to feel that he had never been more foolish in his life than he had been that afternoon. He groaned at the thought of his self-confidence, based on so little. A pretty girl had at least a face to justify her hopes.

Mrs. McDonald waved her white apron from the door of her cottage as they sailed out into the Sound and veered north for Loch Innish. The MacIntyre house seemed deserted. Then the Devil's Elbow crooked out, and the village was hidden behind it. Inchnamurren became a lonely island on a lonely sea.

George was watching him curiously. "I had rather a decent time," he said. "Hadn't you?"

"Yes," David said, "Dr. MacIntyre was very good value." And he kept the conversation determinedly on Dr. MacIntyre throughout the rest of the journey to the Lodge at Loch Innish.

chapter v

IN DR. MACINTYRE'S study, Mrs. Lorrimer was finishing her monologue. "And the first thing that frightens away a young man is a girl who sets her cap at him," she concluded.

Penny turned away from the window as the small sailing boat disappeared behind the Devil's Elbow, ignored Moira's superior grin, and said angrily, "I wasn't, Mother. We were walking and talking."

"You missed tea, and that was rudeness to both your grandfather and to Mr. Fenton-Stevens. I am not objecting to walking and talking. I am objecting to bad manners."

Dr. MacIntyre rustled his newspaper impatiently. It had arrived by the afternoon's boat, and so far there had not been ten consecutive minutes to enjoy it. He noticed Penny's angry eyes. Time to change the subject, he thought. He said, "Depression in America, depression here, and the same trouble in Europe. It looks bad."

"Let's see Grandpa." Moira leaned over his shoulder to read the news. Moira had gone political since she had become a history student at Edinburgh University. Her conversation was now a strange mixture of international understanding and what were her chances on the Varsity tennis team. Her grandfather studied her fair hair, her young-pretty face so like Betty's. But neither she nor Betty would keep that prettiness in middle age. They hadn't the bones for it: they had their father's lack of features. Penny was different. She had good bones, something that lasted—if she had a happy life. He stopped thinking about faces as Moira's even breathing down the back of his neck aroused him. He never could bear someone reading over his shoulder.

"Here, take it." He handed the paper to her. "Now go away and read it someplace else."

Moira looked surprised, but obeyed.

"You, too, Penny. Go out and have a walk. Another one. And Moira," he added as the two girls reached the door, "bring that paper back in half an hour, properly folded, with the pages in the right order."

He rose and searched for his pipe. "Bad enough to be disturbed in the middle of an editorial without having the paper made altogether unreadable."

"Then why did you give it to her, Father?" Mary asked.

"I wanted to have a talk with you, Mary."

Mrs. Lorrimer's surprise gave way to a vague uneasiness. She had not heard this tone of voice for twenty years.

Dr. MacIntyre paused, and then he filled his pipe thoughtfully. His intelligent blue eyes looked up suddenly at her from under his thick white eyebrows. "I think you worry too much about the children, Mary. Why don't you go alone with Charles to North Berwick in August, and have a good holiday together? The girls can stay on here for another month. It would do you all a world of good."

"I don't see how it would."

"If I must be frank, Mary, then I shall say that the children are getting on your nerves, and soon you will get on theirs. That is the quickest way to lose their affection, you know."

"Father, I think you are talking nonsense. What nerves? Why should they lose affection for me? I have been a good mother, haven't I?"

"Excellent. An excellent wife, too," he said soothingly. "But damn it all, Mary, the girls are getting big enough to stand on their own feet. You can now sit back and enjoy yourself."

"Not yet," Mary said quickly.

"Certainly with Moira and Penelope. I agree Betty needs you for another few years."

"And then there's no more need for me? Father, you

36

don't know how cruel you sound." Mary Lorrimer was indeed hurt.

"I am *not* cruel," Dr. MacIntyre said angrily. "And remember, I know something about the upbringing of girls." You were not such a bad specimen either, he thought, when you were twenty.

"You see," he went on sadly, "the most a father and mother can do is to give their children a good beginning—health, character, moral sense. You cannot go on controlling their development. That is their own life. But as long as they stick to the foundation you've given them, they won't go essentially wrong. You worry too much. God knows why. If your daughters were sneaking little hypocrites, or cross-eyed gnomes, or nymphomaniacs, you might have some cause for worry. Damn it all, Mary, they have as good a chance of happiness as any girl. Each one's life is what she makes of it."

"But they have such unsettled ideas. Penelope with her plans centered on London and this Slade School. Why can't she be content with the School of Art at home? Why can't Moira find something suitable to do in Edinburgh, instead of thinking of the League of Nations? They are both pretty girls, I must admit. They could marry suitable men, who would give them security and a decent position in life. That would save them a lot of tears."

"Perhaps they don't want your suitable young men. Perhaps they want to decide for themselves, even if it does mean tears. Let them make their own mistakes, Mary. They are old enough to pay for them."

"You didn't let me make any mistakes, Father."

He looked at her. He said quietly, "Well, if you feel you have made no mistakes, you must be a completely happy woman indeed."

Mary glanced at him sharply. But he was relighting his pipe intently. She moistened her lips, pale and thin now—once they had had the same curve as Betty's, ready to laugh, eager to smile—and her eyes widened for a moment so that they lost the narrow, worried look which had robbed them of youth. Then she looked down at her smooth, well-manicured hands lying folded in her lap. She picked a small white thread off her brown shirt (the material was excellent, always a pleasure to look at, she thought), folded her hands again in that very composed way and studied the toes of her long narrow shoes. Even the way she sat, rather erect, with her ankles delicately crossed, annoyed Dr. MacIntyre at this moment.

With an effort, he said gently, "Don't you trust the girls? If you don't trust them, then you must feel you have failed in bringing them up."

"Of course I trust them."

"Then stop worrying, Mary. Why don't you have this holiday alone with Charles? It's good for married people, anyway, to get away by themselves." ... You could even, with the money you will spend at North Berwick, have a holiday in Salzburg or Ragusa. ... But he knew it was useless suggesting that.

"But we all enjoy being together, Father." Her voice held quiet reproof.

"I know that. But look, Mary—" God in Heaven, what was the use? Mary was right: Mary had such well-selected friends; Mary had such a comfortable, large and well-run house; Mary had three healthy and pretty daughters; Mary had a faithful husband with money; Mary was a virtuous woman. How could Mary be wrong?

"But what, Father?"

"Nothing, my dear, nothing."

"You couldn't possibly mean that I am to take no interest in what happens to Moira or to Penelope. It wouldn't be natural ..."

"It wouldn't. I didn't say you were to drop all interest. I said you should not take more interest than they now need. If they want your advice and help, they will come to you. And they will value it all the more then. Look at us, at this very moment. I am giving you advice which you did not ask for, so you don't like it and probably won't listen to it." He smiled. The point was well-proven.

But Mary didn't smile. She rose to her feet, and said, "I must see about supper. We are having one of your old favorites tonight, Father. I must go and find out if Maggie has remembered to put in enough seasoning."

Maggie cooked well enough, Dr. MacIntyre reflected, for eleven months of the year. Strange how incapable she became each July. He contented himself with clearing his throat.

His daughter had reached the door. She said suddenly, "Besides, our circumstances are quite different. I am a middle-aged woman. The girls have their lives before them."

Dr. MacIntyre stared at the door which she closed

38

firmly, gently, behind her. His point had not been so well-proven after all, it seemed.

Penelope brought back his newspaper, neatly folded, and then she hovered round the room, looking at some books, straightening a pile of music, rearranging the flowers on his desk.

Dr. MacIntyre looked at the paper, laid it aside, and said in a resigned voice, "Well, what is it, Penny?"

"Oh . . . nothing. I'm sorry. I was just leaving."

"Were you?" Then he relented and said, "Come and sit over here. Only, *stop* fiddling around in that way." The end of July would come soon enough, and he would be left in peace then. Besides, he reminded himself, there were days in the long winter when he would have been very glad to have someone fiddling around. After all, he was fond of his grandchildren, fond of Mary too, even if she irritated him more and more. And they did make this effort to come and see him every July. He should be thankful that Charles did not make the effort.

"You aren't disturbing me in the least."

He lied with sudden good grace. Penny was his favorite granddaughter, although he did his best to hide that. He never had to explain his jokes to her. Besides, it flattered his vanity to look at her, to think that he was one quarter responsible for this young woman's existence. How extraordinary the way these young things suddenly grew up! He smiled as she crossed the room towards him. At this moment, she was so very serious: Mary's public lecture must be still rankling.

"I was thinking of the days," he said lightly, "when you called everything 'ripping' or 'marvelous,' from Spenser and Shelley to chocolates and ice cream. And food was 'scrumptious,' and all the boys you liked were 'simply spiffing,' and all the boys you didn't like were—now what was that particularly apt remark?—they were 'absolute drips.' And what was it you felt for your more attractive schoolteachers and film stars? A 'crush'?"

He had made her smile. That was better, much better. "It wasn't so very long ago, either," he went on. "You certainly have grown up in these last three years."

To his alarm, she suddenly came forward and kissed his ear. She must be really upset about something. A display of affection was not in the Lorrimer tradition.

"What was that for?" he asked.

"For cheering me up." She sat down on the hearthrug; her legs lay together sideways, one hand rested on her ankle, the other hand stretched flat on the ground beside her supported the weight of her body. She was a graceful creature, he thought. She reminded him more and more of her grandmother, of his own Penelope. At this moment, he remembered vividly when his Penelope had been Penny's age. And he had been young, as young as these two men who had visited him today. Fastened to a dying animal, he thought. And he looked down at Penny and felt a twinge of old age.

"Well," he said quickly, trying to recall their conversation. Like her grandmother, a pretty creature, graceful. Now she was sitting there, full of life and vitality, forty years of possible happiness still before her. She had sat down there—oh, yes, after she had kissed him. *For cheering me up.* "Well," he asked, "and how did I do that?"

"By saying that I'm grown up. And by letting me stay with you." She glanced towards the door. "Mother is on the warpath, you see. Clouds of gloom everywhere."

"Your mother has a big responsibility bringing up three girls to be intelligent young women. That's quite a strain on anyone, I imagine."

Penny let him enjoy his mild joke. "But," she said, "if we were three boys, she wouldn't worry this way. So it's ridiculous. Because men and women—well, what's the difference nowadays?"

"I believe there is still a slight one. *'Vive la petite différence!'* "

"Grandfather! You *know* what I mean."

That's the reason she's my favorite, he thought affectionately, as he watched her laughing eyes. That jersey was a pretty color—matched them. Gentian blue. Pretty, against the sun-tanned skin and the pink cheeks. Women always ought to wear pretty colors. There should be a law against wearing orange or puce, or all those dirty-looking shades which were just about as subtle as the floor of a cow-byre.

He asked, "What did you really want to see me about?"

Her eyes were now watching him carefully, hesitantly.

"It is all right," he said. "I am in a good mood, Penny."

She smiled for a moment, and then she became very serious. "I want your help," she admitted. "I want you to persuade Mother to let me go to London next winter."

"To the Slade School?"

"Yes. I am not just playing with the idea. I did work hard

40

all last winter in these art classes, you know, and my work *has* improved. At least, I think so. Hasn't it?"

"Yes." Surprisingly so. Penelope had definite talent: she had a sense of line and a quite remarkable feeling for color. She might be a painter, some day, given really good training and hard work. And experience in life. That would come, of course. As he studied her pretty face, now so very serious and anxious, he hoped experience would deal kindly with her.

"Mother seems to think that painting is only some kind of social accomplishment, like being able to play a sweet little piece of music on the piano after dinner. And Father just doesn't like painters. He says they are as bad as actors. Not respectable. 'Bohemian' is what he calls them."

"I didn't know people still used that word," her grandfather said with a smile, and checked her rising indignation. "Your father reminds me of George the First, who hated all 'boets and bainters.' "

"You are just an old Highlander. I suppose the Stuarts always pronounced English correctly?"

"Well, they at least could speak it." He paused. "Even if that was just about all they could do," he added. "So, your father dislikes all boets and bainters, does he?"

Penny regained her seriousness, but the anger had left her face. Her grandfather settled back in his chair, now ready to listen.

"Well," she said, "he hates having them in his family. He says that painting is no good for a career if I want a career. You see, either I stay comfortably at home until I get married, or I choose a career that can support me instead of a husband."

"It is either-or, I suppose?" How like Charles, he thought.

"That is how Father seems to see it. And Mother thinks it a waste of time studying for any career, because women generally have to give up a serious career when they get married. But I thought that painting—well, that's one thing that I—" she hesitated.

"That you could go on with, even after you marry?" her grandfather suggested. . . . "If you do marry." He looked at her mischievously. He would be willing to wager that Penelope wouldn't have to worry very much about a career. And yet, it was good for a woman to have trained her mind: that was something that was never lost. It was so typical of Charles Lorrimer to think that education was only valuable in relation to its earning power.

41

"Yes," Penny said. "Only Father says painting is not a wise investment for the future. That is, in case I don't marry—after all, you just don't marry any man who asks you: you've got to find one you really want to marry as much as he wants to marry you. So Father says that painting is too precarious for a career."

"Well, it is. In that, he is being very practical. It is like all the arts—a good walking stick, but a bad crutch."

"But if I don't mind risking all that? Why can't I at least try?"

Why not? her grandfather wondered. If she were serious and willing to work, why not?

"What do you intend to do, after you finish at the Slade School?" he asked.

"If I am good enough, I may win a traveling fellowship. Please don't laugh. And please don't tell the family. Probably I wouldn't have a chance—not good enough. But, at least," she raised her eyes, and her chin became determined, "at least I can try."

Why not? he wondered again.

"Well," he said at last, "you do know what you want, don't you?"

She sensed his approval, for she began to speak very quickly and enthusiastically. She had found out all the information about entrance into the Slade. She had even made some calculations about the cost of living in London, and did not think it would be more expensive than what her father had to pay for Moira when you counted Moira's clothes and clubs and parties.

"Does that matter? Surely your father has money enough."

"He is always worrying about bills and 'needless expense.' That was what he and Mother said in June, when I had that chance to go to Paris with some friends. They were thoroughly respectable ones, too." She tried to be amused, but there was an edge of bitterness in her voice which worried her grandfather.

"Or perhaps they did not want you to go abroad without the family. Oh, nonsense, anyway!" he said, rising from his chair in sudden anger. "Your father has quite enough money to let you go to the Slade without giving you a sense of guilt. Damn these Lowlanders, they always *will* give you a sense of guilt." He ceased abruptly. Penny was now looking unhappy. She was a loyal creature.

"Sorry, Penny," he said gently. "Blame that little show of impatience on my impractical Highland blood. Your father is a very wise man in his own way. I am sure that he will agree to let you go to London, if he can be persuaded that you really are serious about your work."

"Then you will back me up?"

"Yes." He came forward and held out his hand to help her to her feet, and they walked arm-in-arm over to the window. The sun was now low in the west, and the long warm rays turned the red cliffs across the Sound into a wall of flame.

Dr. MacIntyre was thinking about his promise. I'll see that she gets to London, to any place where she can have a chance to be free. If she stays with her family, she will have all the life crushed out of her. She will be filled with inhibitions. She will be blackmailed by security. And all her vitality will be drained out of her, and her mind will become a dead thing, and she will be—charmingly, sweetly, prettily—only half-alive. Charles Lorrimer has molded Mary. He is not going to repeat that pattern with Penelope if I can help it.

"You will find London hard, you know," he said. "You will be less comfortable than you are at home. And you may be lonely at first. England can be a lonely place."

"I know." She hugged his arm. "But there are other things, too. If I don't make a fight for them now, then I'll never get them. Later on, I'd be too old to fight. Or I would have forgotten how."

"I imagine you have still quite a way to go before you reach that stage. But it is just as well to make up your own mind early in life. One life is too short, Penny; two would be much better. In the second one, you could put into practice what the first one had taught you." He turned away from the window and he walked back to the fireplace. His voice became serious. "Now remember, my girl, if you go to London and have this freedom you are crying for, don't confuse freedom with foolishness. You won't, will you?"

Penny shook her head solemnly. And then she smiled, with so much humor in her expressive face that he smiled too.

"Well," he said, "that's that!"—and settled into his armchair.

"Thank you. You are a darling," Penny said. But she still did not leave. Dr. MacIntyre looked pointedly at his abandoned newspaper.

"Did you have a nice afternoon?" Penny went on.

What's coming now? he wondered. "Very pleasant, thank you."

"I'm afraid your work was badly interrupted today."

To have one's simple pleasures interrupted is worse, her grandfather thought. He answered casually, "Oh, I rather enjoyed it. Bosworth is interesting. What we call 'good material.' I can see why Chaundler takes such an interest in him. The most rewarding thing about being a teacher, you know, is to winnow the grain from the chaff."

"Then you *did* like him?"

The rich light from the western window filled the room. Its colors now became alive, warm and soft, as they lay bathed in the golden rays. It was the best moment of the day, he thought.

Penny said anxiously, "Or didn't you like him?"

He roused himself. "Like whom? Young Bosworth? Of course I liked him. Would I have spent two hours with him if I hadn't?" He closed his eyes. Time for forty winks ... one of the rights of advancing age ... very pleasant, too. He stretched his legs comfortably as the door closed behind Penny, and settled in his chair contentedly.

In the hall, square-shaped and furnished like a sitting room so that the visitors would not be eternally in the study, Moira was sitting with more comfort than elegance on the small couch. Some official-looking periodicals and bluebooks lay beside her, but on her lap was a fashion magazine. She looked up guiltily, and then, seeing it was only her sister, opened the magazine again.

"Don't work too hard," Penny said.

Moira glanced at the periodicals. "I've some notes to make before supper," she said. "Provided, of course, that I am not interrupted." She looked pointedly at Penny, who had sat down on the arm of the couch and had picked up a League of Nations pamphlet on minorities in Europe.

"You'll manage it," Penny told her. "You still have five minutes left."

"As late as *that?*" Moira looked indignant. She said sharply, "What on earth were you talking about in the study? I was timing myself by you."

"About London. I say, Moira—" Penny had picked up a bulletin on white slave traffic, hidden under the other pamphlets, and opened it with interest. "You do have to read pretty widely for modern history, don't you?"

Moira took the bulletin quickly out of her hands and replaced it under the others. "I *wish* you'd leave things alone," she said crossly. "And what about London? Do you

44

mean you really are trying to go there next winter? You could very well put in another year in Edinburgh and go later. As I am doing."

"Are you?"

"Look, stop fiddling with my papers and let me do some work! I've done absolutely nothing all month, and I have *so* much to do."

Penny picked up the fashion magazine, and turned over its glossy pages. For a moment she had been afraid that Moira would jump to the right conclusion.

And then Moira, trust Moira, looked up again and said, "Don't tell me you and David Bosworth were talking economics!"

"Of course not."

"He is taking a degree in something like that, isn't he? Wasn't that what George Fenton-Stevens told us?"

"Did he?" Penny's voice was very disinterested. "Look, Moira, isn't that a marvelous dress? I'd love one like that."

Moira glanced at the advertisement. "Black," she said. "Much too old. You'd never be allowed to have it. What did he talk about, then? You were an awfully long time with him."

"Oh, nothing very much. Just this and that." Penny's voice was bored.

Moira waited, but there was no more information. Had he really been dull, after all? Her irritation with Penny began to pass. She said, her voice dropping into the usual tone of one-sister-to-another, "You know, he is rather attractive, isn't he? Which is strange, because he isn't what you would call good-looking. Of course, he is very tall. Tall men don't have to be handsome, somehow."

"Here is someone still taller," Penny said, showing her sister another advertisement. "The women in these drawings are always eight feet tall, always absolutely slender, always young and beautiful. Do you think that real women imagine they will look like that if they could only buy these dresses?"

"Well, you ought to know. You rather fancied yourself in that black dress, didn't you?"

"It would look nice even on someone who was only five feet, five and a half inches," Penelope said stubbornly. "And it takes a young complexion to wear black attractively."

"Just try that idea on Mummy, and see how far you get with it."

Penny discarded the magazine and wandered over to the front door. Then she walked out over the slope of green grass. She looked towards the Sound. I am as restless as the sea, she thought. How I wish I were old. At least twenty-five, perhaps even thirty. No, thirty was too old. Twenty-five was better. When you were old, you wouldn't have this crushed feeling inside you, you would not need to make up dreams about life. When you were young they always ended the wrong way somehow. How often she had sat on the west shore, painting, dreaming, talking inside to herself. And she had always ended by thinking what a perfect place it was to have someone else to talk to, someone who knew what you wanted to be said, someone who didn't interrupt or laugh at the wrong places and who would talk as if he knew what you were thinking. And sometimes he would not talk at all, leaving well enough alone. Today had been that kind of day. And of course it had to be spoiled. Perhaps David Bosworth had become bored: he must know so many girls in Oxford and London, pretty girls, amusing girls, girls old enough to wear smart little black dresses. Or who wore them, whether they were old enough or not. She looked down at her wool sweater and flannel skirt, at her flat-heeled brogues and smooth stockings. Bare legs were indecent, they said. She shook her head and sighed. If she were old, then she would never feel that she was being laughed at. Had he been laughing at her? "Oh, damn!" she said suddenly, and then looked quickly around. There was no one there to overhear. "Damn AND blast!" she said.

There was only one thing to be thankful for. Moira had not seen how happy she was when she came back from that walk. Then her sister would have questioned and teased for days, until she would come to hate the sound of Bosworth. And how Mother would have lectured: silly ideas, romantic nonsense. Perhaps they were silly and romantic. But that did not explain why she should have been so happy, and then, as David walked away with George Fenton-Stevens and Captain MacLean, not happy at all. That couldn't be explained. And you couldn't ask advice about it, either. Not even from Grandfather. This wasn't something like going to London. This was something you hid inside yourself and never even let anyone guess about. And never, most of all, David Bosworth.

Betty was calling, "Penny, you are late *again*."

Penny turned towards the house.

"What's wrong, Penny? Are you all right? Supper is ready and we are all waiting."

"Of course I'm all right."

Betty blew out of the corner of her mouth at a heavy lock of fair hair, too short to be held in place. Last week, she had cut a fringe to look like Cleopatra's, and then she had not liked it. Now, she was plagued by its refusal to be brushed back.

"I've finished another chapter of my book," she announced. "It's thrilling. You will read it tonight, won't you?" Penny would always read things when you asked her to, but Moira would always say that she would read them when they were published. Some day, Betty thought, I'll be a writer, a real writer with words all in print, and I'll show Moira.

"All right," Penny said, hiding her amusement. For Betty remembered she was going to be a writer every two months or so, and then she would dash off another chapter. Its length depended on the time she had to spare. "How long is this chapter?"

"Pages and pages—three or four. My hero is caught in the rapids. He's almost killed. And I have a new idea for the title. 'Perils of the Amazon.' How do you like that?"

"What was the first one, again?"

"First, it was 'Smugglers of the Orinoco,' and then I thought of 'Dwellers of the Zambesi,' and then—"

"It *is* the same story, isn't it?"

Betty looked at Penny in surprise as they entered the house. "Why, of course!"

"Versatile ...," Penny said. She restrained herself until they had entered the dining room, and then she could pretend to be smiling to everyone around the table. "Betty and I were discussing titles. I say, Betty, why don't you just list all the titles, and that would be a story in itself? You could call it 'Variations on a Theme.' "

"*Sh!*" her mother said warningly and inclined her head towards their waiting grandfather. Penny bowed her head as the others were doing, but her eyes were not closed and she studied her mother's face as it registered thankfulness. It was just as Penny had thought when she had first entered the dining room: her mother had been crying. She remembered, then, that there had been no reproach for being late for supper. She looked quickly towards her grandfather. He had finished saying grace, and he was now admitting nothing beyond the excellence of the food.

Penny was very subdued and very polite for the rest of the evening.

"I wonder if Penelope is catching something," Mrs. Lor-

47

rimer confided to her father as the girls at last went upstairs to bed, and she prepared to follow them.

"Probably just thinking. It is a painful process for anyone. Good night, Mary. And don't worry, my dear."

But Dr. MacIntyre, as he lifted his pipe from the ash tray and stretched his legs before the fire which had been lit against the chilly night air, was puzzling over Penny too. Why had she paid that special visit to him this evening? London, ostensibly. But David Bosworth indirectly? Stuff and nonsense, he thought irritably. And then he tried to imagine how he had felt and thought and acted when he was nineteen. But those years were too far away.

And it was only in moments like those he had experienced this afternoon—Bosworth's energy, his revolt against the state of acceptance; Penny's vitality and warmth—that he could have the fleeting sensation of remembering exact emotions in his own youth. As if each year dropped a thin veil over the preceding year, and as you got further away from the years of youth the accumulation of veils became a thickness substantial enough to conceal and hide. Only in certain moments, when some memory stirred, was that thickness slit through. Suddenly, and only for a brief interval. "There I am," you said, looking at youth. And then you looked at yourself and said, "No." And you added, "There I was." And so you let the slit in the veils close again, and let your thoughts keep the even pace of your body. The veils, some bright, some somber, fell together; and they lost all particular color and merged into a gentle gray.

Dr. MacIntyre looked at the photograph on the mantelpiece. You'll never be a philosopher, he told himself: you were too happy with her. He smiled as he looked up at his wife. "Weren't we, lass?" he said.

chapter vi

THE LODGE at Loch Innish was a pugnacious place. You felt it could face any odds—Norsemen, raiding clans, winter storms, or the yearly invasion of its grouse moors. Even its recent embellishments of lawn and driveway, of tennis court and rose garden, could not alter its essential function. It was the guardian of the road which led from the deep narrow sea loch to the scattered crofts and villages lying inland.

When the mists hung over the loch, blotting out the sharp mountains falling steeply towards its dark waters, this feeling of watchful loneliness increased. With the security of foot-thick stone walls around you, and a solid roof over your head, you could even take a peculiar pleasure in watching the swirling mists, for it was always pleasant to have your comfort and security emphasized. And if you had work to do, the days of mist were welcome. For there was no temptation to go climbing or fishing or swimming, or to have a game of tennis, or to lie among the heather where the air was warm and sweet. Sweeter and cleaner, David thought, than anything he had ever felt around him, so that it became a conscious pleasure just to be alive, just to be able to breathe.

Today was a day of mist, but David found to his great irritation that he was thoroughly unsettled. Here he was standing at the window again, looking out at the half-formed shapes and ghostly outlines of a world which had disappeared and depended on human memory for its existence. This morning, he had thought that the usual daily routine would occupy this mind of his, and that the attack of gloom which had descended on him, very much as the mist had descended on the loch, would clear.

But today, an attack of restlessness had spread through the Lodge. Tea was over, yet the boys were certainly not doing much work judging by the racket they were making in the music room. George had settled philosophically in the more comfortable chair by the lighted fire in the library, with a pile of magazines on the small table at his elbow, although he actually had had enough good intentions to have a copy of *The Greek Commonwealth* lying open on his knees. And David had spent the last half hour reading and rereading the same page in Aristotle's *Politics,* and then had risen from his chair and started walking around the library shelves.

He had picked out a book here and there, glanced at it, put it back into its place in its row. Well-filled rows, too, not only in number but in choice. The library had been stocked by the yard, but adequately, thanks to the advice Lady Fenton-Stevens had taken from the Times Book Club. Guests marooned by the rain would find plenty to read. David had been surprised and delighted when he had first arrived, and had blessed Lady Fenton-Stevens's advisers. It wasn't too cruel to admit ·that she couldn't have made this choice herself. She probably had not read ten books in the last ten years. She knew all about the books being published, of course—enough to make an amusing phrase in conversation. But to read them completely was a very different matter. "One is so frightfully busy, you know," she had murmured vaguely to David last Christmas, just after she had returned from Paris and was about to set out for St. Moritz.

There they were, all in their neat rows: Faulkner, Mann, Proust, Stendhal, Hemingway, Morgan, Romains. . . . Practically virgin, too: David had read them with a paper knife beside him, scanning a favorite page in those he knew, seizing upon those he had not been able to buy or borrow. It was comfortable, pleasant, to sit in the library beside the dying fire, once George had trundled off to bed and the boys were also out of sight and hearing. It was more than pleasant: all the tutoring and coaching and justification for his existence were over for the day. He could spend a couple of hours here in peace, and take his choice in Stendhal or Dorothy Sayers, in Tolstoi or Wodehouse, before going up through the sleeping house to his own room. He hadn't been reduced, like Dr. Johnson, to reading a *History of Birmingham*.

This afternoon, however, even the choice of books hadn't helped him. Here he was, standing at this window, looking out at a wet gray curtain. He must find something to read. He left the window, and went back to the bookshelves. He pulled out *A Portrait of the Artist as a Young Man*, and opened it at random. "Pride and hope and desire like crushed herbs in his heart sent up vapours of maddening incense before the eyes of his mind." David grimaced and turned over to another page impatiently. It always was unfair, he reminded himself, to take a sentence out of context: the easy, the cheap, way to embarrass an author. Ah, here was what he was looking for. . . . . "Now I call that friendly, don't

50

you? Yes, I liked her today. A little or much? Don't know. I liked her and it seemed a new feeling to me. Then, in that case, all the rest, all that I thought I thought and all that I felt I felt, all the rest before now, in fact ... O, give it up, old chap! Sleep it off!" ... Yes, David thought savagely, sleep it off. He closed the book. Bitter advice, which Joyce himself refused merely by stating it. Only those who had never let themselves be possessed by thoughts and feelings, only those could sleep it off. He glanced over at George. George, now, could sleep off anything.

"I say, David, could you stop wandering around? Damned if I can concentrate," George said.

"Sorry."

Something in David's voice made Fenton-Stevens twist around in his chair to look at him. George dropped his book and rose, upsetting the tankard which he had placed on the floor near his feet.

"Damnation," he said, and pulled his handkerchief out of the cuff of his sleeve, and dropped it over the spreading pool of beer. "Lucky there wasn't much left," he said. "Revolting mess." He crossed over to the window. "Nothing much to see out there."

"No."

"Come over to the fire. Have some beer. Chuck that book away. I don't feel like working much, either. It is difficult today, when we had all the arrangements made for that picnic on Inchnamurren. Besides, we worked enough yesterday to make up for any old day off the chain. So let's take it. Come along."

They went back to the fireplace together. George kicked the sodden handkerchief out of sight behind the pile of logs on the broad, flagstoned hearth. He threw a chunk of wood on the low embers of the fire.

"That will cheer the place up," he said. "God, imagine having to sit before a fire in July. We might as well be in Greenland."

David rested his hand against the carved stone panel above the fireplace, and stared down at the flickering small tongues of flame lapping round the logs. Then he became aware of George's puzzled interest. He searched for something to say. The noise from the music room was now at the hilarious stage: Chris and his cousin were happily boring holes off-center on some records, and playing them from that new axis.

51

David said, "How many records do you think these block-heads have ruined? Or doesn't it matter?"

George thought for a moment, and then moved quickly towards the door. "If they've touched any of mine, I'll knock their brains out. What they have of them."

When he returned to the room, he looked pleased with his persuasive efforts. "They've decided to go down to visit Captain MacLean's cottage, so we shall have peace for a couple of hours. The Washboard Beaters and Red Nichols and the new Gershwin are still intact. They were experiment-ing on Wagner, thank God."

"Not the *Meistersinger* or *Tristan*, I hope."

"No, they were concentrating on the Valkyrie and the Rhine maidens."

"Symbolic, perhaps."

George looked at him blankly, and then laughed. "Revolt against women? You are probably right. Chris is at the vulnerable stage, as you call it. If you stayed for the Twelfth when all the girls arrive on the scene, you'd be amused by his contortions. He is fascinated by them and he is afraid of them, all at the same time. Oh, chuck away that book and draw your chair up, David. It isn't a good working day. Pity about the picnic. And the Lorrimers leave tomorrow, so it is off altogether. Probably would have been an awful bore, anyway. Flies in the tea, and midges down the back of your neck."

David said nothing. He was wondering if Penelope Lor-rimer felt any of this strange disappointment which had angered him all day. And then he reminded himself once more that she had probably forgotten all about him by this time. Girls, if you could believe what you read—and how else were you able to find out about them when they all looked as if life were a very simple affair?—girls did not brood over what might be or what might not. Perhaps they did not know what they wanted out of life when they were young. And that was a pity, because when they were young they had poetry in their life: they had intensity and emotion. Later, they lost that warmth: they so often became more like a passage of elegant prose, amusing or thoughtful, but always with the poetry in them well under control. So well controlled sometimes that it had died. Which was more than a pity.

"Penny for them," George said. Then as David looked startled and did not reply, he repeated, "I said a penny for your thoughts."

David drew a deep breath. If he had met any other

pretty girl last week, would he now be behaving in this fantastic way? Possibly, for the island was a magic place and he had been bewitched. Yet, probably not. He had seen plenty of pretty girls. But last week he had seen Penny.

"I was thinking about a topic which men never discuss," he said.

George looked startled. "Just what could that be?"

"Women."

George stopped worrying about David. This was the old David back again, true to form.

"I was thinking," David continued, "about Chris and his agonies in sex. He hasn't learned to hide them yet. You and I have. But that doesn't mean we have lost all our uncertainties or fears. We are still afraid of being laughed at. Because, I suppose, we feel we are choosing by emotion, and we have been told often enough that that is wrong. Yet, frankly, I don't see how else we can choose: meeting a girl you like *is* an emotional experience, isn't it? Reason has nothing to do with it, unless you are a fishlike individual. At a time when we have enough hot blood to enjoy life fully, we are surrounded by a conspiracy of age to settle the rules and regulations as if love were a game or a business. It isn't. It's a state of being. With it, you're alive. Without it, you exist."

"Here!" George said in alarm. He had never heard David talk this way before: he was too damned serious, even if he kept a smile on his lips and a light tone in his voice. "I say, David, you aren't still worrying about Eleanor, are you? As her brother I can frankly say that she isn't worth much worry."

"Good God, no!" David was vehement enough to be believed this time. It was true. Eleanor had now become a period piece. Last night, he had even torn up the verses which he had written to celebrate his disillusionment and unhappiness over that affair. Last night, he had read them and their imitation Verlaine had only made him acutely embarrassed. Tripe garnished with the brains of calf-love. It had been a lucky escape for him, when Eleanor had decided there was more fun in the world than one man could offer. Eleanor, that little nitwit? "Good God, no," he repeated.

"Oh, she isn't a bad scout, really," George said, rising automatically to the defense of his family. "But she wouldn't have done at all. You were too serious about it."

"That's the trouble." David wasn't thinking of Eleanor Fenton-Stevens now. "When *do* you know whether you

53

should be serious or not serious about a girl? You don't, in fact. Either you have to pass her by, altogether, or take the chance of being serious."

"Well, don't take being serious about a girl too seriously," George suggested. "After all, a man knows he can't marry until his career is well established. But there's no ban on following your fancy when you are still at the unmarriageable state."

"Thanks," David said dryly, "but I've no taste for camp-followers. That has about as much satisfaction as pouring your favorite wine into a public drinking-cup. Or helping yourself to strawberries and cream on a plate still greasy from bacon and eggs. How would you enjoy food served that way, George?"

"You needn't argue from extremes," George said placidly. "I wasn't talking about camp-followers."

"It is only a difference of degree, not of kind. What else are women who serve round the same smiles and kisses to several men? They have got a price too, you know, in theater tickets and flowers and chocolates and dinners you buy them. You and five other chaps."

"Look, David, you can't expect a pretty girl to sit at home and not go out. And you can't expect one chap to have the cash to take her out every night in the style to which she has accustomed herself. If she is pretty and amusing, you are damned lucky to be allowed to form up in the queue."

"The true richness of experience."

"Don't be so damned sarcastic," George said irritably. "Besides, you know damned well that you like a pretty girl as much as the next man. You run a mile from the unattractive ones. I've seen you, old boy. In fact, it was only last week that I said, when we were arguing, that after all a plain girl often had rather a good brain. And you said that the trouble was we didn't sleep with brains."

"My trouble is that I know what I want. If I don't make excuses for liking Brahms or Chopin, why should I make excuses for liking beauty in women? That's the trouble: I know what I like, and I don't often find it. That's all."

George searched in his pocket for his pipe, and filled it thoughtfully from a pouch whose striped colors matched the college tie he was wearing. (George had only two ties for day wear which did not belong to school, college, or his five clubs: a gray one for weddings, and a black one for funerals.)

"Well," he said with resignation, "you can't find everything in one woman. It takes all kinds to make experience. If you have several girls, or even a succession of girls if your conscience is squeamish about playing several fish at a time, you'll end your life by having had everything. What more do you want?"

"Nothing. Except that I don't think that is the way to get everything." David looked at him speculatively, and decided to risk going on. "Really, George, you have got to admit that if people put as much thought and concentration into their sex lives as they do into their careers, there would be a good deal more happiness in middle age. After all, why shouldn't we make a real effort to have a successful love life? We aren't eunuchs, and we may as well admit that."

"Hardly. But you can't rationalize like that, David. A job or a career can be planned. But love can't."

"No career is certain of success. We work and hope and aim for something; and often we get it. But we wouldn't have a chance of getting it, if we hadn't done our best. For instance, if a man works hard at medical school, he will probably be a good doctor some day; but no man becomes a doctor by just wishing to be one. That's the point I am making. All I am saying is that if we looked at love that way, we might have a better chance of success in it. And the proof that a lot of us aren't successful in it is not very hard to find. How many burst-up marriages do you know, George? Isn't it all a damned waste of energy and emotion?"

George considered the fire thoughtfully. He said at last, "But we do think and worry about sex all the time. And where does it get us? Certainly not the sure success you believe in. Look, I bet sixty per cent of the human race think about sex and love more often than they think of anything else."

"Ninety per cent," David said, "if you take into account all the disguised approaches."

"All right. Ninety per cent think about it, or purposely avoid thinking about it. And where does that get us?"

"Just thinking about it isn't a real solution. Surely, there's a happy medium somewhere, George, between those who think about sex too much, like some French politician with his string of mistresses, and those who avoid thinking about it and try to convert everyone else to be the same as they are. Surely it wasn't meant to be abused by fools or cowards."

George frowned. And then he gave up trying to answer and said, "I see old MacIntyre's words are taking root."

"What do you mean?" David asked quickly.

55

"All that stuff he told you about living a complete life. Why, a week ago, you sat on that very chair and told me that if a man was serious about his career he had no time to worry about women. Now you have reached the opinion that if love were taken as seriously as a career, it would be a damned sight better for all of us. You aren't by any chance thinking of taking your own advice, are you?"

David laughed, and bent down to pick up his beer mug from the floor. "It's only talk," he said, "talk for a gray day and a warm fireside. Besides," he went on, his voice suddenly casual, "even if a man had an idea of how to be happy though young, in what way could he manage it? Tell me, George, suppose you found that Kitty, or Dorothy, or Phyllis, was just the girl you wanted for life, what would you do? No, old boy, no jokes. This is a serious question—at least, an interesting one. Would you make the effort to keep her, or would you just let her slip away, because you knew it might be years before you were making enough to get married?"

George stared. "Heaven help us if we got into that fix. Better not let yourself fall in love, seriously that is, until you can afford it. If you believe in arranging your love life, that would certainly be the first thing to remember." He thought over that for a moment, and then added, "Here's to the pretty girls who won't take us seriously until we can afford it! Come on, drink up, David!"

"No more for me at the moment, thanks," David said as he looked moodily at the fire. Then he roused himself, and said briskly, "What I need is a walk. Coming?"

"In this weather? No, thank you. I'll supply you with aspirin and a hot toddy when you get back." George settled himself comfortably in his armchair, picked up a magazine, and began to inspect the lovelies of London so invitingly displaying their charms.

David paused behind him, glanced over his shoulder. "Studying the disguised approach, I see."

Fenton-Stevens pointed to one photograph. "Not bad," he said appraisingly. He studied the name underneath. "Good Lord, I'm supposed to know that girl. Well, the photographer certainly earned his money."

David looked critically at an ethereal blonde in her off-shoulder evening dress. "Not bad at all," he agreed. "One more struggle and the lady will be free."

George was smiling as the door closed behind David. Thank Heavens, David was himself again. For a moment or

56

two there, in that last half hour, George had begun to worry about him. A walk would probably do him good: liver, or something.

David followed the path which led him through the gardens onto the moors. There it became a narrow track, a thin ribbon of bleached red gravel, skirting the edge of the granite cliffs through knee-high heather and low blaeberry bushes. To his right was the sea in its grim gray mood. On his left were the rising hills, their crests still hidden by cloud. The mist along the sea edge had lifted and given way to a drizzling rain.

There had been no help from George, he thought. But then he had not asked for direct advice. In any case, what good would it have done? Every man had his own idea about life and what he wanted out of it. Happiness, yes: that was the general ambition. We all wanted to win happiness, but we all found very different ways of trying to reach it. Life wasn't a neat, single track like this path along the cliffs. It was more like a twisting road shut in by high hedges, so that the view ahead was seldom clear: a road constantly broken by side roads, with no signposts, either, to help you out. For direction, you had to depend on your own questions and answers.

He wasn't even putting this question in his own mind openly to himself. He was disguising it with arguments and generalizations. The whole thing was ridiculous, anyway. People did not behave this way. Or perhaps they did, and kept it as their own secret. Certainly, he had never felt like this before. That was what worried him most. His mind might keep telling him it was all ridiculous, an exaggeration, a delusion. But he didn't believe it. All right, you want to see her again, he admitted.

But how?

That, he suddenly realized, was the real problem that was worrying him. He halted then, and stood for many minutes with the strong wind whipping his soaking raincoat around his legs. He stood listening to the strong heavy blows of the waves against the cliff, falling away in front of him into the surging force of water. The perpetual thunder silenced even the high screams of the sea gulls. Out to sea, there was the long dark shape of Inchnamurren.

He stared at it, then he turned away abruptly and started back towards the Lodge.

chapter vii

*T*HAT NIGHT, after the others had gone to bed, David Bosworth wrote two letters. The first was to his sister Margaret.

DEAR MEG,

I shall definitely be home about the eighth of August as we had arranged. Work has been going quite well, and we have been fairly lucky in weather so that I've collected a decent enough tan and stretched the old muscles over a hill or two. The boys are responding to wild curses, and I feel I've earned my money with them. I only hope Lady F-S remembers that some people really *need* cash, and will send me the check in time to bring home as a trophy. Then you can have your holiday before summer gives way to mists and mellow fruitfulness. I wish you could persuade Father to go with you. But if he doesn't feel strong enough for the journey, then it is probably better to let him stay in London with me.

Sorry to hear you have all been sweltering for the last month. But two weeks . . .

Here David stopped and considered. He had been six weeks up here. Meg would count them, comparing the difference subconsciously. She would also think of these six weeks as pure holiday: she didn't consider that tutoring was work. At least, she had never admitted it. He remembered her last letter. How lucky he was . . . to have such a marvelous holiday in such a marvelous place. . . . London was hateful at the moment, the heat-wave magnified all noise and Father objected to the piano . . . he wasn't too well, and this made things difficult . . . she felt too exhausted in any case, after nursing an invalid, housekeeping and cooking, to enjoy playing the piano, far less teaching it to children . . .

David carefully erased the words "two weeks."

But a holiday in Cornwall will cheer you up. I'll look after Father, and finish the rest of my reading.

Tell Father that I have some varied tales for him. I have been collecting them from one of the local chieftains, Captain MacLean by name. Did you know about the MacLeans? They are very proud, it seems. At the time of the Flood, they snooted Noah and had a boat of their own.

I discovered some unusual Gaelic music, pentatonic and strangely sad. Lots of songs about the sea, naturally. The sea dirges are only to be sung by women, as if men weren't supposed to get melancholy about all the drowned sailors. Good psychology this, however, considering the men had to do the sailing. They are allowed the reviving songs, though; all about the wine and women waiting for them on the mainland. (Can't imagine what wine they drank in this part of the world, unless it was something like a mead made from heather honey. Sounds hardly worth reiving for.) I'll try to get copy of these songs for you on my way south.

We called on Dr. MacIntyre some days ago on his island stronghold. He is quite remarkable. And he was most kind.

Again David paused. Better not mention the Lorrimers at all.

Love to Father and yourself. Expect me when you see me. Trains are far away from this wild region, and I'll probably miss at least one connection when I do reach a railway line. It takes almost as long to reach London from here as if I were traveling from Munich. (There are language difficulties, too.)

Yours,
DAVID

He read the letter over carefully. If it gave the impression of rather more fun and games than work, that couldn't be helped. Damned if he was going to start writing Margaret's kind of letters. If she enjoyed writing letters with a neat pin-prick in every third sentence, then that was her loss. He wondered, as he folded the stiff sheet of notepaper and slipped it into one of the Lodge's excellent envelopes, just what she would say if she were to open it and read, "The weather is putrid. The boys are howling dervishes. George is as good-natured as ever, but even that virtue can get on your nerves when there is nothing much else to go with it. I get no real time for my own work. I'll be glad when I get back to London's hot pavements and can be my own master again. If it weren't for your holiday in Cornwall, I would not be here now scrabbling for some extra cash to pay for it."

He smiled grimly, wrote the address—Miss Bosworth, 7 Cory's Walk, Chiswick, London W 4—and then allowed himself to crash the stamp on with his clenched fist.

His second letter was to Dr. MacIntyre, a kind of bread-and-butter letter saying how much he had enjoyed the visit, and that he was sorry the visit to Inchnamurren had been canceled today. That part was simple to write. But the next paragraph took more time. "I promised to bring your granddaughter a book today—the new edition of Gerard Manley Hopkins—but now I must send it to her, and I find that I haven't her address. I wonder if you would be so kind as to give it to Captain MacLean when he takes this note across to you? My thanks again for a memorable day. I hope I have the pleasure of seeing you next year when you come south for that visit to Oxford. . . . " Yes, it was all right, he decided, as he balanced the envelope in his hand. The reference to Penelope was fairly negligible. And he had a copy of that book, brought with him among the others he had packed in Oxford.

He left the letter to his sister on the hall table, where the outgoing post was collected. But the letter to Dr. Mac-Intyre was carried upstairs to his room. Tomorrow morning, he would take it down to MacLean's cottage.

He slept badly, but he could always blame that on his cold.

chapter viii

THE LORRIMER house in Edinburgh was solid and comfortable. It was one of a row of three-storied houses in a quiet crescent-shaped road, each with its broad white steps, polished doorbell, name plate, letter box, and large oriel windows set into thick gray stone. In front of each house was a carriage step overlying the deep gutter at the edge of the pavement. Across the quiet road was a narrow stretch of garden, well-tended and charming with flowering shrubs. The trees that grew there added to the seclusion of the road, for the houses on the other side of the garden were screened from view. There was no one in the garden, and its gate was padlocked. There were no children playing, no people to be seen. Only the rows of large windows looked at you. David felt he was reviewing a line of spit-and-polish Guardsmen, and he did not quite know whether he should tiptoe in reverence or make a run for it.

But here he was, and there was the house. (He had walked past it once already, halted at an imposing lamppost, and then retraced his steps.) The choice was made in any case. It had been made last night when, after a tedious journey by car and then by steamer and then by train from Oban, he had arrived in Glasgow and had purposely failed to catch the London express. He had spent a dull evening by himself in an unknown city, where everything seemed to be closed on

Sundays; and a noisy night at a railway hotel until he could take a train on Monday morning to Edinburgh.

His pace slowed down as he neared the Lorrimer house once more. What on earth had ever made him think of this idea, anyway? He should have posted his letter to Penny instead—it was still in his pocket, soiled and crumpled from five days' handling—or, if he had *had* to obey the mad compulsion which had made him travel home by way of Edinburgh, then he ought to have telephoned first from the station. But after he had written the letter, he had delayed posting it until it was too late. And this morning when he arrived in the Edinburgh station, he had avoided the telephone boxes. As if he were trying to postpone any attempt to get in touch with Penny. As if he had stage fright.

Hell, he thought, don't be a bloody fool. He turned to the house, ran up the broad white steps and pulled the bell before he would persuade himself to walk back to the bus stop. When he released the knob of the bell, he could hear its shrill tongue clattering away into the silent house. He had pulled it too violently. Oh hell, he thought again. Well, either he would see her, or he would not see her. That was all, and it was everything. If he were to see her, he would know whether this strange self-tormenting was valid or not. If he didn't see her—well the thread was already so tenuous . . . a part of one afternoon spent with her, that was all—if he didn't see her, then the thread might snap altogether and he would be free again. He would be able to laugh at the whole brief affair. A girl's face. A girl's way of talking. How easily he had surrendered. Damn fool, he told himself. But as he waited for someone to answer the bell's clamor, he was suddenly nervous, in case no one would be at home at all.

A maid, stiffly correct in a starched dress, white apron, white cap, opened the door. Yes, Mrs. Lorrimer was at home. The maid glanced quickly at his pin-striped gray flannel suit, the long-pointed collar and striped tie, the brown suéde shoes and soft felt hat. Would he come this way?

He entered the polished hall with its thick rugs and clean smell of cedar oil. The large grandfather clock at the foot of the white-enameled, red-carpeted stairs chimed eleven o'clock as if to remind him that he had chosen an unusual hour for his visit. He entered the drawing room, a cool place of green and white with formalized roses to be picked off curtains and chairs, and was left with the three faces in the large portrait, which hung over the mantelpiece, for company. Three girls, heads conventionally together, throats

61

and shoulders bare, with clouds of soft tulle caught carefully, well above breast line, with pink roses. The artist had not captured the right color of her hair, David thought with annoyance. Penny's hair was much less obvious than the painter had made it appear; he had put in far too much of its red lights. Probably he fancied himself as another Titian.

He turned to face the door as he heard the sound of a light footstep. "Mr. Bosworth," Mrs. Lorrimer said and came forward to shake his hand, "this is indeed a surprise."

He colored slightly at her unobtrusive appraisal. He certainly would be found gravely wanting if he didn't explain his visit adequately. His excuse, which had seemed so natural and excellent, now appeared weak in the extreme. His voice lost its assurance as if he were apologizing more for the excuse than the actual visit. But actually, there was no reason for any worry.

Mrs. Lorrimer had her own particular problems: Monday was such a bad day to offer luncheon. Cook wouldn't change the arrangements, either, not on laundry day. And you couldn't give a man an egg and a salad, even if you did not particularly like him. She began to listen to him, worrying now because she had missed the thread of his explanation, something about having a book for Penelope.

"I do hope I haven't disturbed you," he concluded. "It is very rude of me to descend on you like this without warning, but frankly I had no idea how long I would have in Edinburgh between trains."

"When does your train leave?"

"This afternoon. Rather late in the afternoon." He had a very charming smile, Mrs. Lorrimer thought with surprise. He went on, "It seemed very dreary to spend the day here by myself. I don't know Edinburgh at all, you see. I thought that your daughters might lunch with me, and show me the Castle afterwards. I hear it is very fine."

"I'm afraid Betty and Moira are both out. And Penelope has settled down to do some painting in her room. At the moment, she says she is very behindhand with something or other."

"I should be sorry to interrupt," he said. Careful now, careful, he told himself. Gently does it.

Mrs. Lorrimer's sense of guilt at having missed so much of his first conversation now resulted in sudden affability. After all, a stranger in Edinburgh had to be welcomed decently. She eyed the thin book which he had drawn out of his pocket and now held in his hand. "I shall tell Penelope you

62

are here, and she can thank you herself." She rose and went to the door. "We have coffee at eleven in the morning. You *will* stay and have some with us?" He had obviously never expected to have luncheon here, she thought. That was a great relief. She left the drawing room door open, and he heard murmured instructions to a maid who then ran upstairs.

David walked over to the window which overlooked the back garden. Front garden, he corrected himself. It was obvious from the care expended on it that this was really the front of the house. As if it had turned its back on the street to live its own life in contemplation of a long narrow stretch of grass and flower beds and cherry trees within its own high walls. The city seemed remote. Smoking chimneys and tramcars and busses and shops and crowds did not exist. But it was a different kind of peace from that which he had just left in the Highlands. There, it was peace with the feeling of possessive. It was *my* house, *my* garden, *my* peace. His sense of intrusion deepened, and he turned quickly away towards the door.

He heard footsteps on the staircase running quickly down, and then a short halt in their rhythm followed by a thump as she landed neatly on both feet in the hall. She had jumped the last four or five steps. It was so out of pattern with the dignified house and its formal garden that his depression left him. A broad smile spread over his face.

"What *is* it, Mother?" Penny was saying impatiently. And then she halted, and her voice altered, "David Bosworth!" She looked just as wonderful as he had remembered her.

"Hello." He tried to be casual. The result was that he forgot what he had been going to say. And the longer the silence lasted, the more difficult it was to break. He dropped her hand as he heard Mrs. Lorrimer returning to the room, and he spoke then much too quickly.

"I brought you this book. I was passing through Edinburgh and had some free time. I hope I am not being a nuisance."

"Oh, no."

"What about your work?"

"Oh, that's nothing."

Mrs. Lorrimer established control the minute she entered the room. "Penelope, I never imagined you would come downstairs in that disreputable smock. You know, Mr. Bosworth, she won't allow it to be laundered."

"What are you working on?" he asked curiously.

63

"Oh," she said for the third time. And then, half-laughing, "A chest of drawers."

Heavens, he thought, surely she isn't one of those art-and-crafters, painting pretty flowers in between handles!

Mrs. Lorrimer's eyebrows had gone up as her daughter had spoken. "Why don't you show Mr. Bosworth your work?" she suggested. Really, she was thinking indignantly, how silly of Penelope. Mr. Bosworth might have believed her.

"I don't think he would be interested," Penny said.

There was a pause, and as it lengthened David felt he had to say, "I should like to see it very much." He was as embarrassed as Penny. He had never been adept at simulating admiration: he would say inadequate things, and she would be hurt.

Penny stood hesitating for a minute, and then, catching the slight nod of command from her mother, who now was quite determined that Mr. Bosworth should not leave with a wrong impression of her daughter's talents, she suddenly moved towards the hall.

She led the way, without looking back, and David followed quickly. The sooner this was over, the better. She was wearing fine silk stockings today, and the seams were straight, too, on an excellent pair of legs. He admired them all the way up the two flights of stairs.

"Penelope insisted on changing her room to suit her own ideas," Mrs. Lorrimer said as they passed two sweetly pretty rooms belonging to Moira and Betty. There was the slight edge of amused criticism in her voice. Penny said nothing, but her chin was set and determined. David wanted to smile. But instead, a look of surprise came into his eyes as he followed her into her room. The walls were plain, unlike the flower-patterned wallpaper which belonged to the other rooms, and they had been painted a strange shade of clouded blue, almost gray. The carpet, also unpatterned, was the color of sand. Long straight curtains (no frills and flounces here) were striped in white and coral red. There were bookcases, open and low, against one wall, and above them a long deep band of dark green felt over cork had been fixed to the wall. On this were pinned reproductions of pictures cut out of art magazines.

"Good idea," he said involuntarily. This was the kind of thing he would like to have in his room at Oxford. He looked at the pictures. They varied in emotion from Rembrandt's self-portrait through Ingres to Gauguin and the Douanier Rousseau. There was also a magnificent photograph of the detail on the main door to Chartres Cathedral; a reproduction of Dürer's *Praying Hands;* some British Museum postcards of Attic vases. And there was an excellent camera study, cut out of last month's *Vanity Fair,* of a girl's body stretched, with accent on long tight thighs and firm high breasts, against a dark background.

"Here is Penelope's workroom," Mrs. Lorrimer said quickly. I told her yesterday that I didn't like that thing, she thought angrily. She opened the door which led into Penelope's small studio.

As David turned away from the pictures to follow politely, he glanced at Penny. She was watching him anxiously, as if she were afraid that he might laugh, as if that were the normal reaction she had come to expect. He said, most honestly, "I like this room." Somehow, he felt that in these last two minutes he had known her for two years.

"It is so very small, of course," Mrs. Lorrimer said of the workroom. It was very small, but it also looked very adequate. There was an easel, a battered table with sketches and pieces of charcoal and tubes of paint and a jar holding brushes, a high stool, a small electric fire, and some canvases standing on the floor with their face to the whitewashed wall.

"So you paint," he said, half to himself. Chest of drawers, he remembered, and smiled. Penny's eyes were laughing.

"Show Mr. Bosworth your drawings, Penelope, and then we shall go down for coffee," Mrs. Lorrimer said.

Penny hesitated. He walked over to the half-finished canvas on the easel. It was an impressionist study of the west shore of Inchnamurren. By the black rock in the foreground two figures were roughly blocked in, but so far only the sky and the sea had been painted.

"Where are the seals?" David asked.

"At least you recognized it," she said delightedly. "Mother, there you are! You always say that no one can recognize anything I try to paint. I am doing this as a kind of bread-and-butter letter to Grandfather. Do you think he will like it?"

"I like it," David said, and he was being honest. He was a little confused. The sea study was not at all bad. In fact, it was damned good. Surprising. It wasn't just the pretty little picture that you might expect from a girl who liked to paint. He took a closer step to look at the two figures. One was certainly a girl. The other figure might be, could be ... He looked quickly at Penny, but she was now much engrossed in a still-life which she was about to show him.

"Imitation van Gogh, I know," she said and smiled. He had the grace to look embarrassed. He wasn't accustomed to having his thoughts so quickly interpreted.

"And roofs," she said, showing him another canvas. "I do a lot of these. In a way, they are like a sea. A petrified sea."

"Now Penelope, get rid of that dreadful smock, and I'll take Mr. Bosworth downstairs. I am sure the coffee will be cold if we wait any longer."

David and Penny exchanged glances.

"That's all, anyway," she said. She seemed to be urging him to go, as if she did not want her mother to be annoyed. He reached quickly for the door handle to let Mrs. Lorrimer pass through.

"I always think this room is so bare, so masculine," Mrs. Lorrimer said, walking quickly through Penelope's bedroom.

David thought it wise not to contradict, even politely. The colors were not those any man would have dared to use together. The amazing thing was that they made a quiet room and gave it a feeling of space. It would be pleasant to live in a room like that.

"Your house is charming," he said to Mrs. Lorrimer as they went downstairs, and his remark won a real smile. It also involved a quick visit to a dark, book-lined room, all very leather-and-mahogany, with silver cups on the high carved mantelpiece.

"This is my husband's study," Mrs. Lorrimer said.

"Most impressive," he said, and nodded to the silver cups.

"For tennis," Mrs. Lorrimer said. "He used to win everything. He hasn't so much time now, of course."

"Of course."

In the drawing room, the coffee tray was waiting on a low table in front of the couch. As Mrs. Lorrimer poured coffee and hot milk in equal proportions into the cups, she went on talking about her husband. "He enjoys the tennis at North Berwick, you know. We have gone there every August for years. If you had arrived here next week end I am afraid you would have found a closed house."

David, whose chief worry during the last week had been that he might not discover Penny's address before the Lorrimers left for North Berwick, said, "Then I should have been a very lost stranger in Edinburgh."

"I should have thought you would have stayed on for the Twelfth," Mrs. Lorrimer said. "You are missing the chief excitement in the Highlands, you know."

Perhaps she was wishing that he had stayed at the Lodge

for the Twelfth. David felt some of the concealed regret in her voice, accepted a shortbread biscuit, and said quickly, "I wonder if you and your daughter would lunch with me today?" Thank heaven he had his ticket for London already in his pocket, but he wondered if his remaining thirty shillings would be adequate. Less than thirty bob, now: haircut and shave, suitcase in the Left Luggage place, tips, bus fare out to the Crescent. He made the calculation quickly. He set down the fine cup on the silver tray, almost letting it fall in relief as he heard her refuse. Politely, sweetly, but definitely. She was already engaged for luncheon. She was so sorry.

"I am, too," he said, now beginning to worry whether Penny was already booked up in this same party or not. Stupidly, he had not thought of that before. He had been so damned sure that she would be free. He looked so dejected that Mrs. Lorrimer was suddenly friendly. Perhaps, too, her little subterfuge troubled her. Anyway, she began to talk very pleasantly about Edinburgh.

Then Penny appeared at last. Mrs. Lorrimer's quick glance took in her daughter's newest suit, which normally was worn, in the first six months of its existence, only for the most special occasions. That wasn't all, either. Penelope was wearing her smartest high-heeled shoes, and that expensive blouse which had been bought only last week.

"Well!" Mrs. Lorrimer said. "We *wondered* what was keeping you."

David said, "Are you going out to lunch, too?"

"Why, no," Penny said in surprise. She looked at her mother's startled face.

"Then I hope you'll have it with me. You won't object, will you, Mrs. Lorrimer?"

Mrs. Lorrimer found she was helpless in face of the direct attack. If he had said, "May she?" Mrs. Lorrimer could have said, "I'm sorry but Penelope can't manage that, today. Perhaps on your next visit." But now, she would seem rude if she said, "Yes." And she had no real reason for objecting. Except there was just the little feeling that things were moving much too quickly out of her control. She looked at her daughter's happy smile and at the young man's face as he waited for her reply.

"Of course not," she said.

Penny said quickly, "I'll get my hat."

"What about your work? I thought you did not want to be disturbed today?" Mrs. Lorrimer asked.

"Oh, that's all right, Mother. I wasn't making much headway, really. Tomorrow will do."

"Tomorrow—" Mrs. Lorrimer began, but Penelope was already halfway up the staircase.

David Bosworth rose. "You've been awfully kind, Mrs. Lorrimer. Thank you for taking pity on the stranger within your gates."

Mrs. Lorrimer smiled faintly. There wasn't anything else she could have done, she thought worriedly. Only, she did wish that this young man wasn't quite such a stranger. All she knew was that he was poor, clever (this she had learned from questioning her father), and thoroughly determined. Quite admirable qualities, no doubt, if you hadn't a most marriageable daughter. She wondered if there was still time to say that her engagement for luncheon did not matter, and that she would be delighted to accept his invitation. But Penelope came downstairs at that moment.

She was wearing that new hat, with the rakish tilt, which she had insisted on buying. And her smartest handbag, her best gloves. And David Bosworth was saying that he hoped Mrs. Lorrimer would have lunch with him and Mr. Chaundler on her next visit to Oxford. And somehow Mrs. Lorrimer found herself walking into the hall with them, and saying good-by with a smile.

She stood for a moment at the open door, watched them almost run down the white steps and then start walking in the direction of the bus stop. They didn't look back. They were already talking as if they had forgotten all about her. And they looked so exactly right together, Penelope just a head shorter than the man and taking three steps to two of his, Bosworth with his straight shoulders half-turned towards the girl as he talked, that Mrs. Lorrimer found herself thinking for a moment how pleasant it was to be young and walk so confidently.

She closed the door, deciding that this wretched morning was all Penelope's fault. Her father would have to talk seriously to her. If she behaved with such indiscretion in London, goodness knew what would happen to her.

Mrs. Lorrimer, returning to the drawing room, stared at her three daughters over the mantelpiece. If only they were boys, she thought, if only they could take care of themselves, then she would not have to behave like some old tyrant. She looked at their portrait gloomily, as a fruiterer might look at a window-display of highly expensive, highly perishable peaches.

chapter ix

DAVID took a deep breath of relief when they reached the pavement and he still found Penny walking along beside him. Until the very last moment, he hadn't been quite sure that he was going to manage it. He felt as if he had scaled the rocks of Edinburgh Castle itself and flouted every jailer.

"Now what do you want to see first of all?" Penny asked.

"Nothing. Everything. It doesn't matter," he answered. You, his eyes said.

She pretended to laugh, but the color in her cheeks told him that she knew quite well what he wanted to see. He became conscious that he was hurrying her along the Crescent with obvious haste, and slackened his pace.

"Sorry," he said. "I was making quite sure that your mother would have no afterthoughts, and leave me walking along this Crescent by myself. Tell me, does every man who wants to take you out find it as difficult as I did?" The idea, applied to others, seemed rather an attractive one.

"Well, you are sort of unexpected, aren't you? I mean, Mother knows who the others are. She doesn't know you. That was the main trouble, I think."

"And what troubles do the others have to face?" He made a good pretense of joking about it, but he was wondering, with a sudden sharp annoyance, just how many men made the attempt. Looking at Penny, he knew there must be plenty of them, like bees around honey.

"Actually, you avoided the main one."

"And what's that?"

"You didn't phone. You called at our house."

"Is there a ban against phoning?"

"Not exactly. But there's a kind of opposition..." She paused in embarrassment: he must be finding her very amusing, and in the wrong way. "It really is much better to call at our house."

"That makes us respectable?"

"It helps."

He smiled broadly. "Well, I very nearly wasn't respectable."

"We've passed the bus stop," she said quickly. "Shall we go back?"

"No, let's walk. Do you mind, Penny?" They couldn't talk on a bus, and it was a pity to waste any of the few hours he could have with her. Besides, walking helped talking.

"I'd love to walk, David."

They were both conscious of the strange sound of their first names.

"Good," David said with enthusiasm. "Let's head for the Castle. That's the place to see, isn't it? We can find a spot to admire the view, and you can point out all attractions round about."

"You won't see much of Edinburgh that way, I'm afraid."

"I'll buy a guidebook at the station and do some memorizing on the train. Then I'll be able to give a good account of what I didn't see today, if you insist. You look startled. What's wrong?"

"Nothing." She tried to look natural. And then she laughed suddenly and said, "Do you always behave like this?"

He didn't answer that. He had never behaved like this before, he thought, as he took her arm to guide her across a street. He didn't let go either until another fifty yards had been covered and two elderly ladies, in knitted suits, straight-set hats and chamois gloves, smiled and bowed to a most confused Penny.

David lifted his hat with great politeness. "Sorry, that was my fault," he said. "I didn't quite like the sudden gleam of interest in their eyes. Will it cause any trouble?"

"It will be all right," Penny said, looking at him curiously. "They are rather sweet old ladies, not like some we might have met." She gave him the warmest smile that had yet come his way.

After that, David found himself forcing a passage for her through the increasingly crowded pavements. He felt the impulse to punch every man between the eyes who looked a moment longer than necessary at the girl walking beside him. I'm sunk, he suddenly thought as he made some small remark and waited to see the answering smile on her face: I'm sunk, completely and absolutely, and I don't care if I am. He began talking as amusingly as he could. He might groan afterwards at this display of sheer exhibitionism, but each smile and laugh and comment won now was well worth it. And when they had at last passed through Princes Street, broad, welcoming in the morning sunshine, with its fashionable shops along one side and its formal gardens on

70

the other, and then entered a steep street which looked as if it might lead them towards the Castle, he had his reward.

"Why, here we are!" Penny said with considerable surprise. She looked at her shoes, now lightly coated with fine white dust. "It usually takes an hour to reach the Castle from our house. At least an hour, if you are walking."

David glanced at his wrist watch. They had been walking for more than an hour. "What about some food, first? Is there a restaurant near here? I expect we passed several decent places in Princes Street. You should have told me, you know. I'm the stranger, here."

Penny smiled and shook her head. Decent restaurants were expensive. "There's bound to be a restaurant near here," she said, "if you don't mind something simple."

David wondered if he were hearing correctly. "Isn't there some place you'd like especially for lunch?" All the girls he had ever met before chose the best restaurant as a matter of course.

Penny shook her head again, and felt some surprise herself. She had thought, when she had dressed so carefully, that she would make a very smart appearance at one of the well-known places. (Who is the girl with that distinguished man? No doubt one of these foreigners who are now visiting the city. An American? No, probably Parisian—you can always tell by the hat.) But now, it didn't matter. Anywhere at all seemed marvelous, wonderful. He is the most extraordinary man I've ever met, she thought as she looked up at him.

"I don't suppose you have ever missed a meal in your life?" he said with a strange little smile.

"You make me sound greedy. But actually, I don't believe I ever have. Have you?"

"Sometimes. When I'm busy and can't be bothered."

"Frankly, I am not very hungry, now. Perhaps we shouldn't bother. We can have something to eat, later on."

"Good Lord, no!" he said vehemently, and flushed. God, did she think he had no money at all? And that remark of his about missing meals—what a stupid kind of thing to let slip! He had passed so many well-fed, healthy faces in Edinburgh streets that he had begun to think of it as a city of good restaurants, if only he knew where to look for them. One was always inefficient about restaurants in strange places: in Oxford or London, he would have known where to take her to eat. Hell, he thought angrily and looked around

71

him in desperation. He grabbed her arm suddenly and led her towards a sign.

"This looks a restaurant of sorts. Seems all right. Is it?"

"Yes," she said. But she was relieved that there was no one on the street who could recognize her as they entered its door, for her mother would have been horrified. A tavern would have been Mrs. Lorrimer's name for it. But there were white tablecloths and the appetizing smell of roast beef and Yorkshire pudding, as well as the tobacco smoke and the clusters of bowler hats on the racks which stood beside each table.

"Are you sure it is all right?" David repeated. This seemed a restaurant mostly for men. Probably the food would be excellent.

"Of course," she said. Why, she thought with some disappointment, it really looks very respectable!

David was saying, "We might get some decent food here. What chases away my appetite is the tearoom."

Penny seemed intent in drawing off her gloves. She had always thought tearooms, especially the ones on Princes Street, rather pleasant places with excellent cakes. But obviously they weren't held in such high regard in Oxford. She felt suddenly very naïve about her ideas in food.

David noticed her sudden shyness. "Are you sure you don't mind this place?" Good Lord, he thought, I am becoming more Edinburgh than Edinburgh, worrying about what is done or not done. Or perhaps he was being unfair to Edinburgh judging it by Mrs. Lorrimer.

"Do you like Edinburgh?" he asked suddenly.

"Yes," Penny said in surprise, "don't you?" And then she smiled.

"I like its Princes Street," he said, "but I don't know anything about its people. Except you and your mother, and you seem direct opposites."

"Mother was born and brought up in England. She only came to Edinburgh when she married Father."

"Oh," he said. He looked at Penny, and they both laughed, and then she became absorbed in studying the menu.

"If you really don't care for this place," he began hesitatingly, and then stopped. Mrs. Lorrimer's influence was long-lasting, it seemed. He was noticing, for instance, that the tablecloth although white was not well-laundered, and that the menu was thumb-marked. Penny must have noticed these things at once. Damn, he thought, I've bungled things badly: I must look damned inadequate. He scowled savagely in the direction of an interested table. "And who are these young men, anyway?" he asked suddenly. He was delighted when he saw his return stare had routed successfully the watching eyes. He began to feel more efficient again. Well, they asked for it, he thought: bloody rude of them to stare at Penny like that.

"Medical students," Penny said.

David glanced at her sharply. "Do you know them?"

Penny shook her head. She had liked the quickness in his voice, somehow. "You can always tell them. It's their clinical interest."

David relaxed and a smile spread over his face as he ordered lunch. By a skillful process of suggestion and elimination, he managed to make her decide in half the usual time she needed to cope with a menu.

Well, she thought, as the full-bosomed thick-waisted waitress in drab black retired with the completed order, well it is rather nice to have someone to make up your mind for you—especially if he decides on the things you really wanted to have anyway. She wondered if he always knew what he wanted so very quickly; and thank goodness the dye in her new suede gloves was fast and her hands were not streaked with blue as she had feared; and did that medical student with the red hair know her, for he looked as if he did recognize her—students had a way of knowing you without you ever having met them; and was he perhaps a friend of any of Moira's friends? And then she suddenly thought, I don't care even if all the family find out, I don't care if I get into the most awful row. This, she decided as she listened to David's voice and watched the smile in his eyes, this is fun. She laughed suddenly.

"A good joke?" he asked.

"I'm feeling rather good," she said. She told herself she shouldn't have admitted that, but her tongue had outwitted her.

"Are you?" He looked pleased. He said quietly, "So am I. Nice feeling, isn't it?" Their eyes met and held in the same way they had met and held in Mrs. McDonald's cottage. And the effect was still the same. Penny took fright, retreating into words: David was silent, watching her as she talked. She felt suddenly that he knew why she was talking like this and she fell silent, too.

"And what happened then?" he asked. He must have been listening after all.

"Nothing very much. I'm afraid I'm boring you."

He shook his head slowly.

The waitress brought the food, and the intrusion brought them back to earth. Besides, the roast beef was tender and properly underdone, the roasted potatoes were crisp and hot, the vegetables were an appetizing green and did not taste of baking soda, and they were both hungry.

David congratulated himself on his choice of restaurant. It could cook. As he drank the excellent ale which he had ordered—Penny would have nothing to drink—he said, "Thank heavens you are a girl who can eat."

She looked up quickly, horrified.

"No, please don't," he said. "That was a compliment I was trying to pay you. There is nothing sillier than the girl who picks daintily and leaves most of the food on her plate. She probably thinks she is being esthetic or something, although how anyone can be esthetic when they don't appreciate an art like good cooking I can't imagine. Actually, she always reminds me strongly of the princess in *The Thousand and One Nights*. The one who ate rice with a bodkin. Only rice, grain by grain, everything else refused. Remember her?"

Penny, whose knowledge of *The Thousand and One Nights* had been limited to one volume of carefully selected passages, to Rimski-Korsakov's music, and to the annual bowdlerized version of the Christmas pantomime, wrinkled her brow thoughtfully. "I don't know it," she admitted. "I thought I knew the Arabian Nights pretty well, but I don't know that story. How did it end?"

"Well, roughly—without Scheherazade's interruptions—she ate the grains of rice by day, drugged her husband's coffee in the evening, and went out by night with her friend, the ghoul, to tear a few graves apart. Nice clean fun, don't you think?"

Penny thought over that, and then the full implication dawned on her. She laughed and pushed back her empty plate.

"I was only trying to show you that I *was* paying you a compliment when I said I was glad you liked good food. But I suppose I haven't Scheherazade's charm as a teller of tales."

"Actually," Penny said with mock seriousness, "you should not mention ghouls or graves in Edinburgh. Burke and Hare ... Remember them?"

"Why, of course, they worked here .... Good old subconscious: it keeps on going all the time, doesn't it?" He glanced over at the party of medical students, and caught the red-haired man watching Penny again. "Now I know what to say to your medical friend if he doesn't stop looking over in this direction."

"What?" she asked with dawning horror. But she did not need an answer. David's sudden outburst of laughter was enough. It made everyone in the room turn their heads sharply to look at them for a moment; and strangers' faces, as they picked up their own conversations again, still held something of the smile which had been brought to their lips quite involuntarily.

"I believe you would!" Penny said. She imitated his voice: "Doing much body-snatching these days, Dr. Redhead?"

After a while, when she could talk without starting to laugh all over again, she said, "Actually, we *are* being rather cruel. He is probably a most worthy young man."

With a body-snatching eye, David thought.

"I'm sorry," he said, but he did not look in the least repentant.

"What other stories did Scheherazade tell?"

"One thousand and one nights of them." He smiled, thinking of their variety.

"And the king who listened never got bored? She must have been very beautiful as well as having a lovely voice. But I suppose that after a thousand and one nights she had become a habit."

"Probably," David agreed. And a very pleasant one. The three sons which she produced, meanwhile, must have been a help too. "She certainly kept her head, which was more than the King's previous wives had been able to do."

"I don't believe she was afraid of death. She told the stories well because she wanted to tell them. Perhaps she loved the king, and wanted to make him happy."

"Perhaps."

"You think I am being rather silly, don't you?"

David's smile disappeared. "Good Lord, no! I'm interested. Do you really believe she was in love?"

"Why else would she bother? If you had to tell a different story every night for almost three years to someone you did not love, you would probably give up after three months and petition to be beheaded. Wouldn't you?"

David was smiling again. "Probably."

"You are as cautious as a Scotsman. I never heard such a collection of Probably's and Perhaps's."

"All right, I'll abandon caution. When can I see you again? Do you ever visit London?"

She pretended to be very busy pouring a second cup of coffee for him, no cream, three lumps of sugar.

David pressed his question, "No chance of arranging a holiday there?" If not, then I'll just have to think up some old excuse to get to Edinburgh for Christmas. A complicated business. Still, he would arrange it, somehow. If he won that essay prize on the failure of democracy in Greece, there would be enough money to cover expenses.

She shook her head, and then she relented: he was looking quite disappointed enough. "I am coming to live in London," she said very quietly.

"What?"

"I'm going to the Slade School of Art. At the end of September."

He pushed himself back from the table, wrinkling the tablecloth, spilling the coffee. "Well," he said, and then lowered his voice to a more normal tone, "well, that's grand." He studied her face for a few moments. "You know, you can be a devil, too. Why didn't you tell me?"

"You might not have wanted to see me again," she said gently.

Before he had recovered his breath to say anything to that, the waitress, with one eye on the clock and the other on an emptying room, came over and frowned at the tablecloth. Some people didn't know when to stop talking or drinking cold coffee. Imagine them coming to a howf like this, anyway! With clothes and a figure like that, I'd let myself be *seen,* she thought. The man was looking annoyed—did he just want to sit there talking all afternoon, and me with my feet fit to burst? But he tipped well, and that was something unexpected. Usually the students, and he looked like one, left three-pence under the plate. Hard-up, they were, although they did have an extra glass of beer often enough. Funny kind of hard-upness that. That was men for you: suit themselves, me first, me me all the time.

"Thank you, sir." She slipped the tip into the pocket under her apron, and stood there for a minute to watch them leave. Still talking their heads off. . . . And now he had his hand under her arm and was guiding her carefully between the empty tables. Well, she thought grudgingly as she fingered the tip in her pocket, you're only young once. And she wished them luck in her bitter, tired way, as she pulled off the stained tablecloth and mopped up the pool of coffee.

Edinburgh Castle looked coldly down on the last visitors still disturbing its peace. A poor lot, who paid money and stared. Once upon a time, the price of admission had been a good sword arm, a hot-blooded battle cry.

The group of international students was exhausted in everything, even in its good will. Tea had been suggested by Moira Lorrimer, and she was now shepherding her straggling guests towards the Castle gates. Some of the thirstier ones had already started down the twisting cobbled paths, no doubt hoping to find a place where something more to their taste than tea might be found. Well, she had done her best: she had shown them practically everything they should see, and that wasn't a bad day's work. Especially when Joan Taylor, who was supposed to be helping to guide the party around Edinburgh, had done nothing but enjoy herself with the Americans.

"We shall be late," Moira said to the last small group of lingerers, and hoped they would take the hint.

"Superb!" a French student cried, and swept out her arm to the gardens which lay down in the valley between the Castle's precipice and Princes Street. Her sense of drama did not seem to irritate the American who was beside her—as he had been for most of the day.

"On the Rhine, we have many old and beautiful castles. Also beautiful rivers." The German was still informative.

"Have you?" Moira answered coldly for the twentieth time. She was becoming tired of hidden comparisons. What was more, after six hours of listening to foreigners, she found that she herself had started to speak with their intonations. She had caught herself, only ten minutes ago, shrugging her shoulders and saying "But yes!" to a Frenchman. And after two hours of the Germans, who seemed to have adopted her, for they kept coming over to ask questions or make statements, she was saying "So!" as if it were *"Zo!"* and, alarmingly, "Please?" With the Italian, she had found her eyes opening very wide, and her hands fluttering vaguely in the air. Joan Taylor, meanwhile, had been having no difficulties at all.

Now the very handsome Italian who had more often than was truly necessary brushed against her arm—and twice, it had to be admitted, against her hips—was beside her once more. She flinched instinctively, and held her elbows out stiffly, as he walked much too near her, so that she found herself moving forward at a tangent until she was practically against the wall.

77

"I am sorry," he said with his deep, rich smile, as if he had just noticed that she was practically off the path again. "So very sorry."

"Yes, yes," she answered, but still kept her elbows in a defensive position. He had magnificent eyes and he used them well, almost as well as his hands.

"I have a riddle," he was saying, dropping his voice to a friendly murmur.

"But what?" *Stop* talking that way, she told herself angrily. "What is it?" she asked quickly.

"Are the hearts of Scottish girls as hard as the rock on which they placed their castle?"

Moira looked wildly around for help. But, for once, the Germans had left her, the Americans had walked on with Joan Taylor and the French girl, and the Chinese scholar had retired into contemplation of the color qualities of the smoke which hung over the distant rooftops.

She said weakly, "Perhaps they are."

"No, no, no. Impossible!" He halted suddenly, and grasped her arm. "Look, see! There are sensible people here. *There* is a girl with a heart that sings, and a young man who is allowed to listen."

Moira looked, in spite of herself, towards the couple he had pointed out. They were standing at the rampart, leaning forward and resting their elbows on it. They were standing very near each other, for one thing. For another, the man was not even pretending to look at the city stretching out below them. He was watching the girl's face.

"Most touching," Moira said very coldly. And then she stared.

"Are you ill?" the Italian asked anxiously.

"No." She made the effort of giving him a reassuring smile, which he interpreted in all the wrong way. She said, "We are very late. We must hurry."

"Yes?" the Italian asked hopefully, as he steadied her by the arm once or twice and she didn't even notice. But it turned out that they were only late for tea, and his charming blond iceberg was surrounded once more by the phalanx of *Tedeschi* who were still discussing the view, firstly, secondly and thirdly. And what good, the Italian wondered, was a view without a pretty girl to share it sympathetically?

Moira found her conversational powers more strained than ever at the tea table. Her feet felt like burning lead, and her mind kept asking questions. The only answers it found didn't soothe her. Yes, that had been David Bosworth with

Penny. And in full view of the whole city, as it were. Just wait until I get home, Moira thought angrily, and her annoyance turned to outraged virtue. She ate one of her favorite cream-filled chocolate éclairs with as much pleasure as if it had been made of linoleum.

chapter x

TIME to leave," David said. And then he looked at Penny and added, "Of course, I could easily miss this train. Then you might have dinner with me. Would you?"

"I couldn't," Penny said slowly. "I promised that I would be home for dinner."

"I suppose it would be tactless to phone up and say you weren't coming." He hadn't asked it as a question, but he was watching her face for a reply. "All right, then," he said. "Time, gentlemen, time."

They began walking very slowly down the steep Castle road.

"I'll come home with you first," David said. "I'll find a taxi."

"I don't think so, David. Not here. And we haven't very much time left, have we?" She turned back the cuff of his jacket and glanced at his watch, and then she shook her head. She smiled up at him, this time, and said, "Besides, I travel about Edinburgh every day by myself. I am not quite such a wilting lily as all that!" Then, as he didn't join in her laugh, didn't smile, didn't say anything, but just stood still looking at her, she said quickly, anxiously, "What's wrong, David?"

"Nothing," he said then, "nothing." She likes me, he thought, she really likes me. She wouldn't have done that if she hadn't liked me. Damned fool, he told himself, how do you know she wouldn't? You only want to believe that; you don't know a damned thing about any of her gestures, how much or how little they mean. "Penny," he said suddenly, and then stopped himself, in time. Penny, will you write to me, he had been going to say. Better not ask—it sounded pretty silly anyway. Better write to her, and then see if she answered his letter.

"Yes?"

"It *is* Penny, isn't it? Not Penelope? Why?"

"I don't like Penelope," she said. "I mean, I like it as a name, but I don't like it being attached to me. People make jokes about it, you see: they make it rhyme with antelope, or they think up funny things to say about it. I wish they wouldn't. They ruin names, don't they?"

"They do their best. I've often thought that Dr. Johnson was wrong: puns aren't the lowest form of wit. Making jokes on names is quite the easiest and silliest way to raise a laugh."

"We should all be given numbers to identify us until we reach the age of eighteen. Then we could choose the name we really wanted. It is pretty awful at times what parents will think up for the christening."

"Probably, they are thoroughly desperate and bewildered by that time," David suggested. "Anyway"—he looked at her with a smile as he paused—"anyway, Penny it is."

She smiled. And then she said in surprise, "Look, we are walking in the wrong direction! The station is up to our left."

"Is it?"

She wasn't quite sure if he had been trying to lose that train after all. She colored, and looked quickly away.

"I expect your mother will hold it against me if I don't take you home safely," he tried. I'd even risk the horrors of a family dinner if I could see her for four more hours, he thought.

"Mother won't know. She is at the Clinic this afternoon, weighing other people's babies and telling them how to feed them."

"Is your mother a doctor?" he asked with amazement.

"No. It's voluntary work. Mother and some of her friends have been doing that for years."

Lady Bountiful, David thought. I might have guessed that. Still, Mrs. Lorrimer deserved some credit for the will to make an effort: there were those who were rich and never even thought of the poor at all.

"You aren't very impressed," Penny said, watching his face carefully. "Don't you like good works?"

"They are useful in an emergency. And as far as they go," David said carefully.

"But volunteers can be——"

"I know," he said. "They have hearts of gold, and they

80

give up their time, and what would we do without them? And it doesn't matter that the birthrate is low where it should be high, and high where it should be low, or that so many people should be stunted physically and mentally. You would think it would be cheaper in the long run for a state to spend money on professional people to take over everything to do with health. Besides, the volunteer basis doesn't reach far enough. If we depend on people who volunteer to help, then only some of those who need help will volunteer to ask for it. But if it is on a professional basis, then people learn to be businesslike about it, and they'll ask for help knowing it is legally theirs and not a matter of charity."

"But—" Penny began again. She looked at the strange bitterness in his face, and she felt suddenly bewildered and unhappy.

He shook his head. "No," he said more gently, "let's not begin anything we can't finish, Penny. I'll argue with you, if you'd like that, when you come to visit me at Oxford. You will come, won't you? We'll have lunch at the George, and then we shall walk out to the Trout for tea. Will you come?"

"I'd love to," Penny said. It did sound wonderful, although she wondered what on earth the George and the Trout could be.

"That's settled, then." He sounded pleased. He was indeed relieved: he had been worrying how to phrase that invitation for the last fifteen minutes, and for the last fifteen seconds before she had answered he had been afraid of a polite little reply promising nothing.

Then something began to happen to their conversation. They were practically silent by the time they reached the station. They halted at its entrance, Penny pretending to be absorbed in the busy street, David studying the pavement at their feet. He was thinking with some disappointment that this might be as far as the well-brought-up girl could go, and he had better not break any more taboos by suggesting that she should come into the station and see him off. She was waiting for him to say in that easy way of his, "Why are we standing here?" But he didn't suggest that she should come into the station, and he seemed quite immovable. His silence made him, suddenly, appear remote. He is halfway to London already, she thought, and in London we shall probably meet again as strangers. Probably, too, she would never see either this George and the Trout, whatever they were. That was another world—his world. He had come into hers for a day, because he had been passing by, and because it had pleased him. For a day. She watched the hurrying people on the street, noticing neither their faces nor their clothes. She felt miserable.

This is the letdown, David thought. Good-bys were always depressing affairs. You said either too much, or too little. And afterwards you thought of all the things you should have said, which would have been just right, neither too much nor too little.

He roused himself to say very quickly, "Well, thank you Penny. Tell your mother that I think Edinburgh is a lovely, lovely place."

"Good-by," she said. Well, here it was . . . . First you said good-by, and then perhaps good-by again, and you kept using the same phrases as you held out your hand.

"Good-by." He took her hand. "I hope I wasn't a nuisance."

"Oh, no!" She looked up at him, then. "I've had a marvelous day." She said it as if she meant it, he hoped. He still held her hand. Damned if I don't kiss her in front of the whole ruddy town, he thought. But then, at that moment, a stranger's shoulder rubbed his, and a stranger's voice said "Sorry!" and then "Good afternoon, Miss Lorrimer!"

David dropped Penny's hand, raised his hat, smiled and said, "Well . . ."

"Good-by, David."

"Good-by, Penny."

She gave him one of her brightest smiles, and then turned to walk quickly away. He watched her. The worst thing about saying good-by, he decided, was this feeling of uncertainty: would he ever see her again? For that depended on her, too.

The man who had greeted her was waiting at the corner, ostensibly for the traffic to slacken pace. Then he looked round and saw Penny (as David knew damned well he would), and changed his mind about crossing the road. He was accompanying her towards Princes Street, instead.

David lost sight of them in the crowd. He swore under his breath and went into the station.

He bought a newspaper to read in the train, and disagreed savagely with every editorial and article in it.

Then he sat in the gathering dusk and watched the fields flow past his window, and wondered gloomily just what had happened to him. By the time he had reached York, he wasn't even bothering to wonder. He was trying to balance a sheet of paper on a book and make his writing legible. This letter was going to be posted, he told himself grimly.

chapter xi

THERE was an air of distraction about the Lorrimer household that evening.

Betty had come home from visiting her friend, bringing a sore throat and headache. Mrs. Lorrimer, already feeling rather sorry for herself after a particularly trying afternoon at the Clinic, retired to her own room with a tray and a novel. Moira had phoned to say that there was some international dining which she must attend; she would be home by ten o'clock probably.

Charles Lorrimer, worried by Betty, annoyed by Moira, upset by the empty dinner table, finished the sweet as quickly as possible, refused dessert, and when Penny poured coffee for him in the drawing room, found an excuse to go to his study. Penny watched her father march with his long, heavy stride across the hall. He was a tall man, broad-shouldered and erect, so that his six feet seemed taller still, He knew that, and never slouched. Each sign of age distressed him—the spectacles which he now must have for reading, the careful diet which he was supposed to follow for stomach ulcers. How awful to get old, Penny thought, but she was pitying her father and not herself: when you are nineteen, it is difficult to imagine that old age can happen to you. Somehow, you believe that one day you will at last reach the nice satisfactory age of twenty-five, and that you will stay that way always.

Penny felt pity for a full minute. And then she picked up the book which David had given her. He had written her name on the flyleaf. Just her name. That was all. I like his handwriting, she thought. She looked at it critically, holding the book out at arm's length, her head to one side as her eyes studied it for a moment. Handwriting was so often disappointing: it didn't match the person who wrote it, or at least you hadn't thought this was the way they would write.

She carried David's book upstairs to her room. The house was at rest. She listened to its silence for a moment at her door, and then she went into her bedroom with a feeling of contentment and satisfaction. She had peace to think, peace to remember. She would take a long time in getting ready for bed, and she would think and remember and relax in comfort. No one asking questions. No one talking about things which didn't interest her tonight.

She undressed and slipped on a quilted dressing gown, for the night breeze from the open window was cool, and padded downstairs in her white fur moccasins over the thick carpets to the bathroom on the floor below. She had a long bath, with two squares of jasmine bath-salts crumbled into the water as a gesture of extravagant luxury. Back in her own room again, she brushed her hair (and decided to let it grow longer: much more romantic, tied it with sea-blue ribbon to match her nightgown, and even read two chapters of her new book.

Then Moira arrived. She looked tired and angry. Probably Father had had a thing or two to say.

"There's a draught," Penny said, looking pointedly at the billowing red and white striped curtains. Moira came in and closed the door. "Had a good time?"

"Rotten," Moira said. She sat down on a chair with more relief than grace. "Nothing but stairs and steps and stairs all day. Edinburgh was not built for sight-seeing."

"Couldn't you get away earlier than this?"

"Someone had to look after them. Joan Taylor just disappeared with the Americans." Moira looked angrily at her sister's amused face. "If your legs and feet felt the way mine do, you wouldn't think it was so funny either."

"Was there a dance after dinner?"

"If you can call it that. A Frenchman sat down at the piano and gave us 'le jazz hot.' And then I was pump-handled all over the floor, or given a demonstration in the crouch style."

"Never mind," Penny said soothingly. "It may have been trying for your feet, but it is awfully good experience for Geneva—when you get there."

"At this moment," Moira said, "I don't want to see Geneva ever. I've no international understanding left."

Penny rose now and came forward to her sister. "Come

84

on," she said. "Better get to bed. I'll run a bath for you and you can use my bath salts."

Moira didn't move. "If you have left any," she said crossly. "The whole place simply reeks with jasmine. Besides, I didn't come in here to tell you about how tired I am. I've a question or two to ask you. Just how, Miss Lorrimer, do you get away with it?"

"With what?"

"Don't look so innocent. I saw you this afternoon. At the Castle."

"Did you? Well, what's the harm in that? All visitors are taken to the Castle."

"To admire the view. But I didn't notice either of you doing much view-admiring."

"Don't be an idiot. He called here this morning, invited us all to lunch, and I was the only one free to act as guide for the afternoon. That's all."

"So, that's all. Why, he looked as if he was going to put his arm around you."

"He did not," Penny said furiously.

"Just like a soldier with a shopgirl."

"Don't be an idiot," Penny said, and tried to laugh. Moira, she thought, had such a wonderful talent for spoiling everything merely by discussing it.

But Moira had not finished. "This evening," she said in a voice that was much too smooth and charming, "Jimmy Russell came over to talk to me for a moment. He is running the Tennis Club dance on Friday, and wanted me to bring you along. He said, 'I see your sister is now in circulation.' I could have hit him over the head. He is the wildest medical we have had around for years; and that's something."

"I don't know him."

"Well, he knows you. He saw you today. He had red hair and a wide grin."

"Oh!"

"Yes, oh!" Moira said. "Whatever possessed you to go to a tavern like that? What would Mummy say if any of her friends had seen you?"

"There is nothing wrong with the place. It has very good food, and a lot of men enjoying it. That's all."

Moira was silent for a moment. "Men," she said scornfully, still thinking of Jimmy Russell. "Imagine his absolute cheek! It just shows you that you have got to be so awfully careful."

And you take good care that I am, Penny thought angrily:

85

you are worse than Mother, sometimes, as if you wished I were still fourteen years old. She looked at Moira quickly as this new idea came to her mind. No good challenging Moira, though. Moira had always excellent reasons for behaving as she did, even if they weren't the real reasons.

Moira sensed that her sister was amused about something. "But you've got to be," she said sharply. "How do you know that this David Bosworth isn't another Jimmy Russell?"

Penny laughed. "Poor old Dr. Russell. You make him sound a monster. Fascinating."

"Loathsome, I call it. Like that Italian, today. These men shouldn't be allowed out without their keepers."

"What Italian?" At last, Penny thought, the conversation is being turned.

"Another self-appointed Romeo," Moira said airily, with all the superior wisdom of her full twenty years. "The older I get, the more I find out that men deserve the worst being thought of them."

"And how does that fit in with your International Understanding?"

Moira noticed her sister's smile, and her voice sharpened. "It wouldn't do *you* any harm to try a little international good will, instead of enjoying yourself."

"Well," Penny couldn't resist saying, "David Bosworth *is* English."

"Englishmen don't count. Nor Americans. The hard work is with real foreigners. Today, I was absolutely exhausted by them."

"Cheer up, Moira, they probably were exhausted by you."

Moira rose. "We are not amused." she said as coldly as the Widow of Windsor. "I did my best, anyway. Besides, I am not particularly difficult. We have been sensibly brought up, and that makes us very simple to understand."

I wonder, Penny thought, I wonder if that kind of simplicity doesn't cover a mass of thwarted emotions. . . . on the surface, it seemed so controlled; underneath, there were doubts and fears. "I wonder," she said. "if girls like you and me can ever make a man really happy, happy in every way, happy as people ought to be happy. Unless we start re-educating ourselves, of course."

Moira stared at her. "What absolute bilge you talk sometimes," she said sharply. "We have both been stuffed full of education. If any re-education is needed, men can start it on themselves." She moved to the door, slowly as if she were thinking about something, and then paused there for a moment. She said in a hushed voice, "I was talking to Joan Taylor about Italy. And, do you know, she says a young girl, a pretty one that is, with a tight skirt, can't walk down a street in Rome without being—being nipped. Yes, she swears it's true. She was there last Easter, you know. She said she came home all black and blue behind. Can you imagine?"

Penny began to laugh.

"What's so funny? It is absolutely indecent."

"Painful, too, I should think. But where was her powerful tennis forehand? Didn't she slap a few faces?"

"How could she? Think of the scandal in the street. Besides, she often did not know who had done it. In fact, once she turned round like a whirlwind, and the man raised his hat and smiled sweetly. What do you think of that? Who is it that has got to be re-educated, there? Penny, stop laughing!"

Penny regained enough control to say, "Well, I think when Geneva sends you on a mission into Italy, you'd better invest in a bustle." The laughter began to break down her voice again. "Put it on your expense account. Call it your International Underpinning."

"You shouldn't joke like that about it. And you shouldn't laugh at your own jokes, anyway, when they are so bad."

"The worse they are, the better I like them," Penny said cheerfully. "If you won't take my advice, why not ask Mother?" she added mischievously.

At that moment Mrs. Lorrimer's voice said, "Penny, you are waking the whole household. You should have been asleep long ago." The door opened and Mrs. Lorrimer, in her marabou-trimmed gown and a boudoir cap which covered her hair entirely, entered. "Moira, what are you doing here? You should have been in bed by this time. It is almost midnight. Did I hear that you wanted my advice about something?"

"Oh, I was wondering about the color of my new dance frock," Moira said quickly.

"We can discuss that at breakfast," Mrs. Lorrimer said. "Now, to bed with you." She turned to leave the room. "Good night, Penelope," she said severely as she went into the hall.

Moira looked angrily at Penny, who had caught up a cushion and, holding it behind her back, was limping ostentatiously around the room. "Good night, Mother," Penny called. She ignored her sister's undignified face-twisting and said much too gently, "Good night, my sweet." The door closed with a satisfactory bang.

"Moira!" her mother said warningly. And then the murmur of voices, and the footsteps died away.

Penny threw the cushion back on to the bed, went to the window, pulled the curtains aside, and leaned on her elbows as she stood at the sill to watch the night sky. At least, she was thinking, I know how to deal with Moira. For tomorrow, Moira would start her little side remarks. She would begin to hum "There is a tavern in the town, in the town," or talk about "castle walls old in story" until Penny became a package of raw temper and Mother would start asking what was wrong. But now, Penny thought, if she starts any little hidden references I'll start limping. Poor old Moira, how easily her leg was pulled! Joan Taylor had certainly pulled it very hard this time.

Penny looked at the sky. Navy blue with a hint of rich purple, she decided. The soft wisps of cloud traveled over the stars, hiding and then revealing them as the night wind drove on. There was the Plow, and there the Pointers at the edge of its blade; and then a space of sky, and then the brilliance of the North Star. So that was the north, and down there was the south, and four hundred miles south was London. London. She kept repeating the magic name.

She would live in Bloomsbury. She would walk about the streets, and look and look and never have too much of looking. She would see strange things, and eat strange foods in Soho, and meet strange people. She would have a room of her own, a room of her own where no one would come unless she invited them. She would choose her own friends.

And of course she would work, she would be able to paint and think of painting without Moira and Betty and Mother all pulling her away from it. No more interruptions unless she wanted to be interrupted. And if she could get working well enough, perhaps there would be some success, just a little one, and that would be enough to start her. London would be the gateway to a whole new world. She would travel. She could live on an island in the Mediterranean, she could paint in a small village high among the Alps. She would see Paris and New York and Vienna. She would see everywhere. London was the gateway, and she was standing at it. She shivered with happiness.

Perhaps, also, the air was cold. She stopped looking at the North Star, pulled her shoulders back into the room, and drew the curtains together. She removed the quilted robe, stood for a moment looking at herself very seriously in the long dressing-table mirror. Then suddenly she freed her arms from the shoulder straps of her nightdress, and let it fall in its quick satin shimmer to her feet. Now she looked at herself critically, turning slowly around to study the curve of her shoulders, the shape of her back, her slender taut waistline, her smooth round hips. The line of tan, ending so abruptly at her neck and arms, made her skin seem whiter. When I go to the Mediterranean, she thought, I'll have a tan that goes all over, and no white bands of flesh. I'll lie in the sun and feel my backbone melt. I'll wear thin clothes and feel my body breathe: no more sweaters and tweed skirts, and not even pneumonia.

She raised her arms, gently, gracefully. . . . Women look at their best with their arms above their heads she decided. The Greeks had known that. So had the inventors of ballet. She took a slow dance step forward, let one shoulder droop and her waist's curve be emphasized; and then slowly drew her body erect again. Women can be lovely, she thought. And why not? If nature had meant us to be ugly, she would have made us so, with no waist or curves or soft lines flowing into each other. She would have made us squares or cubes with thick gray skin: much more practical for living, if she had wanted us to be practical. She shouldn't have made us this way if she did not want us to be admired. And if we can't find pleasure in the way we look, then we are hyprocrites, and we don't deserve to be made this way: we might as well look like an intelligent rhinoceros.

She stopped being Pavlova, and tried to imitate the Venus de Milo. But it was difficult to hold that double twist of the body for any length of time. I bet the model could have brained the sculptor with his own chisel, Penny thought as she dropped the pose.

She strayed away from the mirror and went over to the bookcase. She searched for the atlas in its bottom shelf, and turned the pages quickly until she found "London and the Southern Counties." It wasn't there: it must be further north than she had thought. She tried "London and the Midland Counties," and found it. She measured carefully with thumb and forefinger and consulted the scale of miles. Why, Oxford was quite near London, nearer than she had imagined. About seventy miles, roughly. That was nothing at all!

She sneezed suddenly, and realized her body was chilled. It was difficult to be romantic in a cold climate: the Greeks would never have produced their sculptors if they had inhabited Iceland. She rose, put out the light quickly, and slid into bed. She lay there a moment, remembering that she had forgotten to open the curtains. "Oh, damn!" she said, and got out of bed, and ran quickly over to draw them apart. Now she could fall asleep looking at the stars.

The linen sheets were cold. It was like bathing in a mountain stream. After the first shivering shock, it was pleasant to stretch her body and feel the cool clear water slip over her. Then she became practical again, but not practical enough to get out of bed once more for the abandoned nightgown lying in front of the mirror, and she curled up and hugged herself to get warm. She was too excited to sleep. She would think about today. It had been a good day. She lay, tightly curled up in the cold narrow bed, and thought about everything that had happened in the order that it had happened. She had reached the restaurant episode, when the growing warmth of the bed relaxed her body. She stretched out her legs slowly, feeling wonderfully comfortable and content. To be continued, she thought drowsily. What a very poor Scheherazade she would make, not even waiting for the dawn of day. She yawned, smiled, fell asleep, all in the same delightful minute.

The train from Scotland pulled into the last station on its long journey, and halted with a final deep-drawn breath. The carriage doors were flung wide open and left hanging on the hinge. The passengers straggled over the broad platform. They moved stiffly as if the long rest in the train had exhausted them. The electric lamps, suspended high overhead from the enormous vault of soot-stained glass, cast a bleak light on the tired faces to make them lined and haggard. "Another lot of perishers come 'ome from their 'olidays," one porter said to his mate as he rolled a heavy milk-can towards his trolley. He grinned as a well-dressed man jumped nervously out of the way as the can rattled ominously near. Out of the side of his mouth he said, "Gawd, Jim, ain't they the walking dead?" There was no malice in his voice, but rather a comic lack of sympathy.

David, following on the heels of the nervous gentleman, grinned too. This was London all right. Same old voice, same old smell of soot and smoke, same old feeling that the air had been breathed a thousand times before it reached his lungs. He had forgotten how warm it could be at midnight when even the breezes were tepid, and the callous lights in the station increased the feeling of heat and exhaustion. Everyone looked as if he needed a holiday. Those who had been spending an evening in town—the girls, with their flimsy dresses, funny hats, bright red lips, and their thin-shouldered young men—were white and listless and did not even try to recapture the crisp gaiety they had felt at six o'clock in the evening. Those who were returning from the country were beginning to walk more briskly as if to assert that they at least were healthy, but the tan on their faces now gave an appearance of incipient jaundice. It must be the lighting, David thought, as he glanced at himself in the fly-spotted mirror of a chocolate slot-machine and noticed the lines under his eyes, too: we can't *all* have kidney trouble. Back to civilization.... Loch Innish was in another planet.

And yet, he was glad to be home. He never knew how much he had missed London until he was back in it again. He changed his bag to his left hand, and searched in his pocket for his exact fare. The sickly smell of the underground, always stronger in summer, reached him while he was still some paces away from its red, circling sign. He hurried down the flight of stairs, walking quickly between white-tiled walls, towards the steadily moving escalator which would bear him deep into the heart of his own city.

chapter xii

DAVID left the bright lights of Chiswick's High Street, and crossed over the small dark common where the trees and dim lamplight gave at least the appearance of coolness. He entered the long street with its rows of neat houses stretching so silently before him. Most of the windows which he passed were already dark. Here and there a top-floor bedroom lamp was lit, dimly glowing behind its pink silk shade. The road was empty except for an occasional man with his pipe and his dog, or a straggling couple walking home slowly with arms linked. He noticed the cracks between the paving blocks and remembered how he used, as a child, to make this long stretch of road seem shorter by counting his paces, measuring them carefully so that he would never step on the black, dust-filled lines.

Twice he stopped to rest his bag and change his carrying hand. Soon home now, he thought as he paused for the second time. Those he had passed on the street had found their houses, and the silence was complete and waiting for his footsteps. A cat, out on its mysterious business, looked at him suspiciously. He could see its eyes, reflecting the lamplight behind him, turn to flat luminous disks. And then they too vanished, and he was left alone in possession of the street. Here was the house with lace curtains, here was the house with the green gate, here was the house with the disastrous yellow door. And here, at last, by the red pillar box under the lamppost, was the entrance to Cory's Walk.

It began as a side street, so insignificant that a stranger—perhaps even the residents in the more prosperous little villas surrounding it—would pass it without remembering it. For it wasn't even a useful short cut to some place more important. Only the people who lived there appreciated its seclusion, its lack of traffic, along with the modest rents which suited their budgets. But even they could not call it charming. The eleven boxlike houses which stood in a tight row along one side of Cory's Walk were of red brick, now dirty and soot-lined at the seams; jaundice-colored plaster framed the narrow doors and small windows; the woodwork, once a possible green, had turned a grayish-black; the railings, shielding the small patches of earth in front of each house, had forgotten the touch of a paintbrush. There they were, the eleven small houses clustered together as if to encourage each other; and the red brick wall which ended the little road; and another red brick wall, longer, higher, opposite the row of houses, separating them coldly from the garden of the mansion which had given the Walk its name. Only the tops of the lime trees, which overhung the long wall in their friendly way, were evidence that a garden did exist. Cory House itself, buried silently behind trees and high walls, preferred not to notice what had happened around it.

It had changed considerably from the Regency days when Nathaniel Cory had built it as a country house, northeast of the Thames and fashionable Kew Gardens. It must have been a pleasant place, surrounded by fields and woods, for many a gay week-end party. Now, it was owned by a lay sisterhood as intent on their future salvation as Mr. Cory had been on his worldly relaxation. And in a few years' time, it was rumored, the ninety-nine-year lease would be ended and the house in the garden and the houses in the Walk would be equally leveled, and there would be a new street with noble

92

buildings, an arcade of pleasant shops and a children's green playground. Margaret Bosworth had laughed when she heard that. She had remarked, "Yes, we talk that way ... until we start building."

David halted by the pillar box at the corner, and felt in his pocket for the letter. He looked thoughtfully at the address, comparing it with the row of silent houses beside him. This forest of brick through which he had walked in the last fifteen minutes looked mean and makeshift. The architect and builder should have been imprisoned for inflicting such eyesores on their fellow citzens. For that was the trouble about houses: they stood there for years, looking at you. Hurting you, too; pulling you down to their level. It seemed monstrous that people who could only afford cheap houses should find themselves automatically surrounded by ugliness. And it did not take many years before they had little sensitivity left in them. It had been smothered to death by the amount of bad taste forced on them by their poverty.

David smiled wryly. Here he was, standing with his letter in his hand, feeling hot and tired, arguing with himself about the obvious in order to postpone a decision. I must be more tired than I feel, he decided, or I would not be standing here like this. Oh hell, make up your mind.

A policeman, marking his solitary rounds with heavy footsteps, halted across the street and walked over to the lamppost. He looked at the bag, and then at the young man standing by the pillar box.

"Good evening, officer." No, I am not loitering with intent.

"Evening, sir." The policeman was more assured as he had a closer look at the young man.

David grinned and said, "I must look a fool standing here, but the truth is, officer, I can't make up my mind whether to post this letter or write another one."

The policeman relaxed. He stood with his feet apart, his hands clasped behind his back. "Important letter, sir?"

"Very."

"Then if you've any doubts, you'd better look at it again. That's my advice. I'm not much of a letter-writer myself, but sometimes things are read different from what they are written."

"Yes," David agreed. It was a rotten letter, now that he thought over it. He shoved it back in his pocket. "Good night. Thanks for the advice."

"That's all right, sir. Breaks the monotony for me. Quiet

93

round here, although we may have a spot of trouble." His voice sounded hopeful. "People away on holidays, you know: houses all shut up. Good night, sir." He gave a forefinger salute and started his lonely march, his thick-soled boots giving their word of comfort to all those who lay awake and heard the steady echo.

One o'clock and all's well, David thought as he picked up the bag and entered Cory's Walk. Yes, it was a rotten letter, full of gush and sentiment.

Cory's Walk had played its little part in bringing him back to earth. He passed the first six houses with sadness rather than distaste. They tried so hard, he thought. The Crescent in Edinburgh had been a row of houses all very much alike, too. But similarity, when it has money behind it, becomes a solid wall of convention, of permanence, even of defiance. Similarity, conceived and born in poverty, becomes an inferiority complex. One had only to look at this row of brick rabbit-hutches to feel that a giant wind might blow them all into crumbling dust. The people who lived in them must be haunted by their own impermanence—jobs that could be lost, money that wouldn't cover necessities unless pleasures were cut to nothing. Their life meant only a round of small worries and distasteful duties, the constant battle for respectability of the lower middle class.

He noticed that Number 2 had planted three small rose-trees in its plot of garden, and Number 4 had painted its railing. But Number 3, into which new tenants had moved last spring, looked worse than ever. Another year or two, and they would succeed in converting their house into a genuine slum.

As he opened the gate to Number 7, took six paces to the three stone steps and then searched for his key, David was thinking that it wasn't enough to be given something: you also had to make an effort to keep it. If you had money, you paid other people to make the effort for you. But nothing could continue to be as it had been, without an effort. And yet, how could Number 3 be really condemned? They were living, by spending money on clothes and pleasure—only on a very reduced scale—as Lady Fenton-Stevens and her friends lived. No doubt, Lady Fenton-Stevens hated housework and dishwashing just as much as the woman at Number 3. But then, Lady Fenton-Stevens had married a rich man. That had turned out pleasantly for her, but it certainly wasn't any mark of moral virtue. She and her friends were just as lazy and incompetent in actual scrubbing and scouring

94

as the woman at Number 3. They were all equals in their search for enjoyment, sisters of definitely the same breed. And as long as people praised Lady Fenton-Stevens's photographs in fashionable magazines, they had no moral justification for sneering at Number 3's dirty doorstep.

I'm certainly home, David thought as he realized his own bitterness. He opened the door quickly, closed it quietly, and stood for a moment to get his bearings in the dark hall. It was small and narrow, with a steep staircase leading abruptly upstairs from the hall stand. In his caution, he knocked against the collection of umbrellas and walking-sticks which stood on either side of its table. He grabbed at them as they moved, scraping heavily on their metal-lined stand, but in the darkness some of them slipped free of the wooden rail which supported them and clattered on to the linoleum floor.

"Damn," he said softly, and had to switch on the light after all. Then he started to mount the stairs cautiously, but the second one creaked as it always did.

"David." It was his father's voice.

David retraced his steps, placed his bag beside the hall-stand and opened the door which lay opposite.

"Sorry, Father. I didn't mean to waken you. I was trying not to."

The shadowy face against the white pillows smiled. "That's all right, David. I wasn't asleep, anyway. Did you have a good holiday?"

"Fine. I'll tell you all about it, tomorrow." David crossed over to the heavy wooden bedstead, carefully avoiding the invalid-chair which stood at its side. He lifted the thin hand which stretched over the counterpane to meet his, and said as he pressed it gently, "Let me draw down those blinds. That lamplight is keeping you awake."

"No. I can't breathe when the windows are covered. That keeps the air out."

"It's pretty warm, tonight," David agreed. He heard the light clatter of heelless slippers on the wooden stairs. "That's Margaret," he said with a smile, "coming to give me a row about wakening you up."

David's father smiled, too, as Margaret appeared in her cotton kimono at the doorway and said, "David, you can see Father in the morning. This is a dreadful hour to come home."

For a moment, the two men enjoyed the shared feeling of innocent conspiracy against female authority. Then David said, "Good night, Father." And remembering the thin face staring so hopelessly up at the ceiling as he had entered the room, he suddenly bent over the bed and kissed his father's gaunt cheek.

Margaret closed the door impatiently. "Really, David!" she said. "We've only one article of furniture in this hall, and you had to fall over it."

"I had forgotten how narrow the hall was," David said. He pulled one of the long dark plaits of hair which hung over her shoulder. "How are you?" he asked affectionately. "You look about fifteen in that rig-out."

Margaret's thin face softened for a moment. She tossed the plait out of his reach. "I'm all right, but Scotland seems to have ruined your eyesight. Now that you have got me thoroughly wakened, what about a cup of tea or something?"

"You'll probably curse me, but I should like some tea. And a sandwich. I haven't had anything to eat since midday."

"Well," Margaret said shrewdly, "they say beer is nourishing."

He laughed softly, and followed her towards the kitchen. Same old Meg, same old house, David thought.

"Why didn't you have dinner on the train?" Margaret asked him as her slippers clopped over the linoleum floor from sink to gas stove. She looked round in her half-worried, half-shortsighted way. David took a box of matches out of his pocket, rattled it to make sure there were still some there, and threw it over towards her.

"I didn't feel very hungry," he said. Actually, he hadn't felt like paying three shillings and sixpence for lukewarm boiled cod smothered in melting lanolin with a dab of green garbage on top. And he hadn't been able to get any beer, either.

Margaret looked at him quickly. "The check?" she asked.

He shook his head. "Lady Fenton-Stevens will no doubt tell her secretary in a day or two," he said bitterly.

"Oh . . ." Margaret sat down on the other kitchen chair. Disappointment chased away that young look: suddenly, she seemed much older than her twenty-five years. Now, you noticed that she was too thin (she was very proud of her lack of breasts and hips) and that the sloping shoulders were round. The bright kitchen light robbed her of any pretension to prettiness. Her skin was sallow; her eyebrows too heavily marked; her lips were too pale, too tight. (In the daytime, she wore her heavy black hair drawn sleekly into a low knot at the nape of her long slender neck. With lipstick to broaden

96

the narrow edge of mouth, and powder to camouflage sallowness, she could look extremely attractive.) David now watched her, half-affectionately, half-worriedly, but with a touch of horror. He wondered how many women looked like this, once the make-up was removed.

Margaret said, "No Cornwall. No holiday. She will never send it in time."

"I've thought it all out," he said quickly, moved by her pathetic face. "If the check doesn't come through before you go to Cornwall, I'll give you the money which I set aside for the first weeks back in Oxford. The check will surely arrive in time to keep me solvent. Don't worry, Meg. This is what is known as high finance. You filch out of one reserve to pay for immediate needs, and then use the money for that to fill up the old reservoir again. Don't worry."

"You and Montagu Norman," Margaret said, but the pathetic look had gone. She was suddenly indignant. "She'll probably forget all about it."

"No, no. After all, she came asking me to take on the job. I didn't go begging her for it."

"What were they like? The boys you tutored, I mean?"

"Decent enough. But between you and me, Meg, there were moments when I thought they were solid teak above here." He placed his forefingers across his eyebrows.

"So it wasn't all holiday," his sister conceded. She rose to deal with the bubbling kettle. She was in good humor again: she was reassured about Cornwall.

"Not entirely," her brother said with quiet irony, which was lost in the ritual of heating the brown teapot. It would have been a wonderful place for a real holiday, he thought.

"You'll find some cold meat in the pantry," Margaret was saying. David took the hint, and went foraging for his sandwich. The pantry window was wide open, protected from flies and marauding cats by a gauze-wire screen. The milk bottle stood on a marble slab in front of the window for coolness, but even so the milk had turned sour. A damned waste, he thought angrily.

"What is Scotland like?" Margaret was saying. "Whom did you meet?"

David brought some cold mutton into the kitchen and the small brown crock which held butter floating in salted water. He planked them down on the table. "Better wash first, and get rid of the grime," he said.

"What's Scotland like?" Margaret repeated. "Not that one, David, that's the dish towel. Over there . . . that's right."

"I'll tell you all about it tomorrow," he said. "You go up to bed, Margaret. I'll have a sandwich and then turn in, too."

"I'm going to have a cup of tea. It's too warm to sleep, anyway, so we may as well talk."

David thought of the letter he wanted to write and post so that it could reach Edinburgh by tomorrow night. He began to tell her about Loch Innish. He talked, too, of Inchnamurren and Dr. MacIntyre. Briefly, because he had the feeling, once he did start to talk, that Margaret's attention was not always focused on what he was saying; it was strange how people could ask you to explain something, and then after the first few sentences they would hardly bother to listen. If you stopped explaining, of course, they would be hurt. He didn't say anything, however, about the Lorrimer family beyond a short reference to their visit at Inchnamurren. He knew instinctively that Margaret would be antagonized by the idea of Penny. She had sulked for weeks when she had learned about Eleanor Fenton-Stevens, for instance: a cool, calculated sulking to show her disapproval. She had never given any reason for it, even after Eleanor and the sulking period were both over.

"It must have been wonderful," Margaret said. "How I envy you, David. You get all the luck, don't you?"

"Well—" he said, and then smiled and said no more about that. "Perhaps we'd better turn in, now. You will have a lot of packing to do tomorrow."

"I've packed everything already. I don't need so very much for two or three weeks. Just as well, isn't it, considering the state of my wardrobe? And Cornwall is so very quiet."

"Well, why not choose a gayer place, if you want it? You will have money enough for a decent holiday," David said, trying to keep his voice even.

"Oh, it is all settled. Florence is expecting me. She has been having a miserably lonely summer, and she would never forgive me if I didn't go. She is counting the weeks until she can be back in London. She will probably be qualified by next spring."

"Qualified as what?" David couldn't resist asking. "A piano mover?" Florence Rawson, the large, rawboned daughter of a country doctor in Cornwall, had met Margaret at the College of Music in their first year as students there. Florence was going to be the composer, Margaret the concert pianist. Time had altered Margaret's plans: when her mother died, she had had to come home here to look after her father, and she could only manage to attend an occassional class once or twice a week. But her friendship with Florence Rawson had increased, and they never seemed bored with each other or their ideas however much these were repeated. They were egocentrics whose thoughts were like a pleasing reflection in a mirror. Narcissus-like, Margaret and Florence would gaze at them for months without any distaste, any self-criticism. Probably for years, David considered. But then, he didn't particularly like Florence Rawson. Her tweeds and booming laugh and hearty step, her perpetual assumption that men were either fools or in league to keep women from the major careers in life, filled him with horror.

"You don't need to be so cruel about Florence," Margaret said in swift defense. "She's as clever as you are, perhaps cleverer."

"That wouldn't be difficult," David said lightly. He rose, and cleared away the cups and saucers. "Come on, Meg, let's get to bed. I am beginning to feel exhausted."

She said suddenly, "You are going up to Oxford the week before term starts, aren't you?"

David looked at her in surprise. "I don't know yet. I might stay here until October." At the end of September, Penny would be arriving in London.

"But you *said* you were going up early to Oxford this term."

"I have been thinking it would be cheaper to stay here: it would save me an extra week of battels."

"Why can't you say 'bills'? That Oxford talk gives me a pain, as if you were all in some secret society or something." Her voice was angry.

"Everyone says battels and has been saying it for centuries: it won't be dropped just because you don't like it, Margaret." He looked at her worried face. "Come on. Out with it. Why do you want me to go back a week earlier than necessary?"

She was disconcerted by the unexpected question. She hesitated, and then came out with the truth flatly. "I've asked Florence to come here for that week."

David stared at her. "You mean she is going to have my room?"

"Don't get angry. You'll waken Father. Besides, as long as you haven't a job, just where *are* we to find a guestroom when we need it?"

He ignored the jibe. "How long is she going to be here?"

"Until she finds new digs. Her landlady last year was horrid. Objected to the piano being played."

"Probably didn't want it to be pounded into matchwood."

"You can save your witticisms for Oxford. You are all so gay and lordly there, aren't you?"

David restrained his rising temper. "Did you ask Father about this? I don't imagine an invalid particularly enjoys a stranger crashing all over his house."

"Florence won't disturb Father. Besides, you might remember that if it weren't for me this house would not exist. Who looks after it and keeps it going? As well as giving those awful piano lessons to make enough money for a little tuition at the College of Music?"

As usual, David was beaten. When Margaret started enumerating her virtues, he was always beaten.

David said, "Look, this is a silly hour of the morning to start having arguments. Come on, Meg." He walked over to the kitchen window, opened it, and promptly let two large moths and a swarm of gnats into the room. "Oh, damn!" he said. "Switch off the light, Meg, and keep the rest of these blighters outside. Why can't there be something invented to let you have windows open and lights on and still be comfortable in summer?"

"Men are so good at changing the subject," Margaret said acidly, as she rose and switched out the light.

And some women, David thought, don't change the subject often enough. Anyway, the light was now out and they could start moving upstairs, and he could have half an hour of peace before he went to bed. But he found himself standing by the window, looking out into the small square of garden turned to silver in the bright moonlight. The rambling roses, which his mother had planted some years ago, now spread over the wooden fences which separated this garden from the others. The grass was worn thin in patches where his father's invalid-chair rested through the day.

Margaret came over to stand beside him. She watched him curiously. "What is worrying *you?*" she asked. Six weeks in Scotland ... Oxford ... What had he to complain about?

David said slowly, "Father. There is a big change in him even in these last six weeks. I got quite a shock when I saw him." David suddenly saw again the thin, hopeless face staring up at the blank ceiling. "Wish we could get him into the country."

"How? James, bring round the Rolls—no, I think the Daimler tonight, and we'll drive down to Little Toad-in-the-Hole." She paused, and then as David didn't reply, the mockery left her voice, and she said: "Don't worry, David. Father is all right. I look after him well. It is probably only

100

this ghastly weather. You know we tried to persuade him to go and live in the country. But he says that London has always been his home, and that he is lonely when he is away from it. He likes the distant noises: he listens for the trains, and for the boats on the river. And he sits for hours beside his bedroom window watching the children playing in the Walk. Besides, what would I do in the country?"

"He has lost heart since Mother died, that's what is wrong with him," David said. "That's the whole trouble." His father had been an uncomplaining invalid, even cheerful, in spite of the long, throttling siege of illness. It had tightened slowly but surely from the time he had been invalided out of the army—he had been one of the survivors of the Kut garrison—partly because of wounds, partly because of some Middle East microbe which continued to attack him long after the wounds had healed. At first, his father had resented the idea of being condemned to illness for the rest of his life: he had tried to pick up his career where 1914 had interrupted it. But that had been impossible. It was then that his mother, the impractical woman, had become the practical leader of the family: they had moved from St. John's Wood to this house in Cory's Walk, and their whole life had been scaled down to meet the new necessity. And his mother had succeeded, with work and care and thought, in making a home where there could even be laughter. But now, his father's will to live had gone. In these last four years, he had become silent and moody.

"In spite of all their bad luck, they were really happy," David said quietly.

Margaret was silent for a moment. "The moonlight is making you sentimental," she said briefly. Wouldn't Mother have been happier if she had never married? She would have made a big success as a concert pianist.

"How could she ever have been happy?" Margaret added in a harsh, angry voice.

"She was," David said quietly. "You had only to look at her face to see that. She never thought she had sacrificed anything, compared to what Father had given up. He would have been a good architect if the war hadn't come along. And he was never as bitter about that as he could have been. Said he wasn't the only one who was left a crock."

"And just how much credit was given us for that? Those who didn't suffer because of the war forgot very easily, it seems to me."

David glanced quickly at his sister's bitter face. "It would have been worse for all of us if we had lost the war. That's what Father keeps saying, and he is right. What angers him, today, is the way we forget that, the way that it has become fashionable not to talk like that. It is a pity, isn't it, that people *will* follow fashions even if it kills them? Like a lot of diabetics insisting on eating chocolates."

Margaret stirred impatiently, and then moved slowly towards the kitchen door. She didn't like this kind of talk.

Father's mind had never progressed beyond the year 1919, but it was a pity that he should influence David like this. David, with all his advantages... (In such moments, she always chose to forget that David had provided for his own education since the age of twelve by winning competitive examinations, that he had already won three scholarships to Oxford which not only paid for his tuition and lodgings and food, but allowed a margin for a careful budget in books and clothes.)

"It is after two o'clock. I'm going to bed," she said.

Good, David thought.

"Besides, the war was all a mistake," Margaret went on, not leaving well enough alone. "We should stop talking about it."

"I've always wondered why a war should have been thought important enough to let so many be killed and maimed, if it can be forgiven and forgotten so easily."

"If everyone had been like the workers, with no vested interests to think of, there would have been no war."

"Aren't you forgetting nationalism? The German workers put on uniforms and marched. The others had to march too, or be marched over. You've found every reason why there should have been no war, except the practical one: what do you do when another nation puts on uniform and starts marching? Just lie down and wave your legs feebly?"

"Don't be so coarse, David. The trouble with you is that you don't take things seriously enough. You are just not politically conscious, that's all."

David grinned. "Been seeing much of Breen, recently?" he asked innocently. Roger Breen, another of Margaret's peculiar friends... Why couldn't Meg choose someone who was pleasant to have around the house just for a change?

Margaret said nothing, but the way she set down her feet on the stairs and the angle at which she held her head described her annoyance sufficiently. She was probably thinking up some corker to give him as a parting thought. David was right: she paused at her bedroom door to say, "It never is any use arguing with your preconceived ideas, David. Your holiday with the rich and powerful has only made you more of a reactionary."

David still smiled, but his eyes had hardened. "See you at breakfast," he said. "I've got a scarf tucked away somewhere in my bag for you; couldn't find that Gaelic music, but we may be able to track it down in London if it interests you."

"Thank you, David. You shouldn't have bothered." She was embarrassed, conscious of the change in her tone of voice. "I'm sorry I was cross. It's the heat, I think. And I've been worried. Just things, you know. My music, and Father, and everything." She turned away suddenly. "Good night, David," she said in a suddenly muffled voice.

"Good night." Poor old Meg, he thought suddenly. There wasn't anything wrong with her which a legacy of a hundred pounds could not cure. That was all most people needed: just a sense of a little security. They could face their problems more easily then.

In his room, he unpacked his writing pad from his bag, and placed his books in their proper place beside the others in his bookcase. The row of titles welcomed him home. Plato, Hegel, Descartes, Kant, Fichte, Mills, Marx, Locke, Bentham, Rousseau, Engels. . . . *not politically conscious,* he remembered. Roger Breen was, of course; although one had to wonder sometimes when talking to him if he moved his lips when he read. Home *Sweet* Home, David thought.

He sat wearily down on the hard chair at his desk. He pulled the crumpled letter from his pocket. Too emotional, too damned cocksure of himself. Yet it said what he wanted to say. If he could see his future clearly, he would say it. But he had nothing but uncertainty before him and he couldn't say it. His sister and his father, each in their own way, had reminded him of that. He tore the letter in pieces. He suddenly felt miserably tired and unhappy.

He wrote a very simple note, beginning "Dear Penny" and ending with "Yours sincerely, David Bosworth." He thanked her for the pleasant day he had enjoyed in Edinburgh, he hoped he would see her in Oxford or in London.

He read the note again. Suddenly he added a postscript. When would she arrive in London and what was her address to be? Quickly, he closed the envelope, stamped it, addressed it. You thought you were a fool, he told himself as he changed his shoes for his thin slippers which would make less noise on the staircase, because you let yourself see her again. But you would be a bigger fool if you hadn't ... or if you don't.

Once he was quietly out of the house, he ran swiftly towards the pillar box at the corner of Cory's Walk. The next collection was 6:30 A.M. Good. Further down the street, he saw the solitary figure of a policeman. It had recognized him. He saluted back, and then hurried towards his house.

It was cooler now, and the night sky was beginning to lighten. He stood by the open window feeling the first stirring of the early morning breeze on his shoulders as he pulled off his shirt. It was strange how natural he could be with Penny, as if he were walking with only himself for company: no feeling of effort, of strain. That came before a meeting with her, or afterwards, but when he was with her ... He kept thinking about Penny as he undressed and prepared for bed. And he kept thinking about her, even after he had fallen into a restless sleep.

chapter xiii

MARGARET had gone to Cornwall and the month passed pleasantly in Cory's Walk. Mrs. Trumble, Margaret's weekly stand-by, now came in for an hour each day to "wash up and dust around" as she said. She was a silent, smiling woman who—with a husband out of work and nine children below employable age—was glad to add a few extra shillings to the family's dole. Beyond the fact that she lived near the river, and that her eldest son was called Ernie and was a bright lad at school (this information was called forth only by the quantity of books on David's desk), David could learn little about her. She did her work quickly and then departed in quiet haste to merge into her own mysterious orbit once more. He would have been amazed to have heard the intricate discussions on Number 7 Cory's Walk, in Mrs. Trumble's kitchen, with her visiting neighbors over a dish of tea. "Give me men, every time," Mrs. Trumble would say, and her visitors, all with at least six children to their credit, would agree.

Certainly, life in Cory's Walk had become very simple. Mr. Bosworth seemed to enjoy it. If meals were not always punctual or even elaborate, they could be digested in peace. And David was happy: his work was going well and the odd hours spent with his father in the garden were pleasant for both men. They talked about the things his father liked to discuss—about the war that was so long over and yet was still so fresh in his father's mind, about politicians' limitations, about the Middle East, about the news in today's paper, about Oxford, about the constant elections in Germany, about David's possible future. He had always got on well with his father, but now he seemed to understand him still better.

And it was easy to be happy with this new background of elation to all his thoughts. He was writing twice a week to Scotland, and twice a week he had his replies. He would have written every day if Mr. Lorrimer had not to be reckoned with. Penny reported that a letter even twice a week was raising eyebrows in one half of the family, and amused comment in the other half. Her first reply had been as stilted as his first letter. And then, as his letters had become fuller, she had gradually thawed out. When he had changed to "My Dear Penny," he had become "My Dear David." She wouldn't have done that if she hadn't, at least, liked him. He convinced himself of that, remembering her upbringing and background. This, in a way, put all the responsibility of future developments completely on his shoulders. But in a way, too, that was how he as a man wanted it to be. The delicate balance of human relationships, of a woman and a man with two separate and well-defined personalities learning to adjust them to each other, would have been overweighted if she had been more confident, more dominant than he was.

He no longer tried to rationalize or justify his summer madness. He was content to feel the excitement which raced through his blood when he saw her neat, decided writing on an incoming envelope, or to hold the happiness which swept over him when he took his pen and sat down to write her. And he knew instinctively that if he once let her slip he would never find her again.

September came at last, with its grayer skies and cool evenings. The mists hung over the river at night, and spread northwards towards Cory's Walk, leaving a few wisps to trail over the gardens in the morning. The roses were fading, and hung full and loosepetaled on the branch ready to be scattered over summer's grave.

People like Margaret Bosworth, who had been out of town, returned with brown and healthy faces to mock those whose earlier summer holidays were already forgotten. She came back with a new store of energy which she proceeded to use in deploring the state into which the house had fallen during her absence. David and his father retired unanimously into their own rooms to read. Mrs. Trumble's hurt feelings developed into sciatica and she stayed away for a couple of weeks, to return when she decided that she had asserted her independence sufficiently and that Ernie needed a new pair of boots for school.

It was bad enough, David reflected, to have this tornado of energy strike with full force, to be made to feel he ought to offer his help, to have his routine completely upset and his work made more difficult, without being conscious of the fact that all this was happening because of the Rawson woman. After all, Margaret said, the house could not just be run to suit him alone. True enough, but still damned annoying.

She had made that remark when they were washing up the supper dishes together. ("If I take time off my own work to cook for you, I don't see why you can't take time off to help clear things up." Again, true enough. But still damned annoying.) Then she removed her rubber gloves, looked at her hands critically, and massaged some lotion into them. "I'll go upstairs, now," she said. "I have some Busoni studies to practise before Roger comes to collect me."

And I'll come and insist you move the piano to another corner of the room when you are in the middle of them, David thought.

"What's amusing you, David? You needn't laugh at piano exercises. They are hard work."

"I know. How's your *Jeux d'Eau* coming along?"

"Slowly. I'll have it perfect in another week."

In time for dear Florence, David thought. Yet Margaret's actions, from Margaret's point of view, were all justifiable. She was the mistress of this house by virtue of her work in it. Her father was the master, paying for the rent and food out of his pension. David was only a boarder, who contributed his share to the household expenses when he was at home.

"What's wrong, David?"

"Nothing. I was just thinking I'm probably rather a nuisance to you—extra trouble and all that."

106

Margaret's thin face looked at him searchingly. "You aren't a nuisance," she said. "Whatever gave you that idea?" Then she tried to assume a more casual tone. "You know, David, I've often thought it was madness for you to go to Oxford. If you had entered an office of some kind, you would have been earning a steady salary by this time. And we'll need that, you know, if Father dies. Remember, his pension dies with him."

David looked at his sister, but her eyes avoided his. He suddenly felt as if an octopus had whipped an arm around his ankle.

"If Father were to die," he said calmly, "then we certainly would not keep this house going."

"We have to live some place. Besides, I can always have a piano here."

"I think this house would be too big for one person." And he saw her eyes again turned towards him, questioning, watchful; he explained, "I am away for most of the year, Meg. And frankly, if Father weren't here, I'd take a job of some kind abroad during the holidays. And after I go down from Oxford, I may not even be living in London."

"But I needn't be alone. Florence could live with me here, and then you'd always have a home to visit when you wanted one."

Had all this been planned in Cornwall? he wondered. He suddenly saw his personal future being neatly arranged for him, all in the name of brotherly love and sisterly care and family duty.

"Suppose I die before Father does? You should think of that too if you have started calculating results of deaths." His voice was bitter enough to startle her. Or perhaps it was this new idea which shocked her. "Wouldn't it be wiser to arrange your life independently of mine?"

"How?" she asked angrily. "I've no money. I wasn't allowed to finish my course at the College of Music. I am qualified for absolutely nothing."

"You did get some education," he reminded her. He didn't add that it had been paid for, too, through careful economizing by their mother. "Why don't you and that woman Rawson look for a job? That is what most young men and women do."

"Then we'll never have the careers we want."

"How many men do have the careers they really want? Even if a man is willing to starve in a garret for the sake of his own hopes, he can't inflict that on his wife."

"He doesn't *have* to marry."

"Mistresses are even more expensive than wives, I believe," David said with a smile. His anger had turned to amusement. Margaret imagined that everyone else should be arranged emotionally into the same watertight compartments as she was. Judging from the shocked look on her face at this moment, it was even possible she thought that men's emotions were as easily controlled and managed as women's.

"Don't be crude, David," she said angrily. She left the kitchen suddenly, and paused at the foot of the narrow stairs to call back, "And don't call Florence 'that woman.' She is my friend. So don't think you can separate us."

"I am not trying to separate you," David said as he entered the hall. Lord, he was thinking, what phrases women use. "All I ask is that you don't inflict her on me."

"You are horribly mean about Roger, too. You just don't want me to have any friends, that's it."

"If Roger is coming round tonight for you, you had better do your hair. The parting is uneven." It had been annoying him for the last fifteen minutes.

"Roger doesn't bother about such details," Margaret said icily. "He is interested in what I think, not in how I look."

He is only interested in what he himself thinks, David would have liked to say. But he didn't. He said nothing, but knocked on his father's door instead, and let Margaret enjoy her last word all the way upstairs.

As he set out the cards on the small table before his father, Margaret was beginning a steady series of arpeggios. Their argument had not affected her playing: the notes were clear, regular, brilliant, machinelike in accuracy and attack.

"We need two packs for bezique," David's father reminded him gently.

"Sorry. I wasn't thinking," David said. He smiled and began to feel better as he saw the anticipation in his father's face. This was the game his mother and father had played through many a long evening. He shuffled the cards and dealt. He waited patiently as his father's thin hands arranged them slowly, and the leisurely game began. He wondered again, as he listened to the unending stream of chromatics, if Margaret's talent was really as first-rate as she thought. Certainly, he couldn't offer any advice. Whether you were really first- or second-rate in your work was something you had to find out for yourself.

He let his father gather a fourth ace to win a nice hundred points. It always acted like a tonic on his father if he could win, not too easily yet definitely. He watched the invalid's thin face, the skin drawn so tightly over its bones, the lack of flesh and red blood to give it shape and color. The gray eyes were, at this moment, interested and alive. Their blank weariness and patience were gone. The weak hands moved slowly.

"Four aces," his father declared in triumph.

"Good for you." David pushed the chips across to his father's side of the table. He rose to turn on the light. The evenings were short, now. He closed the window, for the air turned damp and cold at sunset, and shut out the voices and rushing feet of the children as they had their last game before bedtime.

As he lifted his cards once more, he remembered other September evenings. There had always been eyes at windows watching the children as they played, there had always been the fading trees above the chalk-scrawled walls. He remembered the fine feeling of mist and gathering darkness, the cool touch of the night air on his hot cheeks. And when he had come indoors, his mother and father had been finishing their game of bezique, and upstairs Margaret had been thumping out five-finger exercises. A profound melancholy stirred in him, and he sat quite motionless.

His father was waiting for him to draw and play. "Is there anything wrong, David?" he asked.

David listened to the new burst of rhythm from upstairs. Margaret had abandoned scales for Brahms, but she still played with hard accuracy, as if the heart were not needed to balance the mind's technical skill.

"I was wondering whether I am deluding myself, too," he answered gloomily.

"What's that, David?" His father had been too engrossed in trying to collect four kings. "What did you say, there?"

"What if I'm absolutely no good in the Diplomatic?"

His father did not quite follow his argument. "The Foreign Office needs a variety of men in its service. Inbreeding only weakens. It needs new blood. I shouldn't worry about that, David."

"I could probably fit into the pattern if I tried hard enough," David said, "but that isn't the question. The question is, can I do something more than just fit into a pattern? Or do I want to have to fit into a pattern before I can succeed? Or, can anyone ever really succeed if he has to fit into a pattern? That's what worries me."

"The salary is small to begin with," his father went on,

following his own line of thought. "No more than a school-teacher's. And generally the young men have some private means of their own, or some financial backing from their family. That will be difficult for you, perhaps. But it could be managed."

"That isn't what worries me," David said patiently. "What I am wondering is this: would I be any good? Or would I be just a polite echo with well-trained brains? Thinking correctly, dressing correctly, fitting so smoothly into the damned pattern that I'd become incapable of standing outside of it, if that were ever necessary?"

His father looked at him. "It doesn't hurt a man to worry about these things," he said gently. David wouldn't fail, he assured himself. But David always had these spasms of self-doubt. There hadn't been one major examination yet before which David had not always been uncertain and worried. I'm glad he is that way, his father thought: it keeps him from being overconfident and self-assertive.

He said, "I never wanted a son who aimed at being rich and famous at the expense of other men. And I never wanted a son who would spend his life pretending he was big enough to fill a job, when in his heart he knew he wasn't as good as someone else who might have had that job instead of him. But it doesn't hurt a man to aim high, as long as he never loses the habit of questioning himself. Every now and again, he should get thoroughly worried about himself, try to give himself a few honest answers no matter how painful they may be."

When David did not answer, his father went on, "I've been a spectator for years, David, and I've seen more of the game than those who play it. I would like you to do well, David. Just to make up for me." He paused there and half-smiled. "But I would like you to have a career in which you'd be doing a really useful job. Mark my words, David, there's trouble coming."

"Spengler's century of warring Caesarisms," David said gloomily. "And yet, no one is thinking of war. Disarmament and the depression is all we talk about."

"Here, yes. But in some other countries? I saw the last war begin, and the side that won the initial advantage had been preparing for years. It could pretend it had not, it could try to throw the blame on others, but its first success proved it was lying. Because you can't win an advantage in war unless you are well prepared. Nowadays, to hear Margaret and her friends talking, you would think that in 1914 all

110

nations who were involved in the war were equally guilty. That's the civilian way of thinking: they like to prove the soldier wrong—once they don't have to depend on him to save them."

His voice had risen. Suddenly, he put down his cards. "I had four kings, actually," he said. "I just did not manage to declare them. I'm tired, David. I think I'll go to bed." David looked at him anxiously. He pushed aside the card table, and helped his father prepare for bed.

"You make a good nurse," his father said, and patted his arm.

"It is all a matter of routine," David said. He was thankful that Margaret had stopped playing the piano at last. There was silence in the house, now, and silence in the streets.

"Something more than that, something more than that," his father replied. You could always judge a person's essential nature by the way he nursed, he thought. The selfish ones, the unselfish ones, the careless, the callous, the thoughtful, the gentle ones. "At least, I ought to be a judge of nurses," he added, "even if my ideas on politics seem to be all wrong." He smiled, and closed his eyes wearily. When David asked if there was anything else he could do, there was no answer except a slow shake of the head and a slow look of thanks.

The doorbell rang when he had settled at the makeshift table in his room. (The desk, which Margaret had insisted on painting, was still wet to his touch.) He heard Margaret's heels strike firmly on the stairs as she went down to open the door. Then he heard Roger Breen's high-pitched voice and ineffective laugh. He would have to get rid of some of that affectation in his accent, and his expensive suits and the comfortable allowance from his father, before David would ever be able to take his political opinions at more than mere face value. Thank God, Margaret had been ready, and there was no fear of Breen's sauntering into David's room for a chat while he waited. Breen's idea of a chat was to wander around, picking up a book here, dropping it there, after an amused glance at a page.

"The trouble with you socialists," he had once said, subconsciously justifying his own lack of hard study, "is that you read too much. You see everything but the direct means to get your end. Therefore, you'll never get it. Action, not thinking, is what counts." He had a habit of straightening his tie after pronouncing judgment. He always wore a red

111

one, to annoy his father (a wealthy manufacturer of boots—
a lot of boots had been needed in the war—who had an
accent far removed from his son's) and to prove to the
world that an expensive education at Eton could produce a
champion of the workingman. David had often thought that
it was just this kind of nitwit who did most harm to the
workers, for even the strongest liberal would become a Tory
if he had to argue with Breen.

Once David had asked acidly, "How do you reconcile
taking your father's money with the belief that it's so rotten?"
But Breen had his own brand of lofty answer for that, too.
"He is really trying to bribe me, you know. I am showing him
that my opinions cannot be bought."

That encounter had not ended pleasantly. For David had
said, "You only talk this way to win some kind of private
battle with your father. It is so exciting, too, to feel you are in
the intellectual vanguard, isn't it? If you had lived at the
beginning of this century, you would have worn a green
carnation in your buttonhole. I meet several of you at
Oxford. I'll believe your attitudes when I see you doing something with more self-sacrifice attached to it than just sounding
off among a lot of well-dressed, well-fed people. And I'll be
more reverent towards your opinions when you either stop
quoting your special newspaper's editorial, or at least have the
honesty to acknowledge the quotation. You are as spoon-fed
as the old boys in their fat leather armchairs in the club: you
just get it out of a different bowl, that's all."

Breen had drawn himself up to his full five feet seven
inches, and had remarked that abuse was the only argument
that a reactionary ever offered. That was the last time that
David had seen him. Margaret was always ready, now, when
Breen arrived.

David pushed his work aside and walked to the window.
He looked down on the narrow little gardens, stretching out
like small fingers from the back of the row of houses. How
could she put up with a man like Breen? She chose the
weirdest friends, as if she enjoyed surrounding herself with
misfits. Enjoyed? That was hardly the word to apply to
Margaret. Apart from her own world of music, she did not
know what enjoyment was. We are limited by our own
experience, David thought. We are its prisoners.

He turned away from the window, picked up Plato's
Republic on which he had been working that morning, and
opened it. He read the fable about the Prisoners in the
Cave once more.

"Damned if I agree altogether," David said suddenly, still thinking about Margaret. "We may be prisoners, but many of us choose to be. Plato did not allow for that."

For there were limits around our minds which sometimes we chose to set, not because we could not see but because we preferred not to see. So far we may be willing to go: we know what to expect. But no further; for beyond that boundary we are afraid. Our experience makes cowards of us: we want its security even if it limits us. We know that many who strike out beyond this boundary are lost. But not all. Some manage it. And when we envy them, we forget the risks they took. We think that their boundaries have always been so broad and limitless. We forget that they took the effort of pushing them outwards. Effort and risk. Instead, we talk of luck. . . .

Tonight, when he had been with his father, he had said he was worried. But were the reasons he had given the only true ones? Or wasn't he too afraid because the limits of Cory's Walk were still holding him? If George Fenton-Stevens were to fail, then his friends would laugh and say "Poor old George. Too bad. Better luck next time, old boy." But if David were to fail there would be no second chance, for his own belief in himself would be gone. When you came from Cory's Walk and aimed high, then you had to be so damned good that there was no possibility of failure. You had to be so damned good that you didn't need a second chance. That was why he wouldn't discuss his plans or ambitions with his friends. That was why he was always so vague about them. Yes, it was better to keep quiet about them until you pulled them off. That way, the laughs and the sneers wouldn't be so loud if you failed, and the pity wouldn't be there, either. "Well, David didn't manage it," his friends would say, "but I don't think he was very serious about it. Never mentioned it very much, did he?" That was right: keep quiet, never mention it, and then if you failed it wouldn't seem such a blow. If you aimed high from Cory's Walk and then fell, you fell a long way.

Yet—he had told Penny. Strange how he had suddenly blurted it out while they were leaning over the wall of Edinburgh Castle, as if he had set himself to impress her, win her admiration. The mating display, he thought suddenly. Oh God, did I really behave like that? But she had not laughed at him. She had listened with her large blue eyes watching him sympathetically as if she really wanted to hear him talk.

He moved restlessly around the room. Then he sat down at his desk, pushed the books aside, and lifted a sheet of writing-paper. This was the third letter this week, Mr. Lorrimer or no Mr. Lorrimer. As he dated it, he glanced at the calendar and said to himself, "Another week, and I leave for Oxford. And then Penny arrives. Damn that Rawson woman. If it weren't for her, I could have seen Penny every day until term started."

Then he began thinking how he might see Penny on the day she arrived in London. He would arrange it. He tried to imagine the surprise on her face when she arrived at King's Cross Station and found him waiting there to meet her. Then he glanced at his watch, noted the time, stopped all his wondering and imagining, and began to write her.

It was "Darling Penny" this time, and he didn't even notice how naturally he had written it.

chapter xiv

THE NOTICE BOARD, three porters and a ticket inspector had all agreed that the train from Edinburgh would arrive at this platform in five minutes. David was still only half-persuaded. He watched the giant hands of the station's clock as it jerked eagerly to each new minute, and debated with himself whether he should stand at the gate to the platform or whether he should use the platform ticket which he had bought. He decided to use it, and yet keep near enough the gate so he could not possibly miss her. He hadn't thought of that possibility until he had actually arrived at the station.

The notice board, three porters and ticket inspector had been right after all. The train was pulling in proudly, exactly on time. And suddenly the deserted platform was filled with people. The crowd was much bigger than he had ever imagined it would be, and his nervousness returned. It would be easy to miss her after all in this millrace. He didn't even know what clothes she would be wearing, and she didn't know he was going to be in London. He had liked the idea of a surprise. Damn fool, he thought now. And then, searching the hurrying crowd with an anxious eye and seeing nothing but tall thin men and small thin men and fat men and old women and young women with young men and children dragging at their mothers' arms and a girl who looked like Penny but wasn't, he said savagely, "Anticlimax."

"I beg your pardon?" a man beside him turned to say.

David looked at him bitterly.

"Sorry," the man said in embarrassment and moved away.

Hell, David thought, you've taken your eyes off the crowd. You've missed her, damn you.

And then he saw her.

There was a man with her, too, a white-haired man dressed in well-cut navy blue, carrying a small suitcase which obviously did not belong to him. David walked over so that he would stand in their path. Penny was happy. Her eyes were dancing as she looked at everyone around her: she was missing no details on the crowded platform as she listened to her companion. David found himself smiling. "Well, London, here I am," she seemed to be saying. And he wasn't the only one who thought she was beautiful, either. These passing glances from surrounding males said, "*Mm!* Nice!"

She saw him suddenly, stared blankly, halted, and then, without a word of warning to her companion, ran forward to meet him. "Oh, David!" she said. And there they were, holding each other's hands, gripping them, not shaking them.

"Well," the white-haired man said as he reached them, "I'm glad to see someone did meet you. Yours, I think," he added with a broad smile as he handed the suitcase over to David.

Penny remembered her manners. "Thank you so much for making the journey so pleasant."

"Not at all, not at all. The pleasure was mine." He raised his hat neatly and left them, still smiling, to merge into the stream of people flowing slowly through the narrow gate.

"Who on earth was that?" David said, as they too joined the queue.

"A captain. Navy. He has just been retired. He is sweet, isn't he?"

"Oh, a friend of your family," David suggested.

"No. I don't even know his name. I met him at one of those small tables in the restaurant car. You just can't sit opposite someone all through four courses, concentrating on food like a cow, can you? And after I spilled some salt, and

115

threw it over my left shoulder, he laughed. And then of course, we talked."

"Penny, you are—" He didn't finish the sentence, but smiled instead and shook his head slowly. He took her arm, and led her out of the station. Penny was the kind of girl whose suitcase was carried for her, whose arm was held as she crossed a street. And the strange thing was that you felt she probably was quite capable of looking after herself; she had enough feminine sense, however, to know when to drop her independence.

"You know," David said, still smiling, "you really shouldn't talk to strangers."

"Don't *you?*" She laughed. Then she halted and drew in a deep breath of air. "London!" she said. "It smells and sounds so good!"

"Only Londoners are supposed to think that. But"—he tried to make his voice sound more severe—"men are different. They can talk to strangers without complications. I bet it wasn't the salt incident that made him talk, either. That was merely the first excuse he could find."

Penny laughed again, and said, "David, this is the most wonderful surprise. Did you come up all the way from Oxford?"

"No, I just happened to be walking past this station, and I tripped over some salt and found myself talking to a beautiful blonde, and when I recovered I was wandering on the platform ready to challenge the whole blasted Fleet." He looked down at the suitcase he was carrying. "And am I to be called 'sweet,' too?"

"No," Penny said decidedly. "You are much much nicer than sweet." And then her color deepened and she pretended to be interested in the long row of crawling traffic.

"Where's the rest of your luggage?" David asked, as he managed to get a taxi.

"The trunks were all sent on in advance."

"Trunks? You sound as if you had come to stay."

"Oh, I brought a lot of things from my room at home. I got attached to them, you see."

She settled back in the taxi. She had never been happier in her life, she thought. She studied David's face, believing he didn't notice it, as he gave the driver her address. David had come especially to meet her. Everything was wonderful: London and the smell of petrol and the multitude of noises, the swarming traffic and this wheezing taxicab and its red-nosed bemuffled driver with his draggling moustache and drooping mouth and his shoulders hunched over the wheel. And David.

"We'll dump your suitcase at your address," David was saying. "And then we'll have dinner at a little place I know of, and afterwards we'll take in a theater. How's that?"

"Marvelous." Everything was marvelous. "But shan't I have to report or something at this women's residence? It is a terrifying name for it, isn't it?" She wrinkled her nose in disgust.

"You can do that tomorrow, as if you had arrived with a late train today. I know these institutions, anyway. You just sit around waiting anxiously, and it is only afterwards that you realize that things just arrange themselves anyway, so why all the worry?"

"I wish I could treat it so casually. I'm sort of nervous inside, David. I keep trying to imagine what it will be like."

"It is a place for women run by women, so you'll have chintz and dainty salads and rice puddings and gay girlish laughter all around you. You'll find it pretty awful, I expect. What on earth made you take a room there?"

"Father and Mother. They only let me come to London on the understanding that I'd stay at this place. They think it is 'safe'! And because it is expensive, it *must* be good!" She laughed. "It is funny how one has to keep compromising in life, isn't it? I wanted a room of my own. I've got it, but not just quite the way I wanted it. Still," she looked out of the taxi window, saw that the numbers in Gower Street were lowering rapidly, "it may not be so bad." She stared doubtfully at the row of four houses which had been converted into one building, before which the cab had drawn up. Like the other houses in this part of the street, it had a basement surrounded by iron railings, and a bridge of steps over the deep basement area to the front door on the ground floor. There were three stories of uniform windows above that, and attic windows set into the steep sloping roof with its lines of chimney pots. Three of the doorways had been blocked up, but the fourth was painted a bright green. A large polished-brass name plate informed the ignorant that it was BAKER HOUSE, RESIDENCE FOR WOMEN.

"I'll wait in the cab for you, Penny," David said as he deposited the suitcase in the hand of a stiffly starched maid with a measuring eye. Penny nodded, and stepped into the large dark hall. The door was shut firmly in his face.

When she came out, at last, he could sense her disappointment. She greeted him with too determined cheerfulness.

"Well, did they show you your cell?" he asked.

She smiled then. "No chintz, at least," she reported. Just faded green baize. Walls distempered at least five years ago in a safe cream-color. "And the trunks have arrived." With two of them standing in her ten-by-eight-foot room, there wasn't an inch of free space. I'll have to unpack with my feet up on my bed, she thought. One trunk probably wouldn't need to be unpacked. "I've a window, too," she said. "One of those up there on the top floor."

"The very top floor?" David asked. The attic would be cold in winter, hot in summer. "Do they use the attic, too?"

"They use *every* inch," Penny said. "There was another room vacant on a lower floor, but it would cost two guineas a week more."

She looked at him quizzically. "It isn't only the Scots who count every penny, seemingly."

David refused to be side-tracked. "Look," he said, "this wasn't exactly what your parents planned, was it?"

"Hardly." Not at three and a half guineas a week. "Anyway," she said, "I *am* in London."

"And it is now my turn to be guide." That was a good enough excuse to take her thoughts away from Baker House. The cab had left Bloomsbury, and turned down Tottenham Court Road. Furniture shops, he explained. Then Charing Cross Road. Secondhand books. But as Penny looked interested he added hastily that it wasn't a particularly pleasant place to walk through. And here was Shaftesbury Avenue: gallery queues.

"You make it all sound so much simpler than it looks," Penny said. "I suppose if we were to pass the Tower, you'd just point an arm and say 'Rolling heads.' And Trafalgar Square would be 'Lions.' "

"You see, it *is* quite simple. London is the one city you can remember by Pelmanism. Here is Piccadilly Circus. Now guess what?"

"Eros?"

He paid off the cab. "Let's visit him," he said. He took her arm to guide her through the swooping traffic towards the little island in the center, where Eros balanced on one leg as he reached forward to pluck an invisible rose out of the air. Below his statue, the flower girls strewed their sweet violets. Like the ancient Sibyls that they were, they guarded their mysteries impassively until David's offering clinked into one of their capacious pockets. Then the omens were good, it seemed: Penny became a pretty lady and David was God-blessed.

They came to the restaurant he had chosen. Dusk was beginning, and the lights in the streets were going on. Penny had recovered her first enthusiasm. There was a gaiety in her smile that caught the eye. Several men and women looked at her sharply.

"That's the fifth man we've passed who wishes I would drop dead," David said. "Here's the place. We'll have Hungarian music to help us digest the goulash."

Penny halted. *A little place I know of* ... "Oh, David," she said. "Really ... It looks *awfully* expensive."

"It isn't," David said cheerfully, as he caught her arm and guided her through the doorway. "Come on, don't thwart me. I'm a dangerous man when I'm thwarted. I fall down and have fits. Imagine me reeling, writhing and fainting in coils in Lower Regent Street."

She smiled at that, and offered no further resistance.

"Well," he said, when they had settled themselves at a comfortable table for two, and he had ordered, "this is slightly better than a tavern in an Edinburgh side street, isn't it?"

"I like it," she admitted. "But a man probably enjoys himself more in the kind of place where we lunched in Edinburgh. Doesn't he?"

He watched her, wondering at her good sense. And tact, too: when she had seen that he was set on this place, she had made no further objections but had come in here looking happy, charming and absolutely delighted with his choice.

"I find you very unsettling," he said. Her eyes were puzzled. And blue, so very blue above the simple gray dress. Her coat had been thrown back over her chair, and she was leaning forward slightly with her arms resting on the table. The line of her shoulder was hidden and yet revealed by the well-cut wool dress. Her hair was smoothly brushed and its warm red lights gleamed under the small piece of dark blue felt, curiously crushed into a pretense of a hat, which was tilted just enough over her right eye.

"I believe," he said slowly, "that you would be just as charming if I had taken you to a Lyons Corner House."

"That could be fun, too. If one were enjoying oneself, that is." She pretended to look at a group at another table, picked up the bunch of violets which lay beside her handbag and held them to her face.

119

"No scent, I'm afraid," he said. "They look too perfect. You can't get everything, it seems." His eyes caught hers, and held them. "Only sometimes," he added, his voice now quite serious, desperately sincere. Only sometimes, perhaps . . . by the most miraculous good fortune.

But an efficient waiter chose this moment to serve them with much darting and hovering like an inquisitive humming-bird. Penny, with a smile in her eyes as she watched David's face, began to talk of things to which even a waiter might listen. Her father had won a Mixed Doubles tournament at North Berwick, and then spent two days in bed recovering. Much to his annoyance. Moira was still showing signs of strain from three weeks of International Students' meetings, and she was receiving constant letters from someone who had gone back to Italy. This had been very useful, really, in diverting the family's interest from Penny's own correspondence. Betty was hockey captain of the second team at school this year, and so she had not so much time for her novel. She had decided, anyway, after hearing a visiting missionary's sermon in church one Sunday, to transfer its scene to Madagascar. She was now searching for a new title before she could go on writing. Penny's suggestion, "With Rod, Pole and Perch in Deepest Africa" had not been too well received. Mrs. Lorrimer had become the President of the new Rambling for Health Club (which hoped to persuade girls from shops and factories to spend Sundays on their feet, too); treasurer of the Committee to set up Clubs for Bonnier Bairns (Penny could not convince Mrs. Lorrimer that its title had an ominous ring, likely to frighten away literally-minded mothers); and a member of a Citizens' League for the Preservation and Protection of Ruins.

"The idea," Penny said determinedly, in spite of the waiter as he fussed over their coffeecups and emptied the ash tray for the third time, "seems to be that Ruins should look like Ruins without being Ruins. They are all to be cemented up efficiently so that they will stop falling down, but they still must not look like anything except a Ruin. That would ruin the Ruins."

Then, from discussing ruins, they turned to elder statesmen which, in the condition of the world in 1932, was quite a logical development for such a conversation.

"I'll pay this, and then perhaps we shall get some peace," David said as the bill was unostentatiously presented. Steep, he thought as he glanced at it, but fortunately he had come well-prepared: he had managed to save some money in the

120

last six weeks by resisting most amusements. He gave Penny a reassuring smile. "And," he said firmly to the waiter, "we shall take half an hour over our coffee, and we don't need any more ash trays emptied. We like them as they are. Is that quite clear?"

It may have been the tip, or the belligerent look which had suddenly appeared in David's eye, but at any rate the waiter removed himself to another table.

"Well!" David said as he lit a cigarette with enjoyment. He looked at her with pleasure. "I like that color of gray. And I like that hat or whatever you call it."

"What else could you call it?" She was delighted. She had insisted on buying this hat, in spite of her mother's horror. She had won the argument by saying she could always travel without a hat to London and buy one there.

"I know what's different, now," David said suddenly. "You are wearing earrings. *And* lipstick."

"Then they can't be as obvious as I feel," Penny said, "or you would have noticed them at once." She touched the small pearl studs in her ears to make certain that they were still secure. "My gesture of independence," she added with a laugh. "I put them on just as the train was crossing the Border."

"Gauguin setting out for Tahiti?" David suggested. "And did you put them on before or after lunch?"

"Before." And then she remembered. "David! Really, he was the nicest naval officer imaginable!"

"I am imagining hard," David said. Strange, he thought, how natural, how pleasant all this is: no irritation, no sense of being criticized or of criticizing, only this deep feeling of ease and contentment. "How many times in our life have we sat together like this, talked and laughed together?" he asked suddenly.

She didn't answer him, but her eyes met his.

"Or am I talking nonsense?" he asked with a good pretense of lightness in his voice. "Must be this music bringing out my gypsy blood." There he was, already backing away from the serious into the facetious, afraid of saying too much in case she would be amused or pitying or polite. He waited for her answer, no doubt sweetly phrased so as not to hurt him, and dreaded it. He even forced a smile. Everything, he suddenly realized, depended on this answer.

She said in a low voice, "It isn't nonsense, David."

Watching her eyes, he believed her. He touched her hand.

The waiter drew near once more: there were still other tips to be earned this evening.

"Let's go," David said quickly, and helped her with her coat.

The moment was lost. She was talking to him in her natural voice again, he was being equally matter-of-fact and composed as they passed the crowding tables and at last came into the street.

"We had them specially arranged for you," he said, as they stood for a moment looking at the clear stars which shone in the crisp autumn sky. "Now, what about a theater?"

"Whatever you like," she said. She was still looking at the stars.

"No, it is what you want. Something serious, or something gay?"

"Might we walk, first of all?" she asked. "It is a heavenly night, and I've been sitting in a train practically all day. And I never *have* walked about a city at night. It would be fun. Besides," she smiled up at him as they fell into step, "I've had a lovely time already. You are spoiling me, you know." It *was* awfully expensive, she thought: he can't possibly afford to spend so much money on me as all that in one night.

"Let me worry about that," he said. "Penny, you are the strangest girl."

That was what her mother often said, but David was not saying it in her mother's way. He made it sound like a compliment.

She said in embarrassment, "I ought to worry about it, David. Because you give too much." She thought of this journey to meet her as she looked down at the violets which she carried.

"No one ever told me that before," he said, which was true enough. He had never met any attractive girls who had not accepted everything quite calmly as if it were their due. And then, still thinking over her words, he began to worry: had she meant she didn't want so much from him, didn't want to accept anything more than she was willing to return?

Penny was doing her own share of wondering. On how many girls had he spent so much thought and time and money as he had spent on her today? And why should she use the past tense? How many girls, now, of which she was one? Men were so easy about that sort of thing. All they had to say to a girl if they liked her was, "Are you free on Friday? Good. Let's say seven o'clock." But no woman, however much she liked a man, could say, "Are you free on Friday?

Good. Let's say seven o'clock." Penny was suddenly miserable. She was too proud, she admitted, to take any pleasure in being one of several girls. But most of all, she was probably being a serious fool: men wrote letters to women, asked them out; and it generally meant little more than a diversion, an amusing way to escape from boredom. She wondered, then, why she had not thought of this before, why she should ever have been so confident that David was different. Because she had wanted to believe that? She still wanted to believe it.

They walked on in silence, each aware of it, each worrying that it confirmed their fears. There were few people in this district at this hour. Inside the clubs, impersonal in their remote dignity, men digested their leisurely dinner with no women to hurry them away from their port. The broad immaculate street, the solid buildings, the richly lighted rooms behind the screened windows, all culminated in the feeling of expensive restraint. David quickened his pace, unconsciously.

"I'm sorry," he said, as her ankle twisted and he steadied her by the arm. "I've been walking too quickly."

"No."

He looked at her, wondering what he had done to frighten her away from him again. He halted beside one of the large monuments which decorated Waterloo Place. In front of them were the broad steps which led down to the Mall with its green park and its spaced trees, now a mass of black and blacker shadows. Beyond the grass and trees were the shapes of dark buildings cutting into the night sky, turning the modern city into a stage setting for a medieval play; mounting walls, turrets, spires; and then the moonlike face of Big Ben rising high above its tall tower's solid shadow. To the south, across the river, rose the glow from the clustering lights of unseen streets and crowding houses, a living background to these dark shapes of stone which guarded them so coldly.

"Penny," he said, "Penny, look at me. What's wrong?"

"Nothing," she said, and smiled to prove it.

"Penny," he said, and grasped her arm. "Look, I know this may sound madness, but it isn't madness to me. I'd rather blurt everything out right now, even if I do frighten you off, and for good. At least, I'll know where I stand. You must know that there's only one reason why I came to meet you this afternoon; the same reason why I am going to go on seeing you whenever I can. Any objections to that idea?"

He watched the pretended smile fade, her eyes avoiding

his no longer. For a moment, she stood like that, unmoving, expressionless. And then, a gentle curve came back to her lips. He bent down suddenly and kissed them. As he drew back, as startled as she was, he saw from her eyes that there was no further reason needed, no reason even now wanted. He kissed her again, more slowly, deliberately, and yet with no sense of calculation. It seemed to him that he had never made a more natural gesture in all his life. Then, he heard the footsteps near them, and a woman's high thin voice saying "Really!" He looked around angrily to see an expensively dressed back walking quickly away from them, with her companion hurrying on his short legs to catch up with her retreat.

Damn her, he thought savagely, and looked anxiously at Penny. But Penny was smiling.

"David," she said, and reached up to kiss him lightly on his cheek. He caught her hand as they laughed, and they ran down the flight of broad, shallow steps into the Mall.

Under the plane trees, walking arm-in-arm with their hands clasped as if to double their hold on each other, he said, "I am sorry, Penny. . . . I should have waited until we had crossed over here where it is less public. Or at least," as he looked around and saw the other couples strolling arm-in-arm or sitting together on the seats which edge St. James's Park, "or at least, not quite so well-lighted." Damn that woman, he thought again, and her shocked voice pulling everything down to the level of her own mind.

"I was sorry for her," Penny said. "I saw her face, you know. It looked as if it could do with some kissing."

He laughed, and his anger was gone. He had been afraid, not of what the woman had thought, but of the effect of her open scorn on Penny. It could have pushed her right back into that tight wall of convention which had encircled her for so many years. And yet he could be thankful, too, to that tight wall. He had learned that when he kissed her. Her whole body had stiffened and her lips had been afraid for a fraction of the first moment. He would never need to wonder, when she kissed him, who had taught her so well.

Penny did not appear to notice the couples sitting so closely together, so motionless, as if they were in a drugged dream, but her pace quickened slightly and she started as a policeman's light flickered on and then off. For a brief minute, the light focused on a bewildered young man and woman, looking up in annoyance and sudden worry. But the policeman must have approved of them, for he left them sitting there. Another couple was not so lucky. David noticed the woman's face with the pretty moronic look of the night wanderer. He increased their pace still more. "Too many people around," he said lightly, and hid his disappointment in a complicated description of his new digs at Oxford. This took them through Admiralty Arch into Charing Cross.

"I do believe you are more conventional than I am!" Penny said as she looked back over her shoulder at the comparative peace of the Mall.

"All I am looking for is a quiet spot where we can talk without having to shut our ears to at least five conversations going on around us." He looked wryly at the busy traffic. "And this bedlam isn't much help either. Let's cut down Whitehall to the river. We may find some peace there. Or are you tired? We are too late now for a theater. But what about the flicks? Or some place with music?"

"Not tonight, David. I have to be careful about the time, you see. We are all locked up for the night in Baker House at 11:30. That is, if we get permission. Or else, we must be in by nine o'clock. They insist on our beauty sleep, it seems." She pretended to be amused at the idea, but it still rankled. "Besides," she went on, "we couldn't hear ourselves think in a night club, either."

True enough, David thought. Hell, why should it be made so difficult for two people to be alone with each other? Waiters, women with raised eyebrows, policemen with torches, couples jammed two or even three to a bench along the Mall, no talking in theaters or cinemas, crowded tables and nonstop bands in night clubs and restaurants. What did a man with little money do if he didn't want to share his girl with a hundred or a thousand other people?

Penny waited for his answer, but when it didn't come, she said gently, "I'm sorry, David. I ruined all your plans for this evening. But I did want a walk. And I still do." She looked around them at the changing shapes of silent buildings, and then towards the sky, dark, cool and clean. "Don't you like it, too?"

He answered her this time by smiling, by taking her arm again even if they were in an austerely public street. His feeling of having arranged things so badly disappeared; he relaxed and felt perfectly content.

And Penny, conscious of his arm through hers, conscious of the smile on his face, was happy too. Her feet almost danced over the pavement. Her heart was singing. And in her joy she gave her pity generously to all the women she passed, who could not have David walking beside them.

The Embankment and gardens, south of Westminster, were almost deserted at this hour. The river, swollen by the high September tides, was running smoothly and gently, mocking the sandbags propped up against the Embankment walls at their weaker points. The bright lights of the bridge were strung above the dark water, a glittering necklace of lamps displayed against velvet as black as that of any jeweler's calculated window. Occasional tugs and barges moved in slow, steady progress; if it were not for the reflections of the lights on the water, broken and lengthened as they glanced over the uneven surface of its deep currents, you might not have guessed the strength of the river which held the boats in constant struggle. The stars were clear and high. Their imitators, evenly spaced along the city streets, had distracted your eyes from the real beauty of the night sky. But here, above the dark water, the sky was dominant again. The individual noises of a great city merged with each other into the steady hum of some giant dynamo, into a background of droning power against which you could hear the gentle insistent rhythm of the lapping water below your feet. Here, on the Embankment, with its feeling of distance from noise and light, was a sense of escape from the machine of living.

They reached Gower Street ten minutes before Baker House barred its door for the night. So they walked slowly around the quiet Bloomsbury square which lay behind Gower Street, unwilling to leave each other a minute before they must.

"When am I going to see you again?" David asked. "The difficulty is," he explained, "I am as tied down by rules and regulations as you are. I can come up for an evening, provided I catch the Flying Fornic—the train that gets me back to Oxford in time before the gates are locked. The colleges are all locked up by twelve, you see. After then, you climb over the wall in a dark patch where you won't be spotted easily."

Penny looked at him worriedly. "What about tonight?"

"Term hasn't begun yet, and I'm in digs with no more walls to climb, and my landlady seems to be a decent sort. Only, when term does start, she will have to stick to the rules or lose her license."

126

"You mean she has got to see that you are safely inside her house?"

"Or she would not be allowed a license to rent her rooms to undergraduates. There is nothing like the economic screw to tighten up the good old moral standards."

"What happens if *you* break the rules?" It seemed all so fantastic, somehow. The undergraduates looked like men, they talked like men; was something wrong with them that they couldn't be treated like men?

"You are up on the carpet before the Dean of your college. You can be gated—which is a sort of confined to barracks—for a week or so, or you can be fined. If you collect one interview too many with the Dean, you can be sent down. Permanently, if the Dean's patience has worn out."

"Lord, David! Will you be able to catch the next train?"

"I'll make it. Don't worry, Penny." He smiled at her anxiety, but he was ridiculously pleased by it. "I only told you all this so that you could understand the difficulties in the way. Sunday is the only day I have free from lectures or tutorials. Is it a good day for you?"

Penny nodded. Even her ideas about the days of the week were going to be changed in London: Sundays had always been a day of church, family dinner, duty visits. Sunday looked now as it it were going to be the day in the week when she was happiest. Perhaps that was the way Sunday should be thought of.

David said, "You'll keep them free? All of them?"

"Yes."

"And I want you to come up to Oxford, too. We can walk, there. Not just on pavements, or dodging traffic and crowds. And I'll talk Mrs. Pillington into giving us lunch in my room. How's that?"

"It sounds marvelous."

"It will be," he said. He looked at his watch. "Almost time, now, I'm afraid." They walked quickly back to Gower Street.

At the corner, he halted. "Take care of yourself," he said suddenly. "And have a good time."

She smiled a little as she wondered what time would be good if it were not spent with him. But she said nothing. She seemed half afraid, somehow, as she waited.

He kissed her.

"David!" she said instinctively, glancing towards the forbidding front of Baker House. But her voice was happy, happy and relieved. This good-by was not like the other two:

127

then, they had never been sure that they would meet again.

"Better get used to it, Penny," he said, and took her arm towards the green door.

She ran up the flight of stairs, turned to wave as she waited for the door to open. He waited, too, and waited until it was closed.

He looked up at the row of unlighted attic windows. He looked at his watch. He crossed the street slowly and halted once more at the corner. The house was still dark. His time was running short, and if he missed this train, he would have to spend the night in town and the next day finding excuses which would sound all right in Oxford. But he still waited. At last, a light appeared in one of the topmost windows. He turned away, then, smiling. He began to walk quickly towards Tottenham Court Road. He glanced at his watch again, and he began to run.

chapter xv

BY FEBRUARY, the strangeness of Penny's new life in London had settled into the appearance of routine. It seemed simple enough on the surface, falling into three neat separate worlds: there was David, there was her work at the Slade, there was the group of new friends and acquaintances. But it was David's world round which the other two circled.

At Christmas, in Edinburgh, she had tried to introduce the subject of David. But the family, somehow, had always so much to tell her about Moira's great social success this winter, about all the fun that Penny was missing by living in London, that she had stopped trying. It was discouraging to start talking about an interesting evening at Sadler's Wells with her friend Lillian Marston, and have Moira cut in with long descriptions of three plays she had seen in Edinburgh that winter. Or, when she mentioned lunch with David at the Café Royal, her mother would start talking about the Charity Ball which Penny would have so enjoyed if she could have been there: Moira had met the most charming young men. So after a while she did not mention London or her life there, and the family did not even seem to notice. They all agreed that it had been a very enjoyable Christmas, and how Penelope must be missing Edinburgh really although she had tried to be very brave about it, and once or twice—it had to be admitted—had given herself little airs about London. Giving oneself airs, Mrs. Lorrimer had said, was a thing *she* would not tolerate, not for one moment. Secretly, she was inclined to worry about the number of letters which Penelope had received that Christmas and about the much too casual way in which David Bosworth had been mentioned. Still, better to cut off all conversation about David Bosworth and show that he was of no importance at all. Mrs. Lorrimer was of the school of thought which firmly believed that if you didn't talk about the nasty pain it would just go away.

And so Penny returned to London, after New Year, convinced that as long as she appeared to be the same girl in voice, face, health and mannerisms she would always be considered the same. But there had been changes within change, too. Strangely enough, the things she had been most assured about in September—her work at the Slade, for instance—were those that had caused her the greatest worry this winter. And what she had worried about in September had become completely decided by January: once the major change of Penny-without-David into Penny-with-David had been made, it had become a steady progression of excitement and joy, a climbing graph of happiness which was curving right up into infinity.

But her work at the Slade had been otherwise: here, there had been changes within change with a vengeance. The classrooms, the wandering corridors of University College to which the Slade was attached, the library and cafeteria, were no longer bewildering places where the newcomer felt very much alone and very lost. The art students no longer seemed the forbidding group of genius into which the first-year man could never penetrate. Now she knew that at least three quarters of them were either young men and women whose talents, if they learned and worked hard enough, would secure them a job in teaching, or in design, or in illustrating; or they were rather decorative young things who, judging by the minimum of work which they did and the number of parties which they attended, were only marking time esthetically until they married. The rest of the students were those determined few whose whole lives, for better or for worse, were going to be linked permanently to pure art.

Most of the students were young. All of them disparaged

129

their own work publicly, privately hoped for recognition, talked acidly of those who had become famous, and hid their seriousness under a cloak of superficial lightheartedness. The majority of them calculated the cost of their lunches at the cafeteria down to the saving of fourpence on the dessert (five fourpences would buy a seat in the gods for a new play, three fourpences would take you into one of the less fashionable cinemas) and had a matter-of-fact knowledge of the last inch to which their narrow budgets might be extended. In fact, there was nothing very much to distinguish them from the other students at University College except either the women's conscious hair-styles (a good deal of brushing and sleeking down of hair to turn them into medieval page boys) or the wandering around the quadrangle in oil-stained smocks. And that was counted slightly too much on the local color side, like the younger medical students who always appeared from the hospital across the road in short white jackets with stethoscopes bulging their pockets.

Even her teachers, who had at first seemed so formidable, so distant on their Olympian heights, lost their unapproachable air. They were good artists who could either be good or bad teachers. When they seemed withdrawn and silent, that did not mean they were communicating with their souls in abstract patterns. It was much more likely that they were partly depressed about their own work, interrupted by teaching; partly thoughtful about the flashes of intelligence or the abyss of banality which their pupils could display; and partly worried about the mortgage on their home, the baby's persistent bronchitis, the last bank statement.

In fact, Penny learned, only a very few of the teachers or students could afford the luxury of striking romantic attitudes. Work was quite as urgent as in her father's law office; only, here, because people had chosen a career whose success would rarely be measured in money but rather in doing as well as possible in what they liked to do, there was less feeling of being bound to a machine and more sense of freedom in behavior and ideas. Money was counted as something useful, but it was always the means to the end, the means of being free enough economically to devote oneself entirely to painting or sculpture, and never an end in itself.

Penny began to learn these things in October, and she began to learn about her own work too, but hardly in the way she had imagined. After the first weeks of loneliness, shyness and disturbing fears over her probable inadequacy, she settled down to prove to herself that she was not an object for pity. It turned out to be an extremely painful process.

For after some weeks of proving that her work was not so bad after all, she found that nothing she was painting pleased her. Yet it was still the same kind of work, developed of course, which she had done last year. It had not changed. But it did not please her any more. It was then that she realized that *she* had changed, that her work had not, and that was the whole trouble. Somewhere, somehow, she had adopted ideas and little tricks in painting which had seemed to make her work promising. Now, she was finding that these ideas, these tricks, had carried her as far as they ever would. There was no possibility of growth in them.

That was a very upsetting admission to make.

Still more upsetting was the decision to start almost at the beginning again, to change her conception of painting, to give up much of what had once given her most pride. At first, it was disheartening. She had abandoned ideas which, even if they had turned out to be limited, were certainly as good as any of those held by the average students. And it seemed as if she had found nothing to replace them.

Then, gradually, something began to develop.

Symington, the teacher whom she respected most (his own work was excellent and, strangely enough, was not only admired by his fellow artists and pupils but also by the public) was an interested observer of all this. Because he was a good teacher as well as a good painter, he did not upset her with advice, but waited until she was ready to come and ask for it. "So you have cleared all the furniture out of the room?" he said with a smile, and that was the only reference he made about the battle that had taken her twelve full weeks. But he gave her a good deal of help—more than he usually gave to women students.

By February, she was happy in her work again although she knew she was only at the very beginning. And she knew that she had still to find out whether it would be as good as she wanted it to be; and that gave her just enough uncertainty to keep her from the fault of overconfidence, so that her mind was open and willing to learn.

She would have been both pleased and amazed if she had known that Symington had already picked her out as good material with more than average possibilities. And she would have been more than amazed to hear his comment on her to one of his colleagues. "The pity of it is, she will marry. Then no more painting. As a teacher, I find it deplorable," Symington had finished, "but as a man, I find it highly satisfactory." But then, some ten years ago, he had married one of his prettiest pupils, whose painting had since been confined to funny drawings for four picture-loving children. His colleague, who was listening to this peculiarly masculine remark, had always been able to disprove most of Symington's little philosophies. But that day his arguing power had been weakened, for his mistress (who had never given up her career) had just left him on the charge that he was "smothering her individuality."

Penny might have been amazed and indignant, but it was perfectly true that, although she still took her work with complete seriousness, she had begun to think less and less of winning a scholarship to study in Rome. Or to live anywhere abroad which would separate her from David.

And it was not only her future ambitions which David had altered. There was this strange reaction in making new friends. After the first week, when the students had eyed each other, hesitated, circled vaguely around, given offhand smiles, tried out a few casual remarks, and then suddenly had begun to form the little groups which ate together, went to concerts and theaters together, walked and talked together, Penny had had her share of masculine interest. There would be someone who would drift over towards her place in the classroom and look at her work and begin talking. Or there would be an oblique approach to the lunch table where she sat. Or accidental meetings at the College gates which happened too regularly. She was flattered, for vanity, catlike, cannot resist purring when it is stroked. But that didn't let her fall into the delusion that she should accept any invitations "just to be kind," as so many of the other girls looked at it. What kindness was there in letting a man waste an evening of his life on you? For that was the trouble: she liked several of the men, and some were attractive, but none of them raised more than a friendly smile in her and none of them gave her what David gave her. That was the trouble: she would always make that comparison, now.

Among the women, there were those who sought out her company, and she accepted some of them more readily. They were safer. And yet, even with them, it seemed as if she couldn't give them the same full interest which she would have given them a year ago. It was as if David used up so much of her thoughts and her emotions that there was little left to share out among others.

In Edinburgh, she had made friends easily. But now, she

was neglecting them too. She forgot to write, and then would remember that with sudden attacks of remorse which were intense but brief. Apart from her letters to her family giving them the news of life in London (with mentions of David slipped in here and there to prepare them for the idea that she and David were in love), Edinburgh now seemed a piece of her life which had been amputated and thrown away.

Perhaps it is completely natural that women in love forget everything else. It is not selfishness, for their thoughts are not on themselves but on those they love. It is an absorption, all the more complete as love increases, that shuts them away from any other emotional interests. Perhaps every woman has the devotion of the nun in her, whether it finds expression in beliefs or friendship or her children or her lover. This world of their creating is enough: the rest is well lost.

chapter xvi

ON THIS Saturday in February, Penny was standing at the window of her small bedroom in Baker House. She was wrapped in her heavy dressing gown, because the room was cold and the small electric fire only heated an area of three square feet in front of it. She was all ready for Mrs. Fane's party except for the dress, which lay on the bed until she could press it out. Neri, the Indian student who lived on this floor, was in occupation of the communal ironing board which stood in the little alcove at the end of the passage, and it took a long time to iron a sari.

Penny was thinking that she did not want to go in the least to this party. And yet she must. Mrs. Fane had been at school with her mother. Her mother kept writing, "Haven't you visited Mattie Fane's new house yet? It is so near you. She will be so disappointed if you don't." That, considered Penny, was rather an exaggeration. There was no evidence of any desire on Mrs. Fane's part to make a special effort to entertain her old school friend's daughter. Even this invitation to sherry, today, had come by telephone this morning, and had caught Penny quite unprepared with any feasible excuse, as telephone invitations always did. Still, it would be better to go to Mrs. Fane's and then everyone—her mother, Mrs. Fane, and herself—could relax and not worry about any more duty.

Penny looked at the glistening pavements, wondered if her stockings would be ruined by ugly black splashes before she arrived at the party, wondered about Mrs. Fane (whom she had only seen once in her life, and that was six or seven years ago), wondered when Neri would have finished with the ironing board, wondered what she would wear for David's visit to London tomorrow, wondered if it would be decent weather then. It wouldn't matter, of course, if it did pour with rain. Nothing could ruin Sunday. Sunday was the most perfect day in all the week.

The door of her room opened, and a tall girl with fair hair, brushed smooth in the current Slade School fashion, entered slowly. "I did knock," Lillian Marston said, "but you were dreaming." She was slender as well as tall. Her eyes were large, gray-green, and very direct. Her wide slow smile was lazy. Her movements were slow, too, deliberately so: she moved with a grace that did not seem calculated but gave the appearance of being controlled. Her face was well-shaped, and she liked to keep it quite pale without any hint of color except in the bright lips. All this had considerable effect on the men she met. No one ever guessed that she had even noticed it.

Penny had at first regarded Marston as unapproachable: Marston was in her final year, for one thing. But Marston had started coming in to see her, and a rather curious impersonal friendship was begun. In Baker House, the Slade students kept together, as if they were in some tight trade-union. They viewed the other students who lived there—the scientists, the teachers to be, the future doctors, librarians, private secretaries—with a mixture of alarm and amusement. That they themselves were viewed with much the same attitude would have been a shock to most of them.

Marston was wearing her gray-green suit today, with a dark red chiffon scarf folding softly into its neckline. She never wore jewelry except bracelets, but these she liked to clasp in heavy rows around one wrist.

"Fun and games, I see," she said as she looked at the black dress on the bed. She settled herself comfortably in the armchair. "Or haven't you made up your mind yet whether you *are* going out? Hideous day. I've been sleeping practically all afternoon."

"I'm waiting for Neri," Penny explained.

Marston laughed. "Everyone does. I think she irons one of those saris every day. The joy of living on the top floor: we have one ironing board *and* Neri. Those bloated plutocrats downstairs have two ironing boards to each floor and no Neri or her dresses."

"They aren't dresses. They are works of art," Penny said. "Six yards around the hem. She told me that very proudly the other day. It is the only complete sentence I have managed to get out of her so far." Penny sat down on the bed, for her guest had taken the only comfortable chair, and curled up her legs to keep warm. "Imagine six yards of the thinnest embroidered muslin trailing over city streets in February rain."

"I wonder why she bothers to wear a sari in England? She catches cold so easily. And in any case, the effect is quite ruined when she adds that brown cloth coat with its piece of fur at the neck. I suggested that one day to Neri, but she looked at me in a very hurt way. Hasn't spoken to me since." Marston lit a cigarette and studied her excellent hands. "Grubby," she announced. "I'll have to soak them to get rid of that charcoal." Then she smiled as her thoughts flickered back to Neri. "Meanwhile, I have the room next door to hers and I am kept half-awake all night by that cough she has developed."

"Well, she will look charming in June if she doesn't die of pneumonia before that," Penny said. She was watching the clock anxiously. She looked down at her dress to see if it really needed pressing. It did. It was a black one, bought at the expense of a month's inadequate lunches. It looked smart in its simplicity (Penny had ripped off a lot of the extra trimming) but it did need constant pressing. "I am going to the Fanes'," she explained, "and I have got to look presentable. Mother's friends, you know."

"A party without David?" Marston asked teasingly. "Tomorrow is your day, of course. I forgot that," she added, regarding Penny with a touch of amusement. "Sunday is the one day on which you get decent food in this place, and you always miss it. Of course, they probably calculated that a lot of girls would be invited out on Sundays, so it was a good day to pick for serving roast beef. Never mind, the trustees who pay visits on Sundays must approve of the food we get."

Penny laughed, opened the door and looked discreetly into the corridor. She came back to the bed again, shaking her head ruefully, and glanced once more at the clock. "Now, if that were only you outside, I could say 'Hoy! Let me have that iron for just two minutes.' But I don't like to say that to Neri. She would probably think I was trying to throw my imperial weight about."

Marston nodded. "Makes it difficult," she agreed, "unless you are like me and just don't give a damn." She shrugged her shoulders, smiled, and glanced around the room. She noticed the envelope waiting to be posted, which lay beside Penny's handbag and gloves. She made no further reference to David, but she let herself wonder what on earth those two could have to say to each other that filled a letter every day. Each morning on the hall table there was a fat envelope from Oxford for Lorrimer. Sometimes registered, too, which aroused amusing ideas. She looked at Penny speculatively. Now was the time, she decided, to approach the question which had brought her here in the first place.

"Lorrimer, I like you," she said gravely, "but sometimes I do think you are certifiable."

Penny looked up in surprise from adjusting a stocking seam.

"Let me prove it," Marston said. "Are you coming with me to the dance, tonight?"

"Oh, I have a lot of things to do," Penny said slowly.

"Always some old excuse," Marston said. "That is why you are certifiable. Lorrimer, have a look in your mirror. Go on. Look. Now, see what I mean?"

Penny turned away from the mirror above the small bureau. "No," she said shortly.

"I am only trying to say that there's no possible harm in going out with at least some of the young men who plague you. They are mostly harmless enough. David Whatever-his-name-is couldn't object to you going to the college dances, at least. Besides, why on earth should you do everything he tells you? That isn't good for a man, not good at all. Gives him ideas about being indispensable. Sorry. Lorrimer, I know it is none of my business, but frankly I have been aching to say these things for the last few months." Marston looked at Penny with a sudden warm smile. She's such a sweet innocent, she thought; just the kind to get badly hurt. And she is much too good value to get badly hurt.

Penny said, "In the first place, I don't really want to go to this dance as much as all that. In the second place, David doesn't tell me to do anything." She liked Lillian Marston, or she would not have bothered explaining. Besides, if Marston did not approve of the way Penny was arranging her life,

Penny did not see any particular wisdom in the way Marston arranged her own life. This consisted of frantic bursts of work, punctuating weeks of fun. You could always tell when the affair with Tom had ended: she worked for ten days as if she were driven by a demon. And then the affair with Dick would begin. You could tell when it ended, too. She worked. And then the affair with Harry. And then work. But Tom and all the rest of them remained her friends once the quarrel was forgotten, and even the teachers treated Marston to less sarcasm than might be expected. For one thing, she had a certain good-humor, a certain honesty and such complete frankness in her actions that although there were times to be angry with Marston there were no moments when you despised her.

"I don't quite follow," Marston said. "I thought you were acting under orders."

Penny shook her head. "I am perfectly free to do what I want. And I do what I want."

Marston stared, and then she lit another cigarette. "Struth," she said. "I do believe the girl means it." She spoke with real seriousness. She looked worriedly at Penny, hesitated, looked at her cigarette and then back at the younger girl's face. "Frankly," she said slowly, choosing her words carefully, "I've never known a man who didn't go out with several girls even when he thought he was being serious about one. It is rather a harsh fact about life, but it is just as well to guard against it. Men have their own little way of bringing you back to earth. They are realists, you know. They will write poetry to your eyes, swear eternal devotion and then sit enthralled through one of those Hollywood musicals because they like the shape of the legs in the first row."

Penny laughed. "But I like them, too," she said.

Marston shrugged her shoulders. For a moment, she could find nothing else to say. She was too busy thinking that the extraordinary thing about people was the way they surprised you.

Penny said, "Have you ever thought, Marston, that if his one girl accepts invitations with other men, then that might be the reason why a man is so 'realistic'?"

"Look, I was the one who was giving out advice," Marston said sharply. She rose, brushed the cigarette ash off her skirt, pulled its waistband into the right position around twenty-four inches of firm flesh, and looked critically down at the way the material covered her slender thighs. "Well," she said, suddenly businesslike, "I'll try to grab a place in the queue and get a bath before dinner. I take it you aren't going dancing tonight? I thought so, somehow. Poor old Derek will be disappointed. I came here to plead for him, you know. I'll tell him you have the vapors. And that's as good a description as any."

She walked to the door, turned to give one of her slow smiles, raised one eyebrow. She did this unconsciously now, ever since Derek—the Derek of some three months ago, that was—had told her she looked very much like Garbo. But from the corridor, quite another kind of Marston reported on the ironing-board situation: India had declared and it was now Scotland's innings. And Penny smiled as she remembered Marston's usual pretense that she didn't know one end of a wicket from the other, and thought it quite remarkable how Marston never actually said either "Hello" or "Good-by," and yet one always remembered her coming and going.

chapter xvii

When Penny did eventually arrive at Mrs. Fanes's there were already enough people to fill two rooms. The voices and laughter flowed into the hall and surrounded her there. She would have backed right out of the pseudo-Georgian doorway if the stiff-necked servant had not already taken her in supercilious charge, and she found herself in the middle of the party, engulfed in a sea of strange faces and voices. She looked around desperately for a possible Fane.

The small groups of men and women gave her a brief glance as she passed them slowly, and then seemed not to notice her. Where's my blasted hostess? she wondered, and then saw her, and went forward with a good deal of relief. Mrs. Fane was talking to a group of three men near the fireplace. She was thinner, incredibly so, and her hair had turned quite black, with a harsh outline where it ended and the very white forehead began. In her tight-fitting black suit, she had looked almost young from the distance. But now,

Penny was horrifiied by the two appraising eyes which swooped on her, by the white mask which cracked around the lips as they went through the motions of smiling.

She doesn't remember me at all, Penny thought in desperation, and introduced herself. But at that moment, a crescendo of chatter and trilling laughter came from the nearest group of guests. And Mrs. Fane (she was much deafer than she would ever admit) said, "How d'ye do? So glad you could come." She said it so quickly that Penny's second attempt at introducing herself was stillborn. Perhaps, Penny thought, names don't matter at cocktail parties anyway. She glanced towards the door and wondered if she could pretend she was about to leave. But probably Mrs. Fane's shrewd eyes had seen her come into the room.

Penny was right about that. There was nothing wrong with Mrs. Fane's sight, even if her hearing was becoming hard. She had taken in the girl's appearance with her first glance. Yes, pretty enough, Mrs. Fane decided. Very expert at make-up, with a complexion like that. Simple dress, too simple to show what price it might have been. No hat—how odd. Good gloves, good black suede bag and shoes, though. Probably one of Robert's young things: he liked red hair. Mrs. Fane looked swiftly towards her elder son, who was fortunately within eye-reaching distance. Really, Robert must look after his own friends. "Frightful day," she said to the girl, marking time until Robert could reach them. He appeared almost at once, thank heavens. "Robert will get you a drink," she said with a death's-head smile, and turned to continue her conversation with Mr. Bronway, the producer, and Mr. Winson, the editor of *New Views*. Saying "Yes?" to Mr. Winson at the right intervals, she let her eyes flicker unobtrusively towards the doorway every thirty seconds or so, and concealed her worry that neither the star of the new hit, *Bright Tomorrow*, nor Lady Fenton-Stevens with her delightful Baron Schaudichan, nor Essex Rockfort, the portrait painter, had yet arrived. And soon, Mrs. Fane's instinct was telling her, it would be too late for them to arrive. So she set her smile bravely, and said "Yes? Yes?" Mr. Winson, fortunately, was accustomed to the hostess look, and he talked calmly on, knowing that his reward was his strategic position next to Mrs. Fane when any guest worth bothering about did present himself.

Robert led Penny towards the other end of the room. "Frightful crush, I'm afraid," he said. He was tall, thin and dark, with slightly prominent teeth displayed when he gave

139

one of his slow smiles. The lips would draw slowly back in a lazy curve (that was what you were meant to think, she was sure) and then they would just stay that way, curved and lazy. Surely there must be a time limit.

Penny smiled, tried to look interested, and waited for the next percipient phrase to fall. Robert, she was remembering, was the elder son. Billy was the other one. In between them came Carol. When they all had met six years ago, Robert and Billy had been very offhand schoolboys, Robert a lofty prefect with his new motorcycle, Billy a rather grubby specimen of an overbullied fag. Carol had been a placid blond sausage, with shoulder-length ringlets and shapeless legs that emphasized the likeness.

Robert was saying that it was a frightful day. Everything seemed to be frightfully this or frightfully that. Frightful. A frightful word. Penny smiled again. After that, the flow of one-sentence conversation swept smoothly along for five minutes. Robert did not appear in the least disturbed that he hadn't the faintest idea who she was. And Penny had the impression that he would consider her *frightfully* gauche if she started to tell him. She was remembering enough about Robert, anyway, to keep her amused. He had been sent down from Cambridge because of a barmaid, and had now graduated to actresses in London. In addition to acquiring a very elegant way of wearing his blackish-gray flannel suit, with its broadly-spaced pin-stripe of white, he had achieved the appearance of always being slightly tired. Robert, for his part, was deciding that he hadn't seen this girl's face in any of the right magazines after all. He looked round for Billy—this was definitely his dish of fruit—as Malvina Moore, the star of *Bright Tomorrow,* made her entrance.

"I say," Robert suggested with sudden enthusiasm as he saw his brother obey his summons, "you haven't a drink. Let me find you one."

Billy, in his first year at Oxford, small and dark, with the appearance of always being slightly tired not yet completely established, came forward slowly. And then, as he saw Penny, his pace and his eye quickened.

"Yours, I think," Robert murmured and made his way towards Malvina.

Billy looked thoughtfully at Penny. I believe I know her, he was thinking. "Frightful mob," he said enthusiastically. "I say, you haven't a drink. Let me."

Penny smiled as she watched his adroit progress towards the table at the other end of the room. But he would come back, she knew. She glanced around, interested in the faces that surrounded her. It would not be too cruel, she decided, to say that most had come here either to see or to be seen. One face, round, white, innocent in its lack of expression, had almost looked at her twice. It belonged to a young man in the usual pin-striped suit and suede shoes and negligent tie. Now he gradually drew near to where she stood.

He said, looking determinedly into his glass, "Don't let Billy inflict a cocktail on you. The sherry at least comes out of a reputable bottle."

Penny was uncertain whether the remark was addressed to her or not. She glanced briefly to her right and left, but people there were quite occupied.

He went on talking to his cocktail glass. "The trouble is that English ice has too much warm water in it." He gave her a split-second stare and then fixed his eyes on a music critic's bald head which seemed to fascinate him. "You are the American, aren't you? I think we saw each other vaguely at Nigel's. Or was it at Bunny's?"

"Not even vaguely," Penny said. "And I'm afraid I am not the American, either. But I am a foreigner of sorts, I believe."

Billy, returning from his pilgrimage, overheard that remark. Speaks remarkably good English, he thought. Now, what foreigners had he met in the last few weeks? Where had he seen her?

"Martini, sidecar, or sherry?" he asked, balancing the three glasses with practised agility. "I must warn you the cocktails are Robert's own concoction. That's rather his thing, you know."

"Definitely," the white-faced young man murmured. "All the charm of absinthe." He watched Penny as she chose a glass, shook his head with marked disapproval and said in a shocked voice, "Don't tell me you prefer sherry!" And then, as she looked slightly startled, he added with a bright smile, "Now *do* go on telling me about your father's place in Chile." He was watching her with warm interest. "The smallest one," he said evenly. "The one with the golf course and the ski-run." His interest was now expectant. When he was a small boy, he had no doubt examined a fly on the end of a pin with just that very look.

"Oh . . . ," she said deprecatingly, "it is really so very small. Besides, I haven't visited it for years. I was sent to London. For my health. Lots and lots of fog, the doctors ordered. I simply must have fog."

The young man's eyes looked at her with disappointment. "And in summer?" His interest was waning. He was already looking around the room for a more likely subject.

"Labrador, usually."

Billy smiled easily at both of them. He hadn't the faintest idea of what was happening, but if he smiled and held his glass nonchalantly and looked interested in a polite vague way . . . That usually was enough.

The white-faced young man let his eyes rest on the group around Malvina. "Dear Malvina!" he said with charming venom. "She will choose such ghastly plays. Have you seen the new effort? And there's the chap who invented it." He nodded towards the author, who had, in a moment of weakness, accompanied Malvina to the party and was now regretting it as he stood and drank his cocktail in silence, while Robert Fane concentrated on Malvina and Malvina concentrated on her upturned profile. "It takes a special genius to think up so many cliches in only three acts. And I'm sure he wasn't even *trying*." He looked at the poor unsuspecting playwright thoughtfully. "He needs a little cheering up, I think," he added, with a sudden gleam of interest in his colorless eyes. He moved away as quietly as inconspicuously and crabwise as he had arrived.

"It is always difficult talking to Tony," Billy confessed under the impact of his fifth cocktail. "Brilliant chap, of course," he ended hastily.

"How amusing for him." Penny was watching that little ray of sunshine now circling around the unfortunate playwright.

"Tony writes," Billy went on, as if that explained everything.

"How ever does he find time? What has he had published?"

"Well, he has not actually been published yet. He is in the middle of something."

"A novel about people at cocktail parties?"

"Yes. London life, really. I believe he is putting a lot of us into it."

"That *will* be gay."

"Fun spotting one's friends," Billy admitted. "We are all being made into the most frightful old reprobates, you know."

"I am sure it will have an enormous success."

Billy giggled. Must tell that to Tony, he thought, with just that intonation she had used: Tony would be furious.

Better not, though: Tony might take him out of the book just to spite him.

And then, at that moment, his sister Carol appeared looking definitely peeved about something. Penny recognized her mostly by her voice: it had still the same high-pitched, cracked-crystal tone.

"Billy," it was saying coldly, "Eleanor is here. She and George arrived ages ago." Carol turned to Penny with a pretty smile. "I'm afraid my brother has been monopolizing you."

Billy craned his neck to look round the room. "Why, there's old George. Can't see Eleanor. I'll go and find her." He smiled hesitatingly to Penny. "I'll bring George over. He'd liked to meet you, I know." Then he felt a wave of super-charged annoyance emanate from his sister, and he left hurriedly.

Carol hesitated. There must be *someone* to introduce: Billy was such an idiot—he might very well bring George over. Yes, there was Mrs. Bigsley, the almost invisible wife of that awful Labor M.P. God only knew why father, even if he was a publisher, had to have his parlor pinks to a party. The fact that he made his money out of them, by dolling up Karl Marx for the seven-and-sixpenny trade, was no excuse for inflicting them on the rest of the family. At this moment, however, Mrs. Bigsley could be excused even for her taste in clothes. "Ah, Mrs. Bigsley," Carol said, lightly trapping her by the arm as she passed by. "How nice to see you."

"I must leave," Penny said quickly.

"Must you?" Carol lost all interest in Mrs. Bigsley, who went on her way towards the safe shadow of her husband.

"Good-by, Carol. It has been a most amusing party," Penny said, which was true enough in the wrong way. She could not resist adding, "It has been ages since we met, hasn't it?"

"Yes, hasn't it?" Carol said, and concealed her bewilderment admirably.

Penny relented. She was about to say, "I'm Penelope Lorrimer, you know." But at that moment George Fenton-Stevens appeared at her elbow.

"I thought it was you," he said with obvious pleasure. "And how is Inchnamurren?"

It was at this moment, too, that Mrs. Fane brought Essex Rockfort over to meet her daughter. It had taken her a very adroit half hour of maneuvers to achieve that. Essex Rockfort had reached the plane of success when he did not

143

paint a portrait unless he was interested in the subject. His price was enormous, of course; but it could be adjusted considerably, it was said, if he found a face that stimulated his imagination. Naturally, at this stage in one's carefully planned offensive, one did not talk of prices: money was a vulgar subject which one avoided. "Carol!" Mrs. Fane said with a warning sweetness in her voice.

George said quietly to Penny, "Let's try the music room. It is less crowded, there. Are you down here on holiday?" He led Penny authoritatively away from the little group. Strange, he was thinking, I didn't notice on Inchnamurren what a peach she is. He began talking with enthusiasm to make up for lost time.

Carol watched them leave the drawing room, and her mother's eyes followed her look, and then tried to recapture her attention. But it remained vague and wandering in spite of a sharply sweet *"Darling . . ."* In any case, Essex Rockfort only spoke about two sentences, and after one keen glance at Carol's face let his eyes roam back towards Malvina. Mrs. Fane smiled in resignation and let go: this was hardly the moment to introduce Carol, after all. She looked at her daughter. Really, after all the money spent on that dress, and all the trouble having her hair and skin treated, Carol might at least have tried to put some animation into her face for Essex Rockfort. Of course, her features fell naturally into repose, serene and ladylike only, they didn't have to be such a . . . such a . . . Mrs. Fane put the idea of blank walls firmly out of her mind.

"Carol!" she said sharply, still smiling. And then she looked towards the music room. "Who is she?"

"I don't know," Carol said so crossly that all Mrs. Fane's annoyance disappeared, and she became the defending mother once more.

"Don't worry, darling," she said with decision, and began to move towards the music room.

It took a little time, for a hostess must drop an appropriate sentence to each guest *en passant.* And sometimes the sentence would stretch to a paragraph if the guest was of particular importance. It was quite a feat, she considered, to be able to move about the crowded room at all and remember what fame was attached to which face. (Apart from misquoting three lines of Eliot to one of the quieter painters, and praising the Monet exhibition at the Orangerie in Paris to a self-effacing poet, she managed remarkably well.) A most successful party, she decided: scarcely a face to be seen whose

144

name was not a pleasure to pronounce. And then, her delight in the chorus of "Darlings," so easily given and received as she made her much interrupted way across the room, suddenly faded as she reached the music room and saw George and the girl with no name.

The girl was about to leave. Mrs. Fane recognized the symptoms with a practised and relieved eye. So she halted in the doorway, and made small talk with that awful Bigsley creature, much to his surprise. One couldn't be too obvious, she thought, still keeping an eye on the girl. She would have been amazed to know that Penny had just refused an invitation to dinner.

Penny and George had had a pleasant conversation. George had naturally enough talked about David, once she had brought him carefully round to her favorite subject. It was surprising in some way to find that George had obviously no idea of her visits to Oxford or of David's to London. But she remembered that George and David had not been seeing very much of each other this winter—each was too busy with his own interests and friends. And she also remembered that David had kept her very much to himself when she visited Oxford, because, as he frankly said, he saw little enough of her as it was and he was damned if he were going to share her around.

So she did not mention her visits to Oxford, and as she rose to her feet she was finding a kind refusal for George. "I'm being collected at seven—a birthday party in the wilds of Chelsea."

"You'll have to hurry," George said, glancing at his watch. "What is your address in town? I'll phone you soon and we'll have dinner together then, if my luck is any better."

Penny did not have to reply to that, for Mrs. Fane had decided that it wasn't quite the obvious time to come forward, and smile and say, "George, you must not monopolize all the pretty girls. And I did promise Malvina that you would come and meet her."

It was bait that any young man would rise to. But George's manners were good. He accompanied Penny towards the door. So did Mrs. Fane, pressing her advantage.

"I didn't realize Penelope knew you, Mrs. Fane? I didn't even know she was in London. Last time I saw her was at Inchnamurren, where Dr. MacIntyre has a house."

Penelope. Something at last fitted into place in Mrs. Fane's jigsaw of hidden worries. MacIntyre. Mary MacIntyre's daughter.

Neither Mrs. Fane's step nor her voice faltered. "How extraordinary," she agreed politely. "I'm sorry we had so little time to talk. Parties are always such crowded things."

"This has been a most amusing one. Thank you so much," Penny said.

Mrs. Fane looked sharply at her. "Do come and see us again," she said vaguely. "So nice having you. Give my love to your mother, won't you?"

Penny smiled. George was still totally innocent of the effect which his question had produced on Mrs. Fane.

Near the door, a group had gathered around Carol and another fair-haired girl. Rather a beauty, Penny decided. Poor Carol, how awful to have chosen the same style of hair and the same kind of dress, and to have to stand beside someone who outshone her so effortlessly.

"You did not meet my sister in Scotland, did you?" George asked. "Have you time, now? She is over there." Penny's eyes followed his glance, looked at the girl beside Carol for a brief second, and then smiled at George once more.

"I'm so sorry," she said, and a sudden coldness made her voice elaborately polite. "But I really am rather late."

So that was Eleanor . . . .

Penny walked thoughtfully down the smooth sandstone steps into the street. Then, as she saw its length stretch before her towards Baker House, she began to hurry.

Her excuse to George had been perfectly honest, she told herself. She *was* late.

She arrived breathlessly in the entrance hall as the large gong gave its final warning. Marston was waiting near the notice board. Around her, moving slowly towards the dining room, was the usual Saturday night crowd, some dressed to go out, some dressed to stay in. Faces, pretty and plain, laughing and glum, expectant and resigned. All shapes and colors of faces, thin and broad, short and long, pink, sallow brown, yellow. Marston signaled and Penny struggled through the mass of girls towards the notice board. She smiled to those she knew as she passed them, and some spoke. Fahdi, the Egyptian, was going to the dance tonight, for she had washed her hair and it sprang out from her head in a thick black curling mop. So was Bennett, for she was wearing the new dress and the imitation roses over which there had been an hour's discussion last night. MacEwan from New Zealand gave her friendly, "Hello, there!" Neri in her sari: beautifully ironed, *and* six yards around the hem. Evans from Cardiff wanted to borrow that new Faulkner. Mathers from the West Indies suggested a party in her room tonight (bring your own cup, and spoon if you like guava jelly). And at last Penny reached the notice board.

"That looks simply marvelous," she said, eyeing Marston's long black dress and red brocade jacket. But Marston was looking worried.

"He was here," she said, "an hour ago. He could not manage to come tomorrow, so he came tonight."

"David?"

"Yes. We introduced ourselves, and I told him you would be back around seven."

"Why didn't you telephone me?"

"Darling, it is good for him to find you aren't always sitting about, waiting for him. I told him you were at a party, frankly. And I also said that I thought you might be free this evening, but I didn't know: there was a dance at College which I had been trying to persuade you to go to. Do him a lot of good to realize there *are* such things."

Penny looked at Marston. "Where did he go?" she asked, trying to keep her voice even.

"Out. Don't worry. He will phone any moment, now, and try to persuade you not to go to the dance."

Penny shook her head miserably. "Not David," she said slowly.

"Look, Lorrimer, I was only trying to help you."

"I know," Penny said. That was the trouble: people trying to help. But Marston couldn't know just how much time or money it cost someone, who had little of either to spare, to come up to London. Nor had she rememberd that the Fanes' invitation had come that morning, so that David had not heard about it yet. Penny began to climb the stairs. The hall was empty now. From the dining room came the clatter of plates and the sudden outburst of talk as grace was completed.

"What about dinner, such as it is?" Marston called. And then as Penny did not answer her, had not even heard her, she went into the dining room. "Absolute nonsense," she said to herself.

Penny walked slowly up the stairs to her room, closed the door wearily, sat on the edge of her bed without turning on the light. She wondered where David had gone this evening. And she wouldn't see him tomorrow. He would not phone either: she knew her David. Probably, at this very moment, he was trying not to think that she went to parties all the time and never told him. He would argue with himself that if she wanted to go to dances, he was not going to dissuade her.

"Oh David!" she said aloud. And blast Marston. Her way isn't my way, or David's. Blast her.

She crossed over to the window, trying to calm herself. After all, things could be explained in letters. And things could also be misunderstood. It suddenly appeared to her that a very small, very trivial incident could cause a lot of damage.

Gower Street was quiet now. London's Sunday sleep always seemed to begin here on Saturday evening. A few people hurried to keep a dinner engagement, or strolled out for a pleasant night. Occasional taxis, some cars, but no more trucks or vans: a quiet street, an empty lifeless street, a desolate street. And then a man came out of the darkness, halted under the lamppost at the corner almost opposite Baker House, and stood there looking at its rows of windows. It was David. Penny rapped on the glass sharply, but she was too high up for anyone in the street to hear. She had forgotten to turn on the light, so that he could not even have seen her. But she only remembered these things as she reached the hall, and scrawled her name in the Out-until-11:30 register. He will be gone, she told herself, and dropped the pen, and ran towards the door. The sedate maid on hall duty rose from her chair and stared at the slamming door. Well, reely, she thought, and opened the door curiously.

She saw Miss Lorrimer running, *running* mind you, across Gower Street, and heard the tearing screech of a taxi as it braked suddenly. The cabby was kicking up no end of a fuss, too. So there hadn't been an accident, although that hadn't been Miss Lorrimer's fault. The maid shook her head disapprovingly and closed the door. A fine way to behave, giving people a turn like that. And for what? Just what in the whole wide world was worth that? She sat down in her corner once more, picked up her copy of this week's *Pam's Very Own,* and turned to the third installment of young Lord Utterley's still unrequited passion for the beautiful Muriel Midgeley.

chapter xviii

At first, David thought Penny had been hit by the taxi. But in the next moment she was on the pavement beside him, laughing as if she had not even noticed.

"Damn fool," he said roughly, and caught her arm. Then he kissed her.

The taxi driver leaned forward to add his comment. David turned to the man with an ugly look on his face, but Penny said, "Please, David," and her hand on his arm pulled him gently away. Penny, David had to remind himself, hated scenes. But it would have given him a lot of pleasure to have had one: that was the mood he had been in for this last hour or so.

"It was my fault, David," she was saying in a very subdued way for Penny. "But I didn't see him. I didn't see anything except you. And I was so afraid that you might have disappeared into London before I could run down all those stairs and out of the door."

It was difficult, David thought, to be very polite, charming and just a little diffident. That was what he had intended to be. Remembering too how he had felt in that moment when he was sure she had been hit, he halted, looked at her, and then kissed her so hard that her lower lip was cut.

"Just to make sure you are really here," he said, as he reached for his handkerchief. "Sorry, darling. But I happen to love you, you see. You shouldn't be allowed out without a bodyguard."

Penny hugged his arm. Everything was all right again ... She was with David, and there were at least three hours left to them before he had to catch that train. She would explain all about Marston and the Fanes to him. But not at the moment: at that moment, explanations would only seem like excuses. Later, once dinner had begun, she would tell him all about it. For explanations were necessary. She felt that instinctively. You could reason out that adults did not have to explain to each other, but instinct was so often more accurate than reasoning. At least, Penny thought, when she acted on instinct with David, she was always glad: and when she reasoned things out, she was often sorry she had not followed her first intuition. Reasoning might be good for facts and figures, but it wasn't enough for human beings. For instance, this sort of thing could easily happen again—a trivial thing hardly worth explaining it might seem. And it could happen again . . . and again . . . always small and trivial, always hardly worth explaining. And then, when some really dangerous crisis between David and herself did arise—and human beings always seemed to have periodic crises—it would be all the past difference, unexplained, which might make understanding so difficult. Yes, Penny decided, she would tell David later, tell him casually and amusingly. That would be the best time, once they had settled comfortably at a table in Marinelli's, and dinner had begun.

They crossed over Tottenham Court Road, busy and garish with that early-Saturday-night feeling when women put on their smartest clothes and men have extra money in their pockets, when the evening stretches ahead pleasantly and everything is still to be enjoyed. No disappointments, no disenchantments yet, David thought. A good hour of the week, welcoming everyone with a bright smile, saying "Now go ahead, enjoy yourselves." A good hour, perhaps one of the best hours in the week. Something of the feeling of expectancy in the air caught him up, too. He looked at Penny with pride: once they were inside Marinelli's and seated at a table for two, once he had ordered some food and wine, he would tell her. All the excitement which had accompanied him to London on his train journey began to return to him. God, what a disappointment it had been to arrive at Baker House and find Penny wasn't there. What a hellish hour, wandering around dark Bloomsbury squares by himself, arguing with himself, persuading, wondering, while all the time the amazing news which had put him into such high spirits on the train was turning into a frustrated chunk of gloom.

From Tottenham Court Road, a narrow side street led them to Charlotte Street, empty and quiet at this hour. Only the little foreign restaurants and shops were brightly lit, small oases of warmth and hospitality in a cold dark street.

Marinelli's was crowded, as usual, with journalists and students, painters and writers. When you entered, you felt almost blinded, suffocated, deafened. Then you got accustomed to the bright light, and the warmth was pleasant, and the babel of noise made you feel you were one of a group and not a lonely individual. You could ignore, or you could take part in, the arguments going on around the large tables. No one worried whether you did or did not.

And as well as the voices explaining and expounding and laughing, there were the orders shouted in Italian towards the kitchen window, where the face of Marinelli's oldest son would appear every now and again to shout back. There was the noise of plates and glasses as Marinelli's four daughters served—with generous smiles, Iatlian phrases and flashing glances. There were the sudden burst of conversation between Mrs. Marinelli at the cash desk by the door and Mr. Marinelli moving among the tables.

Now, as Penny and David entered the narrow glass-paneled door with its three missing letters (M RINEL it informed you), Mrs. Marinelli gave them a loud Neapolitan welcome, which would also act as a warning to her husband to find room for two more. Marinelli's youngest son, Giuseppe, balancing plates of steaming spaghetti with its cardinal caps of rich red sauce, shouted that there was a free table upstairs.

"For two?" David asked.

"*Sì, sì.*" He laughed heartily. Always a table for two.

"Near window," Mr. Marinelli put in. He pointed to his legs, shook his head, smiled apologetically for not leading them upstairs personally, pursed his mouth, raised his shoulders, gestured with his hands. Mr. Marinelli had, as he had once explained in detail, very close veins.

As they climbed the narrow wooden stairs, so tightly built against the yellow plaster wall with its hand-painted panels (views of Naples done by Mr. Marinelli's second son, helped by an artist who had needed a month of free dinners) and its bright pink paper flowers (fashioned by one of Mr. Marinelli's daughters, the one with the slow lazy smile of La Gioconda), David said: "There are three reasons why I like this place. No one stops talking to bother looking at us. We aren't expected to leave the minute we finish coffee. And I get you to myself."

He paused, and the lightness went out of his voice. "At least, as much as I can get you to myself at present." Then they sat down at the small table beside a yellow-curtained window, and he pretended to be very matter-of-fact in seeing that she was comfortably settled and that dinner was ordered. Chicken *cacciatore*, he decided: tonight called for something more elaborate than spaghetti. And Chianti, too. Guiseppe, who always made a point of serving them, no matter where they had found a table, took the order quickly and bustled away with his wide grin and cheery "*Sì, sì signore. Subito.*"

David stretched his hand across the white tablecloth and

gripped Penny's hand. "Well," he said, "aren't you going to ask me why I came to London tonight?"

Penny, who had been wishing that Giuseppe would hurry up with the soup so that she could then begin to explain about the Fanes' party and have done with the whole stupid thing, looked startled.

"Darling, I'm sorry," she said quickly, and shook her head at her own stupidity. "I've been sort of worried in a small way, and that makes one slow in the uptake."

"What sort of worries?" he asked, forgetting his own news.

"Nothing important. They can wait until you tell me why you came to London." She looked at him anxiously. "Good news?" she asked hesitatingly. Yes, it was good, she decided. She smiled suddenly, wholeheartedly, and as he watched the deep blue of her eyes he thought of the laughing waters around Inchnamurren on a sunlit day.

"Did I ever tell you how beautiful you are?" he asked.

"Much too often for the sake of my vanity. David, what is your news?"

"Or that I love you?" He was smiling, too.

"David, what is it?"

He was serious again. "Desperately? Forever?"

"Darling, what is—" She fell silent, and the color in her cheeks mounted. She said in a very low voice, "I love you too, David."

He waited.

"Forever, David."

"You don't say that often enough."

"It is about all that I do say in my letters."

"Still not often enough. I want to hear it every day, not just read it. Every day, every night. You know what I want."

Then both were silent, both were thinking of last Sunday. He watched her face, with its emotions changing, following so quickly one on the other. He tightened his grasp on her wrist.

"Don't worry, darling," he said. "It is my fault. I shouldn't have even let you see how I really feel. I tried to write you about it this week, but it is difficult to put it down adequately on paper. Sometimes you need expression in voice or eyes to help words to speak in the way you want them to speak. So I *had* to see you tonight. I began to worry I might have lost you." And tonight, in that miserable waiting room at Baker House, he had believed that he had lost her: this was the beginning of the flight, he had thought. And he had walked for an hour around the squares, watching lamplight on wet pavements and straggling naked branches, feeling the coldness of February strike into his heart. He smiled now, as he looked at her, but there was still uncertainty in his eyes. "Did you begin to dislike me last week?" he asked half-jokingly, but he was never more serious as he waited for the answer.

"David," Penny said gently, and shook her head slowly, and there was so much love in her face that he could say nothing.

"It is my fault," she said. "It is just that I don't want to be—to be rushed. Or perhaps I am a coward, and full of inhibitions. I've got to be so sure in my own mind that I have no fears or doubts or anything. And yet I am sure I love you. I'm full of contradictions, too, it seems. I love you, and I hurt you because I take love so seriously."

"Don't I?"

"Yes. I know you do. That is why I feel so inadequate. I shouldn't need time to decide, I shouldn't have any battle to fight with my mind. I do love you. And you love me. And nothing else matters. I know that. I know that I am so happy with you that every other happiness gets smalled and smaller. And yet, I'm afraid and I hesitate. I let you make love to me, love as violent as last Sunday's. And yet I'm afraid and I hesitate. Although I want you to go on loving me and making love to me. What's wrong with me, David? I am not being honest, am I?" She shook her head slowly, answering herself, disliking the answer. Then she went on, her voice now emotionless, arguing with herself as she had argued all this last week, "Lillian Marston, for instance . . . She has had several men, and she has no misgivings. Yet she has never loved one of them in the way I love you. And she has never been loved in the way you love me either. I don't mean to say that she doesn't know what love is. But there is a casual quality about her way of loving. She calls it freedom."

Penny hesitated again, and then her voice became tense as she continued. "I think that only means she is afraid of going into love so deeply that she could never fall in love again. She feels it is too dangerous, in case he changed and fell out of love with her somehow. One could feel very alone, then, if one had loved so much that there was nothing left to give anyone else."

David had been watching her face. Now he leaned forward and said quickly, "Is that what is worrying you about us, Penny? That I'll fall out of love with you? Good God,

Penny!" The idea was so new to him, so ludicrous, that he almost laughed.

"Penny, there's no answer to that until we reach a ripe old age and I'll say to you, 'See, we are still together, darling.' That's the only answer, I suppose."

She said nothing, tried to smile and didn't, as if she were afraid to let any expression come over her face. She was very near tears.

"Darling, don't!" David said. "Please! It isn't your fault; you must not think that. And all week I've been blaming myself and saying it is all my fault. Do you know, it isn't either of us who is to blame? It isn't your fault that you don't want me enough" —he felt her hand stiffen as he said that—"or my fault that I want you too much. If you weren't so damned pretty, if I didn't love you so damned much, it would be easier to wait until I got a job and money and could marry you. You know that, Penny. And whatever happens I am going to marry you. You know it, and I know it. So I'll get you one day, whether it is next month or next year or five years from now. Only, don't leave me Penny. Never. Hang on to me. Don't . . . "

He stopped speaking, and stared down at the tablecloth. The lines at the side of his mouth had deepened. He looked tired and white. George Fenton-Stevens had said tonight that David was working like forty devils. But she knew now that she couldn't blame that thin, drawn look on his face altogether on work. And if he were overworking, it was because he was driven by thoughts of her, by this desperate feeling of having to start a career and make some money. I am to blame in every way, she thought unhappily. How unfair it was, how cruel to fall in love when you were young like this. Yet everyone praised young love: poets wrote about it, artists painted it, people talked about it and romanced over it and idealized it. In theory, that was. In practice, they discouraged it and condemned it—a man must not marry until he could afford it; a man couldn't afford marriage until he had put in years of training for a career and these years of training were being made longer and longer; any other solution except marriage was wrong: even marriage itself could be wrong. Too young, they said disapprovingly. And then, five minutes later: Ah—young love, how wonderful!

Their silence lasted even after Giuseppe had brought the soup. Penny forced herself to eat. And then, she looked up

154

at David, found he was watching her. "Oh darling," she said, and choked with emotion.

"Please, Penny." David's look turned to one of alarm. "Please darling. I'm sorry. I have no right to make you miserable like this."

"I'm *not* miserable," Penny said. "At least, I am only miserable for you. It is so unfair."

"Don't be miserable for me," David said with a very good imitation of a broad smile. "Have I been complaining? I'm the luckiest man in London at this moment. I was only trying to make some excuses for myself. I didn't behave so very well last Sunday, not according to the etiquette books at all.... Penny, don't! I've heard that *minestrone* doesn't improve with being watered down."

Penny smiled in spite of herself, and used David's tactfully offered handkerchief to wipe her tears. "I do love you, David," she said, avoiding his eyes.

"I know you do. That is why I said I'm the luckiest man." He watched her, anxiously blaming himself for ever having brought up this subject again tonight. And he must teach himself to be more restrained in his letters. Love, he thought bitterly, was pure hell.

"It would be easier for you," Penny said in a stifled voice, "if you didn't concentrate so hard on me, if you went out with other women. But I should hate that. I'm completely illogical, you see."

"No one ever was logical in love. The last thing I want to do is to worry you, Penny, and yet it seems as if I do. We are in love, Penny, and we cannot stifle our feelings. If we did, we'd lose something of what we could have. We might lose much. You have only to look at many middle-aged couples and see that they have lost something in their power to love some are just resigned and queitly unhappy, others keep trying to find the answer with other men and women. It seems such a waste, somehow. You see, darling, when I talked so wildly last Sunday it wasn't just of today that I was thinking I was instinctively reaching towards tomorrow and all the other tomorrows after that. You've got to believe me, Penny." He looked at her anxiously.

She nodded. "Yes," she said.

Giuseppe materialized from the other world. He sadly cleared the unfinished plates away, shrugged his shoulders, and produced an encouraging smile with the casserole of chicken. He set the salad before them with the vinegar and oil bottles, adjusted the pepper and salt and the mixing bowl, poured the wine into their glasses, and stood back for a moment to survey the effect. Too serious, he thought as he left them. Young people shouldn't be too serious. What had young people to worry about?

"Let's not start blaming ourselves, Penny," David said. "It isn't our fault that we are faced with more problems than we bargained for. We've been led to believe all our lives, and the propaganda still goes on, that love is quite a simple formula: all two people have to do is fall in love, be faithful, wait peacefully for marriage and the rest is a matter of living happily ever after. But it doesn't work out like that. The trouble is that young men aren't quite built that way." He repressed a smile at his unconscious choice of words. That's the truest thing you've said tonight, he told himself wryly. He said, "Moralists—and I think the first of them must have been an old man with a young wife—can say, 'You shouldn't do this: you ought to do that.' But if they are talking to young men in love, they might as well tell a typhoid germ not to start a fever. I'm not unique, Penny; you mustn't think that." He smiled openly now, as he remembered the variety of complications in the sex life of all young men he knew. "I am not a case for the medical text books. There are millions of young men of my age going through the same mental contortions at this moment." And physical, too, he thought grimly. "If they have money, love is made an easier problem: they can get married right away. If they live in a less complicated cultural group, they can marry too; their families rally round and they either build themselves a one-room house on their fathers' small farm, or they can share the family house and perhaps the family work. Or they may belong to a group which doesn't worry about marrying at all: they think that getting into bed with a girl is as natural as eating breakfast in the morning. They would probably not understand one word I've said: they would think that men like me are either mad or fools. Are we?"

"No," Penny said, "you aren't mad or fools. You just have a lot more to overcome. And it doesn't seem fair."

Giuseppe appeared once more. He said nothing this time, but he removed the cover of the earthenware dish to remind them.

Penny smiled and David's annoyance over the interruption vanished. In a way, the interruption had been good, for Penny's voice was less despairing as she said, "I am not worth all this trouble, David. How much simpler it would have been for you to fall in love with someone like Lillian Marston."

"And if you were like her, in how many months would you be leaving me? No thank you: not for me."

Penny gave a real smile this time. "Darling, just be patient with me. Just let me argue all this out for myself in my own way. It isn't that I don't want to—to have you and to be yours. It isn't that. You said I didn't want you enough." She paused, remembering how that had hurt. "David," she said with desperate sincerity, "it *isn't* that. I want to be with you all the time. I want you to make love to me. So it can't be that I don't want you enough. It is just that a girl—Oh, I don't know, but she is so influenced by her family and surroundings and everything. Men are so much more free in their decisions, you know. They *are* independent. If men and women were judged by equal standards, then it would be different. We could be courageous too. But for generations and generations we've been dependent and obedient, and that has put a kind of deep fear into us. Isn't that it, David?"

"If you weren't afraid of hurting your family, you would do what you felt was right for yourself? Would you?" He tried to make his voice sound casual.

"Yes," Penny admitted very slowly. "Yes," she said honestly.

David relaxed. It was the family. A man could deal with the barriers which a family had raised. Frigidity could never be dealt with. He said, "I have even thought of giving up Oxford, of looking for a job, any job, anywhere. Now."

Penny shook her head. "Later, if things did not go well for you I'd always blame myself. As I got older and uglier, I'd think I had forced you into a very bad bargain. I'd blame myself for having ruined your life."

David began to laugh. "Men don't ruin so easily," he said. "Not if their wives keep them happy. Besides, we aren't all the geniuses which we like to think we are; we know that."

Giuseppe, looking for the fifth time towards the table at the window, was delighted to see them happy again. The young man was laughing, and the girl was smiling in the way she used to smile. They were even beginning to taste the food. That was a good sign, a very good sign. If they could eat food that was half-cold and not notice it, then they must be still in love. The young man was drinking his wine, now. Good, very good. She wasn't going to leave him after all. These English were very strange indeed: imagine choosing a restaurant to persuade your mistress to keep on living with you. Imágine, even, persuading with words! Still, the young man had succeeded. At this moment, her eyes were filled with sunshine like the water before Napoli. Giuseppe smiled too, as he hurried downstairs, summoned by a piercing scream from the cash desk.

"This," David said as he looked at his glass of wine, "reminds me that I came here to celebrate a decision. You still haven't found out why I am here in London tonight to see you."

Penny studied his face ... "It is good news, anyway," she said. "What is it, David? It is good, isn't it?"

"I think so." He was trying to be noncommittal. The attempt failed. "I have been deciding about this future job of mine."

Penny stared blankly. "I thought it was all decided. You were going to sit the Foreign Office examinations after you finished with Oxford."

"I've changed my mind," he said briefly. "I had the offer of two possible jobs, this week. Isn't it extraordinary how you can think and worry about a job, and then suddenly two arrive almost at the same time? All or nothing, it seems, in this world. I wanted to hear what you thought about them, Penny. That is why I came chasing up here today. Tomorrow I have to lunch with one of the men who is offering me a job."

"David, why did you change your mind?"

David didn't answer that. "The first job," he said, "is one with an oil company. Abroad, of course, in some peculiar place with the temperature around one hundred and ten degrees. But they do offer a princely salary. One thousand a year, flat, to start with. It goes on to incredible heights, if they like you."

"A thousand *pounds?*" Penny said incredulously. "David, that's terrific. But, darling, what do you know about oil?"

"Nothing," David said cheerfully. "The oil firm is picking out two or three young men from the Universities for certain jobs. That's all. What do you think of it?"

"A thousand pounds is an *awful* lot of money," Penny said slowly. "Are you sure they really were in earnest?"

David repressed a smile. "Quite," he said.

"And what is the other job?"

"It is with Edward Fairbairn."

"The economist? The man who is interested in political things?"

"Yes." This time, David smiled. "He has just bought the

old *Economic Outlook,* and he is going to turn it into a weekly magazine dealing with politics here and abroad. He is especially interested in employment and unemployment. He's against the dole, for instance. Says that it is only patting on a soothing ointment to a dangerous cancer: what we need is some intelligent surgery that will get to its root. That's the idea, vaguely, on which he is going to make a fairly large-sized report. He has offered me the chance to join his staff. I'd be working mostly on material for his report on seasonal unemployment, although I'd have a permanent job on his paper. That would give the steady salary. Three hundred pounds a year. Reviewing and articles on the side would probably bring in another fifty pounds, perhaps even a hundred. How does it sound?"

"And after the report was finished?"

"I should then concentrate on political articles and reporting, perhaps with a chance to travel. There is also a definite rise in salary if I am any good. If not, I get chucked out on my ear. Fair enough."

"But, David, I don't quite understand." Penny was really perplexed. "In the Foreign Office, you'd get almost three hundred pounds a year to start with. And you never get chucked out there. Not unless you get all tangled up in some scandal with a woman, or something like that. So why give up the F. O. idea and think of Fairbairn?"

"There is quite a difference in salary, actually," David said. "It costs twice or even three times as much to live as a diplomat as it does to live as a journalist. A journalist can spend just as much or as little as it suits him on clothes or entertaining. But a diplomat has a semipublic kind of life: he has 'obligations.' It is hard on him, harder than most people think: either he must have some small income of his own or he must wait for years before he can get married."

"So that's why you gave up the idea of trying for the F. O. We would have to wait for years ... " She frowned, pushed aside her plate, fingered the stem of the coarse wineglass. Then she said quickly, "Darling, I could look after you wonderfully on almost three hundred pounds a year. On two hundred pounds, if necessary. Honestly, David, I am not so extravagant. We could manage. All we want is a very small place, two rooms even. I can learn to cook. And this year I've discovered how to save money on clothes. We could live simply. We don't need much if we have each other. We could manage."

"There would be something rather hothouse about us if

we couldn't manage on almost three hundred a year," David agreed. "But not attached to something like the F. O. I'm afraid. There's a scale of living attached to jobs like that which is really crippling unless you have enough money. It wouldn't be good for you or for me, Penny, not as the individuals we want to be. Particularly when neither of us believes that money is the proof of a man's worth. It is useful to make life easier, that's all. But it doesn't mean you are superior to the chap who has less money. This price value on a man is becoming more and more a kind of snobbery, just as silly as the older ones about family trees and land ownership. It is all perfectly ludicrous. And you don't have to indulge in vulgar ostentation to be a money snob: there is a particularly insidious kind of money snob, all very quiet, restrained, with fixed ideas of 'what is done' and 'what isn't done'! That is what we would have to battle against, darling: and I just won't waste my energy on that."

"You mean that 'what is done' and 'what isn't done' costs money?"

"Yes. Even on the quietest level. You can make little witticisms about the new-rich who buy diamonds and cars and yards of paintings, and pride yourself on being 'poor' in good taste. But that somehow always turns out to mean that you wear correct clothes which certainly don't cost thirty shillings off the pegs. And you like concerts and theaters, which never means you have gallery seats. And you are a member of a club, which isn't the Y. M. C. A. reading room, either. And the funny thing is that if one hasn't the money to live on that 'simple' scale, the quiet snobs who do live on it are inclined to think your tastes are all wrong, just as they think that those who spend more money than they do are vulgar in another way. They talk with a whimsical smile, of being poor these days. Poor . . . God, they don't even understand their own English language. Give them a taste of really being poor, keeping a wife and children on thirty bob a week, living four to a room: dirt, squalor, disease around you; no holidays, no escape. Give them that, Penny, and watch them yell. I bet they wouldn't be so quiet about it either as the millions who are really poor." He paused, and then smiled and said, "Sorry, Penny. Didn't mean to get onto my soap box. I was just trying to show you that if we tried to live within our income, our taste would be considered wrong. They would need, in order to be considered right, a little help from some quiet gilt-edged bonds."

"But surely if people are doing the same kind of job, they

160

can't be all snobs about money? Surely some of them realize it is only a matter of luck that they inherited or married money? That is nothing to be proud of."

"Not all of them are snobs," David agreed. And then he said with a wide grin, "But it would be difficult for them to imagine that an evening at the theater on their standards can represent our food and laundry bills for the week. That's really my point, Penny. I don't think that it is good for anyone to have to face that disguised competition. Human beings don't wear very well when they have to pretend to live on a scale which would use up three times the money they are actually paid."

"Then careers such as that become a kind of closed shop," Penny said angrily. "A very select trade-union indeed. If you can't meet our economic standards, stay out. Which only means, doesn't it, that the country loses in the long run? Yet you would think that a country would encourage its young men with brains to marry and have children. It is setting a kind of limit, isn't it, on the brain power we *could* develop?"

"We aren't the only country that limits its choice. They all do, whether it is by money, or religion, or politics. And you must remember that any diplomat would only raise an eyebrow, perhaps not even that, and think 'Limiting the country's choice? Nonsense. The best man wins, that's all.' And he'd straighten his tie, look bored with such childish ideas, and he wouldn't even bother to listen to any argument about disguised quotas. He got into his job by competitive examination, and so his conscience is clear."

"How nice for him," Penny said. Then, more gently, "I suppose the truth is that a man can face money worries by himself. With a wife—well, there are other wives? Isn't that it, David? But what if that wouldn't worry me? What if I'd take them all on, and say 'I don't give a herring's leg whether you have a maid or two or three, or a fur coat, a Paris hat, an Alix dress'? Really, David: . . . . "

"It would be much more like having stewed sausages three nights in a row to make up for one evening of decent food and wine for a dinner party. No thank you, darling. I'm damned if I'll play that game. Now let's forget it. I've buried the F. O. idea. What do you want to be? The wife of an oil magnate or of a newspaperman?"

Penny smiled. As long as he is you, it doesn't matter what my husband is, she thought. And then she became very serious. "What did your father say, David? And your tutor? Weren't

161

they disappointed?" They will blame me, she told herself unhappily.

"Oh, just slightly amazed for a moment or so," he said lightly. "In any case, I might never have passed the F. O. entrance examinations, or I might have been a rotten diplomat." He grinned, and put all the memories of Chaundler's discussions with him this week quite out of his mind. His father had not had time to reply to his long explanatory letter; more discussions to come, there. Still, his father had liked Penny when he had met her, and as long as David didn't concentrate on money-grubbing but developed a career with some idea of public service behind it, his father would have no absolute objections. (His father was developing almost a mania for his public service idea: there was some connection between it and his complete belief in a coming breakdown in civilization. That was almost a mania, too. You could not mention Germany now without starting a worrying argument.) Yes, Penny and his father had got on well together. Margaret, however, had been quite another matter.

"My train leaves in sixty-five minutes," he said. "What is it to be, honey? Big business or social consciousness?" He was watching her with a smile, but his hand was tense on the glass of wine.

"David," Penny's voice said gently, "you can't possibly mean you want me to choose."

"Why not? You've got to live with it for the rest of your life."

"But if a man is unhappy in his job, he won't do much good work. You know what you want. You always know." She laughed then. "You know so well what you really want, David."

"Yes." His eyes held hers. "I know."

After that pause, he said, "But to return to the job—and after all it is a luxury to be able to discuss two possible jobs in a depression where even one is hard to find, so we might as well enjoy any luxuries we have—what do you think, Penny?"

"I think . . ."she began, and then stopped short. She looked at him uncertainly. If only she could make the right choice, the choice he wanted. "You don't really worry about having a lot of money, do you David? I mean, as long as we have—Oh, David, I really could run our house beautifully on three hundred pounds a year."

162

"Why do you choose Fairbairn?" he asked. He tried to keep his voice impersonal, to keep his delight out of it.

"Because—well, because it really is your kind of thing, isn't it? The work you are doing now at Oxford leads into it so naturally. Fairbairn is one of the best economists we have, isn't he?" She looked at David worriedly. Surely he hadn't already decided on the other job. Had she made a mistake? "David, I wish you would do just as you really want. I've spoiled one idea of yours already. Don't let me spoil this one, too. If you really want the oil thing, take it." She looked quite unhappy.

He rose suddenly came quickly around to her side of the table and kissed her vehemently. Her ribs felt as if they were broken.

"David!" she said with delight, and the word came out in a gasp as he suddenly freed her so that she could breathe again. He went quite clamly back to his chair, as if he had only been opening a window.

Giuseppe, coming upstairs with a bowl of fruit and coffee, beamed with approval and delight. He approached their table, and then hung back: this wasn't just the right moment. Not that they would have noticed him very much. The young man was now raising his glass of wine towards the girl. Giuseppe turned away and frowned fiercely at an interested table of two men and a woman. Don't you smirk like that, *signora,* he thought: no one would ever want to kiss you even with all the lights out. And as for the two *signori,* you didn't do so well for yourselves this Saturday night: the best you could manage was this leather-faced, leather-hearted woman to share between you. If anyone should be laughing at anyone else, it certainly should not be you. "Coffee?" he inquired, keeping his body so placed that he would block their view. The two men had the grace to realize their barbarism. They began talking hurriedly about poetry. Poetry! Giuseppe thought: how could they pretend to understand poetry when they did not even know it when they saw it? He let the coffee he was pouring slop over onto their saucers. Not frequent customers, anyway; and the tip, which the two men shared between them too, no doubt, was always poor.

David was watching Penny with a smile. He had never been happier. "To you," he said very quietly, and drained his glass.

chapter xix

M R. FANE was in his dressing room, but neither that nor his silence deterred his wife from summing up the events of the day. She creamed her face before the pink-shaded light on the elaborate dressing table, and kept up a continuous flow of comment. Mrs. Fane saw nothing peculiar in the fact that Edward had long since given up the habit of answering her. She tried to ignore a deepening wrinkle at the side of her mouth. It *had* been a successful party, she told herself again. "I'm quite exhausted. Still, it was a great success. You didn't say how you liked my new suit. And how did you like Carol's dress? Well worth the money, really. She *did* look well, this evening. Did you notice how George Fenton-Stevens quite monopolized her? What a pity Lady Fenton-Stevens couldn't come—George said she was leaving for the Riviera. Never anywhere near her husband. All she does is spend his money."

She let that fact soak in. At least, I stay beside you, she thought, as she wiped off the cleansing cream carefully. Then from an elaborately fashioned jar she scooped some heavy cream, yellow with the sheep's fat out of which it was made, scented with the essence of flowers. She smeared it over her face, her eyes following the reflection of the upward movements of her third finger as solemnly as if she were a priestess sacrificing before an altar. Then she rested (five minutes for the cream to penetrate) and her thoughts flickered back to Carol again, and to George. Dear George. It would be so suitable.

"Penelope Lorrimer," she said suddenly. "What a surprise... so unlike Mary Lorrimer. Extraordinary that George should know her. And Billy remembered seeing her too. George was describing the summer in Scotland. He and another man, David something or other, visited Dr. MacIntyre... David Bosfield, that's it. And then Billy said, 'That's who she is.' Do you know, Billy has seen her dining in the George on Sundays with this Bosfield person? George was really most surprised. He hadn't even known! Personally, I think the whole thing looks *very odd*. I wonder if Mary Lorrimer has ever heard of this man Bosfield?"

Mattie Fane picked up a delicately shaped bottle and poured its verbena fragrance onto some cotton wool. She began to smooth away the glistening cream, leaving enough around the wrinkles to help them through the night. "He does sound peculiar, if you ask me. Billy says he is one of those Labour speakers in the Union debates." She shook her head in disapproval and moved across the thick turquoise-blue carpet towards her silk-covered bed.

"Why didn't she say who she was?" she asked indignantly of the mirrored ceiling. And imagine Essex Rockfort walking away from Carol, and asking who was the girl with the dark auburn hair. Auburn? Plain brown with a henna rinse.

"Are you coming to bed, Edward?" she called sharply, and tied on her chin-strap.

He was thin and he stooped, and his eyes narrowed when he didn't wear his glasses. He didn't speak, because he was conscious of his empty gums—his teeth were now smiling charmingly in a crystal tumbler of antiseptic fluid on his dressing table—and a long thin strand of gray hair fell away from the bald crown of his head. She watched him with a sense of dissatisfaction. His age told hers. But she wasn't really old. Men just aged more quickly than women.

Edward Fane climbed heavily into his bed, with the boredom of a man who has long learned to expect no pleasure there. "Good night, Mattie," he said, and closed his eyes. Duty done for the day.

"Good night, darling." Mrs. Fane's voice sounded strangled but chin-straps *had* to be tight. She swallowed her sleeping pills and switched off her lamp. The fireplace glowed gently in the warm darkness.

The strangled voice said suddenly, "Mary Lorrimer and I were very good friends. We still are. I think I shall write her soon." Really one owed it to one's friends to watch their daughters as carefully as one's own.

"Where's Carol tonight?" Edward Fane asked unexpectedly.

"Out. With Eleanor."

There was a mild grunt for answer and then silence.

Mattie Fane listened to her husband's heavy breathing, and began to compose the letter to Mary Lorrimer. "We were quite delighted to see Penelope. How she has changed—amusing how quickly girls adopt London clothes and mannerisms! By the way, you never mentioned the young man at Oxford. Or were you keeping it as a surprise? Do write and tell me about him and his family. How excited you must be! I heard that he was very political, practically a communist,

165

but I am sure that was only gossip for I know you and Charles are such strict conservatives."

Yes, she thought drowsily, I must bring that in. Perhaps not quite so crudely. And then I can give her news about Carol, about the wonderful success she has been having since she was presented last year. Perhaps just a hint about George Fenton-Stevens. Perhaps. After all, Carol would probably be engaged and married long before Penelope Lorrimer. After all ...

At that point, the sleeping pills justified the money paid for them, and Mrs. Fane's worries were tucked up for the night.

Penny, as she climbed the darkened staircase to her room that night, remembered that she had never had time, after all, to explain to David about the Fane party. But it had become less important in face of all the news that David had brought with him. She was still slightly dazed by it: for months she had accustomed herself to have no definite idea of the future, and then suddenly tonight, everything had begun to take a definite shape. Not that everything was settled, as David had been very careful to point out. No job was settled until he had taken his Finals and had produced a good First. But everything was as settled as it could be at this stage: it was certainly more settled than it had been last week. Penny began to hum, and then stopped short and smiled as an angry voice called "Shut up, there!" from one of the rooms which was already in complete darkness. That was someone who had had a very dull Saturday night.

Penny removed her black dress carefully, noticed the creased skirt, and was reminded of her mother who hated cheap clothes because they wore so badly. Well, she thought resignedly, she would just have to reach the ironing board on Monday before Neri installed herself there. She pulled on a woolen sweater and tweed skirt, and over that went her flannel dressing gown, for it was miserably cold in these upstairs rooms at night. She placed the small electric fire as near her ankles as was safely possible, sat down at the brown wood table, adjusted a wad of paper under its short leg so that it would stop rocking as she wrote.

Marston and Bennett, returning from the dance at College, saw the light under Penny's door. "Are you visible?" Marston asked as she came in.

"I'm perfectly decent, if that's what you mean," Penny said and covered the envelope's address negligently with a piece of blotting paper.

166

"Not writing *him!*" Bennett said. "Why, we thought you had gone out with him tonight."

"I was just writing some letters," Penny said carelessly, avoiding Marston's eyes; she rose from the desk and rubbed her cold hands. "I don't know how your circulation gets on with these tuppenny electric fires, but I go to bed each night wrapped up like a cocoon."

"A cardigan wrapped around one's legs does help sleep," Bennett said. At the mention of the word, she yawned, twisting her sweetly pretty face into a strange distortion, and ruffled her fair curling hair with one of her nicely manicured hands. "I had a marvelous time tonight. A medical from the West Indies danced with me all evening. The most divine tango."

"So I guessed," Marston said. "You danced a tango no matter what the band played."

"Well, if you really are dancing a *good* tango—" Bennett shrugged her shoulders. She was thoughtful for a moment. And then she gave one of her small high-pitched laughs and sat down on the bed. "You know," she said, "I've often wondered whether a man who dances divinely with you, so that it just seems impossible to make one mistake while you are following him, might not be a good man to marry. That could be a very good test, couldn't it? What do you think, Marston?"

"I'm too tired to play guessing games," Marston said sharply, and caused Bennett's thin delicate eyebrows to rise in a half-circle. "You certainly are becoming an expert on dancing, anyway: this is the fifth night you've been out this week. And don't go to sleep on Lorrimer's bed. I only came in to ask if she had a good time tonight."

"You obviously didn't," Bennett said. And, contented with the sharp truth of that remark, she stretched herself comfortably on the bed. "How did you get on, Lorrimer?" she asked curiously.

"I had a marvelous time," Penny said.

"Well," Marston said, her voice not troubling to hide its relief, "that's a load off my chest."

"What is all this about, anyway?" Bennett asked with sudden interest.

"Look," Marston said, "it is time we all went to bed—our *own* beds. Come on, Bennett. No one can be as tired as all that."

"I tire very easily," Bennett said with more dignity than her legs showed as they were swung on to the floor. "You

167

look as fresh as a daisy, Lorrimer. All that porridge, I suppose, and heather and things." She increased the roll of her r's. She rather fancied her Scots accent. (When she had first met Penny, or rather *after* she had learned Penny came from Scotland, for at first she had not been altogether sure where Penny did come from, she had giggled and said, "Oh yes . . . . It's a braw brickt moonlickt nickt the nickt." And she had looked so pleased with herself that Penny, in spite of her amazement—for what would Bennett have said if Penny had given an imitation of *her* idea of a Lancashire comedian just because Bennett came from some place near Manchester?— had found her annoyance tinged with amusement.)

But tonight, nothing could irritate Penny. She said, "I feel like someone who can afford to refuse a thousand a year."

"Hyperbole? Lorrimer," Bennett said with a laugh. "Either that or it's the First Stage . . . tomorrow, you will be scattering rue and rosemary from a little basket, and we'll have to watch all ponds." Her arms began to make the appropriate motions.

Marston said, "See you tomorrow, Lorrimer." She looked pleased, knowing now that the evening had indeed been a success. She caught Bennett firmly by the arm. "Look, will you stop being Ophelia and start imitating Lady Macbeth along that corridor?" The door closed and the house was silent again.

It was midnight now, and Gower Street was deserted. It seemed a dead street in a dead town. Yet, only a few hundred yards away was a bright, noisy thoroughfare; in the center of the city the lights and bright signs turned the night into an electric day; people in thousand, there, were walking slowly in the tightly jammed throngs.

Penny turned away from the window, and began to pour cold water from the jug into the washbasin on its hideous stand behind the faded cotton screen. The deep silence from the house all around her seemed to increase: each small noise in her room—the clatter of her toothbrush on the marble top of the washstand, the sound of the water as her hands dipped into the basin, the rattle of the soap dish as its top slipped—was magnified into strange disproportion.

She realized suddenly what frightened her about this house. Too many women. Too many women, crowded into the drawing room and library, trying to look as if this were all a normal kind of life, as if they could go on living this way indefinitely. Too many women all shut into lonely little rooms. All pretending to be so gay, so unworried, so intelligent, or so earnest. All pretending that life was quite simple, easily solved either by hard work or by plenty of fun. Now, in the bleak lonely rooms, the worries were being reviewed, for women always did their worst worrying at night. Strange how normal they could be all evening, and then as soon as they went to bed they lay and worried. Worries about work that was delayed and examinations coming soon; worries about men and parties and complexions and clothes and figures and families and quarrels and pocket-money overdrawn; worries about what was going to happen after this June, or the next June, or whatever June ended this waiting period of their lives. That was the main trouble— this waiting, this terrifying feeling of uncertainty, all emphasized by the loneliness and the silence of night. Tomorrow morning, the pretenses would be back with the bright smile and casual greeting.

Or perhaps the main trouble, Penny thought as she undressed with expert speed to escape the coldness of her room, is that we try to be independent creatures, and we are not. We are dependent on others. And mostly, if we would only be honest enough to admit it, we are dependent on men. They give us the balance that we need. She smiled as she imagined the professional feminist's retort to such an admission. She laughed as she realized she could no longer be convinced by that retort. Perhaps, she thought, I never really wanted to believe the feminists, and that is why I backslide so easily. Last year, she had thought of her future mainly as a career of painting, with her family and friends and some rather attractive men—perhaps even one man in particular (she had always imagined him as someone with fair hair, blue eyes, very perfect features, and a terrific reputation as an athlete and sportsman)—forming an interesting background. But now she thought about David more than she thought about herself, and that was quite a lot judging herself as an average human being. Now, the whole perspective had shifted. It was his career which now worried and excited her. Her own had become identified with his. "Oh, David," she suddenly said aloud, and the darkness and silence deepended the motion in her voice.

She lay thinking about David, about the way he would look at her or speak to her, about all the things he had told her tonight. She laughed softly, and hugged herself with happiness. No wonder she had forgotten to tell him about the Fanes' party. That had been a small incident, a trivial one;

she probably would never see or hear from them again. She dismissed them with a long lazy yawn. She fell asleep thinking of much more important things.

chapter xx

Mrs. PILLINGTON'S lodgings, where David had found rooms for his final year, were in a row of gray stone houses, sharp-gabled, small-windowed, in one of those deceptive Oxford lanes which slip away from the street, twist over rounded cobblestones, promise a short cut to the unsuspecting stranger, and bring him up—just as he is congratulating himself on his astute sense of direction—against high stone walls.

Mrs. Pillington was considered a fairly decent sort by most of the undergraduates who had taken lodgings with her. She was Yorkshire by birth, and she remembered her husband, now that he was dead, with a good deal of pleasure. She had been thoroughly educated in bringing up three outsize sons (two in the navy and one a policeman in London), and a pretty daughter who had now left Oxford, with virtue intact, for a job in Reading Hospital. She provided substantial meals at very little more than what you might expect to pay, the rooms were dusted almost every day, and the College regulations were stretched as far as they would go without actually being broken for those who she had decided were "nice and agreeable." Those she disapproved of—well, that was a different story. Mr. Pomfrey for instance, even if he did have the most expensive room on the first floor, also had a taste for slightly tarnished blondes. So he was kept very strictly to the regulations and he was reported to the authorities for the least infringement. And Mr. Wichell, on the first floor back, would not have his room next term no matter what he offered to pay: the esoteric tastes he shared with his small group of friends had decided that. But Mr. Fillerton on the second floor front was another sort altogether, and so was Mr. Bosworth on the second floor back, even if they did like parties, loud gramophone records, too many beer bottles lying about, and a lot of misplaced objects all over the room. Men, she had discovered in the last twenty years, were peculiar: even more peculiar than Mr. Pillington had been. And if no man could be a hero to his landlady, he could at least be classified as normal or undesirable.

Today was the last day of February, complete with gray sky and a feeling of dampness hanging in the raw air. Mrs. Pillington had gone out into the small back garden to see what damage the heavy rain had done that morning. She was wearing her late husband's galoshes and a shapeless tweed coat which had once belonged to her youngest son. She was bending over one of the narrow flower beds, a stiff square-shaped figure, quite unconscious that "her Mr. Bosworth" was watching her from his high window. He was waiting for Fenton-Stevens to come to see him. They had meant to walk out to the Rose Revived this afternoon, but the weather had postponed that idea to a day when the view could be enjoyed. They had compromised with beer and a talk in David's rooms at five o'clock.

David had stopped his work promptly on the hours, added a lump of coal to the fire in the small black grate, and searched for that new number of *transition* which he had promised to lend Fenton-Stevens. (George always borrowed the books and magazines which he thought he ought to read, and left them lying about his room.) Then he had walked over to the window and looked over the garden's high gray wall.

In a few weeks, there would be a sprinkling of green over these black skeletons of trees, now dripping so mournfully that the sodden earth underneath was perforated with little holes like a nutmeg-grater. And the stone walls would come to life with their particles of quartz and mica reflecting the spring sunshine, turning their cold color to a golden gray. A movement from the garden below caught David's eye, and he watched Mrs. Pillington with a smile as she tried to straighten the stalks of the first few crocuses which the malicious sparrows had pecked, so that the heavy yellow and purple heads had fallen forward with broken necks onto the black earth. She took a large handkerchief out of the coat's deep pocket, wiped the muddied petals and propped the flowers against their stiff spearlike leaves. Then, she suddenly hurried down the muddy path to the house. That must have been George arriving.

David turned away from the window and opened the

door. He heard George's leisurely footsteps mounting the steep wooden stairs. They had not seen much of each other this year. George had increased his clubs and activities in an attempt to enjoy everything while it could still be enjoyed. Next year he would spend abroad, cramming hard for the Foreign Office examinations as well as acquiring a Touraine accent in French. He had given up all hope of getting a First at Oxford, and had decided that a decent Second would just carry him through. David, on the other hand, had cut down most of his activities beyond debating at the Union and paying occasional visits to the Music Rooms in Holywell: this year, he would make sure of that damned First, and next year he could relax and enjoy himself with the Fairbairn job assured. It was a difference of technique based entirely on the little black figures in a bank account. But George's broad grin, his easy way of strolling into David's sitting room, his casual greeting, the way he selected the more comfortable armchair quite naturally, all proved he certainly did not feel a stranger.

"Sorry I'm late, old boy," he said cheerfully, stretching his legs over the hearthrug and reaching for his pipe in his pocket.

"That's all right. I had some odds and ends of work to clear up. What will you have? You look pretty thirsty."

George's face was still a deep red in color. "I am. Beer, I think. I fixed up a game of squash with McIllwain when our walk had to be put off, and he chased me all around the court. Too good for me. I've been trying to cool off in the tub ever since. Still have a boiled lobster look, I'm afraid. Thanks." He took the beer glass and looked at David more critically. "You aren't playing enough squash this term." He frowned towards the desk: too many damned books and papers there. And a large photograph. His interest quickened.

"Oh, I get a game when I need it. I've been doing a lot of walking instead. I like fresh air."

"I've seen you several times in the distance keeping up with old Chaundler. He covers the ground at a surprising rate, doesn't he? I wonder if I'll be able to do ten miles in two and a half hours when I'm his age. To be perfectly frank, I'd hate to do it even now. And what do you talk about, anyway, when you are tearing along beside him? About his book? Eight years on the loom, isn't it? And probably another eight to go. Not my cup of tea, at all."

"No, not about his book," David said. "Walter doesn't talk

172

much about himself, ever." He paused, and then as George was still waiting he added on impulse, trying to keep his voice very diffident, "We've been talking a good deal about the possibilities after June is over, and what I should do."

"I thought Chaundler was quite determined to have you in the F. O., wasn't he?"

"In a way, yes. But something else is brewing at the moment."

George stared, and then recovered sufficiently to say with a smile, "Is it connected with your work, or are you going to branch out as a film magnate or a hat designer?"

David smiled, too. "It's connected with economics, all right. Edward Fairbairn is behind it."

"Oh!" George was obviously impressed. Not that he altogether approved of Fairbairn—one of those brains which never would leave well enough alone, always finding out things that called for reforms and that kind of unnecessary monkeying around. Still, it was a name that made you sit up and take notice. "That might work out very well for you," he said.

"With luck."

"Well, here's luck and plenty of it!" George raised his glass of beer. "Is Chaundler with you or against you in this?"

"He's with me—after we talked it over together." Chaundler had been told about Penny. That had been a difficult ten minutes; but as it turned out, it had been an argument that Chaundler had listened to with a good deal of unexpected sympathy. David had wondered then if Chaundler had not been faced with something of the same kind of problem when he had become a don: it was only quite recently that the colleges had relaxed the monastic tradition that made them insist on the junior dons remaining unmarried for several years. That might be the full explanation of the photograph in MacIntyre's study in Inchnamurren. It was strange how well you could know someone, and yet not know of the tragedies in his life, of the regrets which, though buried away, were still strong enough to affect his judgments.

"He must have been disappointed," George was saying. "He likes to pick out future diplomats and mold them into shape. That's rather his thing, isn't it? He has quite a small collection of his young men now in the F. O., and they all do well. A bit on the radical side, of course. That's why he takes no interest in me, I suppose."

There was a pause. David kicked the lump of coal on the fire to break it up into small warm fragments. George's eye

173

traveled to the photograph on the desk, and this time—with David's back half-turned—he could look at it long enough to recognize it. He cleared his throat and said, "I was at Fane's party in town last Saturday. Do you remember Penelope Lorrimer? She was there. She is looking simply marvelous these days. An absolute peach."

David turned round and smiled. "Yes, isn't she?"

George waited, but David's smile only broadened. George cleared his throat again, reached for the bottle of beer, and became intent in pouring it foamlessly into the tilted glass. He looked up in surprise as David began to laugh. "Well, what's wrong?" he asked with a touch of indignation.

"Nothing at all. I was only admiring your tact."

George said, "I may as well admit that it is being severely strained at the moment. Frankly, I am curious." He rose and went over to the desk and studied the photograph quite openly. "Very nice, too. But what's the idea of hiding her away from your friends?"

"Instinctive self-protection," David answered. "I've watched you, old boy. You've a wonderfully absorbing technique with pretty girls."

"Rot," George said, but he was pleased all the same. "It certainly didn't work on Saturday, anyway. Asked her to dinner. She turned me down flat."

"Did she?" David was delighted, and he couldn't even hide it.

"You are pretty far gone, aren't you?" George said. "That's the trouble about taking things too seriously, you know. I've warned you before about that." He kept a half-joking note in his voice, but he glanced sharply, worriedly at David. After all, there was a big difference for a man between falling in love and being seriously in love.

"Hello, I see you've got that new edition of Housman." He picked up the book from the desk. Nice type and paper: that would be something safe to talk about. And then he saw the written inscription. *To D with all my love. P.*

David, standing beside the fireplace with one elbow resting on the mantelpiece, was watching him at the desk with an undisguised smile. For George's tact had failed him for once: his amazement was quite plain. Only for a moment, though. When he turned away from the desk he was being interested, in his charming way, in the room.

"You've made yourself comfortable here, haven't you?" George asked, and David agreed. The room might be shabby, but it was comfortable. "My own digs are getting on my

174

nerves," George went on. "They are so damned convenient for everyone to find. Can't settle at all to get any work done. People keep dropping in, you know. The traffic is almost as bad as it is outside on the High."

"Well, you are sort of a convivial chap," David said. "And an address on the High has its advantages too," he added ironically.

"It is central," George admitted, "and the food is decent. It has its points." He conceded them so readily that David knew George's first criticisms were not to be taken too seriously. They had only been George's way of trying to compliment David on his rooms, of trying to make David feel that expensive lodgings were something not to be envied. It was only by such small self-deprecations that George ever showed he had a touch of guilt that he should have life made much easier for him than the majority of men at Oxford. And it was all completely unconscious. His whole upbringing had prepared him to take every helping of double whipped cream for granted. But every now and again, the little touch of self-deprecation showed some deeply buried, subconscious realization. (A visit abroad was always "a little holiday." Gadgets, such as his open touring car, were always picked up for "an absolute song." He was now looking for a flat in London where he could escape from the family: "just a small place, probably in some Mews." He would no doubt decide on a flat, converted from a chauffeur's house in central Mayfair, and everyone would be told exactly what it once had been.)

"When I came round here," George was now saying, "I had the idea of asking you to lunch on Sunday." He looked towards the photograph. "Can that be managed?"

"I'm afraid not," David said definitely.

"That is what I expected. Fane said that was your day for wenching."

"What does he know about it?" David asked angrily.

"Oh, he has seen you regularly at the George, I believe. He remembered that detail towards the end of his party. His mother seemed quiet amazed. I think Eleanor was, too."

"What on earth are you talking about?"

"This invitation to luncheon. It is a command performance, really. Eleanor telephoned today to say that she and Carol Fane were coming up here next weekend. She wanted to see you particularly."

"I'm sorry," David said with no disappointment at all, "but I'm afraid I am engaged all this week end."

175

They both laughed, and George said, "If you ask me, Eleanor only had her competitive instinct aroused by seeing Penelope."

"Did they meet?"

"Not actually. But they saw each other. Penelope said she was in a frightful hurry and couldn't meet Eleanor. Didn't seem to notice her at all. Very remote, I thought. But some people are like that."

"Yes," David agreed. Some people are like that. But not Penelope Lorrimer. He was delighted: his vanity was ridiculously flattered. For Penny knew about Eleanor Fenton-Stevens. He had told Penny, and Penny had never brought up the subject again. And that was a sign, he had thought, that Penny really practised the peculiar belief she had—that jealousy was stupid, unnecessary and crippling. It had often made him feel still worse when he was going through one of his bad spasms of jealousy. Sometimes, too, he had wondered how anyone could be deeply in love without being jealous. Now, as George's politely surprised voice still echoed in his mind, David knew that Penny had her own way of acknowledging jealousy. He was pleased out of all proportion to the size of this crumb of comfort.

George watched his friend's face thoughtfully. He *is* far gone, George thought with a mixture of amazement and worry.

"Well," he said, and he was not referring to Eleanor's party, "I see that is that."

"Yes," David said. "That's that."

George pretended to be studying the ring of foam which had collected in his glass, in spite of all his precautions. "Look, old man, I'd like to meet Penelope. Properly. I hardly know her. I'd like to see her sometime. After all—" he halted in embarrassment.

"After all, what?" David asked bluntly. There was a particularly keen look in his eye which was disconcerting.

"Oh, nothing . . . . Even if I did think you were taking everything a little too seriously, it wouldn't have the least effect on you, would it?"

"You are bloody well right," David said cheerfully.

"Well, at least when I do meet her again, I'll have enough sense not to ask her out to dinner."

"You are bloody well right there, too," David said vehemently.

George hid his surprise, but it remained with him after they had begun to talk about other things, about the recent

176

crop of plays at the Repertory Theater, about the newest Marx Brothers' film showing at the Super, about the latest story concerning the Proctor and his bulldogs. It was a story about Pomfrey, downstairs. George insisted on telling it and David, who had heard it two days ago, kept a tactful silence. In any case, everyone was going to hear it being told (and told not so well as one could tell it oneself) for the next week or so.

George had just reached the climax, when two visitors arrived: Burns, American, tall and smiling, with a loose tweed suit and fair hair cut so very short that to the unaccustomed British eye he seemed to be permanently astounded; Marain, thin and dark, with a gentle voice and savage phrases.

Marain switched on the light. "Or do you prefer to be romantic?" he asked.

George halted in embarrassment. He liked Burns, decent chap, played a good game of lacrosse even if it was the sort of thing that girls played at school. But Marain was another cup of tea. Too bitter a brew for George. He couldn't swallow Marain. Strange taste in friends David had. That was the trouble with David. You never knew whom you might meet in his rooms. No doubt Burns and Marain had come to talk politics: Marain talked of little else.

"Do go on," Marain was saying with that smile of his that George never could stand.

George eyed the mocking face. Marain always gave him a feeling of being challenged. He had lost interest in telling the story, but he was determined to finish it now. He cleared his throat. "Pomfrey," he began, and then wished he had not accepted the challenge. He cursed himself for the nervousness which paralyzed him for a moment. "Pomfrey," he went on evenly, "was strolling down the High last Saturday with one of his blondes from Reading." (His voice, his face, his comfortably sprawling body seemed extremely controlled and confident, so that Burns, watching this specimen of young animal, thought of him as the typical example of unjustified English superiority which irritated all foreigners to the point of pushing them into print about it.) "A silly thing to do, really, because she's well known. He was stopped, of course, by one of the bulldogs with upraised bowler. The Proctor came up and said, 'Mr. Pomfrey, would you introduce your companion to me?' Pomfrey said, 'This is my sister.' The Prog recovered his breath. 'Mr. Pomfrey, you *know* this woman is on the University black-list.' And

Pomfrey said gently, 'Yes, we know. Mother and I are *frightfully* upset about it.'"

They all laughed, except Marain. He of course had known the story already. George had become aware of that halfway through the telling. He rose suddenly, placing his unfinished glass of beer on the mantelpiece, "Good-by, David. What about dinner sometime next week? Good. We'll arrange that."

George gave an easy smile all round, and as he closed the door firmly behind him he took a deep breath of relief. David was a very decent chap, even if his politics were impossible, but why did he have such peculiar friends? Burns was all right. Except that he went about too much with Marain. He had certainly got in with the wrong crowd if he really wanted to understand England. Once Burns had admitted frankly that the most difficult thing he had to learn at Oxford was the English. What was it that David had said last summer? "We are becoming a nation of professional eccentrics. Foreigners provide us with a stage, and we enjoy our little appearances all the more because we convince everyone, including ourselves, that we don't even notice the audience." George frowned for a moment, and then he laughed to himself. That was just David being David. Odd fellow, David, and yet likable. But he wasn't normal: falling heavily in love, wanting to get married, giving up all idea of the Foreign Office. Definitely not normal.

George swung his long leg over his bicycle—his driving license had been suspended last week after a normal argument with a normal haystack at the normal speed of sixty-five miles an hour—and pedaled his way briskly to his normal rooms on the High. There would be a decent dinner at the Grid tonight, and it would probably work up to some fun in the Quad afterwards around a bonfire. There were at least two chaps disliked enough this term to have the furniture in their rooms supply firewood. And that little pipsqueak, with the green pullover and the lisp, who quoted Mallarmé at you would have to be debagged. Matter of discipline. All perfectly normal. Yes, George decided, as he found the reflection in the looking glass quite satisfactory and shook out a crisply laundered handkerchief to slip into his cuff, yes it was going to be a very pleasant evening. All normal chaps there, thank God.

chapter xxi

THEY listened to George's heavy brogue shoes clattering down the staircase. David put the copy of *transition* back in its place. George, he was thinking, usually remembered things: he must have been more rattled by Marain than he had looked.

"What's wrong with that guy, anyway?" Burns asked bluntly. "Or are we typhoid carriers?"

"Oh, he's all right," David said.

Marain was wandering around the room, now, picking up the invitation cards standing on the mantelpiece, reading them with well-concealed interest and apparent amusement. David watched him with a grin and paused in talking to Burns to remove some open letters and postcards out of Marain's eyeshot. "Against the rules, old man, when the owner is in his rooms," he remarked, and turned to Burns again. Burns was smiling, too. Marain looked quite unperturbed, picked up a magazine and sat down to read it.

"Go on about Fenton-Stevens," Burns said. "What do you mean by all right?" Burns was a direct man who approached arguments eagerly: he considered them the fair means for an exchange of information. "I've met him half a dozen times, and he always seems a fool. Very much on his dignity, and nothing to be dignified about except what his father has given him."

"Was Marain with you these half-dozen times?" David asked. Burns's eyebrows went up at this new idea.

Marain looked away from the magazine. "Why waste good breath on a first-rate fool? What do you see in such an idiot, David?"

"Perhaps you have a bad effect on him," David said quietly.

"He paralyzes me," Marain said. "He has an infinite capacity for being tedious. He will do well in the Foreign Office. One of our future policy-makers. God help us." He adjusted his body comfortably in the best chair, poured himself some more beer, and turned a page of the magazine. He raised an eyebrow at some statement which caught his eye, and dismissed the others from his presence.

"That's my point," Burns went on. "He thinks he is a natural for the governing classes. Right education, right connections, right everything. Does that make a man a natural for anything except having himself a whale of a time? The life of Riley, *if* you can get it. And those who have it damned well see that they keep it in the family. Take a guy like this Fenton-Stevens. He and his crowd just represent less than two per cent of the population: all the other ninety-eight per cent don't talk like him, or live his way. But he is convinced he is typical of Britain, and so he and his friends have got to represent her. Matter of duty, I suppose. It is also the life of Riley: better than going down a mine, or delivering milk, or wearing the seat of your pants out on a clerk's hard chair. They'll tell you, of course, that the miner or the milkman or the clerk just haven't got the stuff it takes to do the governing or save the country. How do they know that? Who told them, except themselves? If you ask me this country is weighted down with its deadwood—the 'all right' guys who use up the best jobs. And you all keep accepting it, instead of using an ax."

"The trouble about using an ax," David said, "is that it may be used against you, and that isn't according to plan. Perhaps Marain's next editorial would see him installed in a neat six-by-eight-foot cell. That is, if his political opponents grabbed the ax before he could."

Marain looked up to say, "It is quite simple. David wants no action, and is content to continue with things as they are although it is against his interests and the interests of forty million other people in this country. They don't seem to understand where their interests lie. That's all."

"That's all," David said, "except that you did not state my case accurately. I want change, too. But I believe that change will depend on just how much the majority of us want something. If we are content with the second-best because it is 'safe' then we shall just go on getting a good second-best. So the decision really rests with all the forty million people Marain pities so much. That's where I begin to disagree with him. I believe that if there is to be a change, they have to earn it for themselves. Not by violence, but by thinking things out. Get an intelligent electorate, and then an intelligent election, and soon there will be plenty of housecleaning. Provided, of course, that the people go on thinking things out for themselves. As soon as they stop doing that, deadwood will collect again, no matter what variety of political party is in power."

"He would have been a most converting missionary," Marain said to Burns, and his annoyance sharpened when the American did not return his amused smile. Burns was, in fact, still watching David. "It is getting rather late," Marain said suddenly, and rose to his feet. "I'm giving dinner to Furness in Hall, tonight. We are starting a new magazine, and I was thinking of him as assistant editor. He is a sound man in many ways."

And writes like a piece of boiled ham, David thought. No sense of the use of the English language at all. Marain would be editor, of course: Marain played second fiddle to no man.

"I thought of you," Marain went on, "but you are frightfully busy this year, aren't you?" And that meant that Marain had come here with the idea of offering the job of assistant editor to David. I am being disciplined, David thought. Really, Marain, you do like to crack the whip. To hell with you.

Burns looked surprised at Marain's recent statements, and then he said quickly in embarrassment. "We are calling it *Experiment*. Here's the blurb. Wrote it this morning." He pulled out a folded sheet of typescript, which had already been handled a good deal during its short life. David took it, and read it as he was persuading himself that he had indeed no time to be editing a magazine this spring.

"It isn't a purely Oxford affair," Burns was saying. "There will be contributors from Cambridge and London. We hope."

"Better give the Cambridge men more space on the editorial board if you want to keep them interested," David said and then regretted his words. For Marain's smile became real at his obvious annoyance. "Hello," David said suddenly in surprise. "How did he get here?" He pointed to the name of Roger Breen.

"One of the London boys. Marain found him." Burns explained. "He's financing us."

"You mean his father is. And his father won't like your magazine."

"His father can't read," Marain said.

"Look, Marain, why get involved with a man like Breen? He is only using you politically as he is using his father financially."

Marain wasn't smiling now. Burns was looking at him questioningly, as if he believed Bosworth. By attacking Breen, Bosworth was attacking his judgment. "I can deal with Breen," he said coldly.

"What's wrong with him, anyway?" Burns asked. "He is only a name to me."

"He is one of my sister's friends," David said shortly.

"And Bosworth doesn't like him, Marain explained. Sister-fixation, his amused eyebrow said.

"I know what I dislike," David said.

"He must be very grim," Marain said lightly.

"If it becomes fashionable among the so-called intelligent-sia to wear black shirts, Breen would be out there in front of them mimicking Mussolini."

"And if it were fashionable to be a liberal?"

David shook his head. "There isn't enough violence in liberalism for Breen," he said. "He has a mountainous inferiority complex. He has got to justify himself by extremes. He thinks strong methods prove strength. You know, if the revolution he is always talking about did come, he wouldn't find that position of power which he thinks he will get. He isn't good enough. Funny to see all these self-appointed Controllers being left in the rank and file."

"Very funny," Marain said, but he looked at David sharply. David was not only thinking of the Breens in this world, he knew.

David handed back the sheet of paper to Burns, who was silent but interested. He had become accustomed by this time to the peculiar English way of argument, to the hidden conflict, the battle of innuendo, the gently placed barbs. Marain perhaps was just annoyed that David was so damned independent. Marain usually dominated the men he met. Dominated? Burns looked at Marain critically. He felt the blurb in his pocket, and remembered how many of his suggestions for it had been sidetracked, so gently, so smilingly. Hell, he thought, we'll see about this.

Burns rose to his feet. "Must go, now," he said to David. They exchanged smiles. Marain looked slightly startled for one moment that he had not been the first to leave. And then he recovered himself, and with his usual brief farewell remarks left the room. At least, he would be the first to do that.

It didn't matter to Burns. His grin broadened. As he went downstairs by himself—Marain was showing his displeasure by walking determinedly on ahead of him—he was crumpling the blurb for *Experiment* in his pocket as he reminded himself to see more of Bosworth.

chapter xxii

DAVID listened to the dying footsteps, and thought about Marain. It was a strange feeling to have decided so suddenly that friendship was no longer friendship. Either Marain has changed or I have changed, he thought. Once, his clever-cruel quickness was amusing even when it was directed against me. Now, he is becoming rather a bore: you can always depend on him to make remarks in character every bit as much as Fenton-Stevens. And he is becoming rather simple-minded: he judges people by their politics. That, alone, isn't enough. It isn't a man's political beliefs which make him a good or a bad man: it is the way he uses his beliefs, the actions which his own humanity will make him do or refuse to do. Behavior, not belief, is the standard. A man may talk and talk, and be a fake. A man may think he proves a lot by admiring poetry, smiling on children, growing sentimental over charming songs, but he proves a lot more by ignoring or tolerating violence and cruelty. (This is where Father would start the fourth chapter of his lectures on the problem of Germany.) If Marain would only see the whole of a man, and not just—hell and damnation, why waste any more of my energy in coping with Marain? I've changed, David thought. I just don't give a damn what Marain thinks of me. He felt like a man who has decided to clear out a lot of useless furniture from his house and, equally amazed at his own temerity and at the improvement, wonders why he postponed the decision so long. It seems easy enough, now that it has been made.

David picked up his letter to Penny which he would post on his way to dinner in Hall. He began thinking about her and a smile came to his lips and his whole face softened. He no longer felt dogmatic and stupid and inadequate, as Marain had left him.

"You are a tonic, darling," he said to the photograph with its warm smile and laughing eyes. And that was true, a fact which would seem absurd to the cynical. He had only to start thinking about Penny, and all his worries—his father's health, his work, his possible inefficiency in his future job with Fairbairn if he got the job, Margaret, the lack of money, himself, and what he believed or couldn't believe—all these took proper proportion in his mind. He could face any worry if he had Penny. He tried to remember the inflection in her voice when he had said something quite preposterous and she would laugh and say "David!" half-believing because it was he who had said it, half-skeptical as she saw the beginning of a smile in his eyes. He bent down and kissed the photograph.

Outside, the lane was dark and quiet. The row of tall thin houses with their deep sharp-pointed roofs formed a curving wall of shadows, pressing forward into the lane to blot it out. Round the corner the busy little street was quietening, but there were still signs of life in it. Later, it would fall like the lane into its deep night sleep. (Streets are like children, David thought: the small ones go to bed first.) Patches of yellow light came from windows, wide open in spite of the weather. There was the sound of voices and of gramophone records from successful sherry parties which had forgotten dinner. On the pavement, ahead of David and behind him, were the quick footsteps of undergraduates who had delayed too long and now must hurry towards their colleges. Like David, too, they wore no hat or overcoat although there was a dank cold in the air and a chill from the wet pavement. They had slung round their necks, and over their shoulders, the crumpled black cotton gowns (hip-length for commoners, knee-length for scholars) which they must wear to enter their college dining hall. Those whose colleges were some distance away had borrowed bicycles, and were pedaling determinedly up the imperceptible hill (you never noticed it unless you were late) with bodies bent forward over the handlebars and the black gowns slipping off their shoulders. David increased his pace: he must be later than he had imagined. One always was, in Oxford.

This has all become a part of my life, he thought: I accept it as if it were absolutely normal. At first, it had seemed strange—the old houses and crowding towers, the sky filled with medieval spires—and when it had been strange, there had been a constant but well-concealed admiration and awe. Everyone felt that way, to begin with. And then, those who liked phrases would begin to speak of wedding-cake architecture and bastard Gothic. It wouldn't do any of us any harm, he suddenly thought, if we were made to spend our fifth term in some manufacturing town with a Victorian University raising its horrors in a street of smoke and grime. Beauty deserved better than casual acceptance. Perhaps it was time to end this stage of his life. He had a short stab of remorse as he realized he was excited instead of saddened by the idea. For he had been happy here.

The bell was ending its three minutes' warning as he passed through the vaulted portcullis gate into Holywell College. A handful of undergraduates were still lingering in front of the notice boards on one side of the deep entrance, and a couple were trying to borrow a gown for Hall from the Porter's Lodge opposite. He entered the cloisters which led round the green quadrangle, and then slackened his pace as he saw the white-haired, shoulder-bent figure of the Senior Tutor in front of him. Perhaps you had to be as old as the Senior Tutor to feel sadness when a stage of your life was almost over, for then each stage could be the final one.

The mournful bell slowed down as if its strength were ebbing away, and then stopped with a small dim echo, leaving a foolish silence hanging in the air. There was a sudden rush of running footsteps behind David, as the men at the notice board scattered towards the Hall. The Senior Tutor's flapping black gown disappeared into the Senior Common Room's doorway, and David began running too. The large oak door was shut before he reached it. This is what comes of thinking of old age, David reminded himself, and waited with the others until Grace had been said and the heavy door was opened once more. It would close again after the first course had been served, and those who came then would have to find dinner elsewhere.

David's seat was at the Scholars' table. McIllwain and Halsey had kept a place for him he noted, and remembered suddenly that they had arranged to sit beside each other tonight. There was that matter of discussing the programme for the next Musical Union concert, when Myra Hess had been invited to play. He had forgotten all about it, and he had almost turned away from the hall door as he had had to wait outside, and probably would have if he had had enough loose cash in his pocket for a dinner at the George or the Clarendon—he had given up signing checks: they had a way of giving you an extra sinking in the pit of your stomach when you opened your bank statement. But the clatter of plates as the scouts served the long tables at a half-run (four courses were served and eaten within thirty minutes) helped to cover his momentary confusion.

"Thought you had forgotten," Halsey said cheerily, and joined David's smile at such an impossibility.

David listened to McIllwain, talking with Scots intensity about the merits of Bach and the demerits of Delius (Halsey

185

being very pro-Delius at the moment), but his mind followed its own direction.

Overhead, the high ceiling formed a deep vault, dark and withdrawn. The shaded table lamps lit up the rows of faces, intent on mulligatawny soup and light remarks. (The two could go together, it seemed.) The enormous fireplace at one side of the hall had its outsized portion of tree trunk as fuel, and the green baize screens were drawn to protect the spines of those undergraduates whose bench was too near the fire. Those who sat at the other side of the room wore thick pullovers under their tweed jackets to keep them warm. At the end of the hall, opposite the doorway, was a raised dais where the dons' white shirts bulged stiffly out from their low-cut dinner jackets. The junior Fellow who voted Labour and did not believe in all that conspicuous nonsense was appearing unnoticeable in his checked tweed jacket, red tie and determined nonchalance. The three Distinguished Guests of the evening sat with the dons and listened to the conversation which went evenly on, in spite of the rising spate of noise from the undergraduates' tables: the voices always rose after the second course when hunger was partly abated by soup and fish.

David looked at the High Table, tried to distinguish the three guests, wondered what they thought about this zoo, listened to Halsey beside him. Once Halsey and McIllwain started arguing, it was rather like watching two men sawing sawdust. Still, they enjoyed it, and they never allowed it to interfere with the decisions they had already agreed upon. It would be Bach. It would be the *Chromatic Fantasia and Fugue*. McIllwain and Halsey were just working up to that in their own way. David had no objections: this was an evening when he enjoyed being in a crowd of men and feeling completely alone. It was the only pleasant way of feeling alone. To be really alone and feel alone, that was the hour to be avoided. Now, this separation of himself from the crowded hall was a luxury: he could step back into it, when he wanted. He watched the three D. G.'s without appearing to notice them, and wondered about them. At this moment, they were alone too. Really alone in an inexplicable mad-house? Or just feeling alone and comfortably amused as they watched it?

Certainly the D. G.'s were less successful than the dons in ignoring the peculiarities of the young men. The most distinguished of them was a professor from Germany, a Jew who had been declared intolerable, who knew more than most people could understand about nebulae. The small thin one was the Middle East expert who combined exploring with his thirty years of study of the Turkic group of languages. The third D. G. was a Permanent Under-Secretary: rather heavy-going, this one, as the Senior Tutor afterwards remarked to his colleagues. But he, at least, had been an undergraduate at Oxford and had known what to expect. He might even be telling himself that undergraduates were not what they had been. He certainly did not approve of the way they dressed. Thirty years ago, you could have told a man's income by the cut of his coat. The war had made a lot of changes, a lot of changes. He looked at the junior don's red tie, and then took comfort in the fact that the linen was still excellent on the table and that the Charles Second silver was displayed. He took further consolation in the rows of Queen Anne candlesticks and the admirable Montrachet which he sipped from the crystal goblet standing beside the Doulton plate. The Senior Common Room still had its china specially made, he noted with satisfaction as he scraped up the last mouthful of filet and mushrooms, and reached the College arms. He ignored the fact that the junior don was drinking beer like some undergraduate, and concentrated on the fact that the beer was held by a George Second tankard. Perhaps George Third. No, George Second.

The Turkic scholar was telling a very good story about a Rumanian countess at a dinner party in Vienna. He would have been amused if he had known he was the only D. G. who had raised any comment. It had come from one undergraduate sitting at the Hearties' table. (Those in training for rowing sat at this separate table where they had their special beefsteaks and no starches.) "Doesn't look as if he could have lasted eight days in the desert with only a handful of dates, does he?" The tone was derogatory, but the highest compliment was intended. No one said anything about his lasting thirty years in Turkic languages.

The foreign nebulist merely looked slightly bewildered. Afterwards, in talking to his friends, he would probably be very amused. At the moment, he was startled and shocked. All that waste of food, enough to feed a hundred men in a concentration camp for a day. And the science don beside him seemed to be determined to talk about some new experiments at Cambridge with heavy water. Do as the Romans do, the refugee scholar reminded himself, and tried to follow the almost inaudible English voice at his elbow. But he flinched when a roll, and then a pat of butter, was thrown through the air.

Now the circus has really begun, David was thinking. There had been a pause in the running service of roast beef. The first piece of roll had been thrown from one table to another, and a reply was given in kind. Next, the pats of butter were catapulted from the blades of table knives. The first one sailed over his head, aimed at the table behind him. Its near-victim retaliated, aimed too well, and was given a sconce for his success. The quart of heavy ale, to be drunk without pause for breath, was placed in front of him. He did not manage to drink it all, and he had to pass it around the table—and pay for it, too—as his forfeit. David smiled as he watched the fresher's obvious chagrin at his failure. And probably he had been practising for weeks in private. David glanced again at High Table. The nebulae chap looked as if he were indeed in a fog, and the science don was no doubt trying to explain the rules of sconcing to him, judging by his increasing bewilderment. The Permanent Under-Secretary looked pleased for the first time this evening. ("At least they haven't changed in some things," he was saying to himself.) The Middle East man was the least noticing of the three, being too interested in his story of the Italian baroness in Constantinople. (His explorations were of a diversified nature.)

The tide of Oxford reality slipped over David's table. Halsey—who had carried on a continuous stream of conversation from Delius to Ravel, from Ravel to ravishing Garbo, somehow from there (unless under the bam under the boo under the bamboo tree was as good a place to be alone as anywhere) to T. S. Eliot, and then in one easy bound to Kant and the Categorical Imperative, which brought him right into the problem of his tailor's bill (the man had actually forgotten half a dozen ties which had been bought six months ago)—suddenly halted. He stared with distrust and then dislike at the sweet set before him. It was strawberry jelly frozen to almost glacial hardness. "Anemic liver," he said, picked it up in his hand, weighed it as if it were a cricket ball, and then lobbed it down the table. It was well caught, and thrown onwards, and managed to pass three tables before its final disintegration. The German nebulist leaned forward with increasing interest. It was all becoming clear: the medieval tradition of the lords seated on the dais, with the tumblers and clowns amusing the henchmen down in the Hall. The unconscious tradition . . . it was all becoming perfectly clear. He began speaking at incredible speed in German to the science don, who had been unfortunate enought to admit that he spoke that language, and who smiled and nodded when he felt the meaning was beyond his vocabulary—just to keep the old boy happy. He certainly did: there was a nice little footnote of five and a half pages to be added to the dissertation on *The Medieval Mind and Its Attack on the Possibilities of Space,* now in preparation.

An unreal world, David thought. It had become so natural to all of them that, when they left it, they might find the world outside quite unreal in its reality. He thought of the small flat which he and Penny would have, forming their own world of two rooms and kitchen in some place like Notting Hill. He compared it with all this—the high vaulted hall, carved and shadowed; the stone fireplace which would be bigger than their kitchen; the rows of gleaming silver, the hurrying servants; the distinguished guests feeling their prominence at High Table, while the undergraduates ignored them completely and the dons wished the Permanent Under-Secretary would finish his savory and let them retire into the Senior Common Room for dessert and port and—at last—a cigarette, or a cigar, with a snifter of brandy. (The junior Fellow, who must serve round the fruit in the Senior Common Room, was looking at his wrist watch covertly, wondering if he would get away in time to take his wife to that picture which he had promised her. She would be sitting over in his study in College, now, after dining at home on scrambled eggs and a baked apple. If only she would eat a decent meal by herself on the four nights a week he had to put in an appearance at High Table, but women were strange. She said a decent dinner was made to be shared: made her feel more alone. If this old blow-hard didn't finish up that savory, they would never get to that flicker in time. Said to be good, too . . . ."The Blue Light." Damn and blast. And this was its last night.)

Perhaps, David was deciding, I am just a two-room-and-kitchen chap. Yet, that was not quite accurate, he reminded himself as the scout removed his untouched jelly: he had expensive tastes he would like to be able to afford. Perhaps it was just Penny. Even one room and Penny would be the answer to everything. He felt that his happiness was so transparent at this moment, that he looked sharply at the two men beside him.

"Any objection, David?" Halsey asked, noticing the look.

"None at all." He looked at the other men with a sudden

feeling of pity, for not being so madly happy as he was at this moment. With a feeling, too, of relief that they couldn't guess his emotions. And then he wondered how many of these unrevealing faces hid feelings that would have startled the whole room. They talked about everything except what they really felt.

"Of course," he said to McIllwain. "Let's have the *Chromatic Fantasia and Fugue,* by all means." He looked round the long monks' table once more, listening to the interweaving voices, the pattern of laugh, the flow of words adding to a theme or branching from it to give it a new statement or a twist of variation. "Rather appropriate, actually," David said.

McIllwain and Halsey showed a mild surprise, but they did not ask for an explanation. That was one of the best things about Oxford: no one ever need bother to explain.

chapter xxiii

ON SUNDAY, David traveled to London. It was the beginning of March. The whole countryside had been washed by February rains, brushed by brisk winds as if nature had determined to have a thorough spring-cleaning. He ignored the newspaper beside him: it would be filled with further attempts to interpret and cover up the bad news which had trickled out of Germany all last week. News became twice as depressing when everyone was making such a determined effort to hope for the best. That underlined the danger: one did not have to explain away good news. Hell, David thought, I refuse to be depressed today. Today's my holiday from work and worry and what should be done and what shouldn't be done and what does this mean and what doesn't it mean? Today's the day I enjoy myself. In three hours' time, I'll be seeing Penny.

He slipped the small volume of *Religio Medici* back into his pocket. He had thought the rich flow of Browne's elaborate eloquence would be an antidote to the lists of facts and figures, the coldly presented ideas, which he had been concentrating on all last week. A diet of unimaginative prose always depressed him. He had brought the book with him as a matter of habit. Probably he had never meant to read it, anyway. How strange we are, he thought: we buy newspapers, out of habit, which we don't even open, and we cart along a book with us and then ignore it; as if it took a little time for us to persuade ourselves to be completely lazy.

It was pleasant to see the green fields go wheeling past, to watch the white clouds scattering over the cold blue sky in the March wind, to see some occasional patch of wild daffodils at the edge of a sheltered wood, to catch the color of primroses under the hawthorn hedges with their sprinkling of pale green. There were small lambs, too, frisking unsteadily, to bring a smile to one's face. The telephone wires, strung above the railway banks, moved as the train moved, dipped, straightened, rose, dipped, to mark each mile nearer to London.

He went over the calculations he had made last night. Finals were in June, and the thought of them was not unpleasant: a strange realization. Last year, one had thought of Finals and felt a mixture of worry and dislike for June of 1933. Now, he wished that June came in April. For after the Finals came the job with Fairbairn. If he got a cracking First, of course. Three hundred a year minimum, say three hundred and fifty a year with pot-boiling articles. Four hundred a year with luck and some work. Four hundred, then. Thirty-three pounds, roughly, each month. He could live on almost a third of that. He could save about twenty pounds a month. He'd have to. June, July, August. Sixty pounds. Could you furnish two rooms with that? He damned well would. He did not want a rented flat, furnished. A place of our own, he thought. No more lodgings, or college rooms, or a Cory's Walk where his sister Margaret appropriated his room for her awful female friends.

A place of their own ... that had the right sound. Sixty pounds were not exactly a fortune, but at least they could make a beginning with the essentials. Four walls to enclose your own corner of happiness. Four walls with a bed inside them, a table for meals and for work, something to cook with, something to eat with, a bookcase for their books, a place to keep their clothes, a couple of chairs, a place of their own where a door shut meant a door shut. No more regulations cutting short the time that Penny and he could spend together. No more damned interference from anyone.

He laughed suddenly. Marriage, as he was picturing it,

191

sounded like freedom. Perhaps that was the way you should think of it: if it weren't freedom to be with each other, if being with each other wasn't the most important thing in your lives, then you shouldn't even think of marriage. For a moment, he imagined what witticism Marain or some of the other men he knew would think up if they heard him talk like this. He smiled. He wasn't thinking of amusing remarks, either. He was thinking that he had found a very simple truth, and that many a very clever man had never found it; for you couldn't track down truth with words, or analyze it, or explain it. It was there, you felt it, and you accepted it. It was as simple as that.

At Paddington, he jumped off the train before it came to a halt at the long platform. A porter shook his head resignedly. "That's wot we're 'ere for," he said to his mate, "to pick up the blooming pieces."

But David was already halfway down the platform, heading towards the nearest telephone booth.

"Darling," he said.

Penny laughed as she always did. She sounded surprised and yet not so surprised, happy, excited, gay. As soon as he heard her voice, he relaxed. He never could get rid of that fear that someday he would phone and then he would stand and listen to the maid at Baker House, her voice growing fainter as she called "Telephone for Miss Lorrimer. Telephone . . . "And then after a long pause, the voice at the end of the phone would say "Hello" but it wouldn't be Penny's. And instead of saying "Darling," he would listen to the explanation that Miss Lorrimer was out and had left no message. That was the fear that always struck him as he waited. He couldn't know that she had been lounging beside the telephone in Baker House for the last ten minutes, pretending to be most interested in the notice board, wondering if the train was going to be late today, hoping it would be early. (It had been exactly on time, as it always was.)

"I'll meet you in another hour and a half," David said. "I'm on my way now to see Father. Lunch at the usual place?"

"At the *Brasserie?* But that means you will have to come all the way into town again . . . . David, why don't I meet you at Hammersmith? At the main entrance to the Piccadilly line? That would save a lot of time, wouldn't it? And you won't have to rush away from your father. Really, David, I

192

shan't get lost. I'll wear a red carnation so you will know me." And my new spring suit: how will he like it?

There was a short pause as David considered this only sensible suggestion. Then he said, "I love you darling." And he meant it.

"David!"

"It is all right, darling. The girl at the Exchange wouldn't dream of listening in. Would you, Exchange?"

A man's deep voice said, "I'm being completely ladylike."

There was a moment's silence, and then Penny's laughter.

"In that case," David went on, "I repeat I love you and send a hundred kisses, planted generously. I'll add another hundred when I see you. What about Hampton Court for that? That's a good place for talking, too. I've been deciding a lot of things. I hope you'll like them. Keep thinking of September."

"September?"

"Yes, a wonderful month. Best month in the year. Good-by, darling. See you in one hour and twenty-eight minutes. At Hammersmith, Piccadilly side. Take care of yourself. Good-by, darling."

He came out of the bright red booth, and stood for a moment watching the crowd, a mass of hurrying people in Sunday clothes struggling towards the trains and a day in the country. He felt the movement and stir around him, but he saw and heard nothing. It was ridiculous, he thought, that anyone could be as happy as this at this moment. But he was.

David's father was alone in the house. He was sitting in his wheelchair at the window, but he had been reading the *Observer's* editorial so attentively that he had not seen David coming along Cory's Walk.

David's quick glance noticed the untidied room, the sandwiches wrapped in a napkin on a plate, and the thermos of tea placed beside them on the small table. He greeted his father affectionately.

"Where's Meg?" he asked.

"At Communion. Then she is lunching with Miss Rawson, and they are going to some choral society's concert. The 'Messiah,' I believe. She will be home by five o'clock."

"I see," David said quietly, but he looked worriedly at his father. "Well, how have you been?" He had to admit that his father seemed stronger today than he had appeared for several months, now. There was an alert, almost vigorous, look on his face.

"Well enough." Mr. Bosworth held up the newspaper. "There's been enough happening since last Monday to excite a man. What do you think of it all, now, David?"

David glanced at the sedate headlines to the restrained columns, tucked away into the middle of the paper as if to lessen their importance. "Disturbing," he said lamely. "Don't get too excited, Father," he added gently. "If we were Germans, we could do something about it. But as it is—" He placed a hand on his father's shoulder. He was minimizing his own feelings to calm his father.

His father looked at him, and then smiled sadly. "I know," he said, "you have your own worries, and plenty of them. You don't like the news, either, but you are glad to forget it. And it is, fundamentally, the Germans' problem. But they won't face it, for in their hearts they believe that Germany is never at fault. So they will look round for others on whom to blame this Reichstag fire, and persuade themselves that whatever they do—or allow to be done, and that's the next stage to actual doing—is right. And the trouble will grow." His voice suddenly sharpened. "Don't people ever read history properly? Or do they think that if they know a list of dates and what king ruled when, then that is enough? All this has happened before, when Napoleon started his career. Step by step—it is all there for us to read in the history books." Then his voice softened again. "I can't blame you or any of your friends. Most people did not find this news even disturbing. Probably thought it was a little bit of added excitement in the newspapers, instead of the daily diet of divorce cases and dull political speeches. I can't blame you when even the chaps who are paid to *know* write generalizations like this." He pointed angrily at the pages of print, at the other newspapers piled at his elbow. "And all these comments from the world's capitals . . . . They aren't real comments at all. Nothing but a lot of soft soap."

"Yes," David said unhappily. "But, look, Father—some of my friends *are* worried. But what can we do? What magazine or newspaper with any circulation is going to print what we would like to write? What Member of Parliament or diplomat is going to listen to what an undergraduate has to say? And we've got to think of our own personal lives—who else will read the books for us, pass our examinations, get us started in jobs? We have got to concentrate on what we have to do, for until that is done we aren't even treated as if we were adult. Most of us can't vote, and we'd be expelled from the University if we got married. Why, we would be censured by most people if we even got publicly engaged. Funny thing, that. Remember my American friend, Burns? He tells me that a student in America can get engaged if he damned well wants to. And a lot of students are married, too. Are we any less adult than American men? Except, of course, when it comes to a war. Then, by God, we are all considered adult enough to go out and kill."

"Well, David," Mr. Bosworth said slowly, for it was difficult for him to say the things he ought to say when he believed so little in them, "The Universities in this country think that a man's work is disturbed by marriage. He doesn't get such good results if he has a wife to interfere with his work."

"Which is the reason," David said with heavy sarcasm, "that America is such a poor, undeveloped, backward country."

His father had to smile. Life wasn't a debating society, he was reflecting: David was right when he implied that however excellent arguments might seem when they were logically stated, they didn't always produce the only good results when worked out in practice. For a nation that prides itself on its tolerance, we English really like to believe that only our way is the correct way, he thought sadly.

"Besides," David went on, defending the young men who were as powerless as they were made to feel, "none of us wants to start marching, and how else could you deal with Germany? And what's more, how would it look in the history books if we interfered at this moment in German affairs? That would just back up all that Hitler has been screaming: we are jealous of Germany and want to kick her in the teeth whenever possible."

"I didn't mention marching, as far as I recall," his father said sharply. "All I want is that people understand what is going on. We should take the warning signal, and keep watch. That's all."

"I agree," David said, and thought of some way to turn the conversation. His father had never forgiven Germany for her treachery in 1914, and because he was one of a very small minority who still remember—a minority that was argued down and snubbed and attacked by all the broad-minded people who knew better—he had become hyper-sensitive about the whole thing.

And what, David suddenly thought, if they are all wrong,

and Father is right? It was an unpleasant thought, chilling him for the long moment he had unveiled it in his mind. Then he covered it over by walking to the table and lifting the edge of the folded napkin. Sandwiches, as he had thought. "Look, Father, I'll go and forage in the pantry. There must be something to cook there, surely. What do you think about phoning—"

"What we need is a batch of new diplomats, the best brains we have. And with guts and red blood," his father was saying. He looked at David pointedly.

"Well, I've got red blood," David said. "But I don't know about these other qualifications." God, he thought in desperation, here we start *this* all over again. "I was saying, what about phoning Penny? We'll have lunch here with you. There must be something in the larder. Penny says she can cook. Let's try her out, shall we?"

"Perhaps I should be safer with sandwiches," his father said. "And in any case, I rather like being here alone when I have so much to read." No piano today, thank heavens. "Where are you and Penny going this afternoon?"

"Hampton Court." That, David had thought, would be a change from Regents Park and the Zoo. The Tower wasn't too bad, either, if you avoided the popular exhibits. But the museums and art galleries were just as bad as Westminster Abbey; no conversation possible, for the smallest remark had to be delivered in an awed whisper, and if you hadn't whispered with enough awe there was always a sentinel on duty with a reminding eye.

"I do believe you've seen more of your London this winter than in all the other years of your life put together," his father remarked. "You weren't ever much of a sight-seer." He looked at David with open amusement. David had flushed, and then he laughed too.

"You had better leave soon" his father suggested.

"I'll give Penny a ring, and tell her to come over. There are plenty of days for Hampton Court." After the Finals are over, David added to himself: this would have to be his last visit to town this term. Then came Easter, and Penny would be in Scotland. Then his last term, and a damned lot of work too. No time to travel to London, unless his work went miraculously well.

His father's face saddened.

"Now what was that?" David asked quickly.

"Nothing," his father answered. How pleasant to be able to say you had plenty of days to go to Hampton Court or

196

any other place. Plenty of days...He half-sighed. David started towards the door.

"No, David," his father said sharply enough to halt him. "Not today. This is one of my grouchy days. I like your Penny and so I want her to like me. And I also want to read my newspapers, and compose a few speeches that I'd like to be able to make. Arguing with myself is most enjoyable, because I always end up, somehow or other, by agreeing with myself." He smiled broadly. "Come away from that door, David. If you don't, I'll talk to you about Germany."

David knew he meant that, too, so he came back to his chair. He said, "Well, let's have some family news. How is Margaret? She hasn't written very much recently."

"Margaret is concentrating on music, at the moment," Mr. Bosworth said. He glanced ruefully at the ceiling, towards the room upstairs. "Less scales, though, I must admit. And some new pieces too. She has been attending these afternoon classes quite regularly. And she has been seeing a good deal of Miss Rawson."

David looked at his father quickly. What had made him say that. "More than usual?" David asked sharply.

His father considered for a moment. "Miss Rawson is coming to live here, once the Easter vacation is over. Margaret says you won't need your room after that. She says you are obviously going to marry Penelope Lorrimer as soon as you can."

David was silent. "Father," he said at last, "if you were me and mother had been Penny, wouldn't you?"

His father did not answer for some moments. He seemed almost as if he had forgotten the question. Then he glanced at his son. I am sorry for all these young men, he thought, for these young men and women. All planning the beginning of careers, the beginning of their real life. None of them know how little time they may have. None of them have yet discovered that they may plan and work; and all that they have planned, worked for, may be swept away by men they have never seen who appear to have nothing to do with their lives.

He roused himself to say, "Frankly, I don't think you should wait any longer than is necessary. And it is for you and Penny to decide that. You know, when you are happily married, the years become shorter and shorter. Too short."

The newspapers slid off his lap, and David stooped to pick them up. He folded them neatly, placing the pages in the correct order, and laid them carefully on the small reading table beside his father's chair. He said nothing.

"Too short," his father repeated. "So have all the happiness you can before it is taken away from you. That was the chief lesson I learned in life." His voice was low, as if he were tiring. He glanced at the clock. "Don't be late, David. Give Penelope my love."

"There is still plenty of time," David said, but he looked anxiously at the clock. He pretended to be interested in the new books from the library which were on the reading table. "Has Margaret a lot of other women friends?"

"No. Or, at least, I don't see any of them," his father said. And then his voice sharpened, "And you haven't plenty of time."

"What about men?"

"At this moment, she thinks us a bad lot."

"That sounds like an overdose of Rawson," David said worriedly.

"Better leave, David. Glad you came, but I'll see Penny another day," his father urged. He picked up the Sunday *Times*. "Now, let's see what we have here," he said in a tone of voice which announced he knew quite well what to expect.

David let himself be reassured, partly by the renewed vigor in his father's voice, partly by the determined look on his face. He could not have been exhausted, after all. And he apparently was not very worried about Margaret. But I am, David thought. Once his Finals were over, he would deal with this Old-Man-of-the-Sea Rawson. Margaret would never have any chance for real happiness if she had Florence Rawson hanging around her neck, making her distrust and dislike everyone except Florence Rawson. As he picked up his hat from the hall stand, and twisted the knot of his foulard tie to sit squarely against his blue shirt collar, he stared at himself angrily in the mirror. And then he left the house quickly.

He turned to wave to his father, and then, hat in hand, strode down the Walk. After all, his father had said very definitely that he wanted no visitors this afternoon. And there was really no time to telephone Penny now. He should have done that when the idea had first struck him. Hell, he said to himself.

The houses seemed smaller in the bright spring light. Their bricks were more soot-stained. There was the smell of Sunday dinners cooking on the small gas-ovens. One pair of lace curtains quivered gently as their owner watched him discreetly. Opposite the row of neat little boxes, the skeleton branches of the lime tree looked as if they had little strength to bloom this year. David halted at the corner, and turned to wave once more towards his father's window. "All right, all right," he said under his breath. "You were damned relieved that Father didn't want you around, that you could have Penny to yourself today." He gave one last glance at the window. He would be late for Penny, now. He set off at a steady run towards the tube station. That was one way, too, of working off his anger.

He arrived, rather short of breath but in a better temper, in time to catch one of the faster trains. That piece of luck helped, too. He was unworried and in good humor when he boarded the train. And he remembered his father's decided voice and look when he had said, "Glad you came, but . . ."

That reassured David nicely, probably because he wanted to be reassured.

chapter xxiv

THE sharp March wind had driven most of the visitors to Hampton Court inside the palace. There they could wander comfortably through the halls and rooms which lay open, with all their ancient display, to the public.

But David, although he wore no coat, and Penny, in her new spring suit, did not seem to notice the wind. All they noticed, indeed, was the fact that Hampton Court was most pleasantly uncrowded. In this quiet corner of the gardens, they could even feel alone. David slipped his arm around her waist as they paced slowly up and down between the hedges of yew, cleanly trimmed into patterns of neatness. At least, Penny had decided, they must be yew: she could hardly imagine Cardinal Wolsey allowing anything except the very best yew to be planted in his gardens. But now she had forgotten about Wolsey's pride in possession and Henry the Eighth's little piece of sharp practice, which you could forgive because it had been directed against the Cardinal—injustice always seemed comic when practised against the mighty—and she was only thinking about David's plans. By the telling, they were becoming their plans. There was warmth from his body and warmth from the hope in his words.

"Oh, David," Penny said suddenly, and caught his hand and pressed it to her side, so that his arm tightened around her waist. "So soon?" No more dreary months of loneliness, no more waiting and worrying, no more of this awful feeling of time slipping away, of living only for the future. She laughed with equal suddenness. The wind had whipped the color into the smooth skin of her cheeks, her eyes were all the more blue for the blue sky above, her hair was as shining as the spring sun.

"It could not be too soon," he said. He was smiling, but his voice was strained as if all the emotion inside him, so suddenly aroused by her happy laugh, had made simple words almost too difficult to put together in a sentence. He halted and they came to a stop. They were no longer smiling. They faced each other, gripping hands, feeling each other's emotion so intensely that happiness and pain were no longer distinguishable. The long moment passed, their hands dropped, and they began walking once more. David's stride was uneven, and Penny's balance seemed unsteady (but she, at least, had high heels on which to blame that) for she lurched against his arm and then said "Sorry!" in so stilted a way, as if he were a stranger, that he laughed.

"I suppose most people would say we are insane," he said. But if this is insanity, then I never want to be sane. "That woman certainly would." He looked with growing annoyance towards the stranger who had chosen to invade this small corner of the gardens and who was watching them in a frightened kind of a way. And there was another, just behind her, a man who was pacing slowly along the box border of a formal flower bed. Didn't he know that there were much better hyacinths to be seen elsewhere? Never left alone, David thought bitterly. If it isn't relatives or friends, it is a landlady or a strange female with a cold red nose pointed in our direction. Why couldn't she stare at the flower beds as the man beside her was doing?

The strange female, who wouldn't have recognized herself by that description, took a hesitating step and then halted. For the last two minutes she had been wondering if she might ask that nice young couple what time it was. So silly of her to have forgotten to pin on her watch, it had been lying on the dressing table and she had said, "Now don't

200

forget that. You know Emily does not like people being late for tea." And she had forgotten it after all. And really you couldn't trust sundials now, what with all this Winter and Summer Time foolishness, when did you take an hour off or put an hour on, so frightfully bewildering to the poor things? And she had seemed to see only men in the last five minutes, there was one just behind her now, he couldn't be following her, could he? And she couldn't ask a strange man, anyway, what time it was. And tea was at four. And that *did* mean four o'clock. Emily disapproved of people who arrived early, too. And it was a pity, indeed it was, to leave this charming garden even if it was rather cold today, so disappointing for spring, before she really must. Not that the people Emily invited to tea were not interesting too but after all they couldn't quite compare with Anne Boleyn and Jane Seymour and Mary, it was dreadful how schoolchildren today were taught that nasty word before her name, and Elizabeth, and that awful Charles Second. Emily always said that this had been a court of shocking iniquity, and what all these Mazes and hidden gardens were built for was best forgotten, Emily . . . oh dear, she really must ask these young people the time.

She halted in dismay as she realized that they were in the middle of a conversation and a very private one, too. "Not insane," the young lady was saying, "sane at last. I know now, for the first time, why I was born and why I should live at all. It cannot be insanity to find that out. It is the only thing that makes life sane."

Penny stopped and looked at the shrinking owner of the timid voice which had spoken and yet had scarcely been heard. The time, David said, was exactly ten minutes past four. It was their turn to be startled as Emily's friend said, "Oh dear!" in a horrified voice, and rushed out of the garden with her scarf and umbrella aflutter.

"I probably frightened her," Penny said, smiling now, but with the deep color of embarrassment still clinging to her cheeks.

David said nothing. He was wondering why on earth elderly females who wanted to know the time just had to come over at that moment. Why on earth hadn't she asked the man who had been so near her? Why had she chosen to interrupt them? And now Penny was pretending to laugh at herself and her serious phrases, and when she spoke again it would be about some ordinary thing, but not about the moment they had both felt so intensely. He knew that, and yet hoped he was wrong, as he watched the varying emotions in her face. God, he thought suddenly, there isn't an expression on her face that I cannot read now, there isn't one movement of her body that I don't know off by heart, and yet I cannot be sure of her. Knowing, yet not knowing. Perhaps that was what kept people plunging more deeply into love, knowing and yet not knowing. Love was wild contrast: you knew, yet you were unsure; you trusted, yet you were jealous; you were amazed that you had found so much and yet you wanted more; you were content with one woman, yet wanted her to be a hundred women; you were tied to her more closely with every hour you spent with her, here I am happy, here I am at home—and yet you knew tension and constant effort. Constant effort in a love that had been effortless and natural—because you were unsure, jealous, demanding, desirous, painfully conscious of your own lack of worth—perhaps that *was* love. Perhaps love lived on constant effort, however effortless and natural it seemed.

Penny was speaking, and he had been right. She was saying, "I had a letter from mother, yesterday. She is coming to London, and she will probably be here next week end. So, no Oxford next Sunday, David!"

"Are the family coming, too?" David asked. I'll have to meet Penny's father, soon, he was thinking. But it would have been better to wait until he had gone down from Oxford with a job all nicely landed. Three hundred a year, sir, with extras on the side to bring it to four hundred. And prospects. Yes, we are young, sir, but—After all, David admitted to himself at this moment, there weren't so very many young men in Britain who earned four hundred a year to start with.

Penny had been saying that her mother was coming alone which was strange, and so very suddenly which was even stranger.

"Probably she has become exhausted or exasperated by those Bonnier Bairns and Restored Ruins and wants to get away from them all. If she is in London during next week end, why not bring her up to Oxford? I'll be the very perfect, gentle guide."

Penny's frown disappeared. "That's a *wonderful* idea. We could get to know you properly, and—" She broke off, her eyes excited, her whole face alive with her delight in such a chance to show David as host.

"Yes," David said, reading her thoughts. "We could use an ally in your family camp. How much have you written to them? About us, I mean?"

"Only sideways, darling. You see, it is sort of difficult in my family to mention the word 'love'. Everyone would get embarrassed. But my letters weren't very successful. I thought that if I mentioned your name, here and there, sort of slipped it in as it were, that would be their cue. The would start asking questions about you. But they didn't." Penny wrinkled her brow thoughtfully. "I tried at Christmas, too, to let them know how matters stood. But I found that awfully difficult. Somehow, every time I got the conversation around to you it would be snatched out of my mouth."

"Never mind," he said consolingly, "your mother will know as soon as she sees us together. What's that thing women are supposed to have? Intuition?"

"Grandfather MacIntyre has it, too," Penny said. "I am quite sure he has guessed about us from my letters. He doesn't say much, either, of course. He just slips in a little sentence like 'Give my regards to David when you see him.' But that's enough."

David laughed this time. So that was enough, was it, to let Penny know that her grandfather knew? "Does that mean he approves, or not?" he asked.

"Of course he does. He wouldn't mention you, otherwise." Then she stared at him as her lighthearted remark led to a less pleasant idea.

David was following her train of thought. "Perhaps your mother doesn't approve," he said gently, watching the worry on Penny's face. "That would make things rather difficult, wouldn't it?"

Penny didn't answer.

"Impossible?" David asked.

"No," she said quickly, and tightened her hand in his. Then she seemed surprised at her own intensity. "No," she repeated, more quietly. She looked up at his expressionless face, watching her so intently. "No, David," she said with a warm smile, and the worry had left her eyes. "You see, I *am* in love."

David said, "I don't hear that often enough." He had kept his voice light, and his reward was a laugh from Penny. Oh, hell, he thought in sudden anger with himself. The English are as bad as the Scots who won't even mention the word love because it is embarrassing; they've always got to twist the word love into a half-joke, for if they can laugh about it they won't be in so much danger of being laughed at. What's wrong with us, anyway? Who is going to laugh at anyone except the spiteful, and who cares about them?

His voice became serious. "Anyone looking at you, Penny, could tell why I love you. But why you love me is something hard to understand. So keep telling me, Penny, that you do love me. I need a lot of convincing about that. And why do you love me, anyway? Why, Penny?" He put his arms around her and kissed her violently. "And I bet that old boy, over there, studying the box hedge, has been wondering how long it would take me to do that." Hell, retreating into the fatuous remark again. He glanced over his shoulder. "Hello! He's gone. Good Lord, imagine that! We're alone!" He kissed her again. He felt her body relax against his, and then he heard the rush and scramble of many pairs of flat-heeled sensible shoes as a cohort of schoolgirls swept into the garden.

"Hell's bells," David said under his breath. He took Penny's arm and they left the little garden, now a mass of green-and-white hatbands, all volunteering different information in their high-pitched voices to a thoroughly bewildered schoolmistress. "All we want," he said savagely, "is to be left alone. It doesn't seem much to ask, but there must be a conspiracy against it. Lord, perhaps that is why people have to marry ... to be allowed to be left alone."

Outside the Maze, a park-keeper looked at them gloomily from under his peaked cap, and reminded them in the voice of doom that it would soon be closed. Everyone, he said pointedly, was leaving.

"Oh, that's all right," David said encouragingly. "If we get lost we'll wait until you come to fetch us." The keeper did not seem at all cheered by such co-operation.

"Don't worry about him," David told Penny, as he took her arm and led her into a narrow lane of grass bordered by tall clipped hedges. "All he wants is to get home to his tea, or to have a pint of bitter at the Barge Aground. And he couldn't leave here, in any case, until it *is* time to knock off duty. What's more, this is the best part of the day in here: no pack of schoolgirls baying at our heels. And it is warmer, too. Even the wind finds it difficult to reach the center of the Maze."

"Yes, it is warmer," Penny agreed with some surprise. Somehow, she hadn't noticed how cold it had been in the more open gardens until she had felt the contrast in here. When she was with David, she never seemed to notice anything very much, except what he said or how he looked.

"Temperature rising steadily." He halted as they came to a block of hedge. "Well, this couldn't have been the right path after all. Now, either we can start all over again, or we can stay here. If we were very astute and walked a couple of miles we probably would reach the center of the Maze. Or we could quite possibly walk a couple of miles and find ourselves back here. What do you think?"

"I think we ought to save ourselves the trouble," Penny said. "After all, I suppose one path looks exactly like another, so that I've really seen all the Maze in the first few minutes."

"Or we could be very coy, and you could run away and we'd both get lost—you running away, and I giving chase. That used to be one of the chief sports here in earlier days. Maids in waiting or the Windsor Beauties running all around, gay girlish laughter, manly oaths."

"A complicated way of arranging your pleasures. And it would be so very unkind to the old keeper: we'd get lost separately instead of together, and then he would have twice the work to do. He'd be late for that pint of bitter. We couldn't do that, could we?"

"No, we couldn't do that to him," David agreed and they both began to laugh. "We'll get out easily enough, so that we can stay as long as possible in here. We took the first turn to the left, then to the right, and again to the left. Reverse that, and we'll come out in time to let the old boy have his tea at a nice warm fire. I'm all against cruelty to park-keepers." And then David, watching her face, put aside all pretense of joking. His voice became serious. "Penny, darling." He took her in his arms, and kissed her as he had wanted to kiss her since the first minute they had met that day.

The long kiss was over, and he drew back just for a moment to see her face again. She met his eyes, her arms tightened around his shoulders.

She said, in a low voice, intense in its honesty, "Oh, David, I'm *so* happy."

"I love you," he answered. He kissed her again. At this moment, holding her, knowing that she loved him, he was happy too: the only moment, he thought, that one is completely really truly safely happy. Could happiness only be measured in moments? That was the difference of being a man and being a woman in love. A woman in love would say, "I am happy." Being in love was enough. But when could a man say it, and not measure it in moments? When he had possessed her and was sure of her? When she was safely married to him? Or was he ever sure?

"I love you," he repeated. He pretended to smile, but

Penny, looking up at him quickly as she heard the strained note in his voice, saw the lines above his mouth deepen, not with laughter but with some emotion nearer pain. For a moment, his unhappiness in love reached out to draw her into his unsatisfied longing. I don't want to hurt him, ever, ever, she thought. I only want to make him happy as I am happy, yet all I have done is to torture. I am cheating, somehow: I am being dishonest, somehow, and yet . . .

"I *do* love you, David," she said. "I do."

"I know," he said gently. He smiled now, and ruffled her hair—any piece of foolishness to chase the worry out of her eyes. He cursed himself for having let the disguise slip from his face, so she had seen too deeply into his real feelings. He thought, I'm damned if I'll blackmail her with pity. *I cannot go on like this, I cannot bear seeing you and yet not seeing you, loving you and yet not having proof of your love.* That was the easy way to win a girl: blackmail with pity, playing on her desire to have you happy as you want to be happy. And I'm damned if I'll force her into anything, before she makes up her own mind. That was another easy way to win, and then, ultimately, to lose her. When she comes to me, he thought, she will come because she wants me. As I want her. And then I'll have her forever, not just for a year or two years. I'll be sure.

"Forever," he said aloud.

She astounded him by throwing her arms around him, and kissing him with passion as intense as his own.

"Penny," he said unsteadily. "Penny."

And then the bell sounded the closing of the Maze, breaking the moment with its harsh voice.

"A sense of humor," David said, as they retraced their steps, "is obviously a necessity in love. Otherwise, you'd become a solid chunk of frustration."

Penny nodded, busy with the technique of combing her hair, powdering her nose, and looking into the small mirror of her handbag. She was thinking that the short distance to the entrance was considerably longer than they had imagined.

"Or was it to the left, and then the right, and then the left? Or to the right, and then the left, and then the left?" David asked. Yes, definitely, one needed a constant sense of humor.

"We ought to have brought a logarithm table with us," Penny said. "We could have worked it out by *sin* and *cos*.

If one cán find nonexistent lightships by *sin* and *cos*, one surely could find a gate which *does* exist."

In the end, the keeper had to come and fetch them. He was quite philosophic about it, as if he had expected any young man with good sense and a pretty girl to lose his way. And that little practical extra, slipped into his hand as the young man thanked him, would buy him an extra pint or two this evening: that was always a help to being philosophical.

They walked slowly back from Marinelli's to the green door in Gower Street.

"It won't be long, now," David was saying. "Not so long before we do not need to say good-by any more." And stop worrying whether you will see her again, he thought, next week, or the week after, or ever.

"Do you really think I should bring Mother to Oxford next Sunday? She could come some other time, when you are less busy."

"I think it would be a good idea. And quite apart from that, I want to see you. I can work like a stoat all week if I think I can see you on Sunday. I'll invite Chaundler to lunch that day, too. He will assure your mother that I am perfectly respectable, really."

Penny smiled, and pressed his arm. She knew, as he had guessed, her mother's weakness for respectability. Some day, she thought, she was going to ask her mother what it was about people that she called "nice." As a standard, it did seem to vary. Take the Fanes, for instance. Mrs. Lorrimer called them a nice family. They had nice accents, nice clothes, a nice house, and a nice income. Yet, as a family, they were a mockery, and as individuals they were selfish and cheap. They had a very pretty façade of niceness, like a mean building camouflaged from the front to look broader and bigger than it was. Mr. Fane was the only one who had made any claim to reality for himself: if any of the others were to die in their sleep, there would be absolutely no loss to the world.

"I'm sorry for Mr. Fane," Penny said suddenly.

"Because he is the only one of the family whom you don't know? Perhaps if you met him, you'd feel less sorry"

"Well if I were a man, and did the providing and got very little in return for my trouble—well . . ."

"Well, what?" David was watching her with amusement.

"I don't know." She shook her head in bewilderment.

"You see I never thought of that before. Frankly, David, I don't believe many women have thought about it. Either they learn it, instinctively, and their husbands are happy. Or they don't learn."

"I think you chose a pretty good example to generalize over," David said. "But how on earth did the conversation take this turn? Have we just passed the Fanes' house?"

Penny looked in surprise at the number over the fanlight of the nearest house. "Why, yes, we must have passed it. And I could swear that I never noticed it. Didn't even know we were almost at the end of the street. How short it seems then I'm walking with you, David. Last night, Marston and I went to see the new René Clair film; and coming back, we walked up this street and we both agreed it was far too long. No street should be this length and look so much the same all the way. Yet, tonight . . ."

"It's too short. Just as the hours are too short when we are together." He glanced at his watch. "We've been eight solid hours together, today. They seem less than two. Look, when we get married I'll have the days arranged into thirty-six hours, so that we'll have enough time to do all the things we want to do together. That would be pleasant."

"Wonderful."

"Wonderful, too."

They looked at each other. Then, holding arms more tightly with hands clasped and fingers interlocked, they walked towards the green door. David watched her walk up the steps which bridged the basement area, waved to her, waited until the door had closed. He crossed to the lamppost, looked down the length of the long street, long and dreary. It was a lonely street now. He paused to light a cigarette and waited. His eyes were on the top floor of the house. That was her window. He had waited like this every time after saying goodby. But tonight, when the light had been switched on, and she had come over to the window to draw the curtains, she stood there looking down into the street. He knew by the stillness of her body that she had seen him. And then she waved, and he waved back, and it was she who now stood watching him as he turned to enter the narrow dark side-street which would take him to Tottenham Court Road.

The dark street was silent and desolate. The wind was colder. It came from the east, a hard sharp wind that needed the Atlantic to soften its bite.

Christ, he thought, always walking away from her, always leaving her. Would there ever be an end to this? Ever an end

to the loneliness that was more searching than any east
wind? He threw his half-finished cigarette into the gutter.
"Christ," he said, listening to his footsteps' empty echo in
the silent street. Then he thought of the lines he had found
last night when he had been searching through the Oxford
Book of Verse for a quotation that had baffled him. He had
opened the book casually, and there they were. He began to
repeat them as he passed the last stretch of unlighted shops
and dark dead houses.

> O western wind, when wilt thou blow
> That the small rain down can rain?
> Christ, that my love were in my arms
> And I in my bed again!

He thought of the man who had written them. Poor beggar,
whoever he had been four hundred years ago.

And then the lights and noise of Tottenham Court Road
brought him back to the twentieth century and a train to be
caught. He glanced at his watch and began to hurry.

chapter xxv

MRS. LORRIMER sat in Penelope's bedroom, watched her
daughter arranging two teacups on an improvised tea table,
and felt still more unhappy.

In Edinburgh it had been simple to work up a mood of
righteous indignation: her daughter living in luxury in London;
her daughter taking a frivolous life for granted; her daughter,
as return for such pampering, behaving with a ridiculous lack
of common sense, perhaps even ruining her whole future.
But now a good deal of Mrs. Lorrimer's indignation was
turned against the room. It was not worth a third of the
money spent on it. Penelope, accustomed to the Crescent
and its comfort, must have been miserable here.

And yet she did not look unhappy. Mrs. Lorrimer's annoyance increased. We gave her every opportunity, and yet
she is happy in a place like this, Mrs. Lorrimer thought
bitterly. No sense of values whatever, if Mattie Fane's letter
carried any truth. Yes, it was the letter that had brought her
to London. As she had said to Mr. Lorrimer, she simply had

to see Penelope to set her mind at ease. Mr. Lorrimer agreed, with his usual keen legal perception, that smoke usually implied fire. Not that he thought much of that Fane woman, a silly lightheaded flibbertigibbet, but who was this Bosfield anyway? "Bosworth . . . Father likes him," Mrs. Lorrimer had said. Mr. Lorrimer had shrugged his shoulders. So Mrs. Lorrimer had set out for London, feeling the whole thing somehow was her responsibility, and she had a worrying journey during which she mentally prepared several little speeches and various approaches. But now, as she sat here and looked round the room it was difficult to get started on any of them.

"I see you have been doing *some* work," she said, noting the untidy desk. If painting could be called work, she thought. Still that was a good sign. The rest of the room was neat enough, but the desk was an eyesore. Really, Penelope ought to keep all these things in drawers and cupboards.

Penny, who had spent a tiresome half hour at lunchtime making the desk neat, said "Of course." It was difficult to keep the note of surprise out of her voice. Had Mother really expected her to be doing no work at all?

"How is the food here?" Mrs. Lorrimer asked. Penny looked up, her surprise increasing, as she finished arranging some biscuits on a Woolworth plate. Conversation had indeed been peculiar ever since the restrained meeting at the station. Brief comments, unimportant little questions, all made and asked in an atmosphere of cold gloom which had been both worrying and irritating.

"Not particularly interesting," Penny answered with determined cheerfulness, "but no one has died of hunger."

Mrs. Lorrimer, watching the smile on her daughter's face, had to admit in spite of her determination to be critical that Penelope was really becoming a most attractive young woman. Woman? Yes, she was older: she was thinner, she wore lipstick, and she had arranged her hair differently. All that made her look older. What ridiculous fashions were adopted by girls today, as if they wouldn't be old quite soon enough without adding ten years to their ages now.

"Why didn't you write and tell me about this?" Mrs. Lorrimer gestured with a contemptuous arm as she looked around the room. Her eyes avoided the primroses which Penelope had arranged in a green bowl and the excellent reproductions with which Penelope had decorated the bare walls.

"It would only have sounded like complaining," Penny said.

"Besides, you wanted me to stay here. It was one of the conditions attached to coming to London."

Mrs. Lorrimer had forgotten that, somehow, when she had first entered the room. Now her criticism of Penelope's lack of money sense seemed leveled at herself. She said sharply, "I see you have been buying clothes. You shouldn't wear black, Penelope. It isn't becoming: makes you much too old."

Penny looked down with disappointment at her black crepe dress. "I saved some money," she said defensively. And then, "I thought we might have dinner some place decent, and go to a theater. After all, this visit to London does call for some sort of celebration."

"We shall have dinner at my hotel. I have a lot to talk to you about," Mrs. Lorrimer said.

Penny looked worriedly at her mother.

"Is something wrong at home?" she asked. "Is Father ill again?"

"Don't be silly, Penelope. You talk as if your father were an invalid. There is nothing wrong with him that a simple diet won't cure. We are all well and happy, a very happy family indeed. Except where you are concerned. You are the one we have been worrying about a good deal." There, it was said. Mrs. Lorrimer took a deep breath. This was not the approach she had intended. But the opening had suddenly come, and she had taken it, and there it was—a beginning.

But Penelope seemed to be determined neither to understand nor to be helpful. "Why, Mother," she said, "look at me! Don't I look well, even if I do have a cold? And that's only because I thought spring had come last Sunday and wore a suit to visit Hampton Court. Apart from that, I'm in marvelous health. And I've never been so happy. Mother, I have the most *wonderful* news for you!" Penny halted her enthusiasm for a moment. Her mother was not sharing it. At the moment, her mother looked almost on the point of tears. *Never been so happy* ... perhaps that had been a tactless remark. Penny hastened to explain it. The note of gladness came back into her voice and her eyes were shining. "It is about David, Mother, David Bosworth."

Mrs. Lorrimer almost dropped her teacup.

Penny was saying excitedly, "He wants to marry me. He will soon be going down from Oxford, and he has a job, a wonderful job, and we could get married this summer."

The teacup fell. Mrs. Lorrimer did not even notice it, it seemed. It was Penny who picked up the pieces.

"Why did you hide this from us? What have you to hide?" Mrs. Lorrimer asked in sudden anger.

"Why, nothing." Penny was taken aback. Her delight in her news faded. Her voice became defensive again. "And we didn't hide anything purposely. I tried to tell you at Christmas that we were in love. I tried to tell you in my letters that I saw David. But you never seemed interested."

"Isn't it customary for a young man to make himself known to the girl's family before he even mentions marriage?"

"David was going to write, and he was going to go up to Edinburgh to see Father as soon as his Finals were over. Don't you see, Mother, he had to wait until things were more definite, until he could say to you and Father—"

"And I take it," Mrs. Lorrimer interrupted with withering scorn, "that you now count yourself engaged *without* the permission of your parents, without an engagement ring, and without any announcement?"

"Well, you can't become formally engaged while you are still an undergraduate. At least, it isn't much approved. And you can't marry until you have finished your University career."

"I should *think* not," Mrs. Lorrimer said in an outraged voice. She paused for a moment to try to restrain her rising anger. She smoothed the skirt of her brown tweed suit, pulled her beige chamois gloves, all with small broken gestures. Her white face had flushed, her blue eyes stared at her daughter accusingly.

"But" Penny went on firmly, taking advantage of her mother's inability to speak, "that doesn't prevent men at Oxford from falling in love or making up their minds to marry the first moment that is possible."

There was no answer. Mrs. Lorrimer was searching for her crisp linen handkerchief in her brown leather handbag. Her lips were pinched and thin.

"Really, Mother," Penny said indignantly, "this can't be so much of a shock ... For one thing, you saw his letters on our hall table, you've noticed mine to him. And I did mention him in my letters home and I did—"

"I never imagined for one moment that things had gone so far. You are only a child, Penelope, and you don't know how foolishly you are behaving. As for this David Bosworth, we know nothing about him. We don't know his family, we don't know one thing. He might be a Catholic, a Communist or anything."

"They don't often mix," Penny said, and smiled in spite

212

of herself. "Actually, if you feel any happier about it he is Protestant and Labour. And as for his family, he has a sister who studies music and a father who was invalided out of the War. There's no insanity, no drunkenness, no divorces, no prison-sentence; nothing, in fact, that one might be ashamed of."

"There's no need to be facetious," Mrs. Lorrimer said.

Penny took a deep breath. "Look, Mother, David and I had thought up a surprise for you."

Mrs. Lorrimer looked at her daughter almost wildly, as if to say that one surprise a day of such proportions was more than enough.

"You are staying over the week end, aren't you? David would like to have us for lunch next Sunday, at Oxford. Mr. Chaundler will be there. Grandfather's friend. And once you really meet—"

"Have you been going to Oxford to visit this man?"

Penny's patience ended suddenly. "You will see on Sunday that there are a lot of people traveling to Oxford to spend the day. A lot of girls, too. What's wrong with that?"

"And he has been coming to London in order to see you?"

"Of course. When people fall in love they want to see each other, don't they? Our bad luck is that we get so little time together, what with geography and David's work and my classes."

"It has got to be stopped." Mrs. Lorrimer's voice was staccato. Penny, who knew that tone and what it meant, half-rose from her seat on the bed, and then sat down again. She knew what was coming, and yet she couldn't believe it. She knew and yet she wouldn't believe. It is now, she thought; whatever and whoever I am to be, it is to be decided now. Her anger left her: a strange feeling, as if she were standing apart from this scene watching everything with critical coldness.

"You must give me your word," Mrs. Lorrimer was saying, "that you will see no more of this David Bosworth. You are both too young, the whole thing is folly, and if he has any decency he will wait for four or five years until you are old enough to know what you are doing."

"I know what I am doing. Age isn't a matter of years, mother. Some women at forty are sixteen mentally. My grandmother was married at eighteen. You were married when you were twenty. Did that—"

"You are to see no more of him, Penelope."

"Why?"

"Because he is not the kind of man we want you to marry. You will understand that for yourself in a few years. I am only saying this for your own good, Penelope."

"And just what is my 'good'? What good is there in anything if you are not happy? I am the one, surely, to judge what I want, or what I do not want out of life. We've all different ideas about happiness so how can we judge for each other? Moira's idea of being happy would bore me to tears, but I don't think she is wrong. I am just glad I am not Moira, that's all."

"I wish you were half as thoughtful and sensible as Moira. It would have spared me this worry."

"Mother," Penny said firmly, "it is you who are causing yourself this worry. If you only trust me, then—"

"It is obvious that we can't trust you. If you won't give us your promise to stop seeing him, then we shall send you away from London. Not back to Edinburgh. We don't want the embarrassment of inventing excuses why you had to come home so suddenly. You seem to have forgotten how people will talk, or you wouldn't have given them so much reason for it."

"If people have nothing else to do but invent gossip, then that is their loss, not mine."

"Your father and I have decided to send you abroad for a year. We are willing to make the sacrifices to meet that expense. The School of Art in Munich is excellent, and you can stay as a paying guest with Marcia Spiegelberger. You remember, she was at school with me and married that German professor? She has several young girls from England as paying guests. I had a letter from her at Christmas telling me all about it."

"Beating up trade," Penny said drily.

"You always wanted to go abroad. A year in Munich would be delightful."

Yes, a year ago she would have leaped at this chance, but a year ago her family would not even have considered the idea for one moment. Even last summer they had refused to allow her to accept an invitation abroad with a school friend. They had kept her firmly beside them, and it was beside them that she had met David. Now that she didn't want to leave England, they told her to go. She wanted to laugh, but the look on her mother's face checked her in time.

She said, "You don't have to bother with all this trouble and expense. Mother, let's go out to dinner, and I can talk about David to you. And then come up to Oxford with me on Sunday, and meet him, and Mr. Chaundler, and see things for yourself. And really, everything will fall into its right proportion. At present, it is all distorted. You make falling in love sound a tragedy. It isn't something to mourn over. You should be so happy, along with me."

"If you refuse to go to Munich," Mrs. Lorrimer said, ignoring Penny's words—in fact, Penny was thinking, she hadn't listened at all for the last few minutes and this argument was becoming a monologue—"then you cannot expect your father and me to go on supporting you. We shall not pay for your expenses in London. That's decided."

"Then I shall support myself," Penny said quickly. She was angry again. Don't, she thought, don't flare up. Keep calm. Argue. Don't get angry. Argue.

Mrs. Lorrimer gave a short laugh. "How?" she demanded. What a child Penelope was! She rose abruptly, gathering bag and furs and gloves with a hand that was now decided and sure. "I have a headache," she said, "and so I'll go to my hotel. I shall see you tomorrow, and we can discuss this again after you have had time to think about it."

"I don't need time, Mother. I know the answer now," Penny said. There was a hard, hot lump in her throat and her eyes smarted as if they had been stung by salt water. She bit her lip. "Please come with me on Sunday."

"Neither you nor I go on Sunday. This entanglement with David Bosworth ends now. You are not in love with him: you are only infatuated by the idea of love. All girls are, at the age of nineteen. I shall see you tomorrow at half-past eight for breakfast at my hotel. We can make arrangements, then." The dogmatic note left her voice suddenly. "Really, Penelope, you have been such a worry to us. You will never know how upset we have been until you have a daughter of your own."

Mrs. Lorrimer waited at the door, but Penelope did not run towards her to kiss her, to ask her forgiveness, as Moira would have done. Penelope had always been a determined, at times unmanageable, child. Now, she had turned away and had walked to the window. She was saying in a strained voice, "I don't have to come to breakfast to tell you what I have decided. I've decided that you are much more interested in your own peace of mind than in my happiness. You want to regulate my happiness so that it suits yours. You want me to choose the kind of man you would choose, have the same formal engagement and wedding that you had, have a house like yours, furnished like yours, have friends like yours

215

or even share your friends, until my whole life becomes an echo of yours."

"Penelope!"

Penny's voice calmed down, but as she turned to face her mother, her eyes were still angry. "I am sorry, Mother, that I had to speak that way, but you left me no choice."

"I never thought that any daughter of mine—" Mrs. Lorrimer's voice broke. Then she quickly regained control of herself. They remained standing there, Mrs. Lorrimer nursing her hurt pride and wounded affection, Penny openly defiant. It was Penny who broke the uncomfortable moment.

"This *is* really silly," she said and forced a smile. She came forward towards the door. "Look, Mother, come and have a cup of tea, and I'll talk about what I feel, and then you'll understand."

"You have talked quite enough already," Mrs. Lorrimer said, her voice low but staccato once more, as she accentuated each word. "You are being both senseless and ignorant."

Penny's anger surged back, and this time she did not care if she dealt a blow that hurt. "If David Bosworth were George Fenton-Stevens, would you raise the objection that I am too young to think of marrying him? Or that you did not know him well enough? Or would you refuse his invitation to lunch in Oxford?"

"Yes, I should," her mother said. But they both knew, as their eyes met, that it was not exactly the truth.

Mrs. Lorrimer had to walk several streets before she found the taxicab rank. This allowed her anger to cool sufficiently before she entered the musty cab with her dignity restored. Outwardly she was a tall, quietly dressed lady of middle age, who had achieved the right mixture of expensive dowdiness and colorless charm to prove her social position. Inwardly, her emotions were so roused that she could not even think logically. It had been a long time, anyway, since Mrs. Lorrimer had tried self-analysis; so long, in fact, that she had lost that gift.

By the end of the journey to her hotel, she had convinced herself that she had indeed only acted for Penelope's good, that she had been wise and kind as well as right, and that Penelope had been unwise, unkind, and terribly wrong. I am *not* trying to arrange her life, Mrs. Lorrimer decided: I am only trying to prevent her from making any mistakes which she will surely regret. And I am *not* a snob.

To prove that, she gave the driver a gracious smile as she

216

tipped him. The man responded with a pleasant good-day—she always got on well with servants. Her confidence was once more restored by the time she entered the hotel, even if the idea of a revolt against her authority still rankled. The way to deal with any revolt was with a firm hand. She had arrived in London just in time.

Penny was looking down gloomily at the bowl of primroses when Lillian Marston arrived. Marston, who had been invited to the tea party, had thought it would be a good idea to come late: by that time, all the family news would be exhausted, and conversation could become general. There was nothing so boring, Marston considered, as to have to listen to news about people whom you didn't know, unless it was the polite explanation of why they were worth talking about.

"Sorry I'm so late," Marston said, concealing her surprise at finding Lorrimer alone. "Had a good party?" She helped herself from the plate of chocolate biscuits. She chose the armchair, stretched her long slender legs comfortably, and ate the biscuit thoughtfully. "I've had a rotten day," she said. "Everything went wrong." Then she noticed the small pool of tea near her feet. "The roof is leaking or something, I do believe. Have you any tea to wash this biscuit down, or did you spill it all on the carpet, Lorrimer?"

Penny turned away from the primroses and began to search for a piece of blotting paper. Then she knelt on the floor—which was one good way of hiding her face—and, with her head bent, tried to mop up the damp circle on the carpet. "It seems to have soaked in," she said in a stifled voice. She sat back on her heels and surveyed the stain. "Oh, what a mess" she said, and threw the blotting paper on the floor. "What a mess," she repeated dismally.

Marston's smile faded, and her favorite eyebrow curved in real surprise. "Don't worry about the Aubusson," she said. "Another spot or two won't spoil its charm." And just what was the mess, she wondered.

Penny searched for her handkerchief and blew her nose violently.

"Spring colds are a blight," Marston said, and turned her head to look out of the window. "Better take care of it. They go on and on and spoil all your fun. Are you going out tonight?"

"No. Mother has a headache."

"Well, it might be a good idea if we had dinner together.

217

"Or it might be still a better idea if you went to bed and I brought you nourishing jellies."

"My cold isn't as bad as that," Penny said, rising from her knees, suddenly businesslike as she found a cup and saucer and poured some tea into it. "I'm all right," she said, and burst into tears.

Marston looked with embarrassment towards the bowl of primroses. "That is just the right shade of green for them," she decided. "Even the imitation mahogany looks all right underneath them." She studied the desk as a whole. An idea seemed to please her. "It would make a pretty still-life—abstract drawings over a desk; one impressionist painting of a murdered cow, I think, waiting for more impressions to be added; and there at the side, quite unpaintable, a bowl of primroses. Still-lives should have a moral attached: the only excuse for being still is to run deep, isn't it? The trouble is, that although it is a good idea, I could never use it. I keep having good ideas that are no use to me. Just never could paint a still-life. Probably with my present technique, the whole thing would look like a study of a couple of fried eggs. It is a strange thing how a primrose is not a primrose and a pigeon on the grass is nothing but alas, once I start painting them. But then, I've always my camera." She paused, and watched Lorrimer reflectively—who was now standing at the window pretending to look down into the street. "Shall I go, or may I have another biscuit?"

Penny turned away from the window, and gave Marston a small shamefaced smile. "Don't go," she said. "If you don't mind sitting there and watching this performance." Her lip trembled slightly, "Oh, damn," she said, "I must look a complete fool." She sat down on the bed, and looked at the tea tray which she had arranged so carefully. "Funny how your whole life can be altered in an hour," she said. "Everything seemed so perfect, and then it wasn't." She half-sighed. "Oh, well ... Marston, does anyone on this floor have a copy of *The Times?*"

"I must admit that I'm finding this conversation difficult to follow," Marston said. "But I know that Neri has *The Times* if you really want it. She gets it in order to cut out all the small paragraphs of our stupidity—the woman who divorces her husband twice and marries him for a third time; the man who writes to the editor, on the day after the Nazis come to power, about the nesting habits of the yellow-tailed blue-tit; a picture of the long line of feathers bobbing towards presentation at Court, opposite a picture of the unemployment queues in Yarrow; the carefully worded trial, which deceives nobody, of the two guardsmen in Hyde Park. She sends them to her cousin who edits a paper in India. I suggested that she would find us much more ludicrous in some other newspapers, but Neri only smiled politely. I think the prestige of *The Times* lends a bizarre quality to the cuttings which she sends. But she did show signs of alarm when I told her that her sense of humor was becoming quite English."

"I sometimes wonder why she does stay here. Or even why she came, in the first place. She arrived disliking us."

"*And* on a scholarship, donated by an Englishwoman."

The two girls exchanged glances, and began to laugh.

At least, Marston thought, we have reached this stage. No more tears, thank God.

"I am looking for a job," Penny said suddenly. "Hence *The Times*."

"Not much help, there, these days. Quite the best thing is to have a friend who has a friend who know someone. Finding a job is just a matter of the right introductions." Then her voice became serious. "What sort of job, Lorrimer?" And why, she wondered.

"Something to keep me alive."

"You don't seem fussy, anyway."

"I can't afford to be. You see, my family want me to leave London, and I don't want to. That's why."

"I see," Marston said, but she didn't. She searched for a cigarette. Perhaps the family had lost its money, couldn't afford to keep Lorrimer in London any longer. That could be. Lots of people were losing their money nowadays. "Then you really do want a job? Sort of declaration of independence?"

"Yes." And much more so than you imagine, Lillian. This *is* my independence for which I'm fighting, Penny thought. "It all happened so suddenly, I'm still at the stage of hardly believing it."

Money-trouble definitely, Marston decided. "Depressing thing a depression," she said. "Daddy was calculating at Christmas how much longer he could afford a daughter in London. Still, we can't go on being depressed forever. No doubt someone somewhere is thinking up at this very minute another war to end un-employment. Then all you have to do is to make munitions, and you can buy three fur coats." She became serious again as she added, "It is strange, isn't it, that a war produces a boom, when you probably have no inclination to enjoy anything, and that peace—when you really feel like having a good time—produces a depression. It is all quite beyond me. But then, I'm an artist, and artists never solve problems: they only state them. And bewilder people. Which is known as the incommunicable soul. Primroses into two fried eggs."

"Well, I shall have to try and make mine communicable," Penny said. "I suppose I should try for a job where I can use the only thing I've been trained for."

"On the contary. You'll get a *much* better job if you know absolutely nothing about it. Training, if you take it seriously, is only a drawback. If you want to be a politician, then you study pig farming or bird life. If you want to be a diplomat, then you study Medieval History or the Significance of the Vase Shape in the Ping-Wing-Ting Dynasty. If you want to be a journalist, then you take a degree in classics. Quite simple, darling. Throw away your brushes and oils and charcoal and smock, and become a private secretary. You can't type or do shorthand. Splendid. You'll make a wonderful secretary."

Penny smiled obediently, but she didn't answer. She was watching the slate roof of the house opposite and the uneven row of chimney pots with their metal helmets, slashed and shaped like thirteenth-century armor, revolving slowly with the creaking dignity of a knight, or hanging loosely askew, jolted occasionally by the wind into a brief apologetic hiccup. Above them was a sky showing its first real spring blue, with soft white clouds chasing each other and a sun already slipping towards the west. The light held the warm color of evening and the gray walls of the house were less cold. There, just under the drunken chimney pots, were the nursery windows on the third floor. Any minute now, she would see a bright head of curls above a small round face, all freshly pink-and-white from its evening bath, with short pajama-covered arms stretched up to grip the highest of the three polished brass rods which guarded the window. In the daytime, whenever he heard a car's brakes before his house, he would appear (probably he had clambered up on a nursery chair to raise his short body to the proper level); he would twist and crane his neck excitedly to see who it was, losing interest if it were a stranger, suddenly motionless if it were his mother or father. In the evening, at this time, he would watch for them coming home or leaving for a party. And then he would stare out at a world that ignored him, resting his forehead against the middle rod of polished brass, until a crisply starched nanny would catch him under his armpits and swing him off to bed.

"What time is it, anyway?" Marston was asking. "I'll scrounge a copy of *The Times* for you if that would make you happier, and then I've some phoning to do. After that, we'll go to Marinelli's and we can discuss jobs with spaghetti to give us inspiration. It is good for conversation—no need to worry about choking on bones. So bear up, darling. After all, if there isn't a job to be had there is always Edinburgh."

"There isn't," Penny said. "That's quite final. It must be a job. I'll measure ribbon by the yard, if necessary." And I must phone, too, she remembered. I must phone David. Only, I must get my thoughts straightened out first of all. I must not worry him, make him think things are worse than they are. Or perhaps I should wait until tomorrow. Perhaps by that time Mother will have understood that David and I are in earnest, that we cannot be divided and separated. If only she would come to Oxford on Sunday, if only she could see us together . . .

"It's six o'clock," Penny said, finishing her answer to Marston. A small bright head had appeared at the opposite window. It was bent, trying to see who was in the street in front of its house. And then, finding nothing, it looked across to Penny's window. She rose and went forward. The striped arm waved vigorously. She waved back.

"Do you still keep this up?" Marston was openly amused. "Who is he, anyway?"

"I haven't the foggiest," Penny said, turning away from the window. Her voice was normal once more, and she was really smiling. Tomorrow at breakfast she was thinking hopefully . . . everything would come out all right after all. "But he can't be left to stand at a window, waiting for someone to look up and wave. Can he?"

"I'll write a reference for you. Kind to children and dogs, impervious to men. Why, any woman would take you on as a governess anywhere on that recommendation." Marston moved to the door. "I'll scout around for the *The Times*," she said casually. Mentally she was already listing the people she knew who could be useful in finding a job for Lorrimer. She would start phoning them right away. And keep on, until she got some satisfactory answer.

Not so impervious, Penny was thinking. Not so impervious. She touched the soft petals of the primroses, letting her fingers ride over them lightly. To give David happiness, that was her happiness. To have him love her, that was her life. Without him—her heart tightened. The primroses blurred over, their outline was lost as if someone were shaking them in front of her eyes until she could see them no more.

Marston did not return until almost an hour had passed. By that time, Penny had bathed her face and eyes, and was beginning to look natural again. Marston felt a great relief: she had begun to regret her blithe invitation to dinner, in case Lorrimer might be tragic all through it.

As they were reaching the hall, they met the parlormaid, who smiled with pleasure at not having to climb to the top floor after all. It was a telephone call for Miss Lorrimer.

"Probably Mother," Penny said hopefully. "Perhaps—" She didn't finish, but ran towards the telephone. She talked there for a considerable time.

When she joined Marston again, who had been pretending to be interested in a three-months-old copy of the *Tatler*, she was so white and wan that Marston said nothing at all.

Penny broke the silence as they walked towards Tottenham Court Road. "That was David," she said, and her voice was as colorless as her cheeks. "His father is dead."

chapter xxvi

A SENSE of duty is a tormenting thing: if you do what you feel you ought to do, you often wish you hadn't; if you don't do it, you are left worrying in another direction. There is no escape from it because there is no escape from yourself. And so Penny, next morning, dressed carefully and slowly, in spite of a cold that had increased to the point of making her want to stay in bed for the day, and set out for her mother's hotel.

The dinner last night with Marston had been a failure. This theory that one should be very very controlled and oh so brave was all wrong. It would have been better for her in every way if she could have let herself recite her woes in diluted form to Marston, instead of discussing the design of stage sets in the new Komisarjevski production of *Grand Hotel* while all the time she was thinking about David. David and his father. David and his sister Margaret. David and her family. David. The only result had been the worst night in all her life.

She had fallen asleep by three o'clock, worn out by arguing with herself, and had awakened an hour later with the postponed tears drenching her pillow. The dream that had aroused her had been so vivid that she lay taut in the narrow bed, feeling the cramp in her tense body, hardly daring to move because of the sharp pain which would then twist her muscles and threaten in its intensity to hold her powerless forever. The skin on her face was tight, as if it had been sewn up to her scalp, and there was the taste of salt on her lips. She had lain there, watching the green-gray sky, as unreal as a pool of stagnant waters under a threatened thunderstorm, seep into the tight walls of the room. And the dream was played over again, mistily, inaccurately, as dreams were remembered. But still threatening and hideous. They mean nothing, she told herself, as she watched the black hearse and four horses move so slowly over the endless road. She was walking behind it, and yet not walking, for her feet moved without her volition. She was weeping, weeping bitterly, remembering how cruel she had been, cruel wicked cruel to think that a daughter of mine sharper than a serpent's tooth, cruel, cruel to her mother when her mother was alive. And now it was too late, too late for anything except this pillow, wet and horrible to the touch of her cheek. Nothing now, but this endless road and Margaret Bosworth standing black and still against the bleak horizon. Nothing else, no one else on the anonymous background, on the flat colorless land flowing into the abyss of the horizon. No David. It was then that the tears for her mother became tears shed for herself.

Dreams are only dreams, she had told herself. She had turned over the pillow, as if by turning away the wet linen she could blot out its cause.

Yet, it was a relief to enter her mother's room and to hear her calm voice, very much alive, giving instructions for breakfast. Tea, not coffee. Porridge, with salt. Crisp toast, unbuttered. Three and a half minutes for the eggs. Marmalade, bitter not sweet. And out of relief, Penny's kiss on the upturned cheek was more than dutiful. Her mother nodded approvingly. And Penny, with sudden new hope and a confidence to match her mother's, smiled too. It is going to be perfectly all right, they both thought. Both, sure of having won their way, were tactfully thoughtful of each other as breakfast began with charming evasion. Those who won must help those who had lost to feel at ease. Mrs. Lorrimer gave full news about Edinburgh, and Penny listened and asked questions dutifully, privately allowing herself to smile over the dreadful predicament of an Edinburgh ever forced to do without the Lorrimer family.

Mrs. Lorrimer noted her daughter's concentration. She is making amends, she thought, and she went on talking with increasing confidence. "A charming city, Munich," she said. "I know you will love it. And you'll enjoy the family: it isn't the usual dull professor's, he is interested in politics and the house if filled with remarkable people. I believe he is going to have quite an important position in the new government." And then, noticing her daughter's expression, she halted abruptly.

Penny rose suddenly and walked to the window. They faced each other across the strange room. "This isn't much use, is it?" Penny said quietly.

"Because you won't listen."

Penny shrugged her shoulders.

"And you won't even discuss the matter," Mrs. Lorrimer went on with growing indignation.

Penny stirred restlessly, as if she wanted to be free of all this endless argument. Her mother noticed that, and her voice was now angry. "What hold has this Bosworth got over you?" she demanded harshly. "What is there between you? Answer me, Penelope."

At first, Penny did not answer. She stood there, her eyes thoughtful as she remembered David.

"It is time that one of us spoke frankly," she said after the long pause. "I am not David's mistress—if that is what you have been trying to learn."

Mrs. Lorrimer looked shocked, but there was relief in her eyes.

Penny pitied her for the pretense. She went on, "I don't feel proud of that, at all. It only proved I trusted David less than he was willing to trust me. And that I hadn't the courage. I believed that I would be injuring the family if I didn't behave as you trusted me to behave, but now I see that you didn't trust me. Or you would not have made this journey, you wouldn't have insisted on these questions."

Mrs. Lorrimer gestured vaguely in protest as she looked unhappily at Penny. "We trust you, Penny," she said faintly. "Of course we do." Her voice strengthened. "But young men are not to be trusted. Young men of today have no sense of morality. They forget that if a man loves a woman he should never do anything which will make her an object of scorn."

"Then morality must only be a matter of appearance. For it seems that a man may have affairs with other women, and, provided he is discreet, his wife isn't an object of scorn. Aren't cheats to be scorned? And aren't there so many of them, hiding behind appearances? Isn't that more to be scorned than a man and woman who are loyal and honest to each other?"

Mrs. Lorrimer steadied herself by a deep breath. "You talk nothing but nonsense. It is bad enough to inflict it on my ears but it would be worse if you inflicted it on your own life."

"That is why it would be better if I found a job. Neither you nor Father will believe I am serious about David unless I do."

"You father will—" Mrs. Lorrimer began, and then halted as her voice broke.

"And Grandfather?" Penny asked suddenly. "He would not be so angry with me, would he?" She crossed the room then to her mother. Mrs. Lorrimer drew angrily away from her touch.

"Don't come running to us," she began, and once more did not finish the sentence. But she will, Mrs. Lorrimer thought hopefully. She will come back to us.

"When Grandfather comes to visit Oxford, he will see David. He knows that—" Penny stopped explaining, as she remembered that it might not be exactly tactful to say that she had written more about David to her grandfather then she had done to her parents. Penny looked quickly at her mother, but Mrs. Lorrimer had not heard that last phrase. She was lost in her own calculations.

She has never been accustomed to poverty, Mrs. Lorrimer was thinking. She will come back to us. If only, meanwhile, she does nothing rash; nothing to create scandal and ruin her life. And ours. She had talked wildly. But all young people talked wildly. A little of the harder discipline of life, the responsibility and worry of earning her own livelihood, might be what she did need to give her some practical sense, to make her more manageable.

"Promise me you will do nothing rash, Penelope," Mrs. Lorrimer said unhappily.

"Nothing rash," Penny agreed.

Mrs. Lorrimer looked at her daughter's determined face, and felt a sudden fear. "You will finish this term," she told

225

her, "and come to us for the Easter holidays, naturally. Meanwhile, it would be better if you did not see this David Bosworth."

"But I must see David, Mother. His father has just—"

"His father is of no interest to me," Mrs. Lorrimer said impatiently. Still watching her daughter's face, noticing the open rebellion in her eyes, she added angrily, "You have shocked me and hurt me, Penelope. It seems as if you are shameless."

"And what have I to be ashamed about? It seems to me that you would be worried whatever I did. If I went about with a lot of men, you would worry. If I go about with one man, you are worried. If I didn't go about with any men at all, you would still worry. What am I to do? One thing I *won't* do, and that is to live a life crippled by what people think. The issue is not whether I am happy or unhappy in my own choice of life, but what will people think or what will people say. For that is what you are afraid of, Mother. But it seems to me that there are always people in the world who will say unpleasant things about you, no matter what you do."

Mrs. Lorrimer stared in amazement. No one, she was thinking, *has* ever said or *could* ever say anything unpleasant about me! Her annoyance increased with Penelope for even having suggested such a disturbing idea. She made no answer, made no move to acknowledge the good-by and began packing her small overnight case. She waited until the door had closed and Penelope's footsteps had died away. Then she sat down on the edge of a chair, a silverbacked hairbrush still in her hand. "I did everything possible," she told it, but she found no consolation in the words. She glanced at the neat diamond watch on her wrist: the train on which her seat was reserved would leave in forty minutes. She ought to hurry to catch it, for tonight there was the Mathieson dinner party followed by the Benefit Concert for Ruins Restored. Yet, if she caught the later train, she would be able to appear with the Ladies' Committee on the platform at the concert even if she might have to miss the dinner party. Yes, she could take the later train.

The decision made, her movements became businesslike and crisp. Quickly she finished packing, pinned her hat securely onto her hair; furs, gloves, umbrella, nothing left behind except a shilling on the breakfast tray and half a crown on the dressing table.

In the taxi, she gave the Bosworths' address in Cory's Walk. It was an odd address, easily remembered. And the

226

way she had met it had helped to etch it into her memory. She had found an envelope addressed to David Bosworth, stamped for posting, but torn open and empty as if Penelope had wanted to add a postscript and had used another envelope. She had found it, just after Penelope had left Edinburgh when the Christmas holidays were over. She had been doubly annoyed: to think her daughter was still writing him, to think that she treated stamped envelopes so lightly. She had held the envelope in her hand in Penelope's bedroom, wondering if she would send it to Penelope in London with a reprimand about carelessness and extravagance, and the address had become fixed in her mind. Providential, perhaps, as if she had not been meant to fail.

It was a long drive across the heart of London to Cory's Walk, but it gave her time to prepare her brief visit with all the skill of an invading general. When they reached Cory's Walk at last, she was taken aback. "Are you *sure* this is the right place?" she asked the driver.

"If you want Cory's Walk," he said. He shrugged his shoulders, and settled back to wait. She'd never find another cab around here.

The same thought struck Mrs. Lorrimer. "Wait here," she said abruptly. How miserable these brick houses were, streets and streets of little dirty-looking boxes. Yet judging from the children and people she had seen, these weren't slums. The children had been clean, the men and women on the streets were respectably dressed. In Edinburgh, she thought, even the slums look better, even the slums are built of good solid stone. The people who live in Edinburgh slums do not know how lucky they really are. As she waited on the little path which led to the front door, she noted that the curtains were drawn over the windows of the house as in the neighboring ones. But at that moment, the door opened, and a tall, large-boned young woman surprised Mrs. Lorrimer by staring haughtily at her and saying "Yes?" in an authoritative voice. Mrs. Lorrimer found herself explaining that she was Mrs. Lorrimer. Could she speak to Mr. Bosworth?

"I think you had better come in, don't you?" the young woman said coldly; turned on her heel abruptly, leaving Mrs. Lorrimer to close the door and follow. They went into a room at the back of the house. Untidy and not particularly well-dusted. Yet not sordid. Indeed it was surprising to find a room like this behind the unappetizing brick walls of Cory's Walk. Mrs. Lorrimer tried to ignore the books and pictures and other signs of civilization and concentrated on the worn furniture instead. Then she looked at the young woman, and was momentarily shocked to find she was being just as closely appraised. And with resentment, it seemed.

"You are Penelope Lorrimer's mother?"

Mrs. Lorrimer said she was, with a lift of her eyebrows which had routed many a junior committee member.

"I thought so," the young woman went on quite unrouted. "Peculiar name. And then, of course, I knew you were Scotch by your accent. Wait here and I'll find Margaret for you."

Mrs. Lorrimer stared indignantly at the door which had closed so determinedly. What an extremely obnoxious creature, she thought, and ignorant too. Knew Mrs. Lorrimer by her accent, indeed. Didn't she also know that "Scotch" was used only in reference to whisky? Probably she would pronounce loch as lock, and say "Auld Lang Syne" as if it had a zed in it. A most disagreeable creature in appearance as well as in manner, Mrs. Lorrimer decided, quite forgetting that if her own instructions to her daughters were a standard then this young woman's plain hair, lack of lipstick, sensible tweed suit and laced shoes should have seemed excellent.

The door opened. A thin white-faced girl in a black dress said, "I am Margaret Bosworth. Did you wish to see me?" Behind her, the tweed-suited woman loomed like a gigantic bull terrier waiting to pounce.

"I have a taxi waiting outside," Mrs. Lorrimer said pointedly, "and so I shan't keep you very long." She paused, cleared her throat. "Actually," she continued, her voice rising half an octave, "I came here to see your father. But if he is indisposed, perhaps I can talk to you. It is about my daughter Penelope and your brother." She paused gracefully there, but the two young women opposite her remained obstinately silent. She had the feeling that the dark girl's eyes were mocking her—take a good look at me and at this house. Yes, this is David Bosworth's home and I am his sister. And what do you think of us?

Mrs. Lorrimer said hurriedly, "They had been seeing each other very constantly, I believe. Her father and I object because she is much too young and because we feel that she is taking it all too seriously."

"*You* object," the tall girl in the tweed suit said, and then laughed. "What do you think David's sister feels about it all?"

That idea was so new to Mrs. Lorrimer, that she could not even answer.

"I don't think you need worry about your daughter," Margaret Bosworth said. "She seemed to me to be quite capable of taking excellent care of herself. I agree that the whole thing is ridiculous, but for another reason altogether. She will simply ruin my brother's career. In fact, she has begun to do that already. If he must marry, then he could have chosen, much more wisely, someone who comes from a family with 'useful connections.' I believe that's the accepted phrase and custom. And I may add that he has met several girls like that at Oxford. But instead, he is absolutely determined on marrying your daughter. She has ruined his ambition: all he wants is a job so that he can support her. It is a complete waste of a young man of his caliber. That is how we all see it. But it is no use talking to him. I know. I've tried. I suppose that was one of the purposes of your visit—that I should tell David what you and your husband feel?"

Mrs. Lorrimer had risen to her feet. A pink circle burned on each cheek. "And your father agrees with what you have said?" she asked icily.

Margaret Bosworth did not reply. An odd, hollow-eyed creature, restless and unsatisfied, Mrs. Lorrimer decided.

The other girl spoke. "Mr. Bosworth died yesterday."

Mrs. Lorrimer stared at Margaret Bosworth's black dress. "I'm so sorry," she said in embarrassment. "I did not know." But they had not told her, Penelope had not told her, no one had told her anything. She had been put into an intolerable situation.

"I don't think," the other young woman was saying, "that you need worry about your daughter getting married too soon. Not now. It will be years before David Bosworth can think of marriage."

Margaret Bosworth still said nothing, but her silence underlined that last sentence.

Mrs. Lorrimer had nothing to gather up except her composure. There was nothing left of the motions of good-by save to walk towards the door, to bow slightly, to say good-day.

The tweed-suited young woman followed Mrs. Lorrimer and stopped her at the gate. "Your daughter is not only spoiling David Bosworth's future," she said in her brusque voice, "but she is also spoiling Margaret's. I thought you ought to realize that as well." Then she turned on her heel in that abrupt way of hers, and stalked into the house.

Mrs. Lorrimer's hand was shaking as she searched for her

pocket handkerchief in her bag. It took some moments before she could speak without anger and give the driver directions to the station. Her indignation grew as the taxi jolted through city traffic. What right had these two women, anyway, to decide David Bosworth's life for him? Or to pass judgment on Penelope? Of course that was Penelope's reward for having tied herself up with such people. But it really was too much that she should have put her mother into such an embarrassing situation. One thing only had been achieved by that most unpleasant visit: at least Mrs. Lorrimer had found out that Bosworth was serious about Penelope, and that was a healthier state of affairs than if he had been merely amusing himself. Still, it was little consolation. In some ways it relieved Mrs. Lorrimer's mind, in others it increased her worry. *No use talking to him. . . . I know. I've tried.* Remembering the bitterness in Margaret Bosworth's voice, Mrs. Lorrimer felt a twinge of almost-sympathy for David, and then her mounting anger drove it away. All she had left was the very deep, very sincere, and very sustaining feeling of self-pity.

chapter xxvii

On the day his father died, David caught the late afternoon train to London, telephoned Penny, and then spent a painful evening with Margaret and Florence Rawson.

It had been something of a shock to find that Florence Rawson not only had taken over his room, but was also settling herself in the sitting room for the rest of the evening as if Margaret needed her support. David abandoned the idea of privacy and with no more delay began questioning his sister about his father's death. Margaret resented that, as if she found in these natural questions some form of hidden criticism. Her control over her emotions ended, and they broke into violent tears. David found himself suddenly left alone in the room with Florence Rawson, listening with dismay to Margaret's footsteps running up the flight of stairs to her bedroom.

Florence Rawson did not stir from the armchair. She waited, perhaps hoping that he would have to ask her for the information. She had been there this afternoon, and he had not.

"Leave Margaret in peace," she said. "I calmed her down this evening. Now you have ruined it."

"And how delighted you are." He left the room as abruptly as Margaret had done, but he closed the door quietly instead of slamming it, feeling his arm become tense with his repressed anger. He stood in the dark hall for a few minutes, and then moved towards the staircase. The house lay in silence: Margaret's storm of weeping had ended as quickly as it had begun. He paused at his father's door, and his hand half-lifted as if to knock. Habit was hard to break. He entered quietly as he had done a thousand times before.

He sat down beside his father's bed. This too he had done a thousand times before. . . .He stayed there for over an hour.

Margaret heard him as he was leaving. Perhaps she had been waiting for this moment. She came running downstairs, and caught his arm with some show of affection. Why hadn't she done that when he had arrived, instead of treating him as if he had been an interfering stranger?

"Must you go back to Oxford tonight?" she asked half-worriedly, half-pathetically.

"If Miss Rawson allows me to have my room, I'll stay here as I planned."

"She has been such a good friend, David."

"A better friend would have left the family alone tonight."

"But she has been so wonderful. She made all the arrangements about the funeral this afternoon."

David looked very hard at his sister. "I came to town to do that," he said briefly.

"And it was Florence who phoned you this afternoon about Father."

"I know," he said, and this time he could not keep the bitterness out of his voice. "And she spoke with the Vicar, too, didn't she, when he came to call about the church service?"

"She was such a help, really, especially when there was no man in the household to take charge."

David said nothing.

"Look, David, I'll make up a bed for you on the sitting-room couch. After all, we have a lot to talk about."

231

"We can talk about business matters at the week end. After Friday." Friday was the day that Rawson had arranged for his father's funeral. "I'll make plans to stay in town until Sunday."

There was coldness in his voice, and Margaret sensed his revulsion. She drew apart from him, letting her strong white fingers drop from his arm.

"Don't take it so hard, David. After all, we both knew that someday soon he would die. It is a miracle that he did live so long. And he died so peacefully. David, don't!"

David said harshly, "We might have been living on another planet for all the use we were to him when he did die."

"But I've told you already that he seemed better this morning. He was all right when I left to go to the Bach Society luncheon. When Florence and I came back here, we found him—"

"When he became ill last Sunday evening, why did you not let me know?"

"I've told you already that I thought it was nothing serious. You know how he had these ups and downs. He would not let me even call a doctor on Monday. He seemed to be improving. And then, today. . ."

"Yes, I know," David said heavily. But all the telling in the world would not drive away this sense of guilt. Didn't Margaret have it too? He stared at her. In her face, there was more unhappiness than grief. And in that moment, the last spark of affection which he had for her flickered and went out.

"I'll see you on Friday," he said abruptly, and left her.

The lamplight shone meanly over Cory's Walk plunging the end houses in a dark pool of shadow. His footsteps echoed loudly on the lonely pavement, and quickened. But even in the busier street, he still saw his father's quiet face, so white and somehow so much younger with all its surface strangely smoothed out by death. He remembered the still room, the piles of magazines no longer to be read, the books and newspapers forever abandoned.

His sense of failure grew. What he must do for Margaret, he suddenly realized, would be done not out of affection —that had died, too, tonight—but from his sense of having failed his father at a time when his father needed him. He must not fail with Margaret now. That would be another failure towards his father.

He began to see what must be done. Margaret's secret grudge against life was that she never had had a chance.

She felt she had been cheated, first by her father's illness which had impoverished them, secondly by her mother's death. Now, she was convinced that she would have been a brilliant success as a concert pianist if only she had been given the opportunity. And the only way to stop a lifetime of complaint of "might have been" or "would have been" was to give her the chance to prove to herself her real value. The Rawson woman would not be a problem then: she was only a part of Margaret's present pattern of insecurity. Take away Margaret's grudge against life, the feeling that she was the victim of a world dominated by men, and Rawson's power to influence would be ended.

It was a theory at least, David decided as he entered the Underground and joined the small queue for tickets, and it was a theory that might work. Some theory *had* to be put into practice. Otherwise Margaret's life would be permanently wasted. People, who kept telling themselves that they never had a chance, seemed to use up so much of their energies excusing their failure that they had little power left to surmount it.

He looked at the faces of the hurrying crowd around him, wondering curiously what lay behind these masks. It seemed the same kind of crowd which had jostled past him last Sunday. Then, he had been happy and confident and they had appeared to him to be as carefree as himself. Now he realized they hid the knowledge of death and suffering as well as the experience of joy and life. It was strange how a human being could forget that so easily, perhaps because individual man tended to think that his experiences were in some way unique. He would admit that others had sorrow or happiness, too, but not in this way, or at this time, or even to such a degree; for this was the mark of his individuality. It was the reason, for instance, that a man who had never known any serious illness and who entered a hospital for the first time in his life was shocked and amazed to discover that there were so many rooms in so many long corridors, so many wards with endless rows of bed, all filled with suffering. And not only during these days when he knew pain, too, but during the days that went before and the days that came after, when he was well and unthinking of pain. Before, he did not allow himself to imagine, and afterwards he tried very hard not to remember that the suffering was always there. For only by forgetting unhappiness and by concentrating on hope could a man struggle through his

233

life. The determined optimist or the potential suicide: there was only that choice.

A train roared with express speed into the station. A man caught David's arm roughly, and pulled him from the edge of the platform as the train rushed past and the air sucked around their bodies.

"Bit too close there," the man said. He watched David's haggard face carefully.

David nodded.

The man released his grip on David's arm and moved away. Probably it was only by chance that the young chap had walked so near the edge of the platform as the express came through the station, but for a moment it had looked like one of the suicides you read about in the papers. The man, middle-aged, mildly prosperous judging from his neat blue suit and well-fed body, turned at a polite distance to look at that young chap again. He was all right now: the young fool was keeping a reasonable distance from the edge; he was standing still, too, as if he had got a bit of a shock. Here was their train, anyway.

David, suddenly recovering from the paralysis which had attacked him as the express had disappeared with its high whistle into the dark circle of tunnel, moved forward to board the train with the crowd. The man in the blue suit followed him, found a seat, and, after one last glance at the chap who had nearly got himself killed, opened his newspaper. He had almost begun reading it while he was waiting on the the platform. Good job he hadn't.

David, grasping the chromium rail by which he stood, felt the reaction strike him. What a damned silly thing to do, he thought. He could feel, even now, the rush of the train bearing down on the platform, the violent breath of wind which pulled at him as that middle-aged man had held him by the arm. He hadn't even thanked the man properly; but it was only now that he fully realized the danger and only now that he could be properly grateful. He looked at his taut hand grasping the rail, sensed the tenseness of his body. "Well, you *are* still here," he told himself, "and all in one piece." He must be one of the determined optimists of this world after all, for there was relief in his words.

He telephoned Penny from Paddington. The maid at Baker House was not very forthcoming. It was too late for any messages to be delivered to any room. Too late. Against the rules. Too late. She wasted more time and energy in telling him about the rules of the house than she would have done in going to fetch Penelope.

He caught his train with a minute to spare, settled himself gloomily in the corner seat of an empty compartment. It was unheated and draughty, and under the poor light the dusty upholstered seats looked a stained and dirty gray. He had a book with him, but he didn't even try to read. He stared out of the window, his eyes noting the crowding shapes of the tall houses almost edging onto the railway line: the factories, made more ugly by their desolation at this time of night; the rows of poorly lit houses giving way at last to the close groups of suburban cottages and villas with their brighter windows confidently pricking the darkness. Then came the black stretches of fields and hedgerows, lengthening as the houses became more scattered, until the shapeless shadows of the night blotted out distance and outline. The country became anonymous, and the window was a dark mirror reflecting his white, set face and the dim compartment behind him.

On Sunday, he had looked at these same fields. On Sunday his father had been alive. "We both knew that some day soon..." Margaret had said tonight. Yes, we both knew, and our minds were prepared. But sudden death was always a grim shock, for its swiftness proved to those who survived how insecure life was. That was something one's mind was never fully prepared to face. And with that knowledge of insecurity, there came a sense of urgency. What you valued became doubly valuable: what you possessed was to be enjoyed. Your life then became a battle against time.

He closed his eyes wearily....All right, be practical. Stop thinking of anything except the things you must arrange—and arrange in the next few days.... You couldn't even think in peace about those who had died. All right, then. Practical things. First, he must arrange with George to borrow his flat for this week end to give him a place to sleep. Then, Chaundler. He had to talk to Chaundler. There was no one else to ask for advice. He was searching for a reprieve: he had decided already what must be done about Margaret, but he was still hoping that some other suggestion could be made which would be easier for him to follow. For nothing must separate Penny from him. He was not going to lose her, now.

His body was tired and heavy. He was heartsick and weary. Nothing is going to separate us, he thought desperately. The train wheels under his feet caught the rhythm

235

of his phrase mockingly. Nothing is going to separate us, nothing is going to separate us.

And nothing is, he told himself. Nothing, he added savagely. Yet the fear, which had haunted him since he had talked with Margaret, would not lift from his heart.

chapter xxviii

DAVID had decided against Marinelli's tonight. For one thing, it was Saturday when the restaurant was most crowded. And, for another, Marinelli's was enjoying success. What had once been a delightful informality was now becoming a pattern of behavior: the newcomers, having discovered that conversation and laughter were interchanged between various tables, made a determined habit of it. So David had chosen another restaurant in Charlotte Street, where people were less numerous and prices were more expensive. Privacy was always a luxury. Tonight, even if he could afford it less than ever, he must see Penny alone.

He glanced around the dimly lighted room when he had ordered dinner. (Penny, after one glance at the menu and its price list, had decided she wanted only an omelette. David, avoiding her look of refusal, had added hors d'oeuvres to precede the omelette, and a salad with camembert to follow.) He was thinking that the definition of privacy had taken on a strange meaning for him. In order to sit and talk to Penny in some peace and comfort, he must share her with at least thirty other people, the sound of their voices, the subdued clatter of their plates.

Penny, watching him, saw him frown suddenly as if to cover some emotion. She became aware of the deep unhappiness and strain in his face, which until this moment he had disguised very well. But, as if he felt her sudden scrutiny, the frown was forced away and his face became expressionless once more, calm and serious above the dark suit and the black tie. She stretched one arm impulsively across the small table and let her hand rest on his for a moment.

"David," she said, and then could not say anything more.

Only a few minutes ago, she had almost begun to tell him her own troubles. But that would have been a mistake. He must talk first, and once he told her all his worries she could judge how much she could add to them—if at all. It began to look as if her description of job hunting, which she had planned to make as amusing as possible in the telling, was going to be quite unnecessary.

David's hand caught her as it moved away, and held it. "Darling," he said gently. And as his grip tightened, crushing the signet ring he had given her at Christmas into her little finger so that she winced, he said with a sudden rush of emotion, "Penny, I need you. God, how I need you." He dropped her hand then, and looked away as if his own vehemence had embarrassed him. Or was he afraid? And of what? He had spoken as if he had been saying good-by.

Penny, easing the ring on her finger, felt an echo of his fear. "But you will always have me, David."

"No matter what happens?" His eyes searched her face. His voice sounded almost desperate.

"No matter," she said. She tried to smile. "You will always be stuck with me. Poor old David."

He caught her hand again and held it. Gently, this time, but firmly.

"Every day I am away from you, I keep imagining you as I last saw you. I keep remembering how wonderful, how truly wonderful, you are. Then I meet you again, and you look the way you do, and you speak, and your eyes light up for me; and I realize that when I was thinking of you, wanting you, I never had imagined how wonderful you really are. You are better than any dreams of you."

There was a pause. Penny's hand stirred in his, and then relaxed.

"What were you thinking?" he asked, watching her eyes.

Penny's color deepened. "That I want to hear you say that just as vehemently when you are sixty." She thought over that. "Darling, I *do* sound overconfident."

David shook his head. "You haven't even begun to know you own power over—" He stopped, released her hand. The waiter wheeled the table of hors d'oeuvres before them.

"Well," Penny said with pretended lightness as the waiter eventually departed, "if we *are* in a restaurant, I suppose we may as well eat. Besides, I had no lunch today .... And if we weren't here, where else could we talk? It is cold in the streets tonight."

David glanced at her quickly. "So you are in rebellion too?" he asked quietly.

Penny nodded. "You know, David, sometimes I feel as if we were being hounded. As if the whole world were in a conspiracy to interrupt us, or interfere with us, or even to separate us. Sometimes it is accidental, but sometimes I feel it is really done on purpose. We just are not allowed to be alone, are we? And when you come to think of it, not one single person has tried to make things easier for us. Even our friends give us advice against marrying, against concentrating so much on each other. You can *see* them thinking, 'It won't last.' And the nicest of them, the kindest—well they feel sorry. David, we'll show all of them, won't we?"

He pushed away his plate. He said with a sudden return of bitterness, "Perhaps your friends are right. I've asked too much from you, and I give you too little in return." He pushed aside the glass of water and felt its coldness spill on his hand. I've nothing to give, he was thinking. Nothing. And now, less than ever. Just words and waiting and talking and promises and words. "I have had a lot of decisions forced on me in the last five days, Penny."

She kept silent while the waiter served the omelette. She thought of Margaret. I expected this, she realized, but I hoped it wouldn't be so. Margaret....

"Let's begin at the beginning," she said more calmly than she felt. "I know very little of what actually has been happening, you see. I guessed from your letters that there were difficulties."

David began to tell her the brief story of this week. As she had hoped, the telling of it did him good.

Now, he was talking about Margaret.... After the funeral, there had been a long discussion about her future. She had had her own proposals all ready, of course. They were the same old ideas that he should share the house in Cory's Walk with Margaret and Florence Rawson, and be responsible mostly for its upkeep once he had a job. Margaret needed only a few years, and by that time she (and Rawson, too naturally) would have had some success, and David would not have to worry about anything. And everyone would live happily ever after. Margaret was quite confident about that.

Then David had stated frankly that a much more concrete plan was needed, something practical and not merely a vague kind of ambition. This suggestion had not been well-received. So David had left them and gone back to Fenton-Stevens's flat, which had been lent him for this week end.

The very fact that neither Margaret nor Rawson had seen the ridiculousness of this arrangement convinced him still more that it was no good discussing anything with them. And so, this morning, he had gone to see Margaret's teachers at the School of Music.

He had told them exactly what he could do for Margaret. They had been understanding and frank in their turn. Margaret was a good student, but her chances as a concert pianist were highly doubtful: she was efficient, but not inspired. Besides, success would not come overnight. It was a matter of years, and even after the first success, a career was not established. That was a slow, painful business. On the other hand, Margaret could complete her courses in one more year of tuition and then be qualified to teach in a school of good standing. That kind of work could be pleasant enough if you let yourself accept it: it would allow free time for her own work at the piano as well as financial independence. Most musicians did combine teaching with their own work: there were few artists in any field who did not have to face that economic problem.

"Yes," Penny said. "And what did Margaret say?"

"She doesn't want to teach. She says that once you begin with compromises, you never get rid of them."

"I suppose you didn't tell her what her teachers had said?"

"I could hardly do that. You can't tell people that they would be a failure."

Penny shook her head slowly. "I don't know... Perhaps better now than later. Some day she will have to find out, anyway."

"But Penny, she wouldn't believe me. She would think that this was only an excuse of mine to do nothing at all about her. She is a complicated problem, you know, at this moment."

And a complicating one, Penny thought bitterly. "Frankly, as long as she has two hands and a head, I don't see why she is so helpless. Why doesn't she look for a job?"

David looked at her in surprise. He had never seen Penny quite so indignant. "What kind of a job? She has had no training except in music."

Penny did not reply to that. Her indignation increased.

"After all, Penny, you would not like to give up your painting for bookkeeping, would you? That is, if you were in Margaret's position and had to worry about your own future."

"I would," Penny said angrily. Then she restrained herself,

239

and tried to calm her voice. "So what did Margaret decide? The year's tuition and expenses, or a job to make her independent?"

"I wish you wouldn't think of it that way, Penny. It only makes the whole thing more difficult for me." He was hurt, too, now. The fact that he had asked himself through a sleepless night why Margaret had not the guts to look for a job, why she had to be so helpless and abandoned in a century when women could earn their own living, did not help to smooth his temper.

"Well, that's that," Penny said. Her voice was abrupt. She stared at David unbelievingly. She thought of several truthful things to say about Margaret, but she stopped herself in time.

"Yes," David said gloomily, "That's that. I can see no other way, Penny. I've tried thinking up plans until I felt I was going stark raving mad. It means," he paused, and his voice became cold and emotionless, "it means that I shall have to support Margaret for a year. We have two relatives— Mother's brothers, both married, each with families of their own. They came to the funeral of course, and they were kind enough to make some gestures, but—Well, one is a lawyer in Wales; the other is a doctor in Yorkshire. They invited Margaret to stay with them until she had decided what to do. Their wives looked quite relieved when she refused. She doesn't want to leave London, you see."

Penny said nothing.

"I went into the cost thoroughly today," David continued in the same cold voice. "It will take, altogether, more than half of what I earn. After a year, she will be fully qualified and can teach. Anyway, she will be on her own, then."

"I wonder," Penny said bitterly, and then wished she had not said it. For a moment, they looked at each other across the table as if they were strangers.

Then David looked down at the plate of salad, and laid aside his fork.

"I don't want coffee either," Penny said in a strangled voice. She knew she was unreasonable, even petulant. But it seemed to her as if David was treating his sister with more than necessary care. It paid to be helpless, Penny thought with rising anger: if only women were sufficiently helpless, then they could always rely on men being foolish enough to rise to their defense.

Then, as she watched David pay the bill with that tight, tense expression on his face which terrified her, her anger vanished. She rose quickly, afraid that her emotions were going to make her break down in this restrained and elegant restaurant. She hurried into the street, not waiting for David, and began walking quickly away. Then she realized that she had taken the wrong direction, and halted. She stood there, with her face averted, not knowing what to do now, feeling what a fool she must look and was.

"Penny," David said beside her. He took her arm, and held it firmly, ignoring the slight movement she had made to draw away from him. "Penny." He kissed her. "I should have done that in the restaurant," he said. "There isn't any problem that a kiss can't begin to solve."

She laughed happily through her tears. He gave her his handkerchief, and smiled as he watched her blow her nose. Then he folded her arm through his, and they retraced their steps. "I'm sorry, Penny. I told you tonight that I've asked too much of you and given you too little in return. You have every right to be bitter. You would be better off if you had never met me."

"I wouldn't. And I'm not bitter. Not with you. Oh, David, how *awful* it is to feel we are hurting each other. How easily a quarrel can start. Just suddenly. Out of talk."

"Yes," David said, with a smile to take the edge off his words, "that had all the beginnings of a good one, hadn't it?"

She nodded. "We hurt each other. And it was all so stupid, for neither of us deserved to be hurt." She gripped his hand, as she wondered what she would have done if he had not come after her, if he had not taken her arm and kissed her. She suddenly reached up to kiss his cheek. "I adore you," she said.

They halted at the corner of the street. The wind was shrewd and the passers-by looked at them curiously. David glanced at his watch.

"Shall we go into another restaurant and have some food?" he suggested teasingly.

"Let's walk. I have some news for you too, David." She drew close to him as they walked, ignoring both the wind and the passers-by. "I thought I wouldn't tell you this evening, because you were so depressed. But it would explain a lot ... why I was so angry and stupid and all the things I don't want to seem to you." She halted, suddenly aware of the street which they had entered, crowded with Saturday-night holiday-makers. "Where *can* we talk, David? How far away is George's flat?"

He looked at her, unable to conceal his amazement.

"Not too far," he said guardedly. "Ten minutes by taxi." He made no move. He stood there looking at her, watching her face, asking her a question, just standing there, saying nothing, watching her.

"There's the taxicab rank, David," Penny said, pretending to be practical.

"So it is," he said with an equally good pretense of surprise.

He smiled, raised one hand and hailed the first cab just as he had wanted to do ever since he had seen the row of taxis some five minutes ago. With the other hand, he tightened his grip on Penny's arm.

The view from George's flat was one of rooftops. When they entered it from the tiny square of hall, David switched on the light automatically, and then wished he hadn't been so quick to cut out the magic of the clear night pouring through the large double windows. But Penny must have sensed the sudden nervousness which had attacked him. She walked into the room, looking around it with careful interest. He was amazed at her calmness.

"Some day," she was saying, "we'll have a room like this, and a window like this. Only better than this, for it will be ours." And how happy we shall be. . . . Not for just one day here, one night there, but for always. People who were married did not know how lucky there were to have a home, a place to be together, four walls around one life.

"Put out the light, David; we are blotting out the stars." She crossed the room to the windows. "I like rooftops," she said. "When you have rooftops, you have the sky." She turned almost instinctively to meet David's kiss halfway. He caught her in his arms.

They stood there, straining against each other with pain and desperation of unfulfilled love. And then, suddenly, he released her, dropping his arms as if they did not wish to touch her, moving his body as if to step away from her. But their eyes did not leave each other. Penny's hand rested on his shoulder, then it tightened and her arms slipped round him, drawing him back to her again.

"I love you, David," she said. Tonight, as she looked up at him, holding him, sharing the pain and anguish she found in his eyes, the words had become a promise. Not a promise to be taken lightly. A promise to be kept and repeated forever.

"I love you," he answered, and in his words there was all the feeling of a vow.

The room's darkness was broken by moonlight. Its pale white light spilled in a pool on the floor before the window, overflowed gently into the shadows, diluting their depths into ghostlike transparence.

Penny stirred and then relaxed against David, feeling the strength and peace of his body, the peace in her heart. His arm tightened around her as if to reassure himself. He gently kissed her eyes and lips and throat, and then his head rested against her breast. From this couch, the sky with its sprinkled stars was all that could be seen of the world outside. There was only the sound of fading traffic coming up from the street below: dim, distant, remote from this silver-shadowed room. Time, itself, seemed to have stopped.

chapter xxix

WHEN the curtains were drawn and the lamps switched on, and Penny had combed her hair, they sat down together with lighted cigarettes. Penny was in one armchair, David in the other across from her, on the opposite side of the hearth; because, as he said, he wanted to look at her.

"How domestic this all is," Penny said with some surprise and glanced round the room. "I don't feel at all like an abandoned woman."

"As long as you only abandon yourself to me for the rest of your life, I shan't object," David answered. He smiled, and then saw that Penny was watching him. "Well?" he asked, "You too?"

"Yes, I'm so happy, David." He need only look at her shining eyes, at the soft eager smile on her lips, to find the proof of her words.

"You are so much more beautiful that I ever dreamed," he said suddenly serious. "Penny, why should you love a chap like me? What makes you?"

When she didn't answer that, but only watched him with

that warm smile on her lips, he went on, "You know, Penny, I've always been afraid that I'll lose you. Even now. . . ." His voice hesitated. "Even now, at this moment, I suddenly realize what a nightmare this life would be if, having known you, I lost you."

"We shan't lose each other," Penny said, "For we shan't hurt each other. That is the promise we made, isn't it?" Then she became serious, thoughtful. Her voice was hesitant in its earnestness. "I realized, tonight, something that I hadn't realized before. I don't think girls do realize it until they meet a man like you. No one tells us, you see. All we are told about men is that we should distrust them because they have the power to hurt us. Yet, tonight, I know that I have every bit as much power to hurt you as you have to hurt me." She paused. "It is a terrific responsibility, this being in love."

David rose and came over to her. "If we remember that," he said, "we won't ever lose each other." He took her cigarette and stubbed it out in an ash tray. He sat down beside her in the armchair, pulling her legs over his lap, sliding his arm around her waist. "It is a pity to waste the mercies," he said and kissed her ear. "Now, be co-operative. Look at your arm, quite useless. Put it around my neck. That's the girl."

"But, David—" She tried to sit up and look businesslike. "We have so much to talk about, to decide."

"It seems to me as if we've made the only important decision in all our life," he said, and kissed the curve of her neck. "And look here, Penny, when you're married to me, you had better not interrupt me when I'm making love. I'll beat you with the poker if you do."

Penelope laughed delightedly as if she enjoyed the idea and let herself relax on his lap.

"Still, David, we have a lot to discuss," she said mildly. "In my handbag on that table is a letter from Father, for instance. It came this morning. But first of all I must tell you about Mother's visit, and that I am now hunting for a job. *And* a room of my own."

David looked at her in amazement, his interest now fully awakened. Penny began her story.

At its end, he was silent for some moments. Then he kissed the hand he had been holding, and said quietly, "I'm sorry I lost my temper in the restaurant. I'm sorry, Penny."

"But I hadn't told you, darling, so how could you know? You must have thought I was hardly qualified to talk, with my parents providing a nice comfortable life for me. I should have told you at once, I suppose, but you were so unhappy and gloomy."

"I was," he admitted. But no more. All the desperately unhappy thoughts of these last days had vanished. Tonight death had once more gone back into its proper proportion to life. We lived, not in fear of death, but in spite of death.

"Everything seemed useless," he said. "Even my work. It is behindhand, as you may guess. Yesterday I thought that proved I could never manage it anyway. Tonight," he kissed her hand again, "I know I'll manage it. I'll go back to Oxford and work harder than I've ever worked." He kissed her on her lips. "Now I *know* what I'm working for, he added quietly. "And we'll manage everything. We'll get married, sister or no sister."

He tightened his arms around her as if by crushing her this way he could hold her forever.

"If we had only my people to struggle against, or only your sister to cope with, we could get married this summer. But my people and Margaret together are going to be a difficult combination. You see, one complicates the other."

"But I don't see, darling."

"Father's letter says quite frankly that I can't get legally married without his consent. And I can't, David. Of course a lawyer would think of that. Now, if we could have shown him that we *were* in love and that we had three hundred pounds a year to live on—perhaps even more, but certainly three hundred—he would probably have relented in the end. But I know Father, and he will never allow me to get married on three pounds a week, and that is what we shall have left after Margaret is taken care of. And he wouldn't allow me to get married if I had to have a job in order to add to our income. He doesn't believe in that. And if I pointed out that a home might suffer just as much from a wife who spends so much time on committees and concerts and bridge clubs and good works, he wouldn't listen. He would only be furious. And that's no way to win him to our side."

"Damn it all," David said angrily, "If it is only money they want..."

"Darling, darling," Penny said, and kissed him. "Don't, please don't. I agree with you. People are not logical. For instance, Mother thinks George Fenton-Stevens is charming and would make a most suitable son-in-law. But look at this—" she waved her arm around the room. "He has this flat." She glanced at David with a smile. "And you probably know what I found in that cupboard beside the

245

bathroom. I was looking for a towel; I thought that cupboard was the linen cupboard and I opened it. A very nice black lace nightie; a pair of slippers, all pink and fluffy." She laughed openly. "So, supposing I had got engaged, *formally* of course, with the correct ring and the correct announcements, to a man like George; supposing after a very correct period of waiting I got married in white, with engraved invitations and three hundred guests in the very best church—well, I know Mother and everyone would think it was all a most moral arrangement. A most excellent marriage. Tenderhearted ladies would weep with happiness for the bride. Mother would be delighted. Yet at the same time she would never want her daughter to have a second-hand husband. So what's logical in all that?"

David was still silent.

Penny said, "You see, darling, I've been thinking things out all week. If we are serious about each other, we must take ourselves seriously. Not let ourselves be persuaded by anyone or anything. We are our own conventions, our own morality. If we keep faith, then nothing we do is wrong. Do you believe that?"

"If I didn't, you would not be here now." He repeated slowly, "If we keep faith . . . " That was the whole foundation. "Without it, we can build nothing. And marriage is a house you build, not a hotel room you can rent and move into. It has to be well built, too. Not a ramshackle affair." He raised her face gently towards him, and bent forward to give her lips along, slow kiss. "Speaking as a man," he said at last, "I don't know a better start on that foundation than the proof you gave me tonight: you love me for nothing but myself. That is what all men want, and damned few get it." This time he kissed her with a violence that startled her. And then pleased her.

"And what do women want in love?" he asked. He watched her face, now. It was one of her greatest charms that her thoughts should sometimes be so unconsciously revealed by her expression.

"To be judged so wonderful in love that the man you love will never think of anyone else," she said at last. "You see, darling, if you were to stop loving me, it would be a dreadful confession of failure on my part. And women always like to think they are a success. Oh, David," she tightened her arms around his neck, "let's make it a good house. A strong and wonderful house, a lovely house."

"Yes," David said. "And to begin with, did I ever tell you

246

how many ways I love you, and why, and how much?"

"Never sufficiently. But, darling, we haven't finished discussing problems."

"Remember the poker!" David warned. "They can be discussed—what is left of them—in letters. What are letters for, anyway, except to say all the things you hadn't time to say when you were talking? And we have done enough talking tonight."

He rose suddenly, switched off the lamp on the table, and turned towards the window to open the curtains again. "Quotations seem in order," he said, looking at the stars. "I should now begin with Shakespeare and work down through the lesser poets. Or should I?"

"What are letters for anyway?" Penny asked, leaning her head back against the chair. "Besides, in letters we can always make the quotations word-perfect. Darling, do you remember how I used to quote chunks and chunks of poetry in my first letters to you? I was trying to show an Oxford man that I really might be educated, even if I did come from Scotland. I'd remember the first line or two, quite fairly. And then I cheated: I copied out the other lines from the texts. Sounds awful, doesn't it, but I was trying so hard .... And, at least, give me the credit for having the texts, and for knowing where to look in them."

"Scholars would say that was more important than having a parrot memory. They are purists, you see. Just as you are, but in a different direction." He came back to her. "In a very different direction, thank God." He paused, looking down at her.

The room's silence grew under the silvered light from the windows. The traffic in the street had now ceased. In the deep quiet, Penny looked up at David. She was startled for a moment. There's so much about men that I never knew, she thought in amazement; but if I am to be as happily married at the age of fifty as I am now, then I must learn. The age of fifty, viewed that way, seemed even attractive. David had taken hold of her hands. He was trying to be so impersonal, so impersonal, so thoughtful, that a wave of love flooded her heart and broke out into her smile.

"Tired, darling?" he asked.

"Yes," she said truthfully. And then, her smile deepening, "No."

He laughed. His momentary nervousness had gone.

"Darling," he said, with a sudden deep emotion which held

247

them together in a tightening grip. "I love you. I love you forever."

chapter xxx

DAVID's life at Oxford became austerely simple. He set himself to work with an intensity that surprised even Chaundler, who found himself in the strange position of advising a pupil to take things more easily. David would answer with a smile, "But it seems to agree with me, Walter." And Chaundler would have to admit to himself that Bosworth seemed happier than he had been last year, and that he was less worried and more sure of himself than he had been last month.

"Besides," David said one day, after another fatherly lecture by Chaundler on the wisdom of working with black coffee until four o'clock in the morning, "I have to make quite sure of this job with Fairbairn, you know." Walter Chaundler agreed, but he also suggested in that halting, quiet-voiced way of his that David was practically sure of it already. Fairbairn had lunched at length on two occasions, and had dined once, with David; and during these meetings—as Chaundler well knew, although David was not supposed to realize it—David's brains had been skillfully though subtly examined, and David's personality and capabilities had been carefully reviewed. So Chaundler contented himself by smiling, when David looked skeptical at such confidence and replied, patting the books he held under his arm, "Well, this is one sure way of making sure."

David had to make sure. There was the competition of Marain, for instance. Marain, until he had discovered that David was Fairbairn's possible choice in his search for talent in this year's crop of graduates, had been thinking of a career combining writing with politics. Now he suddenly decided that a job with Fairbairn would be interesting and useful, and entirely suitable for his own talents. His plan of campaign had been quite simple and direct. His uncle owned a small but important economic quarterly, which

Fairbairn would like to buy and build up into a monthly magazine. And although Marain would not work on the staff of his uncle's journal, for he was always scornful of nepotism, he somehow had no compunction about arranging a luncheon in town where he uncle played host to his nephew from Oxford and Mr. Fairbairn.

David learned about this luncheon from Burns. David and the American had come to know each other in an easy, casual kind of way, and Burns liked David enough to make a special visit to Mrs. Pillington's lodgings and drop the news about Marain in the middle of a conversation about Dos Passos.

David looked sharply at Burns, and then said as casually as possible, "Well, of course, Marain's a good man. Clever. Probably get a good First, if he will only allow himself to appear to work." He paused, trying to disguise the worry which this piece of news had started churning, and forced himself to say, "He would probably be very good in the Fairbairn job."

Burns looked at David with irritation. "Well, I wouldn't let myself be beaten with thoughts like that." Hell, he thought, I'd fight Marain every inch of the way. And no quarter. Marain has asked for it. Didn't Bosworth see that he had told him about this straw in the wind not as a piece of Oxford gossip but as a warning? Hell, didn't Bosworth know that he liked him? There was a real warmth in Bosworth that attracted Burns; if there were more Bosworths in Oxford, he wouldn't be so damned homesick for America. It was not the coldness of the climate but the coldness of the people which depressed him over here. You could never relax and stop worrying, either about the way you spoke or the way you liked to dress or the way you liked to eat. You could not be natural, without feeling you had to apologize for it. You couldn't even talk about being natural without someone quoting Oscar Wilde at you in a most unnatural voice—"The greatest affectation of all is that of being perfectly natural." You were always trying to behave as people expected you to behave. England expects . . . Quite, as they would say. And, he reflected as he watched David's impassive face, you might as well not waste your breath in warning an Englishman. For warnings implied knowledge that he did not possess and that, of course, was unthinkable. And if you were fool enough to make the gesture and waste your breath, what did you get? The glacier stopped moving a couple of inches each year and froze dead in its tracks.

"Stop worrying," David said with a smile. "I shan't."

Burns relaxed. He liked the look of that smile, the look in David's eyes which had been allowed to appear for a moment before it was hidden again. "Fine," Burns said, and he meant it even if he had to revise a nicely-building theory. He didn't object. If these people only knew, he wanted them to disprove the theories they aroused. He wanted to like them. The trouble was that few of them cared whether they were liked or not. Their attitude was that it was just too bad if foreigners didn't like them or behave as they did; too bad for the foreigners, of course.

Burns walked slowly over to the window, and stood there looking morosely down into the garden. "What was it like here all through Easter? This place must have been a graveyard then. Nothing but monuments left. Why didn't you take a week off and come to Paris with me? It's nice in the spring."

"Nice at any time. Not this Easter for me, though. Perhaps next year . . . " David glanced almost imperceptibly at Penny's photograph. "I'm hoping to break the back of this work by May. Then, if all goes well, I'll have a week end in town." And then, six weeks later, Finals. Thank God. His voice was casual. There was no hint of the trouble that had hindered his work so badly. Anyway, it was all over now. Margaret was living in a room near the School of Music, and had started classes there. By cutting his own expeness to the bare minimum, he had enough left of his scholarship money (together with Glendale Prize Essay money which he had won in January and the proceeds of the sale of the Cory's Walk furniture) to finance Margaret and himself until he started earning a regular salary.

But how long was it since he had seen Penny? It felt like years, years all the longer because the distance to London was so short: the next train would take him there in one and a half hours. He had to keep remembering Penny saying, in that serious way of hers when she was arguing out something inside her own mind, " . . . The only *intelligent* thing is that I should let you work in peace." Then she had sighed, tried to smile. "Oh, darling, how I *hate* doing the intelligent thing!" And then, as he had said nothing, only looked gloomily at her hands lying in his, she had said quickly, "But we'll have that week end in May as a kind of prize to cheer us along." Yes, it was the intelligent thing to do, but it also was hard. My sweet Penny, he thought now, as he looked openly at her photograph, you keep tying me to you in every unexpected way, without even knowing that you have got me bound hand and foot.

Burns was watching David. Time to move, he decided. The trouble was that the people you wanted to know were all so damned busy; and even if they were doing nothing, they had always those private little worlds of their own into which they would pop and leave you. Perhaps that was what made them seem so well worth knowing. *If* you ever could get to know them.

Burns crossed over to the door. "We must get together, sometime," he tried.

David said, "Yes." And then with a frankness and warmth that both astonished and pleased the American, he went on quickly, "I'd like that very much. This is a difficult year for me, you know. But after June is over, it will be different. I'll have time then to do the things I want to do. I'll be in London, and we'll get together. You are going to be here for another couple of years, aren't you?"

"If I don't freeze to death." Burns grinned widely. "I'd like to meet her, too," he said, looking at the photograph. "You're a lucky guy, Bosworth. It wouldn't be hard working for that." He saluted Penny as he went out.

David's thought echoed Burns's last remarks. He settled, still smiling, at his desk.

He looked at Penny's photograph, moved it so that she seemed to be looking directly at him, and picked up his pencil. The sheet of paper before him, fresh and white, invited clear headings, neat notes, numbered paragraphs. He opened the *Critique of Pure Reason*, forced himself to abandon romantic imaginings and concentrate on the unbroken page of small print. He began making notes, and as he wrote he felt a sense of pleasure. There was a lot of satisfaction in getting a job done as well as possible.

chapter xxxi

Penny was writing, too, at that moment. She looked around with a touch of pride as she noted the window measurements, and waited for Lillian Marston to verify them. This was her room. A few weeks ago, it had been an empty forlorn place on the top floor of one of the dingier houses in Fitzroy Square. But it was a quiet room at the back of the house, and its rent was a reasonable twelve shillings a week unfurnished, and it possessed two tall, wide windows. The Square, itself, was useful for quick, cheap shopping: Charlotte Street and the open-air markets lay near by; that was something to be remembered when one's free hours were regulated by a job.

Now it was hers, becoming less forlorn with each week. The shabby walls and woodwork had been disguised by a coat of pearl-gray paint, coconut matting in its natural shade made a modern-looking covering for the uneven floorboards. These had been the biggest expenses. The few pieces of furniture had been bought cheaply in Tottenham Court Road and transformed, by a good deal of sawing asunder, sandpapering and careful painting in the same soft shade of gray as the walls. And at last the important stage of curtains and coverings had been reached, and Marston's long arm was now obligingly measuring the height of the windows.

"If I could find a design in green and white, large enough to balance that size of window," Penny said, "then the place would really begin to look decent. Sort of formalized bamboo trees in green," she added, eyeing the coconut matting, "rather in the way the Douanier would have painted them."

"You must like your new job," Marston said with unconcealed amusement. "You are learning the jargon quite naturally. What is it like being an interior decorator?"

"I've no idea ... I only work in an interior decorator's office."

"I make this window almost two yards and one foot, again. Two yards and ten inches to be precise. From the top down to the window sill, that is. Doesn't Bunny let you try out any of your ideas? I know he *is* the boss, and a prima donna too, but still—he didn't just engage you as

252

a bookkeeper, did he?" Marston sat down on the topmost step of the ladder, and lighted a cigarette.

"No, but I'm still very much in the apprentice stage. I'm learning a lot, too. It really is quite an experience to see Bunny swing into form with his prize customers. They begin by retreating to the safe position of brown, and then they end by agreeing that off-white is the only possible setting. Although why people insist on off-white for a room in town, unless they are willing to keep the windows tightly shut and die of suffocation, is something I haven't quite solved."

"But it keeps decorators in business. If they weren't, then you wouldn't have this room, and you wouldn't be able to write home saying how wonderful everything is. You know, Lorrimer, I think your family must be quite frantic."

"Why?" Penny was finishing her calculations. "From the floor to the window sill is two feet. I'll need double width. That makes. . .Good Lord, Marston." She held out the notebook with her calculations.

"Put your little sums away, darling, and answer the nice lady."

"But they *can't* be frantic. I am not sleeping on the Embankment and I did find a job. Thanks to you, Lillian, and your friend Bunny Eastman. Really, you must have pestered him over that telephone until he had no breath left to say 'No.' I still feel guilty when I think of the jobs I couldn't find for myself, and of all the other girls still searching the newspaper columns each morning."

"Don't be so damned Scotch. You don't need to spoil the job by having guilt. I knew Bunny needed someone with a few brains attached. And he *isn't* a willing martyr to friendship. He can be as hard as nails, even if his hair waves and his voice curls. He is quite anesthetized to all women, so he is completely businesslike and unsentimental. In one way," Marston concluded, thoughtfully, "that's a Good Thing."

"Definitely," Penny agreed with a smile. "But you did make things easier for me, Lillian."

"Nonsense," Marston said brusquely. She was always embarrassed by thanks. "You still haven't given the proper answer to my question."

"About my people? But they can't possibly be worried about me. I'm happy. I never felt better in my life."

"Exactly. You should be miserable, you should hate all this worry and effort, you should be lonely and homesick. And instead you probably write letters filled with the joy of living. Do they write much to you?"

"My sister writes," Penny said shortly. Her face hardened for a moment. "She is bursting with curiosity."

"*And* with disapproval. She'll never forgive you for doing what she had not the courage to do. Here, Lorrimer, steady this brute while I climb down. I'm getting cramp up in this crow's-nest."

Penny held the stepladder, looked at the windows reflectively and said, "If I could find fifty-four-inch material and allowed—"

"Lorrimer! I love you dearly. But I have had quite enough work for one evening. Besides, you have probably decided everything already in your own little head, and I'd only give you advice you did not really need."

"Well . . ." Penny said, and then smiled. She couldn't deny that. She looked round the room again, seeing it as it would be when everything was in place. She would place the large plain table in front of the windows, and she would work there, so that the excellent top-floor light would come in leftwards. Against the wall which lay directly opposite to the windows and worktable there was the bed, low, without headboards, waiting for a simply tailored cover to make it look quite impersonal. In the center of the third wall there was a small fireplace, with a bookcase and an armchair (later, with luck, there would be another) which she would also cover once she found time and the right curtain material. The fourth wall was so broken by doors—one entrance, two cupboards—that all one could do with it was to put a low sideboard, painted gray, in the one decent-sized panel of space. Not even Marston had guessed that the sideboard was the base of a one-time kitchen dresser, whose top shelves, sawn off, now stood near the window wall to hold Penny's folios of drawings and the large books on art which never fitted into normal bookshelves.

"Well . . ." Marston echoed. She walked around the room. "I shouldn't say it was exactly cluttered with furniture."

"Of course, it isn't finished yet," Penny said.

"Of course." People were always funny about their houses and gardens: this was never the moment to see either of them—if only you had come next week, the rugs would have been down or the petunias would have really been blooming. Nothing ever was finished or completely perfect to the owner.

"I think it is all simply marvelous. But I'm afraid that when I live alone I'll just take a furnished room in a hotel."

"Expensive," Penny said.

254

Marston looked mildly surprised. "Oh, a *cheap* hotel, darling"

"Horrid."

"*Don't* be so realistic. Now, I suppose you'd like me to admire all the other improvements you have been making around here. Shall I make a tour of inspection of the kitchen, scullery and other offices?" Marston did not wait for an answer, but strolled out into the narrow landing. In an alcove there was a sink, a small gas oven and some narrow shelves.

Marston said, "Hm!" as she looked at the well-equipped shelves. "Domestic creature at heart, aren't you?"

"Thanks to Woolworth's," Penny said. "Now let me make some tea to show how well I can cook."

"And meanwhile I'll visit the other offices."

When she came back, she said, "Well, the abominable bathroom hasn't grown, but it looks altogether different. Don't make things too nice, Lorrimer, or you'll have the rent raised." She looked at Penny with concealed surprise, as she carried the tea tray into the room. "Perhaps you *did* find your right career after all, even if you got into it by accident."

Penny was pleased by Marston's praise. Marston had been first alarmed and then gloomy when she had seen this flat before Penny had actually decided to take it.

"My trouble is," Marston went on, "that I see things as they are and not as they could be. I expect the next time I come to see you, I'll be amazed by curtains and colors and things."

"Next time, I am going to ask Bunny Eastman to come along with you."

Marston sipped her tea thoughtfully. "That might be a good idea." She waited for the explanation, but Penny went on with careful unconcern:

"First, this room has to be ready. I have been doing it gradually. Partly because of lack of time, but mostly because of money. I got Bunny to pay my salary by the week: it makes things easier, to start with. I also used the remainder of my last quarter's dress allowance from my people. Later, I can start gathering some money to pay it back. I hated using it. It would have been such a grand gesture to hand it back intact. But I needed it, and you can't afford grand gestures when you are desperate. False pride is much too expensive, really."

"I've been ill-mannered enough to wonder how much all this *has* cost."

"Fourteen pounds and six shillings, so far. I am allowing myself twenty-five pounds, altogether. Which brings me to an idea I have been developing in the last two weeks. Have another cup of tea and I'll tell you about it."

"No sugar, this time. And no cake either, thank you. A horrible thing happened yesterday. I put on my black skirt and the waistband would scarcely fasten. It is all these dinners with Chris." Marston lit a cigarette, watched Penny pour out tea, and then said unexpectedly, "What amazes me most is the way you know exactly what you want. All these ideas and things... What is this one?"

Penny described it in detail, and over a third cup of tea they discussed it.

"Yes," Marston said, "it is good. But you'll never get Bunny to listen to it. His name is expensive and he'd rather die than lose *that* reputation. You'll see."

"He can start a new firm with a new name altogether to develop this idea. He won't lose by it, financially. That might sound attractive to him."

Marston smiled. "You know him quite well, already."

"And that is why, some day, you will bring him here for a glass of sherry. I shan't mention my idea at all to him, at first. I'll let him look around. Can't you see him, sitting in that armchair (which will look quite different with its cover in just the right shade to emphasize or contrast with the curtains), glancing around him while he pretends to notice nothing? If he says he likes it— 'I *do* like this, I really do. I *adore* it,'" Penny gave a good high-pitched imitation, and leaped up to stride about the room in the way Marston had seen the blond, beautiful Eastman do when his interest was excited. "'Most amusing. Definitely amusing'—then I shall start talking about the room. I'll give him the cost, analyzed, if he demands it. He will, if he is interested. And *then* I'll produce my idea about the new firm. We could give it a ham name like *Moderate Modern*. Oh... isn't that awful? Still, something like that. That will catch the fancy of people who have to furnish a house for less than Mrs. Whosit pays for her curtains or fireplaces alone. No one likes to think they are furnishing cheaply. 'Moderate' is a much soothing word, isn't it? But we wouldn't be bogus, for anyone who did come to us would have a pleasant house for their money. And they'd be all the happier for it, too. There is nothing more dismal than dull, stereotyped rooms: it makes people

256

into a pattern of dimness. The trouble is that unless you have lashings of money to spend on a house, it is almost impossible to have an exciting one. It's silly. Charm and taste don't, that is they shouldn't, depend on money. In fact, money often kills them. Funny, isn't it, how poverty or wealth can both kill taste? One, because it crushes people—you reach the stage when a loaf of bread on the table is more important than a vase of flowers on the window sill. And the other, because it takes away the need for any personal effort—you can hire people, can't you?"

"Yes, my sweet," Marston said with a smile. "But Bunny isn't given to philanthropy. And he would have to raise your salary. He couldn't go on paying you that miserable three pounds a week. He's an astute blighter, really: he only pays you so little because he knows that jobs are so scarce."

"Well, even if he did have to pay me more he wouldn't lose money. The idea would make some profit; I know it would. For there are far more people with little money to spend than there are with lots of money."

"But it all means a lot of work and effort for a comparatively small profit. Can you imagine Bunny's genius thriving on anything less than a guinea a yard? Can you imagine him giving up any time or thought to selecting good-looking designs and textures and colors for half a crown a yard, as you suggest? See, darling?"

"Yes. But I could do it. I'd love it. It would be fun beating the ramp on prices, and helping others to do it. I wouldn't decorate rooms of course, so Bunny need not fear that I'd steal any of his thunder. I'd just choose fabrics and furniture that looked good, and weren't expensive, and have them all there for the customers to select as they pleased. In any case, people ought to choose their own rooms, just as they choose their own clothes."

"That's heresy, if not blasphemy. Don't ever say that to Bunny or he will blow up into fragments. The only good taste is his taste. Or didn't you know?" Marston asked with mock gravity.

"Well, I suppose we all feel that way."

"You are much too loyal ever to succeed in the interior decorating business. Or any business. What are bosses for, except to sneer at? One good sneer a day keeps the doctor away." Lillian Marston laughed. Strange, she was thinking, how I always find being with Lorrimer such an easy way to spend an afternoon. Here I came up, all full of problems about Chris, and I've only mentioned him in asides as if everything were going swimmingly with us. Of course, it was really no good asking Lorrimer for advice: people who were happily in love always thought life was so simple and why aren't you like me, look, it's easy. Not so damned easy. Not by a long chalk.

"And what if Bunny doesn't like this room?" Marston said suddenly.

"I have thought of that, too. If he looks around, and then concentrates on his sherry—and at the end says, 'It is *too* divine, darling. Now, I must really run'—I shall say good-by with a sweet smile. And I'll say nothing at all about my idea."

"But you'll go on thinking about it."

"Of course. It *is* sound, isnt it? And I'd probably start going cuckoo if I had only clients at twenty-five shillings a yard to deal with in my job. Either cuckoo, or cynical like Bunny." She paused, hesitated, looked at Marston again, and then rose to get a large folder from the other end of the table. "Here is something else I've been wondering about," she said in a much too offhand manner. "Not very much here to show you, I'm afraid, as yet. But later, when I've more time ... They are designs for rooms, whole rooms, not just furniture and fabrics and colors."

Marston raised an eyebrow as she looked through the folder. "I'd like this one," she said in a mixture of surprise and pleasure. She held up the drawing and studied it from all angles. "Yes," she added, "I do like it. I'll have one like that, Lorrimer. But where do I find a house with such an excellent room ready for all these pleasant shapes and colors? Rooms are not built like that, my sweet." She shook her head regretfully, almost pityingly. "It would have been so nice."

"But supposing people who were about to build a house, or alter one, were to choose the kinds of rooms they wanted from these drawings? Then they could show them to their architect and say, 'Fit these rooms together and surround them with walls.' "

"And the architect would clap his hands with joy."

"If he's a good architect, he probably would be glad to find a customer who wanted an intelligent house."

"I've only one more touch of gloom to add, though. Ideas, even good ones, don't always work."

"We don't know that until we try them. If they don't work, then what is needed are better ideas obviously, and not less of them."

Marston smiled and rose, shaking down the skirt of her

black suit into its neat line, pulling the waistband round to the correct position on her elegant waist, patting the imagined extra inch in disapproval. "God," she said, "we're beginning to sound serious. How frightful! I must dash, I'm afraid. I have to dress. Chris is giving a party tonight. His aunt has just died and left him some money. Scads of it. Isn't it surprising what the old girls hoard up? Why don't you come along? There will be lots of people you know."

"Well," Penny began, "I—I have some things to do, you know. I—" The usual mixture of politeness and hesitation always gave her voice a slightly worried tone when she was trying to refuse an invitation. Marston never failed to be amused by this. Why worry about not doing what you didn't want to do, anyway? Really, Lorrimer could be so quaint at times.

"I'll make myself presentable," Marston said. "Where's that hidden boudoir of yours?" She opened the wrong cupboard door, and then the right one.

"How's your David?" she asked unexpectedly as she finished powdering. She watched Penny's face light up with sudden interest.

"He's well. I had a letter this morning." And one yesterday, and one the day before. Wonderful letters.... Wasn't Marston ever going to leave? Penny wondered.

"Don't you ever run out of things to say to each other?" Marston asked teasingly. "I suppose you are going to spend the whole evening quite happily writing a letter to him. Most touching." Her attitude had always been one of tolerant amusement combined with unexpressed liking for these two. At least, it had begun that way. But now, although she kept up the pretense of amusement, she was no longer so very amused.

Penny colored slightly and smiled. "It can be fun writing letters," she said.

"Not my cup of tea." There was the slight edge of irritation in her light voice.

"How is Chris?" Penny asked quietly, suddenly realizing she had been meant to ask about him from the start of this visit.

Marston shrugged her shoulders. "Oh, he's all right." She stubbed out her cigarette half-finished, and began pulling on her gloves with exaggerated care.

Penny looked at her friend in dismay. "I think Chris is charming."

"He can also be rather tiresome."

259

Penny said nothing, but she was thinking that Marston would not always be twenty-two, or look like Garbo.

"He has become so possessive recently. All this money from his aunt makes him dream of a nice place in the country and settling down. Can you imagine it? He is in such deadly earnest nowadays. To tell you the truth he is becoming rather a bore."

Penny began to speak, and then changed her mind.

"Now, what was that?" Marston said, her good humor returning.

"Don't you ever want to be married? You always seemed to have such a lot of fun with Chris."

Marston managed to produce a laugh. "How embarrassing we are becoming, like Buchmanites or something. What a quaint idea, Lorrimer. Of course everyone wants to be married. Some day. But not yet. Unless, of course, you have the luck to meet someone like your David, and then I suppose you grab him while you can."

"I didn't grab him." At least, not that way.

"Don't lose your hair over it, darling. After all, you are damned lucky. And you know it, old girl."

"I know it. But I never thought you did, Lillian. You always think I'm rather a fool about it all."

"I must admit that you could have a lot more fun than you do have. What harm is in that?"

"I probably wouldn't have David for very long."

"Nonsense, darling. You'd always have him. One sees that kind of man every now and again. It is easy to live with him: one has only to look at his wife to see that."

"And one always thinks how lucky she is."

Lillian Marston looked quickly at Penny's expressionless face. Was she being sarcastic? How odd, for Lorrimer. "Isn't she?" Marston asked sharply.

"Of course. And perhaps he is lucky too, although it may take other men to see that. But there is something more than luck attached. Oh yes, I agree, the first meeting is a matter of pure luck. But after that, it is something else."

"Is it? Darling, I'm boring you. We are talking in circles. Besides—" She glanced at the wrist watch which Ronald had given her last year. She still wore it, not from any sentimental reason although Chris never quite seemed to believe that, but because it was such a pleasure to look at its charming design. "Oh, I'm late. . . . I must fly." Her voice returned to its naturally light tone, and she gave Penny one of her slow controlled smiles. "Don't worry about me, darling. Life is really very gay and amusing—if you don't think about it. Don't forget to ask me to that party for Bunny. I'd adore watching his concealed emotions. But don't make this place too attractive, or he will think you must be overpaid."

Penny was smiling again. "Oh, he isn't such a monster as that, Lillian."

"Darling, he is the kind of man who calculates whether his friends are worth a five- or a ten-shilling dinner before he asks them out." Marston picked up her handbag, took one last look at herself in the mirror, and said, "Now don't work too hard. After all, no room is worth too much effort. And it will look marvelous, I'm sure, once you get the smell of turpentine out of it. What does David think of all this?"

"He hasn't seen it yet. He is coming here some time in May."

"You know," Lillian Marston said, half-teasingly, half-accusingly, "I'd like to meet him properly some time."

"Of course you will," Penny said conventionally, but she must have also shown some embarrassment—she remembered David's point-blank refusal to meet any of her friends meanwhile: *I've little enough time with you to waste it on other people*—for Marston jumped to the obvious but wrong conclusion.

"Oh, don't worry, Lorrimer," she said with amusement. "You know he will be perfectly safe. I have my rules, you know. I never poach on my friends' preserves."

That was what was known as a good exit line, Penny thought, as the door closed and Lillian's footsteps began their promised flying: there was no answer one could think up in time. But as Penny walked over to her table, and cleared a space for writing-paper and elbowroom, she was thinking of several replies. "I suppose David wouldn't be safe if she hadn't her little rules? I suppose he would fall for her if she decided to raise an eyebrow? Of all the—" Her sense of humor began to reassert itself. She was even smiling broadly as she dated her letter. And then she began to laugh. The only thing that spoiled this joke was the fact that she couldn't tell it to David, somehow. She stopped laughing then.

She rose and walked restlessly around the room. The open cupboard door reminded her to close it, but she paused there for a minute to look at her reflection in its mirror. What am I, who am I, that a man should love me forever? Why should I expect such happiness, so much more than many girls ever get? Am I as vain and selfish in my way as

Lillian Marston is in hers? She stared at the reflection facing her so seriously. Her eyes were tired with worry and too little sleep. Her hair was untidy; she found a comb and tried to make it look better, but tonight it wouldn't go the way she wanted it. "You look a fright," she told herself cruelly. Why, she thought again, should I expect so much from life? She closed the door quickly, and walked back to the table. She brushed the sudden tears from her eyes with the back of her hand. Stupid, she accused herself; you are overtired.

After a space, when she could start thinking again, she knew the real reason. It was this separation. If she could see David, she wouldn't have these attacks of gloom. If she could hear his voice, she would be confident again.

She picked up his letter and began reading it. She could feel the sudden attack of doubt and depression lifting from her heart. "I *am* hearing his voice," she told herself. She could even hear the urgency of his words. *Keep writing me, Penny. Tell me you love me over and over again. Tell me in fifty different ways. Keep telling me.* He too was never sure: he too wanted reassurance.

She remembered their last night together. She had awakened at dawn to feel his arm around her waist, to find him raised on one elbow, leaning over her, looking down at her, watching her as he had drawn her out of sleep. He had not moved, had kept looking at her, searching her eyes with his. At last, he had said quite simply, "Why? Why, Penny?" She had smiled, stirring happily in his arms, not knowing what to say. There were a hundred reasons, big and little. Where could she begin? Then she had put her arms around him and drawn him down to be kissed. "Because I love you," she had said, and kissed him again.

When we are together, she thought, a look or a touch is all that is needed to reassure us. But when we are apart, we need all the courage that only words can bring. He feels that, too. And realizing that, she was happier again: if they were both in need of reassuring, then that was good. That way, they would never forget the miracle of being loved.

She began to write. There was a soft, warm smile on her lips as the words flowed on smoothly. This was her first real love letter in the true sense of the word. It had taken a long time to find courage enough for it, she thought. How afraid we all were, and out of fear how we held back what should be given without asking. And as she wrote, it seemed as if her thoughts filled the room with the warmth of memories recalled, with the excitement of future hopes. Its loneliness had vanished.

chapter xxxii

By MAY full summer had come that year. It astounded and delighted foreign visitors and added another topic of conversation to English dinner tables. A poor view was taken of the drought—in the Cotswolds, cottagers were fetching water by the bucket from far-off wells—and of this appalling heat-wave with the temperature soaring around seventy-six degrees. (People who tried to introduce a description of Singapore or of New York in summer were politely listened to, but equally silently disbelieved.) Penny was much too occupied to worry about the weather and enjoyed the luxury of open windows and the view of green leaves, already at midsummer growth, on the back gardens' trees. She had become accustomed to the breathless quality of London air. She would probably shiver now in Edinburgh's bracing climate.

Strange how we adapt ourselves quickly, she thought. Last May, my whole life was centered round Edinburgh. Now, it is here. And things, which I hadn't even dreamed of then, are opening up before me. She thought of her first ambitions, and found she was smiling at herself. It was such an obvious reaction to want to live on the Continent in romantic places and become a great painter. Instead, there was that folder growing richer with designs, more carefully worked over than when Marston had seen them. And there was this room, at last completed and ready for her visitors this week (Lillian Marston and Bunny were to be the first—they were coming this afternoon), which had given her a very practical lesson in her new career. For now it was more than a job of work which gave her economic freedom; now it was the beginning of a career. Bunny Eastman would decide that today. Or would he? If he didn't like her ideas, then someone else might some day.

Penny, arranging sherry glasses and decanter on the birch tray, paused to admire the natural grain of the wood and its silver blond coloring. She was smiling at herself again: last May, she would never have had the thought that an idea can go on to live after others reject it. Last May, she would have accepted Bunny's refusal or his scorn. Now she would question it and act on the answer she would find. Still, she was nervous: rejections were always depressing, even if you didn't accept them as the final verdicts.

She tried the tray in two different places, decided it looked best in a third. She arranged the deep yellow roses on the mantelpiece for the fourth time. She gave a last practical look around the room. I love it, she thought happily. She danced across the room, sang five high' notes of no song in particular, and ended with a full circle swing on one foot. Happy, happy Penelope, she thought, and danced for an imaginary David. He is coming on Friday, on Friday, she sang. And then she heard footsteps on the stairs. She stood breathless, collecting her delightfully scattered wits, and then she dashed to the cupboard, catching a glimpse of her face in the mirror before she closed its door once more. Yes, it is he who brings the stars to your eyes, she thought.

When Marston knocked and called a casually cheerful greeting, Penny was seemingly calm again. She opened the door, concealing, with some difficulty, her pride in ownership. Even Marston, although she had hardly expected Penny to be placarded with "All My Own Work," was surprised at the perfect offhand welcome. And then, as she entered the room somewhat dubiously with Ernest Boniface Eastman, she was still more surprised. "Well!" she said, and both eyebrows went up. She had taken care to tell Bunny before they reached Fitzroy Square that really Lorrimer must have been quite mad to have chosen such an impossible flat, and she had described it accurately as she had first seen it. Her eyes met Penny's, and there was an amused glint in them.

If the strategy was good, the tactics were superb. Penny talked of everything and anything except the room. Bunny, his long legs curled round each other, his thin greyhound body slouching half-sideways in the armchair, now covered in dark green linen to pick up the leaf color in the curtains, rested one hand against a slightly drooping head and balanced a glass of surprisingly good sherry in the other. This was his favorite attitude when he was charmed—"the wilting-rose position" Penny called it. Suddenly, as he finished his fourth glass of Bristol Cream, he could bear this no longer. He leaped up. He leaned an elbow on the mantelpiece, and stood there for a moment. No detail in the room escaped him. Probably cost next to nothing, probably no more than a hundred quid all told. Still, most people would not guess that: it took the professional eye to add up the cost.

"I *do* like this, I really do," he began.

Marston bent her head to search for matches in her

handbag. Now we're off, she thought. She lit a cigarette, and looked at Penny with increasing respect. If only she doesn't become too serious, Marston hoped. But Penny was suiting herself admirably to Bunny's tempo. "Moderate Modern" was explained, lightly, gaily, practically, and she even avoided arousing Bunny's petulance. But he was, as Marston had predicted, extremely wary.

"Amusing," he was saying, "yes, an amusing idea. But, my dear, I simply haven't the time. Or the energy. Life is crushing enough as it is. Imagine sweating over designs and colors at five shillings a yard, when the amount of creative energy put into them should bring eighteen-and-six at least."

Penny looked at her curtains pointedly. "One-and-ninepence a yard," she admitted frankly, and then smiled with all her charm. "But you wouldn't be spending your energy on designs for this idea. That would be a shocking waste of your time." She cleared her throat, and kept her eyes determinedly turned away from Marston. "No, Bunny, the good cheap materials are all there, ready for sale, just waiting to be picked out from the bad cheap materials. All one has to do is to think of using them differently. These curtains of mine are made of material which was sold for dresses, which would have been hideous; but it is all right for curtains. Of course, the whole room was done on practically nothing. *You* would see that at once."

Bunny acknowledged that fact modestly.

"Thirty-one pounds," Penny said, "and that includes pots and pans and things. Thirty-one pounds, two-and-ninepence, to be exactly exact."

Bunny's usual quick phrase was somewhat slow in coming. Then he said with a bright smile, "Yes, that was more or less what I guessed." He looked round the room once more. "Amusing, really."

The visit ended with Bunny still resisting slightly, but obviously attracted to the idea. It would take three or four weeks before Penny would learn whether it had been successfully presented to him or not. And then, if he did accept the idea and financed a new branch of his firm, with quite a new name, to cater for people who had more taste than excess money, Penny would probably have to fight in her own way to keep the idea as she had imagined it.

"So far, so good," said Lillian Marston, after Bunny had left with protestations of regret at having to simply tear himself away. "He never makes a song and dance out of his good-bys unless he feels rather good about something. I think you hooked him, sinker and all. But why didn't you show him the folder?"

Penny, busy clearing the overflowing ash trays, straightening the cushions where Bunny had slumped all over them, poured another glass of sherry for Marston. "Here, you deserve this," she said, bringing over the glass to Marston. "The folder—Frankly, I thought he had as much as he could swallow at one time."

Marston regarded her curiously. "You know, you get on surprisingly well with him. Do you really like him?"

"As much as he likes me. Which is limited, of course, for he is a limited kind of man. I suppose we do get on quite well together. You see, he isn't afraid of me."

"Is he afraid of me?" Marston asked.

"Terribly," Penny said with a wide smile.

"You make me sound like a predatory female," Marston said lightly, and rose to go. She thought she was changing the subject when she asked, "When is your David coming to see all this?" she waved a graceful hand around the room.

"This week end," Penny said, and then regretted her frankness for no thinkable reason at all. "My grandfather is arriving tomorrow," she added quickly. "And Bunny has given me the afternoon off. Isn't that marvelous?"

"Amazing," Marston said. "And your grandfather is coming all the way from his island?"

"Well, he is really going to visit Oxford. He and Walter Chaundler are thinking of collaborating on another book, you know. But of course he is spending a day or two in London to see me."

"An emissary from the family? An advance scout, as it were?"

"Quite possibly."

Marston caught some of the anxiety which lay behind the brief answer. "Oh . . . Well, he is bound to see that you are happy here." Happy. There was that word again, blast it. It had slipped out as usual. She went on quickly, concentrating on the room, "Now I begin to see how you must have hated Baker House. I really wouldn't mind having a place like this, myself. Bunny was very acute when he said that you had given it some of your charm."

She was relieved to see Penny's smile come back. She glanced at her watch. "Late again," she said cheerfully. "I am meeting Chris for dinner." And then, with comic emphasis on dark omen, "We are going to Have It Out, tonight."

But later, in the street, she felt a touch of irritation. Why did she always have to bring in the word "happy" when she was talking to Penelope Lorrimer? Of course she didn't want a room like that, or a life like that. Then why say it? Poor old Penny, she thought and felt better. Poor old Penny, she had to be cheered up some way: she had undertaken far too much. My rôle, Lillian Marston thought, will become more and more depressing: Lord, how awful to have condemned myself to a future of acting the sympathetic aunt. God, I couldn't bear it. When David and Penny break up, I'll disappear on a holiday to the Continent or something. I couldn't bear it.

chapter xxxiii

THE first greeting was affectionate, but restrained. They both said, much too politely, how well each was looking, and how were they? Dr. MacIntyre then walked about the room, pretending he was stiff after so much sitting in a train. Without any comment, he noticed Penelope's drawing board with a half-finished design tacked to it, her bookcase with its well-filled shelves, the reproductions of Utrillo and Rousseau on the walls, and David's photograph on the table beside her work. She was nervous, he realized as he turned away from the photograph, and that too depressed him. He did not like London, he hated nowadays the fuss of traveling, and he had left his last two chapters in very bad shape on his desk in the study of Inchnamurren. For weeks now, his daughter's worried letters had invaded the peace of his island. And, if only to stop their dirge, he had visited Edinburgh. There, in spite of a lot of discussion (once Moira and Betty were out of the room), he was still no nearer to understanding the problem of his favorite granddaughter. "I shall go and see Penelope," he told Mary and her husband finally. "And that is what you both ought to have done weeks ago."

But now, watching his granddaughter, he suddenly realized why Mary had been so worried over her. It was *not*, as he had been told in Edinburgh so repeatedly, that Penelope needed advice and help, that she was living in great un-happiness, carefully disguised in her letters out of pride and pigheadedness. But rather, it was only that Mary had begun to realize that Penelope was now in no need of advice or help, that the child-parent relationship had been broken, and would never be resumed. He was beginning to wish he had never attempted the journey at all. I am a curious interferer, he thought: that is how I must seem, and that is how I feel.

He sat down in the green armchair, and elbowed a yellow cushion out of his way. "Hm!" he said in some surprise, "comfortable!" That was his only remark about the room.

Penelope sat down on the floor, as she always used to do when she came to see him in his study. There she was, wearing a neat black suit instead of a sweater and skirt, looking thinner, paler, but somehow prettier. Pretty? Stupid word. She was reaching beauty, now. And no woman ever looked beautiful unless she had some inner happiness. Beauty was not a surface quality. He studied her covertly. She was not so anxious now. There was even a hint of amusement in the deep blue eyes watching him so steadily. As if they were saying, "This is a joke which you and I are sharing without even needing to tell it." The little monkey, he thought with affection and pride, and smiled openly.

"Well," he said, looked around the pleasant room, looked back at Penny, and then drew his pipe out of his pocket and stretched his legs comfortably. Penny relaxed too.

"This is wonderful," she said, her eyes sparkling with delight. "How *glad* I am to see you!" She rose, hugged him, and then sat down once more in front of him, her legs sideways, her right arm supporting the weight of her body, her left hand clasping her ankles. She wore a plain signet ring on its third finger. She began to talk, answering his questions, plunging with all her old enthusiasm and frankness into the details of her new life—her work, her friends, her interests, what she had seen and done since she came to London, the Slade, Baker House, this room, the new ideas which her job had stimulated. Her grandfather listened crit-ically, but he was surprised in spite of himself. He was glad now that he had made this journey to London. She has not thrown away her chances, as Mary and Charles insisted. She was developing new ones, through new influences, that was all.

He purposely kept off the subject of David. It was em-barrassing anyway to think that the girl, still so much the

Penny he had known at Inchnamurren, had become a woman. It is always a shock to older people, even to the most sympathetic, to realize that the children they have loved are now capable of a quite different kind of love.

But the subject of David did crop up, and afterwards Dr. MacIntyre was inclined to consider it had been no accident.

Penny had been talking about painting, and about the present dominance of the French schools. She was beginning to believe that to repeat their techniques, to try to paint in their manner, might produce an adept canvas, but at best it was only being an echo. "If there is anything of real value in a painter," she was saying, "he has got to find his own expression. He should *learn* from others, but he shouldn't become an echo, or a part of a fashion. That is true of poetry, too. Perhaps that is what is so wrong with so many young poets, today. They *must* be in the fashion, even if it kills their own natural inspiration. It is the thing today to write uglily, they seem to persuade themselves. So let us have no more beauty. That would date us: we'd be called Georgians or something equally damning. As if beauty could ever be outdated."

"Poets reflect the times," her grandfather said. "The world is ugly and harsh, today." He was listening with concealed amusement, a touch of pride, and much pleasure. Where had she picked up that idea? he wondered.

"*Anyone* can see that. We need the poets to show us the beauty that still exists, however hidden. That's what poets are for. . . ."

She looked, and looked naturally enough as her grandfather had to admit, at the top row of the bookcase beside the armchair.

"I see you've been collecting some poetry, there," he said as his glance followed hers. "Isn't that something new for you?"

His hand went out automatically, and he picked up a volume, and let the pages ripple slowly through his fingers. He halted at the group of poems called *Michael Robartes and the Dancer*. Yes, he was thinking, let a poet clothe his conceptions with new images of striking beauty. Let him give richness and life to his ideas, phrased in such sound that those of us who listen will remember their music. Penny had said *That's what poets are for. . . . Yes, that is what poets* are for.

His eyes paused at *The Second Coming,* and he turned

over no more pages but let himself read it once more, silently, slowly:

> Turning and turning in the widening gyre
> The falcon cannot hear the falconer;
> Things fall apart; the centre cannot hold;
> Mere anarchy is loosed upon the world,
> The blood-dimmed tide is loosed, and everywhere
> The ceremony of innocence is drowned;
> The best lack all conviction, while the worst
> Are full of passionate intensity.
>
> Surely some revelation is at hand;
> Surely the Second Coming is at hand.
> The Second Coming! Hardly are those words out
> When a vast image out of *Spiritus Mundi*
> Troubles my sight: somewhere in sands of the desert
> A shape with lion body and the head of a man,
> A gaze blank and pitiless as the sun,
> Is moving its slow thighs, while all about it
> Reel shadows of the indignant desert birds.
> The darkness drops again; but now I know
> That twenty centuries of stony sleep
> Were vexed to nightmare by a rocking cradle,
> And what rough beast, its hour come round at last,
> Slouches towards Bethlehem to be born?

Penny let him read and said nothing; and because she saw that something had moved him deeply, for when he was finished he let the book lie on his lap for a moment, his eyes fixed broodingly before him, she did not even dare ask what poem it had been. Then he suddenly closed the book, replaced it quickly in its narrow place on the shelf beside another volume of Yeats and was once more back with her in the room.

She said, "David has been giving me these books. I am sure he thinks—although he has never actually said it, of course—that I don't read enough poetry. So this is his way of propagandizing me."

"And does it work?"

She smiled and nodded, and then she laughed. "Yes," she admitted.

Dr. MacIntyre lit his pipe very carefully. And then, as his silence became too obvious, and Penny would not speak, he was forced to say, "And how is David?"

And that was the way in which the subject of David and Penny was introduced. Now, Dr. MacIntyre asked no more questions, but let her tell him what her good sense chose to tell. He had only to watch Penelope, to listen to the earnestness behind her words, to see the light in her eyes when she talked of David or the worry there when she spoke of her family, to know that she was neither irresponsible nor thoughtless. That was what he had wanted to know.

Now, he realized that this "affair," as Mary and Charles Lorrimer would insist on calling it, was not something flaunted as a piece of youthful bravado. "Temporary affair," Charles had said, emphasizing both words bitterly. Temporary was the one word which Dr. MacIntyre, himself, would not have forgiven.

"So you see, Grandfather—" Penny ended. She left her words there, adding nothing. She was watching him anxiously.

He measured his words carefully. "I see that you have a considerable enthusiasm for this young man," he remarked dryly. And my journey is not yet over, he reminded himself. I shall have no peace of mind now until I see David Bosworth, to discover for myself if his enthusiasm for Penny is equally considerable and permanent. That is all I want to feel. Then I shall write Mary and Charles that the only thing they should worry over is this refusal of theirs to let Penelope and David be married. "Now, what about some fresh air? I always feel suffocated in London," he said, and rose to his feet.

Penny suggested Hampton Court. "I was there in March with David," she said. "You'll get plenty of fresh air. I remember I caught a cold." She spoke the words happily, as if catching a cold could be an enjoyable experience.

"I haven't been there for almost thirty years," her grandfather admitted. "But if you have visited it so recently, you'll make a very good guide."

"I'll be responsible for the geography," Penny promised, "if you, as the historian, will supply the dates."

But strangely enough, once they did arrive out at Hampton Court, Penny was not a very good guide. Her memory, usually clear and accurate, seemed to have deserted her. Faced with Clock Court, Base Court, Fountain Court, Chapel Court, Round Kitchen Court, she became bewildered. And inside the Palace of almost a thousand rooms she was even less capable. From the Colonnade at the south end of the Clock Court, she led her grandfather up a large noble staircase which surely was the approach to the Great Hall. Instead, they found themselves in an oak-paneled room surrounded by weapons.

"Well," her grandfather said philosophically, "I suppose I

271

had to see the King's Guard Room, anyway. Much more important than the Great Hall, I'm sure. Now we shall try for Queen Anne's Drawing Room and end up in Henry the Eighth's Wine Cellar."

Penny looked at him ruefully. "I'm awfully sorry," she said. She was remembering that her grandfather prided himself on wasting no time if he had to go sight-seeing. Once he had suggested that the *New Oxford English Dictionary* should bring its definition of tourist more up to date. *Tourist:* a man who gets lost, a man with shortening temper, a man with sore feet. *Cf. detour—*.

"Not at all," he said with a smile as if he were highly enough amused by an idea, now forming, about her last visit here. "And this kind of sight-seeing really is a great improvement over the usual variety: this has all the joy of the unexpected."

"I *do* remember the Board Walk and the gardens and the Tijou Screen," Penelope protested. She added, with a smile to match her grandfather's, "Once I find them, that is."

They did, eventually, with the help of a guidebook and directions from two guides.

"There's the screen of panels," Penny said with relief, looking towards the set of tall wrought-iron gates leading to the river.

"Extremely sharp memory, considering how unobstrusive they are."

Penny's cheeks reddened, and there was an amused apology in the way she glanced at him.

Then she settled her arm comfortably on her grandfather's, and paced slowly with him through the gardens. "At least," she remarked appeasingly, "you are getting fresh air."

"Is that what it is? I was puzzled for a moment."

Penny thought: Everything is all right. He isn't angry with me about David. He never is angry when he starts teasing me... She smiled at her grandfather. He was walking, she suddenly noticed, more slowly than she remembered.

He was saying, "Now that I have begun this journey, I shall probably make the most of it. I am going to Oxford to see Chaundler, probably for a week or two. Then, I shall go to Paris to see Latisse at the Sorbonne. There are some points about the summing-up in my book which I want to discuss with him. Then I shall return to London by July. Unless I am tempted to take a little trip with Latisse into the

Beaune country. That might help to inspire me in that lecture at the Sorbonne if I *am* asked to give it."

"Will you see David in Oxford?" Penny asked.

"I hope so. You told me he was working hard, but perhaps he can spare an hour or so for me."

"Of course he will. He wants to see you, I know."

"That was what he said in his last letter to me." Dr. MacIntyre paused, and then asked quite simply, "When are you going to see him next?"

Penelope looked squarely at her grandfather. "He is coming to London this week end," she said. "Then after that, I shan't see him until his Finals are over."

"And then?"

"We have still to discuss that. We shall probably make the decision this week end."

"I hope it will be the right one, Penelope."

"What *is* 'right'? Right for Mother and Father? Or right for David and me?"

Dr. MacIntyre hesitated. "It is a pity—" he began and then halted.

"Yes, I know. There did not have to be any choice like this. It was forced on us."

"Out of the best of motives, remember: your father and mother love you."

Penny was silent. "I know," she said at last. "That is what makes everything so very difficult, so. . ." Her voice trailed away in dejection. She watched the white and yellow butter-flies fluttering so undecidedly over the green lawn and its wide border of flowers. Then her voice hardened, and there was her first touch of bitterness when she said: "They have had strange ways of showing their love recently. They don't even write, but set Moira to find out what she can about me through her letters. Why don't they write, themselves? Why don't they realize that even if they were back in the days of shutting up a daughter in an attic room with bread and water, I still wouldn't change my mind?"

"Now, now, Penelope," he said sharply. "When you have children of your own, you will begin to understand all the things that worried your parents when you were young. Frankly, I never appreciated my mother and father until I had to sit up night after night with Mary, when she was three years old and had diphtheria. It was then I remembered being five, myself, and having my father sit up with me when I had scarlet fever. Yes, I began to understand a lot of things then."

"But, Grandfather, I am no longer a child. And that is what Mother and Father forget."

I warned Mary last summer about that, Dr. MacIntyre thought; I told her that she must stop being so possessive towards the children.

"You are angry with me," Penny said anxiously.

"No, Penny. Not angry. Worried, certainly."

"Please don't. Not you too." She looked abruptly away from him, stared fixedly at the garden. The rose trees, in perfect formation, advanced and retreated through the mist of tears over her eyes. *Alice in Wonderland* rose trees, round circles on straight lines, and frantic gardeners splashing paint to turn them red. A rose is a rose, and by any name. All that matters is appearances... Grandfather couldn't be one of the people who thought like that.

He patted her arm awkwardly, knowing then how much he could hurt her. *Not you too.* If he failed her, like the others...

"I'm sorry, my dear. We who are old forget so very easily that young people are capable of dealing with life by themselves. They don't need us as much as we should like to believe." He paused, and then asked, "You *are* confident?"

"I know what I am doing," Penny said slowly. She was groping for words to explain what she felt. "There are some things in life which men and women have got to decide for themselves. Not impulsively. Arguing it all out, really believing in what they do. Isn't that true?"

"Yes," her grandfather agreed. It was equally true that those who did not argue their actions out, for themselves and by themselves, lost control of their own life. Even the first decision of a four-year-old child, whether to tell a lie and escape punishment or to be truthful and take the consequences (a hard decision, for the right one meant pain and the wrong one meant no reproof), went towards building the future man or woman.

He suddenly realized that Penny was speaking again. "I'm sorry, my dear," he said. "I digress mentally, nowadays. Something is said, and I agree or disagree, but that isn't enough, it seems. I must go wandering off." He smiled. "What was it you were saying?"

"I was saying that sometimes in life there's a crisis forced on us."

"Not sometimes. Always. At repeated intervals."

"If we accept it, don't fight against it, we may have

274

tragedy. And we have only ourselves to blame. I mean—Oh, I am putting this so badly."

"Give me a practical example," suggested Dr. MacIntyre shrewdly. "Take David and yourself, for instance."

"Well, we could have been separated by our families. If we had accepted that, then we would always have regretted what we had lost. I mean, if we hadn't made sure that nothing was going to separate us, if we hadn't—I mean—"

"You mean that you were faced with what might have been the elements of tragedy? And that, by adjusting your lives to beat them instead of accepting them, you have averted the tragedy? But what of other things—what of worry, malicious gossip, scandal? They could mean tragedy, too."

"The only *real* tragedy would be to forget the value of what David and I have together."

"Did David say that, or is it you?" Dr. MacIntyre asked with a wry smile. He had been hearing echoes of David all afternoon. As it should be, of course: two people fell in love, and if they were to stay in love, then a third personality, a joint one to which they each contributed, was created between them. No doubt when he saw David in Oxford, he would see this third personality shaping, too. If he didn't, then he would have real cause to worry about his grand-daughter.

"David," she admitted. "But I came to believe that too, in my own way, in my own time. So we are both saying it to you. We believe it. And each day we are together proves it. And all the days we aren't together prove it, too. That is why I said that it could only be our decisions that mattered. We are happy when we are together, we are miserable without each other. Only we can know how much."

"I see," he said gently. He suddenly wished that he could live to see what his Penelope and her David made of their lives. . . . Then he realized that, even by this regret, he was expressing his confidence in them.

He said happily, "Well, anyone listening to us this afternoon could tell that one of us was very young and one of us was very old."

"Why?" Penny slackened her pace to match his as they turned to leave the gardens.

"Because we have been talking about Life. What is the next subject up for discussion? Religion?"

Penny laughed, pressing his arm. "I want to hear all about Inchnamurren. I shan't be able to visit it this summer, you know." Never again shall I have the long days there, she thought. Long holidays were a thing of the past, which you put away with your childhood, lazy unhurried days in a magic place. "How are the seals? Do they still lie on the black rocks on the white sands?" And the sun, sinking slowly from the wide flaming sky, leaving on the horizon a searing line of red for one moment as it slipped into the Atlantic waters. And the waves, no longer roughly beaten copper but suddenly dark and cold as lead, with fading purple lights... And as you turned back to the village, the west wind behind you, the taste of salt spray still on your lips, the last gulls silenced in the darkness, there was the low moon rising over the red cliffs of Loch Innish to welcome you. And the arm of the sea, flung round the island, was silvered and black. "Tell me about Inchnamurren," she said.

And she knew by the way he talked so easily, telling her affectionately of the things she wanted to know, that he had decided for David and for her.

chapter xxxiv

DAVID paid off the taxi, trying to appear nonchalant. Yes, this was the Square, this was the number. But as he stood looking at the house, his heart beat with sudden unsteadiness and his excitement, so controlled on the journey from Oxford, now mounted.

She won't be home yet, he reminded himself. You are early.

A middle-aged, untidy woman with a stained apron covering her skirt came up from the basement to let him enter the hall. "Third floor back," she said. She was too tired even to be curious. But he didn't need the directions. He had imagined it a hundred times. He mounted the steep narrow staircase, taking two or three steps at a time. Then on the top landing, facing the door with its neatly printed card, looking at the name, he paused.

She won't be home yet, he told himself again. For a moment, as he raised his hand to knock on the door, he had the cold fear that she wasn't there and wouldn't ever be, that the card with her name was a lie, that she had left and never would return. Then he heard her voice saying, "One moment. Who is it?"

"David," he answered. And she was there, as he remembered her. She wasn't just a dream to soften a lonely night, to ease him into sleep. She was there, and his arms were around her, and her hair had the same soft perfume, her skin had the same touch of silk.

"Oh, Penny." He held her close and closer to him, straining the young soft firm body against his, tightening his grip as if he would never let her go. He kissed her again, feeling her arms around his neck, her lips answering his. Her eyes were shining.

It's true, he thought, it is all true. He relaxed, loosening his grip on her waist, sliding his hands along her arms to grasp her hands. He stood back to look at her. "Hello, my beautiful," he said.

She laughed, uncertainly, with a catch in her throat. "Hello darling," she said, and she hid her face in his shoulder.

"Well, I hope it's happiness," he said half-worriedly, half-comically, and succeeded in making her laugh. He drew her towards the nearest armchair, pulled her gently onto his knee, and reached for a handkerchief. "Blow hard," he told her. "That's better." But he was still worried. "Now what was that all about?"

"I'm just happy, darling." She was smiling now as she tucked the handkerchief back into the cuff of his sleeve. "It hit me suddenly: I realized then how lonely I had been without you, David."

He smoothed her hair with his cheek and tightened his arm around her waist as she tried to rise. "Relax, darling. Let me enjoy myself," he said.

"But David, look at me! I haven't finished dressing. We'll be late."

"So we shall." But he made no move to release her. Her hair was loose as if she had been brushing it, and had not yet had time to comb it into place. She wore a dressing gown of some kind of dull gleaming cloth, smooth to the touch. "So we shall," David repeated firmly, and tightened his arm still more.

"The concert?" Penny asked.

Two tickets were standing proudly on the mantelpiece. In Oxford, planning this evening, it had been an attractive idea to write, "Let's have dinner at Giovanni's; you shall wear your smartest dress. And it might be an idea to try for tickets to that Queen's Hall concert. I see Sargent is to conduct the Holst, and I've always wanted to be with you when you first heard it. The London Choir is singing, too; the effect should be *astronomisch* indeed."

But now he wondered why he should ever have been so insane as to suggest any plans. They weren't needed. Not with Penny. Just to be with her was plan enough. He kissed her hair and then the side of her brow, gently lifting her face so that it turned upwards to him, and his mouth followed the line of her cheek to her lips, resting there, owning them, declaring his love more fully than a thousand words could ever do. He felt her body stir gently in his arms, and his murmured name was lost in the long kiss.

They arrived at the concert at the end of the interval. ("*The Planets* are last on the program, anyway," David had said. "What is played first doesn't usually matter. It is generally *Oberon* or *Leonora No.* 3.")

They raced into the Queen's Hall, hand in hand, and then slackened their pace to a decorous walk down the aisle towards their seats. An excitement stirred in their blood which was not merely the sharing of the expectant tension around them. The crowd and the lights only emphasized their secret happiness. Penny's eyes turned from the platform with its massed array of musicians and singers, and gave a glancing smile. David bent to pick up the program which had slipped from her lap, and his hand rested on her ankle for a moment. She was smiling openly as she watched the conductor take his place, and then bent her head to study the program notes.

David settled comfortably in his seat and prepared himself for the opening chords with their grim, relentless rhythm. The audience around him slumped into their self-chosen listening postures. Penny, sitting so quietly, unmoving, smiling no longer, stiffened in fear as the marching feet hammered into her emotions. Feel, the music said, feel what can destroy all happiness; hear what can be the end of all hope. And then, even at the height of its warning, the music relented, changed, slipped into the serene long descending chords of "Venus, the Bringer of Peace." After the noise and the tumult, it became the vague shimmering beauty of repose, the last trembling note of happiness achieved.

David felt the music attack him as he had never been weakened by it before. The muted chord, the liquid notes shivered down his spine. His hand tightened gently round Penny's, and he felt it tremble within his. We have given each other this experience, he suddenly realized. In some strange way, our minds and bodies are alive to every note, every change in tone, every breath and sign in the music. The emotional and spiritual revelation each added to the other as the climax mounted. In this moment, evil and ugliness were banished from the world. In this moment, all thought and emotion were purified into absolute good.

> For if such holy song
> Enwrap our fancy long,
>   Time will run back, and fetch the age of gold.

Even when the choir's voice, soaring in the music of the crystal spheres, the ninefold harmony, had died away into a silence as vast and living as that of eternity, they sat together quite motionless. It was the young man next to David who brought him back into the hall of shuffling feet, of sharp coughs, of surging applause.

"How did you like it?" the young man asked too loudly of his companion. Perhaps he was unwilling to pass any judgment until he was sure how the other felt.

"Gay, but noisy," his friend said, in the clipped decided voice which never gave any right of appeal. The other man nodded in agreement and stopped applauding. Then they both rose, crushed their way across Penny and David, murmured the conventional but meaningless "Sorry," and walked leisurely up the aisle. All need for haste was over, now that they had made complete nuisances of themselves, David thought angrily. Certainly, they had broken the spell. David looked at Penny, still silent, as they emerged into a world of honking taxis; jostling crowds; voices telling each other how marvelous it was, and by the telling losing something of the marvel; the smell of a warm city packed with human bodies and movement. The spell was broken. But the experience, felt so deeply, was his to be held and remembered.

"Hello, Bosworth," a voice said out of the crowd. It was Marain with a strange young man. There were brief introductions. Marain, after a slight stare in the direction of Penny, seemed not to notice her. He turned all his attention on David. His companion remained quite silent, aloof from everyone, perhaps even from himself.

"I hear you have been working hard," Marain chided David, reminding him, too, that he had seen very little of

Marain in the last few months. Marain would never admit that he did any work whatsoever.

David ignored the slightly amused smile, and said, "How did you find Germany? You were there at Easter, weren't you?"

"There will be a revolution," Marain said cheerfully. "The people won't stand for the present régime. Besides, the German Left is the best organized in Europe. Are you catching the train? We can share a taxi."

"I'm staying in town," David said.

"Well, what about lunch some time next week? You haven't abandoned all interest in politics, have you?"

"No," David said. He was thinking that this invitation was, after all, Marain's way of offering an apology. For, last month, the magazine *Experiment* had died a natural death, and from the very causes that David and Marain had once quarreled over. Breen's father had at last found the solution to all the problems of his son. He had stopped paying any allowance, and Breen could no longer afford to play at being earnest. He was pushing a pen in an office for three pounds a week. In the evenings, so Margaret had reported, he was running up a good-attendance card at the nearest Oswald Mosley meeting room, no doubt taking lessons in the manly sport of knuckle-dusting.

But Marain, quite unaware that David knew all about the trouble over *Experiment*, was speaking again. "Good, good," he was saying. "Let's say next Wednesday. I've an idea which we must talk over. There is no doubt that the Germans are damned suspicious of us. If we could make them understand that there is no reason to be, then the Nazis wouldn't have a chance with their propaganda to the German people."

"You mean with the myth that Germany is surrounded by enemies and must prepare to defend herself?"

"Exactly. But we all have to make some kind of gesture which will be publicized in every country. If we say that no young man in Britain is going to fight in any circumstances and pledge ourselves to that publicly, then that will prove to everyone, Germans included, that Hitler has absolutely no case."

"Will it?" David asked. He did not want to start discussing it now, anyway. He made a remark about the concert, drawing Penny into the conversation.

But Marain went on, "Of course, it is only the germ of an idea, and it will take some time and a good lot of thought to work out. The Nazis will be cynical to suit their own purpose, but then the Nazis are not the German people."

"No?" David asked, looked at Penny, saw the expression in her eyes. She knew instinctively what he thought about all this. He realized then how close they had come to each other, when even thoughts could be listened to as understandably as words.

The silent young man beside Marain stirred gently to say it was getting rather late ... train ...

"Wednesday," Marain said. A slightly relaxed muscle in his face suggested a smile. And then he and his friend disappeared as quickly into the crowd as they had emerged from it.

"He didn't like me," Penny said after she and David had walked some distance in silence. She was hurt. She wanted David's friends to like her. "Not that he gave me much of a chance. Or perhaps I should have been one of the German people."

David laughed. "You have more effect than you think, old girl. He did not have to talk to me tonight at all, you know. He could have come to see me in Oxford."

"Why was he so rude, then? As if he resented me, as if I were an intruder."

"He didn't think he was being rude, and he probably could give two or three reasons why he ignored you like that and none of them would be right. The true one he wouldn't like to recognize at all. What do men feel, do you imagine, when they see a competitor with a pretty girl on his arm? Especially if they don't happen to know many pretty girls?"

"You always restore my vanity, darling. What *would* I do without you?"

"You've got that slightly wrong. You mean, what would I do without you? And the answer is Marain. That would have been me if I hadn't met you."

"No, David. You couldn't ever be like that." She was both horrified and amused.

"A year ago I was developing nicely into something closely resembling our friend Marain." Then David smiled and said: "I had quite an escape, hadn't I? If you had met me tonight for the first time, would you have disliked me as much as you disliked Marain?"

"If you had met me for the first time tonight, would you have ignored me?"

David laughed. "I should have lost the train," he admitted.

But she still wasn't persuaded. "I really am inadequate, David. About your work, I mean. And politics. I should be listening to you for hours—what you feel should be done about this or not done about that." Yes, Marain had conveyed that quite clearly: David with a girl was less important than David as one of Marain's circle.

"Heaven forbid," David said in genuine alarm. "You've been reading the advice paragraphs on the woman's page, all about sharing his interests," he teased her. And then he added quietly, "You do share mine, old girl. But we didn't choose each other just to have a suitable audience, you know. Later, when we are married and have each other day in, day out, I'll probably begin to bore you with all my thoughts that are only half-argued out. Be careful, then, or I'll start practising my speeches on you, too. How would you like that?"

"I'd love it," Penny said, and she did look as if she meant it. And that pleased him, somehow, however much he had protested against it.

As they crossed over Oxford Street to follow the wide curve of Regent Street down towards Piccadilly Circus, he said with unexpected anger, "But damn Marain's eyes. This was one night I didn't want to think about politics and problems. I wonder if he sat through that concert only finding social significance, or lack of it, in the music." He suddenly felt sorry for Marain. It was a new feeling, too. His annoyance left him, then.

Penny said, "If it had not been Marain, it would have been something else: those two young men who were in such a hurry to leave and then blocked up the entrance; or the street noises; or something." She looked at the brightly lit red bus as it roared down the sweep of Regent Street. At this hour of night, the pavements were less crowded, the shops were shut, the traffic was lighter. But that only reminded you of the busy street in daytime, when it was fully alive. A sleeping street always seemed unnatural. There was no real feeling of peace, even when it rested. It was full of latent energy, ready to burst into noisy demonstration.

"Because a city is a practical place," Penny went on. "Everything about it pulls us back into a world where practical people live. We should have been on Inchnamurren, and then the music would still have been around us long after it had ended."

"Only," he pointed out, "we couldn't go to a Queen's Hall and hear that concert on Inchnamurren. Life doesn't have

282

cut-and-dried classifications like a library: you don't find perfection all complete under one heading. Not even on your Inchnamurren, Penny."

She looked at him, thinking now about their love. "Nothing is perfect?" She was half-puzzled, half-worried.

He didn't answer. Perfection, that strange experience of unexpected moments: moments which came often unsought, released you as irrationally as they had gripped you and possessed you, leaving you with a sense of wonder over the unexplainable.

"Nothing?" Penny asked again. "At the concert . . . " she went on, and then she saw his eyes and realized she did not have to explain her idea of perfection. "And before the concert," she said quietly. "In spite of the Marains, I haven't forgotten. Even in a city street it is still here, David." She raised his hand which held hers, to touch her heart quickly, lightly.

"Yes," he said. Each experience we share, even my hand on her breast at that moment, is something which cannot be taken away from us. It is always ours, if we keep it this way.

He looked down at her. "For two pins, I'd kiss you right now," he said. He paused suddenly, and did kiss her. To two passing women, watching with shocked curiosity, he said, "Yes, *most* enjoyable, thank you."

To Penny, he said, "We'll keep it this way. Always."

They exchanged the little smile of knowledge, of experience shared, which needs no explanation. And then arm in arm, they swung down Regent Street—oblivious to Indian silks in Liberty's, South African diamonds in the goldsmiths' window, French perfumes and laces in the Galeries Lafayette, Harris tweeds and Shetland wool in Jaeger's, Balkan cigarettes, prints from Brussels and Vienna, glass from Sweden, silver from Denmark, movies from America—towards the Café Royal, as if indeed the world was stretched before them.

chapter xxxv

MRS. LORRIMER entered her drawing room, looked
around it with pleasure as she always did, and walked
over the thick green carpet to her private writing table. For
a moment she stood looking out of the window, postponing
the moment of sitting down.

The heavy shower of rain had ended, and there was
enough blue in the sky to patch a Dutchman's trousers: so it
would clear, and with this warm summer breeze, the tennis
courts would be dry enough for the last day of the champion-
ship. It would be nice if Charles could win this year: it had
been five years since he had won the finals. Mary Lorrimer
smiled tolerantly as she reflected what children men were,
always attempting more than they should try to do.

The sun was shining now: the patch of blue sky was growing. Yes, it would clear up nicely, after all. The trees in the
Crescent's locked garden were fresh and crisply green with
the look of June. But soon, it would be July. She remembered
what she had been trying to forget: the letter to be written
to Penelope. "Before July," her father had warned her. It
had been an unpleasant warning, as unpleasant to her as the
rest of Dr. MacIntyre's letter. She had been so shocked, so
scandalized by some of his ideas that she had been ashamed
to show the letter to Charles. But when she did, his reaction
had been bewildering.

He was still against this marriage. He must be. (He had
not answered that letter which David Bosworth had written
to him at Easter, asking if he might visit Charles's office in
June when his future would be settled.) But Charles had
made no comment at all on Father's letter, not even at the
mention of Bosworth's probably brilliant future. That had
been Mr. Chaundler's phrase, quoted by Father. But of
course a don would always think that of any favorite pupil.
"So, as a prospective son-in-law, if you insist on thinking
only of the practical side of this marriage, you could do very
much worse than accept David Bosworth." Her father must
have written that with a wry smile. And Charles, always
angered by sarcasm used against him, had said nothing at
all after he had read the letter. If he had been shocked
or horrified by it, as she herself was, then he had not
allowed that to be seen. Nor did he allow any more dis-

cussion. When she had begun to talk about Penelope, he had said suddenly, "No more, Mary. I'm tired of hearing this dramatized." An odd remark, and an unjust one too.

Suddenly, Mary Lorrimer felt uncertain, as if somehow she now stood alone in this matter. It's unfair, she thought miserably: he won't discuss anything, and it *is* important to discuss it. It's unfair to leave everything to me. He's evading it now. He can't possibly start siding with Father. Or *is* he? And is he only unwilling to admit that he is? Impossible, she told herself. She turned abruptly away from the window and sat down at her writing table.

Before July, her father had said. She glanced unnecessarily at the calendar.

She began the letter. Then she abandoned the half-written sheet of paper. She must deal with this tactfully. She must think clearly.

She opened a small drawer, unlocking it first, where she had placed her father's letter. She unfolded it again, her eyes following its small neat writing impatiently. Yes, she knew it all off by heart. First there was the paragraph about Penelope. Well and happy. (How could she be happy in a single room, cooking, cleaning, and at the same time working in a furniture shop?) Then a paragraph about David Bosworth: his work, his family (*that* ridiculous sister with her superior airs), and his prospects. Prospects! After that, there was a paragraph giving her father's own impressions of Penelope and David Bosworth, formed not from their answers to his questions— "A crude and cheap way of getting information"—but by just listening to them talk about each other. "Not only what they said, but the way they said it."

But it was the last pages of the letter which had upset her most of all. Even yet, she could scarcely believe her eyes.

All this has been most distasteful for me to write, but I have set down everything as honest evidence for Charles to consider. And now, I am going to set down a few thoughts which are directed frankly at you, Mary. I have no control over Charles's decisions; they depend on his conscience. But I can at least give you, Mary, some advice, for that is a father's privilege. If you take it, I shall be happy: Penelope's future will then be her own responsibility. If you don't, then Penelope's future is your entire responsibility.

I should not need to tell you the facts of life at your age. But there is one real purpose behind falling in love, even if those who never could call a spade by its own name have done their idealistic worst to disguise that fact. A man does not fall in love in order to have a pretty companion to take to a theater or a football match. He can enjoy that without having to love the girl. But he cannot love a girl without wanting to possess her, and marriage is the solution that civilized society has found for that very natural phenomenon. It is the logical solution because marriage is the simplest and strongest way of living together, and a man and woman in love will live together.

Don't write back saying that living together is immoral. You and Charles have been doing it for twenty odd years, now. And I am not discussing people who experiment with love as if it were a fashion, a whim, or merely a physical sensation. If that is all they want out of life, let them have it. That's punishment enough. I am talking about men and women who are in love and therefore want to live together for the rest of their lives. Like you and Charles. I put no objections in the way of your marriage (although I could have, for you were young), and so you both got what you wanted. But what about the less fortunate people in love? Those who must face the lack of money, or their families? In their desperation, they will find their own solution. It isn't done with the childish idea of being daring, of wishing to prove they are "modern," unconventional, contemptuous of accepted behavior. I am talking about men and women in love who have discovered that the outward symbols of marriage are of less value than the essential love which is the solid core of lasting marriage. And to me, that is the most important thing in anyone's life.

Now, Mary, pick up this letter once more and smooth it out where you crumpled it. It is no good throwing it aside. You would always want to know how I ended my fatherly talk to you.

I can hear your objections, even at the distance of some four hundred miles. "What about control, discipline?" What about it, Mary? Doesn't it take self-control and discipline, and hard work too, to make love a success?

You say, "But why can't they wait?" Wait for what? What have you given them to wait for?

You say, "But they are young, impetuous. They have all their lives before them. There is no need to hurry." How can anyone be so confident of the time left him that he can afford to waste any of it? As for being young and impetuous—the more responsibility given to youth the better for them *and* their country. There's a growing weakness in Britain when we call young men "boys" and young women "girls"; when middle age and falling hair is considered the first stage of trustworthiness; when old age and thinning blood is reserved for praise and distinction, as if the number of years which a man endures must raise him automatically to the intelligent, capable class of men. We forget too often that youth is a reservoir of power and energy; that it has a sincerity and a longing to prove itself that should be used. Instead, we ignore this potential strength, or we discourage it, so that its vital quality is lost.

If, at this moment, you think I am being fantastic, I should remind you that our country was not built up, either in its history or its literature, by the "typical Englishman" we have so popularized. We forget too easily the kind of men who gave us our heritage; their energy, their vitality, their passions, vehemence, wild emotions. Yes, I know these can be vices as well as virtues. But better strength which has its mistakes than no strength at all. And there is a high courage and generosity in youth, which can accept the risk of mistakes and even turn it to success. There is no need to be afraid for the man or woman who keeps that high courage in his heart.

So put your fears aside, Mary. Penny has her job; David will have his; together, they will have enough to live on. And later, when Miss Bosworth has finished her education, Penny need not keep her job unless she wants to. They are, as you see, not without plans.

Write Penny. Better still, go down to London and listen to her. But write her, certainly, before July.

And that is the last piece of fatherly advice which I shall ever give you. It is much too painful a pleasure.

Mary Lorrimer let her father's letter fall on the desk. She stared at the note she had begun to Penelope. I won't write, she thought. I won't. Then she picked up her pen again. She heard Betty's footsteps running downstairs. Her youngest daughter burst into the room with her usual imitation of a volcano in eruption.

"Betty! Please!"

"Sorry, Mummy. Still writing old letters?"

"I thought you had gone with Moira to see Daddy play. Pull up your stocking, Betty, it looks so slovenly."

"I'm going out to the courts now," Betty said with slight difficulty in breathing as she twisted a leg and looked over her shoulder to see the stocking seam. She had grown taller in this last year, and the shapeless body had begun to assume its proper proportions. Mrs. Lorrimer stared in amazement. It was really so noticeable now.

"Betty," she said sharply, "why aren't you wearing your jacket?"

Betty's cheerful face clouded over. She looked down at the white blouse, the striped tie, the navy skirt, black stockings and flat-heeled lacing shoes. "But Mummy, it's a *clean* blouse."

"Do as you are told, Betty, and don't argue. Why were you so long in dressing, anyway?"

"My watch stopped when I was working. I must have forgotten to wind it again. I've finished my novel, Mummy. It's wizard, it really is. The hero finds a witch-goddess guarding the temple, only this girl isn't a witch or a goddess really, she's just a—"

"Yes, darling. You'll be late for Daddy's match. Why didn't Moira take you with her?"

Betty stared incredulously at her mother. "Moira didn't want me."

"I am sure your sister wouldn't dream of leaving you behind," Mrs. Lorrimer said indignantly. I must speak to

287

Moira, she thought; she must not hurt Betty's feelings in this way, always running off and avoiding her.

Oh, *wouldn't* she? Betty thought, but she did not dare say that. Besides, who wanted to go along with an old sister, and sit in the grown-up part of the veranda? "I've promised to meet Barbara and Jean Mair anyway," she said in an offhand way. And Bobby Turner and the Lang boys.

"Well, you had better run along then." Mrs. Lorrimer suddenly stared at her youngest daughter incredulously. "Betty, have you been putting powder on your nose?"

Betty looked startled. "Powder?" she asked carefully. And then, with emphasis, "Oh no, Mummy." Golly, she thought, that was a narrow squeak. Did I put on too much oatmeal flour? She waved her hand and ran out of the room, saying, "I must simply *dash*. The girls will be waiting for me. 'By."

"Good-by, dear. Come home with Daddy, won't you? And put on that jacket."

"Yes, Mummy," Betty called back from the hall. If it got too warm, as it would, she could always take the jacket off when she reached the tennis grounds. It made her look so *fat*. Why couldn't she have a fitted one like Moira's, and silk stockings too?

Mrs. Lorrimer picked up her pen once more. How easy it was to understand Betty. If only she could stay at this age forever, instead of having to grow up and go out into the world. As Penelope had done. You brought up girls carefully, made them sweet and innocent and trusting. And then they met men, and you did nothing but worry. Why were men like that, anyway? Look at her own father and these shocking ideas he had expressed about men and women in love . . . Why, if an elderly scholar, a quiet gentleman, could have thoughts like these, what must younger men think of life? Charles—surely he did not think like that, or rather feel like that? For Father's letter had emphasized emotion rather than thought. Yes, that was where he was wrong: he had not talked about rational human beings, but only those who were driven on by—she thought of the word "passion" but slipped it quickly out of her mind into the deep cellar where all disturbing thoughts must be buried, walled-up, not discussed, not even imagined in privacy.

At that point, the parlormaid brought in the silver tea tray, and Mary Lorrimer abandoned her writing table. The letter could be written after tea. She must rest now, and put her feet up as the doctor said, and try to stop worrying. She picked up the new novel which Boots's library had recommended to her this morning. It was really so difficult, today, to find suitable books, what with all the violent thoughts and words and monstrous ideas that so many writers were using. She felt irritation at her father's possible reply to that: what about Chaucer, or Shakespeare, or Balzac, or Tolstoi? As if one didn't know that those were classics. Classics were different.

Now she must stop thinking about such things, or she never would forget her worries. She had to get her mind calm and clear before she wrote Penelope. She opened the book on her lap, looking at the first page then at the last page and then at a page near the middle. Yes, it did seem a pleasant story; about a pleasant house and pleasant people. How nice...

Mrs. Lorrimer poured herself a second cup of tea, and began to read.

The front door opened rudely. There was a low murmur of confused voices. Moira was calling to her. She laid aside the book with regret. Moira must have brought some of her friends in for tea: late, too. Goodness, it *was* late. Was there never any peace in this house with all this perpetual running in and out, all these unexpected guests? Really, she must speak seriously to Moira about this kind of thing.

She rose as Moira entered the room with her hat in her hand and her hair ruffled. "I'm just about to write a letter," she said, trying to convey a broad hint in her words without appearing rude to any listening guest. And then she stood quite still as Moira was standing. Moira's face was tense and white. The murmur in the hall had given way to shuffling feet.

"What's wrong, Moira? Betty... Has something happened to Betty?"

Moira shook her head. "It's Daddy," she said in a stifled voice, and burst into tears.

chapter xxxvi

Mary lorrimer was alone in the silent drawing room. It was the third day of Charles Lorrimer's illness. Everything was under control again—the alarm, the tears, the terrifying emotions which threatening death arouses. The capable nurses had established their territory in the Lorrimers' bedroom, and Mrs. Lorrimer had found herself exiled. She disliked illness, anyway, regarded it as a worrying nuisance, a disturber of routine. She wasn't, therefore, a particularly good nurse. Yet, she resented the nurses' authority. "But Charles needs me," she had said pathetically to Dr. Morrison. "Well, you are here if he calls for you," the doctor had answered soothingly. Which was true. So she put her energies into superintending the whispered footsteps and lowered voices even down to the basement kitchen.

The doctor had just left after his late evening visit. He had held out more hope than before and, at the same time, his cheerful words had thrown her into a panic. "Definite improvement, today. There's a good chance now that the first shock will not be followed by a second one." And Mrs. Lorrimer, who for three days had not even been thinking about the possibility of a second shock, stared in amazement at Dr. Morrison. She had thought the worst danger was over when they had brought Charles home from the club. Now she realized for the first time the full meaning of the nurses' overofficious watchfulness, of the doctor's guarded phrases, of the serious words which Charles's business partner had spoken. They had all known the danger, but she had never thought it possible that Charles would die. Charles couldn't die, so much of his life was still before him. She had glanced sharply at Dr. Morrison's thoughtful face. "Won't Charles ever be fully recovered?" she heard herself ask. Dr. Morrison had hesitated. "Never fully; never quite the same again," he had answered gravely. "He will have to take care, perhaps give up much of his work, rest for a long time, look after himself." And as he left her he added, "I warned him about that blood pressure of his, last summer, you know. I told him to cut down work and exercise, and I prescribed a diet for him. Didn't he follow it?"

Yes, Charles had followed it—to a certain extent. But it was difficult for a man with so many public engagements to be able to keep that strict diet. And Charles had never told her why he was supposed to keep to a diet: he had let the family think that it was simply indigestion which troubled him, a case of stomach ulcers. He had not told them the truth, perhaps wanting to spare them worry, perhaps refusing to believe himself that he could be made a helpless invalid overnight. Charles had been so proud of his physical strength. Overnight? In a few minutes. For that was how it had happened. He had pleaded a sudden attack of cramp towards the middle of the match, had walked firmly by himself towards the Club Room; and there the shock had struck him down. Thank Heaven, Mary Lorrimer thought, remembering Charles's horror of scenes, that he had been inside the Club House and not on the tennis courts at the time. And if he had not taken the warning signal, if he had gone on playing? She suddenly realized that he would have been dead. Charles dead, and Mary Lorrimer a widow with three daughters to provide for. She grew white-lipped at that thought.

Mary Lorrimer faced the drawing room, seeing its value for the first time since she had come to live in this house. She had looked at it then, and wondered delightedly that it was hers. Now she looked at it, this pleasant room symbolizing a pleasant way of living, and she knew it was lost to her. In a few minutes, she repeated. It only had taken a few minutes to end everything built up through years. And then the new feeling of humility, of fear, of insecurity struck her its full blow. She sat down on the nearest couch and buried her face in a cushion as if to shut away the lost room.

Moira was saying in a hushed voice, "Mummy! Daddy's awake now. The nurse says you may see him." Moira, embarrassed, trouble at the sight of her mother's unhappy face, was saying over and over again, "Don't worry, it's all right, Mummy." But she knew it wasn't all right.

I wish I were Penelope, Moira thought suddenly: Penelope with a career she really likes, not just forced into teaching to help support the family. Penelope with David Bosworth. Penelope is free, and I am tied to the family. It is unfair, unfair. Penelope is always the lucky one.

"He said one word," Moira went on. "He said 'Penny.' Mummy, you *should* have let me write to her."

The two women looked at each other. Then Mrs. Lorrimer rose and made her way to the staircase.

At the bedroom door, she halted. What, she wondered miserably, had made Charles think of Penelope? Was it possible that lying there, so motionless on that bed, he had been conscious some of the time, conscious of his nearness to death, conscious of the problem of Penelope which must not be left unsolved if he were to die? Charles will blame me, Mary Lorrimer thought: yet, it wasn't I who was against Penelope; I was only doing what Charles wanted to be done. He was always so busy with his career. Everything I have done has been all for Charles. He must know that. And on that resolution, having persuaded herself she was telling the truth, she opened the bedroom door.

The nurse smiled encouragingly. Charles looked so weak, so white, so helpless, so unlike Charles that Mary Lorrimer again felt the terrifying fear. She took the limp hand in her own. Charles, I love you, get well, get well, she thought. She slipped to her knees beside the bed, and tried to smile.

"Don't worry," Charles," she said when she could control her voice. "Don't worry."

The white lips were forming themselves slowly. "July," she seemed to hear. July. He was remembering her father's letter.

"I know, dear," she said. "I've written the letter to Penelope, saying we agree with Father. Shall I post it?"

He tried to say something, and then she saw that his eyes were happy. They, alone in his face, could still communicate with her. The look of trouble and worry had gone in them. They were happy.

She kissed him, even if the nurse was watching them, and murmured close to his ear, "Get well, Charles, and everything will be all right. That is all that matters."

Then the nurse was signing to her, and she had to rise to her feet and move to the door. He had closed his eyes, and there was a subtle change, almost an expression of relief, on the blank face.

Mary Lorrimer sealed the letter to Penelope.

After four weeks of deliberation it had taken her four minutes to write. And now it was ready to post, and the white lie told upstairs in the bedroom had become truth. Well, she thought, that was that. . . .

She tore up her father's letter. That was that, she repeated; another problem decided. Now she would only have to worry about the future of two daughters: one, at least, was off her hands.

Not that I'll ever be able to like David Bosworth, she admitted frankly to herself. But if Penelope was determined to be in love with him—well, what could parents do? Penelope's future was Penelope's responsibility.

I hope they will be happy, she added, doubtfully.

chapter xxxvii

FINAL examinations were over; the results had been posted that morning; and Chaundler asked David to lunch with him and Fairbairn in order to celebrate David's excellent First. After that, David would catch the afternoon train to London. Most men had gone down from Oxford already: and the few who had stayed there until the results were out, shared the quiet town with visiting sightseers. As Chaundler sat with his two guests in his dark, cool room, the desultory voices of the tourists visiting the chapel came drifting in through the opened casement windows. The chestnut trees spread their broad leaves in the warm, breathless air. Even the bees were lazy in the strong July heat; a fat black one bumbled his way slowly into the room through the open window, and then lazily, almost heavily, moved out towards the sun-splashed chestnut trees again. It was pleasant, David thought, to sit in a quiet room, to feel as lazy and unhurried as the world outside. He drank Chaundler's admirable Amontillado, listened to Fairbairn discussing the differences in climbing in the Austrian Tyrol and the Swiss Alps, and thought of the journey to London this late afternoon.

At last Chaundler rose and moved towards the table at the oriel window. His guests followed him. His scout watched anxiously to see that everything was just right—the silver cups and bowl that Mr. Chaundler liked for special occasions, the hock properly iced, the ground ginger well mixed with sugar for the melon. Everything was just right. The four men relaxed, each in his own way. And then Fairbairn produced his latest idea: David, before he settled in London to work on a survey of seasonal unemployment, was to make a tour. He was to go to America, to the United States, to see how the problem of unemployment was being tackled there.

Then, having let the idea explode in the quiet room, Fairbairn began to explain it in more detail. The United States, probably because of the advanced specialization of its industry and agriculture, had always had a serious problem in seasonal unemployment. But it was only when the depression reached a climax that general and seasonal unemployment combined to produce a first-magnitude crisis. With their usual violent energy, the Americans had faced the crisis and formed plans to meet it. It would be interesting to see how far the plans would work; and next year would be the testing time.

What interested Fairbairn most were two things: how far had seasonal unemployment tipped the balance towards disaster; how could seasonal unemployment be regulated? There were other things, too, which would be interesting to watch: these projected camps for young men, for instance, where they were taken off the street and trained for jobs; the Public Works Administration, which intended to avoid the evils of the dole; the balance of state planning, which must be carefully held if a country of the size and potential strength of the United States was not to degenerate into a totalitarian machine. But it was the problem of seasonal unemployment which interested Fairbairn most. For he had a theory that there would always be cycles of unemployment in the world, but that if seasonal unemployment were more recognized, and better controlled, then these cycles would not degenerate into the grave danger and threat of a really fulminating depression.

He talked on and on, with all the enthusiasm of elaborately dressing one's own brainchild. And it was a good idea; he knew that. Fairbairn—his alert brown eyes shining with enthusiasm, his thatch of white heavy hair falling untidily over his brow as it always did when he was excited over something, his shoulders hunched, his hands clasped before him, his elbows on the arms of his chair—gave the details in his crisp, complete way. Originally this tour of America had been arranged for himself, but a crisis had arisen here in London with one of his publications—his favorite one, the *Economic Trend*—and he had better stay at home for the next month or so to control matters. If David were going to work on seasonal unemployment, he was certainly the man to send as Fairbairn's eyes.

David sat quite silent. He was too dazed even to listen coherently.

Fairbairn halted his exposition to glance sharply at David's face.

"It is a wonderful opportunity for any young man," he said. "You will have a chance to travel through all the States. You will be helped by official sources. Your expenses will be paid by me in addition to your salary, of course. And they will be paid on the American scale while you are there. That is only fair. Everything costs twice as much in America, and British salaries cannot cope with that. I found that out when I traveled there two years ago." He smiled at the memory, and paused, waiting for David's response.

David forced a smile, too. It was more than fair. It was a chance in a thousand, the kind of dream that would have excited him as much as Fairbairn, if only there hadn't been Penny. If only we could get married, he thought. If only . . .

"How long do you expect this tour to last?" he asked quietly.

"Probably about a year," Fairbairn said cheerfully. He looked as if he expected David to share his enthusiasm. "America is a big place, you know. We often forget that. Even if you spent one week in each state—and most of them cover more ground than the British Isles—that would take you eleven months. The United States is not a country, remember: it is a continent. You will send me a monthly report of facts and figures. And I shall also expect a weekly article for the *Economic Trend*. I want that written of course in a more interesting way than the matter-of-fact reports, and you don't have to confine yourself entirely in your articles to seasonal unemployment. Anything that touches the social problems will be the sort of thing I'll need for that page. You'll find it a varied and interesting job."

A year, David was thinking. And after that? Probably there would be always some other excuse in life to separate him from Penny. Some other excuse to separate them for another six months, another three months, another year. His instinct told him to fight against this: it was the beginning of a series of dragging separations stretching into a permanent one. For if he were a good reporter Fairbairn would use him as that: he had been talking only last week of the need to observe methods in European countries, of the need to forget Britain was an island. Fairbairn was thorough. Fairbairn was the man, so interested in a job to be done, that he would drive his assistants with the tight unrelenting purpose of a general. No favors could be asked of Fairbairn.

"Well?" he was now saying.

David glanced at Chaundler's quiet, watchful face. Chaundler knew. He was worried too.

"I must think about this, sir," David said haltingly.

Fairbairn stared uncomprehendingly at the young man. "It is a chance in a thousand," he said, with a hint of rebuke in his voice.

David flushed. "Yes," he agreed unhappily.

Chaundler said, "First of all, you need a holiday, David." He looked pointedly at Fairbairn, who nodded. David gave Walter Chaundler a look of thanks. He was trying to buy David some time, some time to think over this whole business.

"Yes, you need a couple of weeks or so," Fairbairn agreed. "But you would have to sail by the middle of August."

David stared at the fallen cigarette ash on the carpet at his feet.

"Let me know by Saturday," Fairbairn said with marked finality. "If it is the responsibility of such a job that is worrying you, you can put your mind at rest. I should never have suggested it, if I had not thought you would shape up very well in it." He began speaking of other things, but there was just the touch of disappointed tolerance in his whole manner. He had been so sure that David was the kind of man to seize opportunity, and to do well. Perhaps, of course, he did need a holiday: he had been working hard and he looked tired. And when you are tired, Fairbairn thought, then you hesitate before new ideas.

Chaundler gave David a quick look of encouragement. He said quietly, "Why don't you go to bed and nurse that cold of yours? It looks to me as if flu were developing."

"Oh, I'll be all right," David said. "I suppose I'm more tired than I imagined." He roused himself to carry on with the rest of the conversation.

David found a letter for Penny lying on the table of the dark hall in Fitzroy Square. He lifted it. It was from Edinburgh he noticed, as he climbed the stairs slowly. All his movements had become heavy. Yes, I am tired, he thought. But what else could I expect, anyway? Another week of that strain and I would have cracked up. We all would have.

He remembered the rows of white serious faces bent over examination papers day after day. Outside the Examination School there was sunlight and green trees. Inside, there was the race against time, the scraping of pens, the worried coughs, the shuffling feet, the rows of desks. The judgment day. The weighing in the balance, the found wanting. The sheep and the goats. No matter how brilliant you had been in editing a magazine, in producing a play, in contributing verse to anthologies; no matter how original you had seemed with your decided tastes in clothes and food and conversation; no matter how well you had played music or Rugby or at politics in the Union, this was the day of rendered accounts. It was the same test for all, and the same lesson: first-rate brains without the capacity to work would get you no further than those who worked but had second-rate brains. It was the day of painful self-revelation, of regret for some, of hope for others, of exhibitionism, of frustration, of submitting your inner pride to the outside verdict.

David paused to rest his heavy suitcase on the first landing.

Well, that is all over anyway, he thought: the written papers, and then the oral, and, at last, the posted list of successes and failures. All over, thank God. Another chunk of life put in a box, wrapped up and labeled: "Past. Not to be reopened. No second attempts." But a rare chunk in its way, for other periods in life did not end so neatly, so completely, with an examiner's clear mark to tie up all the loose ends. No wonder I feel lightheaded, he thought. And this damned cold which keeps hanging on—how did I get it anyway? Too little sleep for weeks, a sudden drop in temperature in the early morning while I was working at an open window? His head at this moment seemed made of lead and it was an effort to lift each damned foot and place it on the next step. His shoes seemed to be soled with cast iron. Oh hell, he thought, I'm just tired and worried. That's all. If I can get some rest I'll be all right in a couple of days. There had not been much rest in these last days at Oxford. After the orals, there had been the packing up, the last removal, the payment of bills, the farewells to be made, the summer plans for Margaret to be arranged. Hell's bells, he thought, doesn't life ever become simple? One thing over, and another begins.

He thrust the letter into his pocket and changed the suitcase to his other hand. As he paused again for a moment on the top step of the long staircase, he admitted for the first time that this cold was worse then he had realized. And the lunch party in Chaundler's room had not exactly been a cure. It was funny how anxiety could deal the last blow to your health, could crumple it up as surely as any germ. Then he called himself a bloody fool for even allowing himself to think that, and he knocked at the door, and he was smiling as he heard her clear voice saying, "David? Is that you?"

Her light heels ran to the door to open it. He forgot about Fairbairn and America. He was only thinking how lovely she was, standing there at the opened door, her face flushed, her eyes shining. He had no feeling except the eternal one of surprise that she was always so much lovelier than he had dreamed in his loneliness.

"Darling," she said. Her arms were tightly around him. He held her closely, saying with the stupid inadequacy which attacked him when he was emotionally upset, "Darling Penny, I love you." He kissed her neck and her brow and her ear, and explained, "I mustn't give you this cold. I'm full of germs."

"I wouldn't mind," Penny said. "If we share triumphs then colds will be shared, too. But you didn't tell me in your letters that you had a cold." And then, seeing that he didn't want to talk about it, she said, "Our celebration supper is all ready. I cooked it in advance so that I wouldn't meet you all hot and bothered." She tried to look not too proudly at the table. There was a cold duck with orange salad, a Brie cheese beside a salad bowl, a basket of French bread covered with a napkin, strawberries piled on vine leaves, and a bottle of Liebfraumilch. "There's only the asparagus to drain and cover with butter," she said. She smiled with delight at having timed everything so well. "Oh, David, I am *so* happy!" She threw back her head and laughed with pure joy. "How wonderful to have won a victory. I feel like Caesar after a successful campaign. No, you should be Caesar and I'm the wife who shares his triumphs. No, not Caesar: he was a bald-headed old reprobate with husbands hiding *their* wives from him whenever he entered a town. Who was the victorious general who loved only one woman? Surely there must be some? The trouble is you never hear about virtue, only about vices."

David's smile broadened. He noted with pleasure, too, that his telegram giving the results of Schools was displayed in the middle of the mantelpiece. The happiness and pride on Penny's face made him aware of his achievement. "I'll rush out and sit fifty more examinations," he said, "if you give me a welcome like this when I get back." God, it *was* wonderful to accomplish something, and then see your girl more triumphant than you were. Her laughter, her gay remarks, her dancing steps done in a moment of bursting joy, her excitement and happiness, were infectious. He forgot his throbbing temples and the coldness of his body.

"Stop it, old girl," he said smilingly, "or you'll give me swelled-head." But he loved it, and then, like all men when they are enjoying the height of their triumphs, he added diffidently, "It was nothing, anyway."

"Of course, Penny said with a laugh, "nothing at all. Absolutely nothing!" She went out into the landing, saying that it would be a pity to ruin the asparagus.

He remembered the letter which he had slipped into his pocket as he climbed the stairs. "I brought a letter up here for you. From Edinburgh," he called through the open door. "back-slanting writing, square-shaped, with elaborate capital L's."

"That will be from Moira. Throw it on the mantelpiece, darling."

David placed the letter near his telegram, and went out into the hallway where Penny was busy measuring coffee in the small alcove kitchen. He lifted the dish of asparagus, which made a neat pyramid on the slices of toast draining the last drops of water. He put his other arm around her waist, hugging her as he said, "This is what I needed," and made her lose count of the spoonfuls.

But at dinner, in spite of determined efforts, he could eat very little. He hadn't eaten much lunch, either, but he had blamed that on Fairbairn's conversation.

"Sorry, darling," he had to say at last. "Everything is perfect. But I seem to be unable to—" He pushed back the nauseating plate of food. "This cold of mine—"

"David—" Penny began, half-rising.

"No, don't!" he said sharply. "There's no need for any fuss." He rose and crossed over to the armchair, feeling the slowness of his movements. "I'm just tired, that's all."

And he is ill. And he is worried, Penny thought.

"Sorry, Penny," he said, trying to keep his voice even. "You see I *am* a bad-tempered blighter."

Penny resisted the impulse to follow him, to find out by talking what was wrong. He was tired, he was ill, he was depressed. More depressed than being tired or ill warranted. Something was wrong.

She looked down at the gay table now so forlorn. "I think you are a very independent blighter," she said in a low voice, keeping her eyes fixed on the pattern of the tablecloth. Water lilies. Only half an hour ago, they had seemed enchanting with their cool white crispness blocked on water-green linen. Something had gone wrong. But what? Something to do with me? But he loves me just as much as ever, she told herself. And then she wasn't sure. Yes, he loved her—she had seen that in his eyes when she had opened the door, but perhaps he did not want to be tied to her. Now that he was a free man with a new world before him, perhaps he resented subconsciously the ties that she represented. He *was* an independent kind of man.

She knew that she was only letting herself express, at this moment, the fear that had lain at the back of her mind in spite of her belief in their love. People could believe, but they could never feel absolutely sure; they were always haunted by the fear that they would lose what they valued most. The more they valued it, the greater the fear of losing it.

She said very quietly, "David, why don't you tell me whatever it is? I'd rather know definitely than imagine things."

David leaned his head against the back of his chair. He took a deep breath. "Penny, I am not taking this job with Fairbairn. I'll look for something else."

She rose then, and came over to his chair, kneeling beside it.

He touched her hair. "You don't seem very upset," he said in surprise. "Didn't you want me to get the job?"

"Yes. I'm relieved because I was jumping to quite wrong conclusions. I thought you were depressed for another reason."

"What reason?"

"Us. After all, darling, you could have changed your mind about us. Men do, they tell me."

"And damn their eyes, whoever they are." He stared at her incredulously. "Good God, Penny. I can worry about you changing your mind about me, but *you* don't have to worry that I ever shall. Just take one look in a mirror. Or reread the letters I sent you. Good God, Penny."

She kissed his hand, and then slipped hers into its grasp.

"Well," he said ruefully, "that's a good lesson to me. I shan't spare you any worries from now on, my girl. I'll pour them all out before you, so that you can join me in worrying over the real thing and not over an imaginary piece of foolishness. How would you like that?"

"Very much," Penny said cheerfully. "Besides, when we share worries they don't seem half so bad, just as when we share good news it seems twice as good." Then she became serious, watching his face thoughtfully.

"Why give up the job?" she asked gently.

"Because I don't want it."

She was worried now. "But why? What do you really want to do, David?" she asked.

He didn't answer. So she imagined he was just being temperamental about a career, uncertain of what he wanted to do? And then he grew angry with himself over his bitter thought: his temper was on the short side today. He hadn't told her why he was giving up the Fairbairn job. She had every right to be worried about him. No girl would like the idea of tying herself to an unstable man who changed his mind too often about how he was to earn his daily bread. Bread didn't get earned that way.

"I am not being a prima donna," he said savagely, his voice still angry from his own self-accusation. He paused, and his tone became more gentle but there was still intensity behind it. "I'll take any job that gives security and the chance to develop a career I won't be ashamed of. I must have security. And I must feel that whatever I accomplish today will be less than what I can accomplish ten years from today. Not in power or in money, particularly. But in myself."

"Fairbairn offered that kind of job," Penny said. In the next moment she regretted her too quick, too accurate reply as she saw the expression on David's face. "Well, darling," she added hastily, "what job will you look for?" Jobs were scarce: she had found that out for herself. It was said that no man with a good Oxford degree was ever unemployed, but it might take a lot of worry and heartbreak to prove that. She sat quite still, trying to hide her unhappiness, and not succeeding very well. She managed a smile. "Don't worry, darling."

David said, "You know, Penny, you are taking this rather well. Why don't you lecture me for the spineless chap you must think I am?"

"But you aren't, David."

"You can't think that I am exactly a strong-minded character at this moment. Why don't you try to manage me, make me take the job for my own good whether I wanted it or not?"

"If you don't want it, then it wouldn't be for your own good. And that means it would be bad for me too. Besides, darling, I shouldn't dare try to manage you. You do the managing in this household. Do you know a most extraordinary thing? I rather enjoy it."

"If you make me believe that, you've learned how to manage me completely." He regarded her with a smile of pleasure. "Mrs. Bosworth, as well as being in love with you, I have a great affection for you."

"Mr. Bosworth, my regard for you is only equaled by my constant devotion."

They both laughed. Penny said, "Good. I've got a laugh out of you at last. David, you do worry me when you don't laugh easily. You're tired. You've got a rotten cold—oh yes, you have; that cough you are trying to disguise is almost a graveyard one. And your eyes are—well, peculiar."

"Like the things you see staring up at you from the fishmonger's slab of ice?"

"Almost. What you need is bed, aspirin, a hot toddy, and twelve hours of solid sleep. How much sleep have you been getting?"

"Oh, enough." Sometimes five hours, occasionally six hours a night for too many weeks. And that last night, before the orals, when he had had a sudden attack of worry over the possible floaters in his written papers, he hadn't been in bed at all. He had kept himself awake with potfuls of coffee, and he had worked by the open window enjoying the cool breeze after the hot mugginess of the day. That was the night he had caught this cold, although he hated to admit it. "It is only a summer cold," he said determinedly. "Annoying things. Hang on and on."

Penny said equally determinedly, "Bed, David. Now. With aspirin and toddy."

"Look, darling, that's the wrong way to phrase that invitation. Besides, I've got a job to think about, instead of sleeping myself dizzy in bed. I have to wire Fairbairn by Saturday that I am not available. I hadn't the brass neck to turn him down today. It is always easier to wire a refusal."

"What did Fairbairn want you to do?" Penny asked quickly.

"To do some traveling, make a monthly report using lots of statistics and facts, and write a weekly page for the *Economic Trend.*"

"But you expected some traveling, didn't you? I thought your headquarters were to be London, and that you would go on little jaunts into the provinces. That sounds fun. The report would be hard work, but the weekly article would be a marvelous thing for you. What is it you don't like, David? The traveling?"

"Not when it takes me three thousand miles away from you

302

for a year, perhaps longer. I bet it will actually take every week of fifteen months, or I'm a Dutchman. Fairbairn wants facts. They take a long time to gather accurately."

"Three thous—Where are you to go?"

"America. For one year. At least one year."

"Oh," Penny said slowly while her thoughts raced. There was a pause. Then she said, "You must take this job, David."

"I don't want it," he said quickly, angrily.

Penny said quietly, "If we could have got married, then you would have taken it?"

"Then we could have gone together. Fairbairn would have paid my traveling expenses—American scale, too. We could have just managed it financially, even allowing for Margaret."

And I could have let this flat to Marston, Penny thought. That money would have balanced Margaret on their budget. She sighed.

"It would have been perfect," David said.

"Yes." She rose to her feet, and leaned over to kiss him. Then she moved silently away to search for some aspirin in the bathroom. She was searching for aspirin, thinking of fifteen months and no end to the worry, thinking of jobs, what kind, what next, and what was she searching for now? Her mind went blank and she could neither remember nor think at all. She gripped the cold edge of the washbasin, stared at nothing, feeling nothing. Suddenly she came to life again, remembered the aspirin, found the small bottle. She held it, looking at it, saying aloud, "What shall we do now?"

Then she knew what she had to do.

She would wire Walter Chaundler: he would know where Fairbairn was to be found. She would wire Chaundler telling him that David was ill and could not send a telegram, but that he would accept the job in America. Chaundler would understand the telegram's hidden meaning. He would help her persuade David. For he knew, as she had just realized, that it was too late now to refuse this job. And David knew, too, even if he would not admit it.

She bathed her face with cold water, powdered it carefully, and returned to the room.

David was sitting as she had left him, his head leaning against the back of the chair, his eyes fixed on the Utrillo reproduction above the mantelpiece as if he could find some end to their troubles down that silent street of quiet houses with their shutters drawn against the midday sun. Penny began to fold the linen cover off the divan, to strip the cushions and turn them into pillows.

David roused himself, and made the effort of rising. It seemed to take his mind a long time tonight to tell his body to move. And his body wasn't one piece, as he had imagined: he realized he was made up of several parts, all of them in conflict at the moment. He knew then that this was more than a cold.

"Look, darling," he said, "if I am going to be ill, I'd better catch the first train back to Oxford. I probably should not have come here, today. Only, I've had this day circled on the calendar for weeks, and—"

"I'm going to buy some whisky and lemons for you," Penny said with a smile. "Get into bed quickly, won't you, darling? I want to see you there when I get back."

"But—" David began without conviction, looking at the cool white sheets. That pillow was just the right invitation for a throbbing head.

"Darling, *where* could you go in Oxford? To hospital? Or to hospital here? Nonsense, darling. The sooner you are in bed, the more quickly you'll be cured." And hospitals cost money. All illness cost money.

"But all this trouble—" He was weakening in his protests: he didn't want to talk, to argue; he only wanted to get into that bed and get to sleep . . .

Penny smiled, shook her head, and picked up her handbag. "Shan't be a minute," she said lightly, and left the room before he could offer any more objections. *Trouble* . . . how strange a man could be. Nothing was trouble if you loved him. If you were in love, all the work and worry in the world was no trouble at all. When women started complaining about trouble, they were already half out of love. She shook her head in gentle amusement. Then, as she reached the front door, she was serious again, planning what was to be done. She opened her handbag and counted the money in it. She looked at the coins in her hand. Five-and-nine-pence . . . all that was left of the pound note broken this morning for tonight's dinner. Mercury should have been the God of Money. She searched for the emergency ten-shilling note which she kept tucked safely away in one of the bag's pockets. There was a moment of panic when she couldn't find it; and then she did. That made fifteen-and-ninepence altogether: enough for whisky, and a thermometer too.

She hurried into the Square, and turned towards Tottenham Court Road. Fortunately, this was not a wealthy district, and shopkeepers on the side streets were apt to keep longer hours. The Wine and Spirits shops would be closed, of course. But there was always the carrying-out department in the local public house. If my people could see me now, she thought bitterly, what would shock them the more: David ill in my room, or me visiting the jug-and-bottle department in a pub? It was easy for them to criticize; they had whisky in the house as a matter of course, and money for doctors and nurses and private nursing homes. But what did you do when you didn't have money for a doctor or a hospital? Quite simple: you did everything yourself without outside help, just you and your two bare hands.

Her hurried step broke into a swift run as if to match the urgency of her thoughts.

chapter xxviii

DAVID had fallen into an uneasy sleep marked by heavy breathing. There was a dark flush on his face, and his hair lay damp on his brow.

Penny rose stiffly from the armchair which she had drawn over beside the bed. He was too restless. He was getting worse. This wasn't a cold, this was something which could be, perhaps was now, much more serious. She had a sudden attack of panic, standing there, looking down at him, her fears refusing to be silenced any longer. She ought to have insisted on calling a doctor, she should not have let David talk her out of it. And now, it was too late: it was midnight. She did not know of any doctor who lived near here. The one who had attended the girls at Baker House lived miles away. And he was highly expensive. Hideous, she thought angrily, to be forced to count the cost of being cured. David, well again, was worth more than all the money in the world. But it was a case of logic, not of meanness. Either you had the money and could buy what you needed, or you hadn't, and couldn't.

She stood there, looking down at him, trying to persuade herself that this stage of illness was necessary: you didn't get better from flu until it was sweated out of your system; you had to go through this high fever. She felt the sheets. They were quite wet. That would never do. She moved over to the bureau drawer where she kept the linen. There were so few sheets there, really, if many changes were necessary. She laid the fresh linen on the small table, now cleared of the abandoned dinner party, and stood still as she thought of what must be done in what order. She felt almost too tired to arrange the details in her mind, yet the long night had scarcely begun.

"Stop standing there!" she told herself angrily. She began unfolding the sheets to have them ready for the quick change which would be necessary. She searched in David's suitcase for another pair of pajamas, and found them with two buttons, jagged and useless stumps, broken off by the laundry. Blast them, she thought, and searched for two possible substitutes in her sewing box.

As she sat on the arm of a chair and sewed the buttons quickly and securely in place she comforted herself by remembering all the things she *had* managed to do this evening. Mostly telephone calls, but each had meant a separate journey downstairs, for she had not wanted to leave David too long alone.

She had phoned Bunny Eastman and told him she couldn't possibly come in to the office tomorrow, and would he please post her weekly check to her?

She had telephoned Lillian Marston, and found her in the middle of excited packing. "Darling, couldn't possibly see you tonight. I'm catching the boat express from Victoria tomorrow at ten, and I haven't got a thing inside the suitcases yet. To Paris and then to Barbizon, to stay at a little inn and paint the forest and sky. Isn't it marvelous? Chris's idea. I call it bribery and corruption. I'll probably end up by marrying him after all." So Penny had said it *was* marvelous; and she did not mention that David was ill.

Then she had telephoned two of her Slade friends, but they had already left town. The long vacation was here, and everyone she knew was scrambling out of London, pitying those who were tied to it. David's friends, too, were either scattered over the British Isles or had gone abroad. Chaundler was preparing to leave for Salzburg. Her grandfather was giving an address to a group of medieval historians at the Sorbonne.

She had telephoned Margaret Bosworth, too. She was out at a theater, so Penny had left a message. There had been no reply to that message, but when Penny had telephoned again, only twenty minutes ago, Margaret was there.

"Oh," Margaret had said when Penny had told her about David, and then there was a pause.

"Could you come here tomorrow?" Penny had asked, swallowing her pride.

There was another pause. "It is rather difficult. You see I am leaving for Sussex on the day after tomorrow, and I have so much to do."

"Oh," Penny had said.

"It is probably only a summer cold. I had a very bad one last week."

"Did you?" Penny had asked, and hung up the receiver.

It was only now that Penny's sewing on the last button, realized that Margaret had possibly been trying to be polite. Otherwise she would never spoken so much; she would just have said "Oh!" in that noncommittal way of hers. But what strange ways people had of being polite or comforting: Margaret had had a very bad cold, too, so David's was absolutely nothing to worry about.

I give up, Penny decided. I've tried to like her, but I give up. Mother dislikes David, Margaret dislikes me. And Mother and Margaret developed a cordial dislike for each other when they did meet. Yet David makes excuses for Margaret, so he must be fond of her. And I defend Mother when we talk about her. How on earth, then, did David and I ever fall in love?

She half-smiled, and then thinking of Margaret Bosworth's cold voice she stopped smiling and her face became quite hard. What I resent most, she thought, is this hidden battle between us. As if I were opposition to her. And I am not. I don't even compete with her, the silly thing. How idiotic some women can be, going around with martyred expressions as soon as their son or brother thinks of taking a wife. Freud, of course, would have his usual answer. But if he had been a woman, he could have added a little footnote pointing out the strange fact that men who were drunks or jailbirds did not have to worry about any silver cord.

Penny snapped off the tight thread angrily, placed the sewing box on the mantelpiece. She touched David's telegram to straighten it. A FIRST A JOB AND YOU ALL MY LOVE ALWAYS DAVID. Her face softened and became young again. How happy he had been when he had written that. She turned quickly away. The letter from Edinburgh, in the usual blue deckle-edged envelope, was left lying face down on the mantlepiece. She would read it when she had time. But now, there were too many things to be done.

She heard David stir restlessly. He was half-awake. Yet she still hesitated. The danger of a chill, if he were moved, was very great; the danger of lying between damp sheets was even worse. She knew so little about nursing. She was only remembering how she had been nursed when she was ill. Then suddenly, she became decided. She caught up the extra blanket which she had laid in readiness over a chair, and went over to the bed. She shook David's shoulder gently, firmly.

"David! Please get up. Help me, darling."

He shook his head dizzily, looked at her as if he did not recognize her, raised himself onto one elbow, and then sank back on the pillow as if he were falling asleep again.

"Come on, darling. Help me. David, help me." She raised him until he sat up in bed, half-wrapping the blanket around his shoulders. This time he really was awake. He obeyed her urgent voice, now, but when he rose to walk to the armchair he seemed to be moving in some heavy dream.

"Help me, darling," she said, and the urgency in her voice roused him. When he had changed his pajamas, she wrapped the blanket tightly around him, and sat him down gently in the chair. Then she turned to the bed, stripping it quickly, changing the soaking linen, and as she stretched the cool fresh sheets smoothly in place she remembered the burning heat of his body. At least, she thought, he will be able to rest more comfortably now. But her worry increased as she helped him back to bed. She bent and kissed his forehead as she tucked the bedclothes neatly around him. It seemed to be on fire.

She wept then, silently, so that David would not hear her. She felt lonely and afraid. She found she was kneeling beside the bed, burying her face in the blanket. She was terrified of her loneliness, of her fears.

That was just after midnight.

At two o'clock, she again roused David, again changed the sodden linen.

And again she did all this, when it was almost five o'clock, and the pale light outside cast a cold look into the dreary room. This time, David was less dazed, smiled for her, watched contentedly, and said, "Dear Penny, all this trouble—" before he fell asleep. This time, too, it was an easier sleep; his brow felt more normal, his breathing was lighter.

She sat on the chair beside the bed, so that she could

cover him with the bedclothes whenever he threw an arm outside of the covers, or when he flung over on his side and exposed his back and shoulders. But now, suddenly, his sleep was deep and peaceful, and all the wild restlessness had gone. She relaxed in the chair, watching him as he lay so quietly, folding her arms tightly to keep her body warm in her flannel dressing gown for the morning had brought coolness to the room.

And then, as he still slept, sudden relief surged through her with the biting sharpness of pain. She rose and walked to the window, stood staring at the gray-blue rooftops. Their sloping slates rippled sealike as they gleamed with dew under the early sunlight. The day promised well. Loneliness vanished with the cold shadows of the night.

"He won't die," she said, at last giving words to her fears; "he won't die now."

The doctor, gray-haired, thin, sharp-eyed, noncommittal, was preparing to leave.

"Don't worry about him," he said, not unkindly. "He still has some fever, but really nothing to worry about now. These things go up and down, you know. All we have to do is to keep an eye on him. If he gets any worse again tonight, you can call me, and I'll send round a woman to help you. She isn't a qualified nurse, but she is very capable."

"It developed so suddenly," Penny explained. "We thought it was only a bad cold, and then suddenly it was something much worse. And I didn't know of any doctor, until the caretaker downstairs gave me your address this morning. Thank you for coming so quickly."

The doctor repressed a smile. He found her anxiety amusing, and a little touching, too. Newly married, he thought, glancing at the heavy signet ring on her left hand. Just wait until she had five children, two down with mumps, another with asthma, and the baby with croup. Then she would know what a night's nursing was like. Still, she hadn't done a bad job. She had managed to stave off pneumonia. Her husband would be all right now.

"You had better get some sleep," the doctor said, he who hadn't been to bed all night himself. "And let him sleep as much as possible. You may not need to call me again." His patients weren't the kind who wanted repeated visits.

He paused at the top of the stairs, and said, "If you *could* stop him from worrying, he will get better in no time. He is a healthy specimen, you know." And then, as if he felt that he had intruded too much into some personal problem, he gave a brief good-day and hurried downstairs.

David, who had been pretending to be asleep, opened his eyes as she came back into the room. He said, "If you don't get some sleep, I shall start some real worrying."

"I shall sleep. That's all arranged. Mrs. Lawson, the caretaker, has found a camp bed; one of her neighbors is lending it to her. I just can't manage the two-chair technique it seems—they slip and I slide. Strange how kind people are when you are in difficulties. There had been a sort of communal rallying-around going on here, ever since Mrs. Lawson sent the neighbor's small boy for the doctor. I gave Mrs. Lawson all the food and wine which we didn't touch last night—in a round-about way of course, so that her feelings wouldn't be hurt. And I've a length of flowered material which will make some bright cushion-covers to cheer up the neighbor's parlor. She came up here with some broth for you when you were asleep, and admired our curtains. And the small boy gets tuppence, which seems to be the union rate for running errands in this neighborhood. Mrs. Lawson said I was to give him no more than that. But I did give him the chocolates you brought me. You don't mind, do you? His eyes went into big circles. And he has been running so many errands for me all morning. But to balance the box of chocolates, which he seems to have taken home and shared around, his mother arrived with the bowl of broth. Strange, isn't it?"

"Only because you have never lived with the poor, Penny. They'd never survive if they didn't lend each other a helping hand."

Then he frowned, trying to remember what he knew must be remembered. "It is hell to be ill at this time," he said irritably. There was a job to be found, a job to begin. And what kind of job, now? "Penny, would you send a telegram to Fairbairn for me? There's some money in my pocket, and his address is in the small diary you'll find in my jacket. Get the boy with the big circles of eyes to take it to the post office."

"Don't worry about that, darling. We've still a day to decide."

"I've decided already."

So have I, she thought sadly. The telegram had probably reached Chaundler by this time. What else could have been done? Saturday was tomorrow and Fairbairn was Fairbairn. David could not change his career a second time because of her. But she was glad that he had not made that decision, that it had had to come from her.

She smiled, gave him her hand obediently. He stretched himself lazily, drowsily. If you had to be ill, he thought, it was good to be ill with all this kind of care around you. Dimly, he remembered last night. He looked at her tired face.

"You must love me a lot," he said, and kissed her hand.

"And you must love me a lot, too," she said, still thinking of Fairbairn. "Sleep and get better, darling. And don't worry." She turned away quickly, and pretended she had to tidy the room.

The telegram from David had fallen forward again on the mantelpiece. She picked it up, and the letter too. She turned the envelope over in her hand, and saw the address for the first time. The writing was not Moira's. It was the same kind of handwriting, but with more decision, more strength.

"It's Mother," Penny said incredulously, and she ripped open the envelope. There was a single sheet of paper inside.

David watched her face. It was white and tense.

"Father is ill," she reported. "He had a shock, brought on by his 'great worries.'" She looked up at that moment. "My fault, of course, I suppose." She pushed a lock of hair away from her eyes and forced herself to read on. Her impulse had been to stop reading the letter altogether.

Then David saw her whole face change. She was young again, young, incredulous, happy.

She held the letter out to him, but she couldn't speak. The smile had changed to laughter, a laughter that was very near tears. But her happy eyes, her happy face, told him that the news was good. She held out the letter to him, not speaking, not moving.

"The old brain is slow, today," he said quickly. "I can't guess." There was a glimmering of hope in his mind, but he repressed it. Too many disappointments recently: better not add another. Better repress all hope. "I can't read it from this distance, Penny," he said with one of his old smiles.

She came forward to him saying, "David, oh David."

They stared at each other, still not quite believing. Then he caught her wrist and pulled her down towards him. "They'll let us get married?" he asked, incredulous.

"Yes, David, yes! Oh, darling, careful! You'll have another temperature attack."

"And by God it couldn't be for a better cause. This is one temperature I'll enjoy having." He tried to sit up in bed.

"Don't worry, old girl, nothing is going to kill me now. Not now."

"I know I'm a rotten nurse, but I'm not quite as bad as this," Penny said and made him lie down again. He didn't rebel, so perhaps he wasn't quite so well as he had suddenly thought he was.

"How strange women can be," he said. "So calm, and practical."

"Calm?" She laughed then, unevenly, happily. "Just wait until you are better, and you'll see how very uncalm I am." She covered his shoulders carefully, smoothed the top sheet under his chin, turned the pillow around for coolness, and felt his brow.

"Well, nurse?" he asked with a grin.

"Some more aspirin, darling. And a lot of sleep. And no more talking. I don't want any more frights like the kind I had last night."

"Strange, I can't remember much about it except that you were there, hazily, and that the bed seemed to have an oven going full blast underneath it."

"No more frights, thank you," Penny repeated firmly, and placed a kiss on each eyelid to close them.

They didn't stay closed. "Darling. America. For both of us!"

"Yes, David."

"Send Fairbairn a telegram. His address is in my pocketbook in my jacket. Tell him I'm ready to start any time."

"Yes, David." She smiled and added, "Get some sleep, now."

"We'd better see about getting a marriage license. It takes ages sometimes, I believe. Get a quick one, darling. And I want at least one week on dry land with you, before we sail. I'm a rotten sailor. I want a honeymoon on solid ground."

"Yes, David." Her smile told him to stop talking, to fall asleep, to get well quickly.

She left him then, to make sure of these things.

She sat outside on the top step of the staircase, her arms hugging herself, her eyes looking at the blank wall dipping down into the dark house. She made herself think of all the things to be done, all the practical things which must done, and for once they seemed neither too difficult nor exhausting. She wasn't even tired, now.

I must write Grandfather at once, she thought. "He must know that I am so happy," she said aloud. She laughed as her voice startled her. It *was* so happy.

She rose and went back to the room. David was asleep. She picked up her mother's letter from where it had fallen on the floor beside him. "We've managed it, David," she said softly. "We've managed it. In spite of everything."

She went to the table and found her pen and some paper. She watched the sunlight turning the blue tiles on the opposite roofs to shimmering heat, and imagined Inchnamurren with the sun on the waters. If they had time to travel there, that would be a wonderful place to spend David's week on solid ground. Inchnamurren...

And thinking of the island and its quiet loveliness, she began to remember the summer day when she had met David there. She smiled with the delight of remembering, but the wonder in her heart grew. "What *is* love?" she asked herself suddenly, and could find no answer that was complete enough. Her smile lingered, giving warmth to her lips and depths to her blue eyes. "It just *is*, that's all," she said. She turned for a moment to look at David.

Then she drew the sheet of paper in front of her, and began to write the letter to her grandfather.

chapter xxxix

THE wedding, in spite of Mrs. Lorrimer's dismay over its suddenness, its simplicity, its lack of invitations and white satin, was an enormous success. The bridegroom felt less sick with apprehension and nervousness than the usual bridegroom is forced to feel; the bride was neither as exhausted nor as short-tempered as the usual bride is forced to be. Their only worry—each of them had it, concealed it from the other, and then admitted it a week later with laughter—was that one of them would be killed or injured in a traffic accident on their separate ways to the ceremony, and that they would never really get each other after all.

Dr. MacIntyre, after giving away the bride, was host at

the luncheon in the Savoy. It was a small party, but a gay one in spite of Mrs. Lorrimer's determinedly brave face.

At first, she had said it was quite impossible to attend the wedding. And then, just as David was secretly congratulating himself, she had decided to come. She reengaged a nurse for her husband, and spent three busy days organizing clothes for the occasion. She also found time to write a great number of explanatory letters before she set out for London with Moira and Betty. The one to Mattie Fane in Salzburg gave her a certain amount of pleasure. " . . . So *very* exciting . . . leaving at once for America . . . Fairbairn, *the* economist . . . *most* important mission . . . such a lucky girl, isn't she?" (This was a most successful letter and quite spoiled Mattie Fane's holiday. In addition, her guest, George Fenton-Stevens, received a wire from David, and immediately said that he must leave for London "to see old David through this." Even the fact that it was such a hole-and-corner wedding gave Mattie Fane little comfort.) But to Moira, on the nervously gloomy journey to London, Mrs. Lorrimer voiced her forebodings. Imagine traveling to America, not having a settled home or anything; Penelope must be quite mad. However, at the proper moment in London, she was sentimentally upset, and called Penelope "My dear daughter," and wept with grace and real affection.

Margaret Bosworth made her dutiful appearance too. She said very little, but watched everyone acutely. The Lorrimers were a silly family, she told herself, noting the new hats, remembering their new circumstances. "David seems so ridiculously young to be married," she said to a tall American called Burns who had come back from Paris especially for the wedding. Ridiculous too, she thought, that people had traveled so far just to be here today: it made her own journey from Sussex, a frightful nuisance, seem so very small and not half the sacrifice it really was.

Burns looked at David's sister in frank surprise. "I wouldn't say that," he replied, "I'm all for it. Why, some of my friends get married when they are still at college."

"That's America, of course," Margaret said coldly. She thought for a moment, and added, "Besides, how can they afford it? Or are they all millionaires?"

Burns decided to ignore that crack. He smiled down at her and said evenly, "Oh, they get along. If they can't, their families chip in. Say, don't you *like* people getting married?" His tone was so easy and friendly that Margaret,

314

feeling she must prove that she *did* like weddings, went on listening to him talking about America although her first impulse had been to walk away. Later, after the third glass of champagne, she even became talkative herself. Burns listened politely, agreed heartily at the right moments until he felt sure that the thaw had set in. He managed to draw Halsey and McIllwain adroitly into the conversation, and eased away leaving the three of them discussing Scriabin. Then he set out to do what he had wanted to do ever since he had first seen Lillian Marston.

Lillian, slender (too thin Moira decided, smartly dressed, too dramatic, Mrs. Lorrimer thought), had arrived that morning from Paris. "Simply had to be here," she said to Penny. "Good Lord haven't I nursed you through the other stages?" As for the holiday at Barbizon, she shrugged her shoulders. "Thank Heavens, I didn't marry Chris. I really don't approve of divorce, you know. Find me another, David, that's a good girl." She had been very quiet and thoughtful all through the marriage ceremony, but she recovered her old sparkle as the party left for the Savoy, and devoted herself not to the men from Oxford ("I adored them when I was sixteen"), but to Dr. MacIntyre and Edward Fairbairn. They found her charm not undelightful. "Perhaps," she said to Penny, "I am just an old man's darling." There was a slight edge in her voice, so that Penny looked quickly at her friend. But Lillian was smiling. "Don't worry, my sweet," she said. "I'm going back to Barbizon tomorrow. Chris is leaving this week, and I'll devote the rest of the summer to My Art." She laughed then, and suddenly kissed Penny lightly on the cheek. "Have a wonderful life, darling," she said. "I'll bring all my funny friends to visit you and David, to show them I do know some really original people."

After that, Penny had not much time to talk to Lillian again, but she did notice that Bunny Eastman, who had chased Fairbairn away, was in turn ousted by Bill Burns. She remembered that Bill was also returning to France tomorrow. What had he called David when he first met Penny? A fast worker? Bill Burns wasn't a slow one, either. Then Mr. Fairbairn came over to talk to her, and she stopped thinking about Lillian.

Edward Fairbairn had been delighted by the wedding. Like all bachelors, he was a great romantic at heart. As an economist, he approved of early marriage and young men who were men. He glanced bitterly at that fellow Eastman, now talking so engagingly to Mrs. Lorrimer about Jacobean embroidery. That, Edward Fairbairn thought angrily, does not solve the problem of the falling British birth rate. He looked at the bride's charming face, nodded approvingly to what she was saying, decided to double that check which he would give them as a wedding present.

George Fenton-Stevens was enjoying himself as one should at a wedding. (Besides, accepting that invitation to Salzburg had been a grave mistake.) He was taking all the credit for having arranged the meeting on Inchnamurren. And he had just managed to do some unobtrusive bribing, with results that were most pleasant to contemplate as he stood so innocently here. At this moment, confetti and rice were being liberally disposed in all the pockets of David's and Penny's traveling coats. An obliging chauffeur was tying an assortment of cans, a boot and a placard to the rear of the car which David had hired to drive them so quietly to the station. One of the chambermaids had sewn up all the pajama legs with large strong stitches and frequent giggles. Everyone was co-operating beautifully. Nothing like a wedding to bring out the gay conspirator. All in the day's sport.

George restrained a smile of triumph as he looked across the room at an unsuspecting David, who thought he had hidden everything damned well from practical jokers, and made easy conversation with Moira Lorrimer. Not such a peach as Penny, and not such fun, but pretty enough and a good listener. But as he talked to Moira Lorrimer, he glanced over from time to time at Lillian Marston and Bill Burns. And as if to prove something to Lillian, he made not one move towards her and was as charming as possible to Moira.

Moira had never imagined she could possibly enjoy herself so much at her younger sister's wedding. Still, she did have the very considerable consolation of the diamond solitaire on her own left hand. (That was Peter's—the son of the shipping Barries, not the brewing Barries. He was nice: really very sweet.) She would be married in a year's time, and she would not have to teach after all. She was really very happy. As she talked to George Fenton-Stevens, she would glance down at the ring, for after all it was only four days old. It was a perfect stone, sparkling beautifully, set in platinum. How strange Penny was: she never had liked platinum, said it was cold and ugly, and people were silly to spend money on it just because it was fashionable. Just as she hated chinchilla, and said that if it were called rabbit no one would want to wear it. Yet, Penny liked sables quite frankly, and said they would be worth wearing even if they were called rabbit and sold for five guineas. How strange she was! Moira looked around the small party, thought it didn't look like a real wedding at all, and began to enjoy herself thoroughly.

Betty, sitting beside her grandfather and her mother, looked around at the smiling faces and listened to the talking voices. She was waiting impatiently for the end of the luncheon: that was when the strawberries and cream were to be served. Penny had promised her that. Penny was smiling across to her now. Golly, Penny *did* look pretty today in that blue dress. When I'm grown-up, Betty thought, I'll wear a little flowered hat and pearl earrings, too. And lipstick. She looked at her mother. Yes, I will. She looked once more at Penny. She let her eyes slide to David. He has married my sister, she thought. Golly! For a minute she sat very still, hardly breathing.

David looked up suddenly to find his new sister-in-law staring at him with wide eyes. He smiled. Betty felt her cheeks turn scarlet and she turned her head quickly away, but not before she saw him glance down at his watch again and give a little nod to Penny. Then they both rose very quietly. Grandfather had a laughing look on his face at something David was saying to him. And everyone was pushing chairs aside and rising and going into the busy hotel lobby. Betty followed them. We'll miss the ice cream, she thought miserably. All this fuss—why, you *didn't* say good-by to people going away for a week on Inchnamurren!

When they returned again to the room, the waiters were already standing beside the serving table. I *knew* it, Betty told herself. The ice cream was almost all melted.

She looked around the table, but no one else seemed to notice. They were all talking twice as loudly as before, and laughing about things that didn't seem funny at all. Her grandfather was being very amused as he told Mr. Fairbairn something that David had said to him. She listened. Silly, she decided. No joke at all. She concentrated on spooning up the liquid ice cream.

David, alone with Penny in the locked compartment of

the express to Scotland (ticket collectors were quick to spot a newly married man and the tip he so unobtrusively offered), was remembering the incident, too.

"You know," he said, "I had the feeling that your grandfather was highly amused at the end. I spoke to him, as we were coming away; thanked him and all that. And I said, 'Well, *that's* over, thank God. We've got married, and there's nothing left to worry about.' He looked at me very quickly—you know that quick sideglance he gives—and his eyes were twinkling, and I really had the feeling that he was trying very hard not to laugh at me." David paused, tightening his grip on Penny's waist, holding her left hand in his, looking down at the wedding ring.

"He must have been thinking about something else," Penny said, and kissed David's cheek happily. She glanced up at the neat labels on the suitcases in the rack. Mrs. David Bosworth. Mr. and Mrs. David Bosworth. "There is *nothing* left to worry about, now, is there?"

"Nothing," David agreed. The last ten days had been a nightmare of arrangements, of things to be remembered, of things to be done. Yes, everything was settled. Even Margaret. At that last moment in the Savoy, amid the exciting warmth of friendly good wishes, she had even said, "Have a marvelous time in America, David," as if she had really meant it. She had laughed when he had kissed her and knocked her hat all sideways—it was one of those large black affairs, difficult to negotiate—and suddenly she had looked ten years younger.

"Nothing left to worry about," he said firmly, and bent to kiss Penny's lips.

She threw a nervous glance towards the carriage door.

"Locked," David said. "Half a crown and a kind heart did it. No escape, my proud beauty. I have you in my power."

"At last. You forgot to say 'At last!' I was waiting for it, frankly, the very moment the ticket collector locked the door and pretended to be looking down the platform at something more important."

David laughed. "I did think of saying it," he admitted. "And then, Penny, I couldn't make a joke of it. I really felt that way too damned badly."

"Well, say it now. I think I'd like the way you'd say it. I expect every husband, even if clichés embarrass him, finds there is one time in his life when he can turn to his wife—"

She paused, smiled, repeated firmly: " . . .wife, when he can turn to his wife, and all he can say is 'At last!' Isn't there?"

David watched her vivid, laughing face. Under his serious eyes it became serious too, desirable in its promise.

"At last," he said very quietly, and they kissed each other.

About the Author

Helen MacInnes was born in Glasgow, Scotland, and was educated there and in London. She and her husband moved to the United States in 1937, and in 1939 her first novel, ABOVE SUSPICION, was published. It was an immediate success, and she was launched on the spectacular writing career that has made her an international favorite.

Ms. MacInnes died in New York City in October, 1985.